Kaye Dobbie has been writing professionally ever since she won the Big River short story contest at the age of eighteen. Her career has undergone many changes, including writing Australian historical fiction under the name Lilly Sommers, to romance written as Sara Bennett and published in the US and Australia. Her books have been nominated for a number of awards and translated into many languages. As Kaye Dobbie she is published in Australia and Germany. Kaye lives on the central Victorian goldfields, where she creates her stories despite the demands of three privileged cats. You can find her at kayedobbie.com.

Also by Kaye Dobbie

Sweet Wattle Creek
The Road to Ironbark

THE
Keepers
of the
Lighthouse

KAYE DOBBIE

Fiction HQ

First Published 2022
First Australian Paperback Edition 2022
ISBN 9781489249180

The Keepers of the Lighthouse
© 2022 by Kaye Dobbie
Australian Copyright 2022
New Zealand Copyright 2022

Except for use in any review, the reproduction or utilisation of this work in whole or in part in any form by any electronic, mechanical or other means, now known or hereafter invented, including xerography, photocopying and recording, or in any information storage or retrieval system, is forbidden without the permission of the publisher.

This book is sold subject to the condition that it shall not, by way of trade or otherwise, be lent, resold, hired out or otherwise circulated without the prior consent of the publisher in any form of binding or cover other than that in which it is published and without a similar condition including this condition being imposed on the subsequent purchaser.

All rights reserved including the right of reproduction in whole or in part in any form.

This is a work of fiction. Names, characters, places, and incidents are either the product of the author's imagination or are used fictitiously, and any resemblance to actual persons, living or dead, business establishments, events, or locales is entirely coincidental.

Published by
HQ Fiction
An imprint of Harlequin Enterprises (Australia) Pty Limited (ABN 47 001 180 918), a subsidiary of HarperCollins Publishers Australia Pty Limited (ABN 36 009 913 517)
Level 13, 201 Elizabeth St
SYDNEY NSW 2000
AUSTRALIA

® and TM (apart from those relating to FSC®) are trademarks of Harlequin Enterprises (Australia) Pty Limited or its corporate affiliates. Trademarks indicated with ® are registered in Australia, New Zealand and in other countries.

A catalogue record for this book is available from the National Library of Australia www.librariesaustralia.nla.gov.au

Printed and bound in Australia by McPherson's Printing Group

For Selwa, who has been on this journey with me from the beginning.

Hobart Recorder, **18 April 1882**

On 12 April, 1882, Mr Albert Munro of New Norfolk married Miss Rochelle Fernley, only daughter of the late Colonel Fernley Esq. of Mallowmede. The ceremony took place before a small gathering of friends and family, in consideration of the bride's father's recent death. The wedded pair will be leaving Tasmania soon for Mr Munro's property in western Victoria, where they plan to settle.

Hobart Recorder, 15 May 1882

The schooner *Alvarez* departed Hobart yesterday and is expected to arrive in Melbourne in a day or two. The vessel was chartered by Mr Albert Munro, and is under the command of Captain Roberts with an experienced crew. Mr and Mrs Munro are on their way to their new life in Victoria. Also on board are Mr Edmund Bailey, a visitor to our shores from England, and Mr Richard Jones, travelling to Melbourne on government business. We wish all of them well in their future endeavours.

LAURA

*17 May 1882, Benevolence Island Lighthouse,
Bass Strait between Tasmania and Victoria*

'Can you see it?'

Laura peered through the storm, as lashing rain struck at the thick glass windows of the Wilkins lantern room. Twenty-one small, fragile lamps shone out brightly through their polished reflectors, despite the weather. Well-kept machinery moved steadily, taking the light through its five-minute rotation—fifty seconds of light and fifty seconds of darkness. Every lighthouse was unique in its clockwork movement and this one belonged to Benevolence. The granite lighthouse tower had stood solidly atop rocky cliffs for over thirty years, and it still felt strong and safe, even when the world outside was chaos.

Her father pointed again, shouting to be heard above the screaming wind and the pounding waves that had come with what had started as a westerly gale. Not uncommon at this time of year, but the gale had turned into a raging storm.

Laura caught a glimpse of a small ship. Close to the rocks that stretched out from the base of the cliff below the lighthouse.

A faint light blinked as the crests of the waves gave way to troughs.

'There!' she shouted back.

Leo Webster nodded, his teeth clenched around the stem of his pipe. It was not lit. It had gone out hours ago. 'They're too close,' he said. 'They can't see us.'

It was an unfortunate fact that the lighthouse on Benevolence Island, standing at one thousand feet above sea level, had been built too tall. In good weather, its warning light could be seen for close to thirteen leagues, all the way to the Victorian coast. In bad weather, however, when clouds or fog hung low over the island, it was often invisible.

Laura leaned forward again, trying to catch sight of the vessel she had spotted a moment before. She and her father had been up here, tending to the light and keeping watch for most of the afternoon as the weather closed in and early darkness fell. Now it must be almost midnight and the violent gale showed no sign of abating. Her father's assistant, Rorie, had refused to leave his fireside to take his turn up here, claiming he had a bad cold, and her stepmother, Miriam, was in the head-keeper's quarters with Noah, Laura's five-month-old brother. No doubt Miriam was worried sick, but neither Laura nor her father could leave the lighthouse. There were lives at stake out there on the wild water. Lives that were in their hands.

Benevolence Island lay between Tasmania and Victoria, in the shallow waters of the treacherous Bass Strait. The island's lighthouse had been built to warn ships away from the savage line of rocks that stretched out from the northern side of the island. The Tiger's Teeth, as they were known, and for good reason. They could rip out the bottom of a boat and slice open the flesh of its passengers. Since Laura had come to live here nine years ago, there had been several wrecks, one in a storm like this one, where the revolving light had been hidden by the low clouds, and the other when a fog had shrouded them. On both occasions, Laura remembered vividly the wreckage strewn along the shore, and the bodies that her father and his two assistants toiled to give a Christian burial in the island cemetery.

They were down to one assistant these days, and with Rorie playing possum, it was just Laura and her father manning the lighthouse.

'She's on the rocks!' Laura's gaze shot to her father's. His face looked greenish in the candlelight, full of anguish and memories of the past as he murmured, 'God help those poor souls.'

Dread filled her at the sight of the string of sharp-toothed rocks. Briefly, the gusting wind eased and the spray cleared, long enough for her to see the disaster unfolding in front of her. The small ship— it appeared to be a schooner—was definitely on the Tiger's Teeth. Laura winced to imagine what damage had been done to the hull. Pinned and incapable of escape, the vessel was being thrown about by the elements. Her main mast was down, sails trailing in the boiling sea, and she was listing badly to port as she took in water. It was only a matter of time until she would break apart and sink.

When next the beam of the lighthouse flashed, she could see the frantic efforts of passengers and crew as they struggled to remain aboard, clinging to their tattered ship, while others moved in the water. Her heart ached for them.

Her father's hand grasped her shoulder and tightened painfully. 'We must go down and save as many of them as we can.'

'How?'

'We'll go to the cove with a lamp. Guide them to the safety of the beach.'

Thankful Cove was the safest anchorage on the island. It faced to the east, away from the violent westerly and northerly gales, and therefore giving shelter to stricken vessels. On one side, a low headland of flat rocks circled around to shelter the inlet, rather like an arm, while to the north another jutting headland separated it from the fury of the Tiger's Teeth. Thankful Cove was difficult to spot if one was coming in from the sea during daylight, but at night the lamp would guide survivors.

'We won't put the lifeboat out, then?' Even as she said it, she wished the words back. Such a heroic act was impossibly dangerous in this weather. Ten years ago, on the east coast of Scotland, her parents had gone to the rescue of a sinking vessel in the cold waters of the North Sea, and her mother had drowned. Laura had watched from their lighthouse, and she would never forget her terror and pain, nor her father's anguish when he returned to shore after a long and fruitless search.

'We wouldn't get any boat close enough,' he said, interrupting her thoughts. 'When the storm has passed we'll have more of a chance.'

He did not need to add: *If the schooner was still in one piece, and there were still survivors to be saved.*

Once more her father checked the lamps and the reflectors, making sure they were working properly, and that the oil burned by the lamps would not need refilling, or the clockwork mechanism rewinding. He would have been happier if Rorie was here—there was always the chance that something could go wrong—but Laura knew they needed to save those who could be saved. She made her way down the narrow set of stairs that led from the lantern room, and then the cast-iron spiral staircase that took up most of the utilitarian inside of the tower. She was sure-footed, and had made this journey many times since they arrived on Benevolence. Her father had brought her to the colonies shortly after her mother's death, when she was just fifteen, determined to make a new life for himself and his young daughter. He had tried, worked at many jobs, but when push came to shove, lighthouse keeping was what he knew best. And so when he was offered a position as head keeper on isolated Benevolence Island, he had gratefully accepted.

To the surprise of them both, Leo had met Miriam, the daughter of a merchant, while in Hobart three years ago. He had been seeking explanations from the Hobart Marine Board as to why the items he had carefully noted as urgent in his letters to them were either ignored or did not arrive on the quarterly supply steamer.

Leo had been introduced to Miriam when attending a dinner with a former lighthouse superintendent, and, Laura gathered, they had fallen in love between the soup and the pudding. All the same, her father had not asked Miriam to marry him immediately. He had returned to Benevolence and Laura first, looking uncertain and a little sheepish, but happier than she had seen him in a long time. She had given him the blessing he'd asked for, and Miriam had come home with him on his next trip. Laura had expected to love her stepmother for her father's sake, and so she did, but she also loved Miriam for herself, and she knew that feeling was reciprocated.

Father and daughter had reached the base of the tower. Laura was wearing the loose trousers that Miriam abhorred but which were so much more practical than skirts in situations like this. Now she donned her waterproof coat over her thick sweater, and tied her hood under her chin, tucking back her blonde curls. Her hands were covered with gloves while her feet were encased in strong, sturdy boots. A lighthouse-keeper's daughter valued warmth and long wear in her clothing rather than fashion. She needed to be prepared to venture out in the foulest of weather, while the social engagements that other young ladies her age dressed to attend were nothing but dreams to her.

'Ready, lass?' Her father's gloved hand was raised to open the thick wooden door. Outside, she could hear the thump of the surf and the wail of the wind. It would be dangerous, but something in her rose to the occasion. Her father often said she had her mother's courage, which was counterbalanced by her father's caution.

'Ready,' Laura said, and the next moment they were out in the storm. The wind must have been at least nine on the Beaufort scale, probably a ten. It tugged violently at their clothing and whipped their breaths away. She leaned into it, forcing herself forward, as she followed her father's broad back to the track that led down from Lighthouse Hill to Thankful Cove.

The first section was very steep and slippery, and she took her time, clinging to the rope that had been strung alongside, not willing to risk injury. Soon they were on gentler ground, and to her right she could see the sheltered valley where the head-keeper's cottage stood, the lights visible through the shuttered windows and the grove of trees. Miriam would be safe inside with Noah.

The cove was beneath them now, and on the far hillside were the trolley rails that led straight down to the jetty. At the top was a whim. When the steamer carrying supplies docked in the cove, and those supplies were unloaded, one of the island's horses was harnessed to the whim. The turning horse would bring the trolley to the top, and then a bullock-drawn dray would carry the supplies further on to the lighthouse station.

Leo and Laura hurried down the final stretch of track to the beach. She could see the tide was on the turn and the exposed poles of the jetty were covered in foam blown in from the stormy sea. Down here they were sheltered from the full force of the wind, although she could still hear it screaming around the cliffs above.

The oil lamp swung in her father's hand, the flame inside the metal casing protected from the gale. Laura smiled when she saw that he still had his pipe clenched between his teeth.

'Let's hope some poor soul sees this and makes their way to safety!'

On closer inspection, his beard was wet and tangled, and his face pale with cold and exhaustion. Laura's hood had been tugged off by the wind, despite the cords that were supposed to hold it firm, and now she reached to pull it back over her hair. The rain had stuck strands to her face and her lips were numb with cold. She could taste salt on them. When they got back to the keeper's quarters, Miriam would fuss about her husband, drawing him to the fire and drying off his clothing. She would fuss about Laura, too, if she let her, and Laura rather thought that she would.

As they made their way further down the beach, Laura could see beyond the steep headland to her left, to the Tiger's Teeth and the turbulent waters that had brought grief to the schooner. Out there, the salt spray and driving rain made visibility difficult, but above the sound of the storm, she could hear the agonised groans and creaks made by the vessel as she struggled helplessly to free herself from the tiger's maw. How much longer could anyone stay on board? Once the little ship broke up, the only option was to risk the wild sea. To strike out for calm waters and dry land. In that regard, Thankful Cove was well named.

'There!' Her father pointed.

Three dark shapes, moving. Survivors fighting their way through the choppy waves as they waded towards the beach.

As Laura hurried forward, she saw that two of them were supporting the third, who hung slumped between them. As the trio reached the shallows, Laura noted that one of the helpers wore a skirt. A rogue wave hit them as Laura and her father approached, sending the injured man face first into the water. Voices were raised against the wind and rain, and one of the two began to tug the limp body towards firmer ground. The other, the woman, began heading out to sea again.

Quickly, Leo put down the lamp and ran to help support the injured man. At the same time, Laura ran past him to reach the woman, who was by now almost waist deep in the water. Laura caught her, and then grappled with her as the woman tried to force her back.

'Albert!' the woman sobbed, struggling to be free. 'I need to find Albert!'

'Albert will find you,' Laura said breathlessly, the first words that came to mind. 'Now come with me before we both drown.'

The woman's hands were icy and her teeth were chattering. Her dark hair hung heavy about her face and shoulders, while her sodden clothes clung to her. The coat she was wearing was heavy with water and pulling her down. She looked at Laura with wild eyes just as another wave washed hard against them, and they only just managed to stay upright. She seemed to give up then, and she and Laura fought their way out of the waves to stumble up the beach.

Laura grimaced. Her boots were filled, sloshing, and her wet trousers clung to her legs. She loved swimming, loved the sea, but this was not the weather to be out in it. By now, her father and the other survivor had lain the injured man down onto the sand.

Her father was kneeling beside him, trying to reason with him, while the stranger sought to hold the man down as he twisted and groaned, clearly not in his right senses. Eventually he quietened, and Leo ran his hands over limbs and torso, and then carefully examined the fellow's head.

When they had first come to isolated Benevolence, Laura's and her father's medical skills were rudimentary at best, but they had only themselves or a succession of assistants to rely on and help might be weeks away, so they had had to learn. Since Miriam had come, with her soothing voice and gentle hands, she had dealt with many a cut and scrape, and worse. Normally, she was the person they went to when there was need.

The injured man was muttering to himself, but at least now he lay still. The stranger who had been holding him down fell back upon the sand. He lay there for a moment as if too weary to move, and then with a groan he sat up and began to pull off his boots. He tipped the water out of them one at a time, frowning as he did so. Unlike Laura's boots, they seemed expensive, and were probably more for show than of any real practical use. His clothes, though wet and stuck with sand, looked equally expensive. He could have passed for one of the gentlemen in the books or illustrated papers she kept in her room.

As if he had felt her watching, the man glanced up, and she saw he was young, about her own age. The wet hair he pushed back appeared black in the light of the lamp, his eyes just as dark. He was clean-shaven, unlike most of the men she encountered with their beards and moustaches, and as she continued to stare his mouth quirked at one corner.

Embarrassed, Laura looked away, but his voice, very English, drew her back. As well as dressing like a gentleman, he sounded like one, too.

'Where are we?'

'Benevolence Island,' Laura told him.

'Not the State of Victoria, then?'

'No. We are halfway between Victoria and Tasmania.'

As he examined her, she became aware of her drowned-rat appearance, not to mention her male attire. She tugged her waterproof jacket tighter with a shiver. The water had been cold.

'What is your name?' he asked, still watching her.

'Laura Webster.'

'Edmund Bailey.' He held out his hand to her. It was probably automatic, something he did all the time, but in these circumstances polite introductions seemed incongruous. He gave a huff of laughter as if he realised it, and dropped his hand just as she was about to take it. The moment felt awkward.

'Were you alone on board, Mr Bailey?' she asked, remembering her role. People were drowning and there was no time for silliness.

'Yes,' he began, and then frowned again. 'That is, my dog ...' She saw grief in his eyes, and he opened his mouth as if to say more, but instead bent to tug his boots back on.

Suddenly remembering the woman she had rescued, Laura panicked, fearing she'd gone back into the water. She was relieved to see her standing at the edge of the tide, facing the sea, arms clasped about herself and shoulders hunched. Laura went to her and gently urged her further up the sand to where the oil lamp sat. In its comforting light, she could see that the woman was hollow-eyed and ghostly faced, her teeth chattering violently. She swayed and would have fallen if Laura had not been supporting her. It did not help that she kept twisting her head to try to catch a glimpse of the stricken schooner.

'Are you hurt?' Laura asked. 'Ma'am?'

Rather than answer, she whispered with a wild sort of grief, 'Albert. Where is Albert?'

Laura gave up trying to get through to her and concentrated on the two men kneeling beside the injured survivor. Leo was speaking to Edmund Bailey, their words broken up by the keening of the wind overhead, but Laura heard enough to make sense of them. 'He was on deck ... unconscious. Got him into the water. To shore. Told to abandon ship, but ... we didn't have time to take to the lifeboat.'

Edmund coughed, his voice grown raspy, no doubt from swallowing sea water. Laura moved closer.

'What is the name of your vessel?' Leo asked.

'The *Alvarez*. Out of Hobart and bound for Melbourne. Mr Albert Munro chartered her. That is his wife there.'

Leo looked at the huddled figure.

'Father?' Laura dropped down beside Leo and the injured man. 'Can I help? Is he alive?'

'Yes, lass, he is. But he's been hit hard on the head and there may be worse. I won't know until we get him inside.'

Three survivors. It seemed little enough and Laura knew they still had to get these people up to the quarters and out of the weather before they died of cold. A furious gust of wind flung rain against the hillside above the cove, reminding her that before they could reach safety a climb awaited them.

'Should I fetch Nelly and Ted?' she said.

The two horses were strong and reliable, used for spinning the whim to pull the trolley up the haulage tracks from the jetty, or performing other tasks about the island that required brute strength. They were stabled on the south side of the island, near Rorie's cottage, where the lay of the land was lower and tended to be protected even in the worst storms. Unlike the lighthouse, which was built on the highest point. As head keeper, Leo needed to be closer to the light, and although his quarters were comfortable enough, Rorie's would have been better. But Leo would not change places with a man who could not be trusted.

'Or we can wait in the boatshed until the storm has passed,' Laura went on.

The boatshed was tucked into the hillside beside the head of the jetty, and although it would give shelter, time had wrought its toll on the building. There were gaps between the planks that made up the walls, and the repairs her father had planned to finish over the summer were yet to begin. It was certainly no substitute for the solid warmth of the keeper's quarters.

Laura was not surprised when her father shook his head. 'The boatshed won't do, and this is no weather to fetch the horses and bring them down here. We'll just have to do our best on the track.'

'Track?' Edmund, opposite them, was watching and listening.

'It's a narrow road, really, and the quickest way up from the cove to my quarters,' Leo explained. 'But it means a bit of a climb.' He looked again at the injured man.

'We can carry him between us. I doubt he'll last long out here. The same goes for Mrs Munro.' Another glance at the woman and he lowered his voice. 'She and her husband were on deck and he pushed her into my arms. The next thing I knew, he was gone.'

'Why didn't he come with you?' Laura asked.

He ran a hand over his mouth, with an expression on his face that might have been regret.

'We had had a conversation at dinner before we sailed. I told him I could swim and he told me he could not. I can only speculate that is why he did as he did.'

'You saved her life.'

He looked as if he wanted to dispute it, but before he could answer his gaze snapped to her side and with a muttered word he lurched to his feet. That was when she realised that Mrs Munro was in the process of fainting. Laura struggled to her feet, hampered by her wet clothing, but he already had hold of the other woman. He sat her carefully down onto the sand and then pressed her head to her knees.

'That's it. Wait until the dizziness passes,' Laura heard him say as she stumbled over to them.

Foaming sea water swept up the beach towards them, stopping just short, before sliding back. Above them, the tall red-and-white tower of the lighthouse stood sentinel, its revolving light illuminating the tragic scene for its allotted time. Edmund glanced at Laura as the illumination washed over them and she realised how close together they were, both hovering over Mrs Munro. She could feel his warm breath on her frozen cheek, and see the shine of his dark eyes.

'I'm sorry about your dog.' It sounded awkward, but the kindness was well meant. Laura had had a dog once, only to lose it in tragic circumstances.

'Thank you.' He bowed his head and suddenly he seemed even younger than she had thought. Twenty, perhaps. 'He was in my cabin. I left him there, safe I believed, and went to see what was happening on deck. It was rather chaotic, as you can imagine. The mate informed me that we were abandoning ship and asked me if there was anyone else still below.' He spoke slowly, as if reliving it. 'I told him about Seal, my dog, and the other passengers I knew were in their cabins. I thought … Well, the captain was ordering a lifeboat to be launched and I was helping when I realised the mate hadn't come back. I went to get my dog, but it was too late. The next thing I knew we were being driven onto the rocks.' He looked up at her. 'The captain did not see your lighthouse.'

As her father had feared, the storm clouds had hidden the lamp from the *Alvarez* until it was too late.

'Do you live here?' he asked her, and this time when she met his dark eyes she could see they were puzzled. As if the thought of a young woman being here on an island mystified him.

'I'm the lightkeeper's daughter. Mr Webster is my father,' she said with a nod towards Leo, who remained by the injured man's side. 'I've lived on Benevolence for nine years now.'

'Nine years?' he said, astonished. 'I thought my life was ending when my father sent me to the colonies last year. Nine years. Don't you get bored, Miss Webster? There cannot be much gaiety here.'

Now it was her turn to be astonished.

He went on in a teasing voice. 'No parties to attend, no friends to visit, no shops to browse through. My sisters would be wailing to be set free of such purgatory within five minutes of stepping ashore on your island.'

Was he flirting with her? Some of the sailors on the supply steamer liked to flirt, but usually it was in a shy way, and if not the captain soon put them in their places. Laura had a feeling that

Edmund Bailey was used to ladies enjoying his company. Young as he was, he had a self-confidence that implied he was also used to getting his own way.

Laura's voice was stiff and unfriendly. 'I'm afraid I don't have time to be bored, Mr Bailey. I am far too busy doing things that matter.'

Instead of taking offence, he gave a soft laugh. And he was still staring at her in a way that made her wonder if, like the mate, he too had hit his head.

'So cold, so cold …' Mrs Munro was shaking with what Laura knew must be shock as well as the cold. She unbuttoned her wet-weather jacket with numb fingers and put it around the other woman's shoulders, before slipping an arm around her and holding her against her own warm body. 'You're safe now,' she said, close to the woman's ear. 'Can you hear me, Mrs Munro? You're quite safe.'

'My husband. Albert … Where is Albert?'

Laura could hear the agony in her voice. At the same time, something about the name struck a chord, as if she had read it recently. Laura was a voracious reader, and as well as her bookshelf, she had a collection of newspapers and magazines, clippings from which she kept in her room. It was her way of being part of the outside world despite her isolation. She had always told herself that she did not need to attend the picnics and parties in Hobart like other girls, because she could read about them. Abruptly, she wondered what Edmund Bailey would think of that. Would he stare at her even more?

'Albert went out on deck to see what was happening,' Mrs Munro was speaking again, her voice low and rambling. 'Then he came back and took me up with him, and I could see how awful things were. There was no hope at all. I thought I was going to drown, but that man,' she indicated Edmund, 'saved my life.'

'Ahoy there!'

The shout brought their heads around. Laura felt a leap of excitement when she saw two men wading through the water towards them. Jumping up as her father heaved himself to his feet, Laura hurried to help. One of the men, a broad-shouldered fellow, wore the practical clothes of a crew member.

'Are you hurt?' Leo called.

'My arm,' he said in a gravelly voice. He was holding his right arm to his chest, as if it might be broken.

The other man was smaller, his belly protruding beneath his waistcoat as he panted and gasped, stumbling out of the water and onto the beach as if he was at the end of his strength.

'We would have drowned if the dog hadn't swum with us,' the seaman said. 'He pulled me along, and when I came upon Mr Jones here, about to sink, I dragged him up.'

'Dog?' Laura asked, wondering if this was Edmund Bailey's pet. Just then, a sleek, wet body pounded out of the water and speared past her.

Laura gasped, and then gave a shocked laugh as she realised it was indeed a dog. A large dog. It began to shake itself wildly, sending out a shower of salty droplets.

'Seal!' Edmund cried, and she heard the joy in his voice. Seal also heard him, and jumped at him, almost knocking him over with enthusiasm.

The sailor with the broken arm sank down on the sand as if too exhausted to walk another step. 'He was barking from your cabin, sir,' he said to Edmund. 'I let him out.'

'You have my deepest gratitude.' Edmund sounded close to tears. 'I ... he may be a mere dog, but he is my dearest friend.'

The portly man shot him a disbelieving look before bending over to catch his breath, back heaving from his exertions.

'Where's your coat?' Leo slung his arm around her shoulders.

'Mrs Munro needed it more than I did.'

'Four men and a woman,' he said, as if cataloguing the extent of the survivors.

'Do you know how many were aboard?' She leaned in to share his warmth.

Leo scratched his beard, his handsomely rugged face creased in its weathered lines. 'Mr Bailey isn't sure, lass, but I don't think there were as many as we feared. The *Alvarez* was chartered by Mr Munro to carry him and his wife to Melbourne, and it was taking only a few paying passengers, along with the usual crew. I'd say eight or ten all up.'

Five saved and perhaps five drowned, Laura thought. No doubt the morning light would reveal the full extent of the tragedy.

'Don't forget the dog,' Laura said with a smile.

Her father grinned back. 'Aye, our fancy Mr Bailey's dog.' He gave her a sideways look as if he wanted to say more about Mr Bailey and then changed his mind. 'He's the only able-bodied one among them, so he'll have to help me get the mate up the track. Can you help Mrs Munro? The rest will have to shift for themselves.'

'What about …?' She turned and stared out towards the rocks.

Her father did the same, grim-faced. 'If there are more poor souls still alive, we can't do much for them now. I'll come back after we get this lot to safety. Let us hope that the storm blows itself out soon, and we can put out the lifeboat.'

Times like this must remind him of the past, when Laura's mother drowned, but he was right. Hard as it was, there was nothing they could do now but care for those who were alive.

Mrs Munro was struggling to her feet and Laura went to help her. 'Albert should be here now,' the woman said, looking about wildly. 'We need to call to him.'

'Mrs Munro …'

'He's alive,' she insisted. 'I know he is.'

'Come with me,' Laura said gently. 'Our cottage has a fire to warm you. You can't help Albert if you're frozen.'

'This wasn't supposed to happen.' The woman was staring at Laura now. 'Our lives were only just beginning. We had so much before us, years of happiness. Years together. Why did this happen? It's as if we're being punished.'

Laura had no answer for her.

The small man with the round stomach seemed to have regained his breath and now trotted up alongside them. 'I need to get to

Melbourne,' he said, peering about him as if he had not heard a word anyone else had spoken. 'I have urgent business there.'

'I'm afraid your business will have to wait,' Leo retorted, bending to heave the mate to his feet with the help of Edmund. The mate groaned, his head dangling, his body slumped between them.

'But …' The little man's eyes were wide. 'Surely there will be a ship sent to rescue us?'

Leo grunted, holding the mate upright, while Edmund adjusted his own hold. Seal danced around them as if this was a game. Leo shot the man an impatient look. 'We get supplies by steamer every three months from Hobart, and you're in luck. We're due for a visit any day now. But I expect the storm will delay them, and if it does, then maybe we can intercept a passing ship. I can't promise, though.'

'I can't wait! I must insist—'

'Save your breath for the climb,' was Leo's gruff advice.

He and Edmund started up the beach, moving slowly, supporting the injured mate as best they could. Laura and Mrs Munro followed, and then the seaman with the broken arm. The self-important little man stood a moment, glaring at their backs, and then with a huff joined their party. Seal ran ahead only to double-back again, as if to see what was keeping them.

The beam from the lighthouse shone over the sea, but Laura did not turn to follow its path over the shipwreck. She kept her eyes firmly on the track and gathered her remaining strength. She knew that Miriam would be waiting, with a warm fire and food and sympathy, and that was comforting enough to spur her on.

Mr Edmund Bailey might be horrified at the thought of life on the island—no parties, no shops, no visits to friends. He might look at her as if she was a specimen in a jar, but unless the supply steamer came on time or a passing vessel could be stopped, for the next few weeks he would be sharing that life. Sharing their food and shelter, and their kindness. She hoped he would be suitably humbled.

NINA

May 2020, in the air above Benevolence Island
Day One

A gust of wind buffeted the helicopter, making Nina's stomach dive. She leaned to look down as the aircraft banked into a turn and took another sweep around Benevolence Island. Below them waves struck rocks, spray spurting up and drifting far into the air until she was sure she could taste the salt. She pushed her sunglasses back up her nose and tucked her fair hair behind her ears. She had found the flight from Hobart invigorating as they passed over craggy scenery and wild water, but now all of her focus was on her destination.

The small islands off the coast of Tasmania were mostly solitary and rugged places, and even to travellers in this modern era, they could seem like the end of the earth. That was the appeal, she supposed, for those wanting to get away 'from it all' and explore their thoughts in seclusion. Before the coronavirus lockdown, the island had been booked up for months ahead, but all that had come to a grinding halt now. Isolated islands with decommissioned lighthouses relied heavily on volunteers and visitors to keep them going. Add that to staff members sitting around in offices or taking Zoom calls alone at home, and Island Heritage had decided that this was a perfect opportunity to do some much-needed maintenance.

Nina worked for Island Heritage, and for the next fortnight, she would be the team leader for a small group of employees and volunteers, along with their support crew, living here on the island. Quarantine had been managed as meticulously as possible, but once they were declared healthy and virus-free, they were sent out to Benevolence and would be left to their own devices.

The helicopter did another pass and Nina felt a spike of adrenaline course through her body, trumping her need for sleep. She'd lain awake last night worrying about things, which was nothing new. Nina was the sort of person who worried, and if there was nothing to worry about then she'd find something. She suffered from anxiety, which often came in the form of panic attacks, but over the years she had learned to manage it. Mostly, she kept it hidden, removing herself swiftly from an escalating situation. Although there were still times when it got the better of her, she was determined this wasn't going to be one of them.

Because this was her last chance. She'd transferred from the Tasmanian Department of Environment and Tourism two years ago knowing in her heart she had always been more of a conservationist than a bureaucrat. She had taken on the role of project manager, working on logistics and making certain everything was in place for the field workers. This was her first opportunity to get out into the field herself. There had been an incident in early March, but Nina was determined to rise above that. Lockdown had given her a reprieve and this was her chance to show Island Heritage what she was made of, and she meant to shine.

Her little crew consisted of a construction expert, volunteers to supply the grunt work, and a cook to feed them all. They had been flown over Bass Strait from Flinders Island by light plane yesterday to the private airstrip on Benevolence. Nina had been held up, so she and Elle, a last-minute addition, would be the final team members to arrive, and she was looking forward to settling in and taking charge. With one exception.

Jude Rawlins.

Jude, an up-and-coming travel writer, had been compiling a book on the islands of Tasmania. That had morphed into a television series with him fronting it. His association with Island Heritage was new, and Nina hadn't expected to see much of him. Or maybe that was just what she had hoped for. To keep her distance. Until he had pulled strings and wangled a place in her team. When she'd complained she was told he was paying his own way, and from the fawning attitude of her superior, she suspected Jude or the television production company had made a large donation to the perpetually cash-strapped Island Heritage. He'd bought his way in and she wasn't at all happy about it. The last person she needed on the island was Jude. Another reason for her sleepless night.

They both had been at a dinner in Hobart, before everything had closed down. Jude had won an award for one of his travel videos—he had branched out recently from writing about places to filming them, and his success on YouTube was probably why there had been interest in a series and Island Heritage promptly had jumped aboard. There were times when Nina sneaked a look at him on the video platform, although she'd never admit it. She and Jude had a past she visited as little as possible. She'd managed to avoid him for nearly ten years and suddenly he was everywhere. A conversation that had started off icily polite had soon become nasty.

'There are plenty of islands. You might have joined Island Heritage, but I hope we never meet on any of them.' Nina had heard herself say, only just this side of bitchy.

'Sweet-natured as ever, Nina,' he'd replied, his handsome face twisted into a smirk. She'd wanted to stab him with her cake fork. That or hide in the bathroom.

'If we ever do end up on the same island, then please make sure you stay on one side. I'll stay on the other,' she'd said.

'You make it sound like reality television.' He'd grinned, those dark eyes filled with their surprisingly familiar wicked gleam. Too familiar. Her stomach had taken a dive. Just then, someone had come up to congratulate him, and while he was distracted, she'd taken the opportunity to examine him properly. He was aging well at thirty-two, his hair still dark, his face tanned with lines fanning out from his eyes and smile lines around his wide mouth. If anything, he was even more handsome than he had been when they were together. *Probably knew it, too*, she told herself. It seemed to her that these days Jude was not above using every weapon in his armoury to get his way.

Had he always been like that? Her stomach twisted now, but she refused to let herself fall into the trap that lay in their past. When his admirer had moved on she was ready with another snarky comment.

'Reality television? Well, it certainly won't be *The Bachelor*.'

'*Married at First Sight*?' he'd mused, and then he'd given a chuckle at the glare she had shot him. 'All right, all right. Truce, Nina. Can't we just act like professionals? So, we'll be working for the same organisation. You'll be doing your job and I'll be doing mine. I can't imagine we'll be cosying up over the campfire.'

Nina had almost said yes to the truce. Shockingly, and rather worryingly, she had almost agreed and put their feud to rest. Shocking, because what would she do then whenever she bumped into him? How would she react to the man she had loved with all her heart, only to have it broken? It was too dangerous to get close to him again and she knew it.

Thankfully, they had been interrupted by another bright-eyed fan, and Nina had moved away so there was no need to come up with a suitably snarky answer. Snarkiness verging on nastiness was what coloured their meetings these days, when they couldn't avoid them altogether. She daren't let that change.

The meeting with Jude had soured her evening. She'd watched him go off with the beautiful publicity assistant from the network, and told herself she was being ridiculous. What did it matter what he did after all this time? They had moved on and he was no longer important to her. The past was just that. She would be professional; she would be *distant* and professional.

No matter how sometimes, in the middle of the night, the memories still hurt enough to make her cry.

Anyway, she had enough to think about with organising their stay on Benevolence. She'd employed the professionals needed, and then put out the word for volunteers. Plenty of them had been eager to come to the party, their enthusiasm making up for the lack of pay. She had tried to present the idea of lowly paid work as a working holiday, away from the constant news of COVID-19, and it had seemed to strike a chord.

The helicopter hovered and the pilot's voice came through her headset. 'I'm going to land on the beach,' she said. 'A bit risky nearer the lighthouse. You'll have to carry your gear up. Okay?'

Nina gave the thumbs-up sign. Beneath her, Thankful Cove came into view with its white sandy beach curved into a crescent. Once the helicopter dropped them off, it wouldn't be returning for two weeks. That was the plan, at any rate, but with Bass Strait being notorious for unpredictable weather, they could only trust the forecast—fair weather for the first few days, with the possibility of it changing.

Behind her, Elle was chattering away to the pilot on the headset, her short dark hair feathered about her pretty face, and her camera safely fastened around her neck. Elle would be taking photos during their time on the island, documenting the place, while Nina made notes. They were hoping to post their progress online, internet connection allowing, so that they could get interested parties back to the island when travel resumed. The thought of two weeks on Benevolence didn't appear to concern the younger woman, but Nina had found most of the team were in their twenties, young and enthusiastic. The oldest person in their group was Brian Mason, the construction manager, who was in his late fifties, and then there was Paul, the cook, who was in his thirties.

At thirty-one, Nina's career was her main focus these days. She found relationships increasingly difficult to negotiate. Too many hidden rocks and sharp reefs, ready to sink the unwary, a bit like the waters around Benevolence Island.

The cove was sheltered, a safe anchorage with a jetty, while the dangerous rocks the lighthouse had been built to warn against—the Tiger's Teeth—stretched out from the headland on the left. A short jetty had once received supplies from passing ships, while the rusty railway tracks had been used to pull them up to the top of the island. In recent times, helicopters or light planes had taken over that task.

Nina peered up at the lighthouse, level with them now as they began to descend. White, tall and decommissioned. It was the second-tallest lighthouse in the southern hemisphere and had once been the domain of the lighthouse keeper and his family. There were probably plenty of stories about those days and Jude would know them all—interesting gossip and heart-tugging tales. Jude was all about family, being so close to his own.

She reminded herself not to ask him more than the most superficial questions about the Rawlinses. Not that she needed reminding. Jude's family was another reason for her sleepless nights.

The water in the cove looked calm, a gorgeous turquoise with darker patches of seaweed beneath. She could see some of her team up on the hilltop above the beach, watching her arrival. The existing buildings were grouped up there and they had decided to use them for shelter, as much as was possible—two of the modern cottages had been damaged in a storm last summer, but there were tents set up to take their place. They'd be sharing, apart from Jude, who had managed to snaffle another cottage south of the cove all to himself.

One of the figures, his bright red hair visible against the blue sky, lifted his arms above his head and waved. Nina grinned, recognising Paul. There was a trickle of smoke from behind him, and she knew preparations for lunch would be well underway. She waved back, relieved that there was someone she could rely on totally.

He was an old friend, from back in the days when Jude had been around, and Nina knew he still saw Jude but he never mentioned him. At the time of the breakup, Paul, after a few heartfelt attempts at reconciling her with Jude, had put himself firmly in her camp and he had never given her reason to think he had wavered from his decision.

The white sand of the cove was pristine apart from the scuffed footsteps made by her team. Seabirds sailed around the cliffs, screaming out warnings. Her gaze dropped back to their landing spot, and that was when she noticed the dark figure of a man standing there, watching their approach, his hand up to his forehead to shade his eyes from the sun. The way he stood, that amused and arrogant tilt of his head ...

Jude.

What had happened to keeping to their own sides of the island? Him standing there, watching her land, felt as if he was throwing down a challenge.

Sand whipped up as they came to a soft landing. Nina felt Elle's gaze on her from behind, and wondered how much the girl knew. Jude was a celebrity now, even if she wasn't, and there probably had been gossip about their romance in the distant past. It was annoying, and distracting, but she reminded herself yet again that she would just have to shrug her shoulders and do her job.

Jude ducked down, leaning in to the pilot's side of the craft, and laughing words were exchanged between the two of them. Nina hopped down from her seat just as Jude came around to offer her his hand. She ignored it. Jude lifted an eyebrow. He was wearing khaki shorts and a red-and-white checked shirt, and his feet were bare. He looked completely at home with his windblown hair and the faint flush on his cheeks, as if he had been here for years instead of a day. Nina, who until now had thought herself casually dressed in navy pants and matching cropped jacket, her fair hair in a chignon, felt suddenly overdressed and out of place. And he'd already put her on the back foot and she didn't like it.

Elle was disembarking too, and now there were numerous bags tossed onto the sand. Nina moved away from the gritty storm the rotor blades whipped up.

'What are you doing here?' she said, keeping her voice low. Best not to add to the gossip. 'I thought we were going to keep our distance.'

Behind her she heard Elle laughing at something, and she could see that a few members of her team were negotiating the track down the hill to welcome the new arrivals. She had five minutes, maybe ten at the most, before anything she said to Jude would be overheard.

He watched her, hands dug into his pockets now, and she noticed the wariness beneath his normally confident expression. 'I thought we could clear the air. This island doesn't belong to you, Nina. We have to share.'

'You should have thought about that before you pushed your way into my project. I know you paid off my boss, Jude.'

He raised that eyebrow. 'I persuaded the production company to make a donation. I'd think you'd be pleased. You know I've always been a keen supporter of environmental issues.'

'When it suits you.'

His face hardened, the attempt at a conciliatory smile gone. 'You never give an inch, do you?'

He was angry, and she wondered if she made him angry enough would he jump into the helicopter and go away? That was probably too much to hope for. Like her, Jude would never give in. They were as stubborn as each other. And the thing was she knew why he felt as he did, and she could do nothing about it.

'I don't know why you want to be here,' she said. 'You could come at any time. Why now? Why when I'm here to do my job.'

'Don't you?' He stared back at her, then he seemed to deflate. 'You know, Nina, you've been holding onto this grudge or whatever it is for too long. I'm tired of dealing with it. I just want us to get past it. Because it's always there whenever we meet. Like a bloody great storm cloud on the horizon.'

Shock stilled her. 'I don't know what you mean,' she said automatically, but she did know. The problem was that he didn't. Not the full story. She could see the frustration and puzzlement mixed with hurt in his dark eyes, and she found she really didn't want to explore why he still felt like that. It was like a bruise and she knew if she pressed it, the pain would start all over again. It always would. And she could never tell him why.

They were still staring at each other when Elle cleared her throat just behind Nina. 'Sorry to interrupt. Will I take the bags?'

Nina dragged in a deep breath and turned around. 'There are too many for you, Elle. I'll take these two and we'll come back for the rest.'

'Hello there!'

It was Paul, striding down the beach towards her. Relief swept through Nina at the sight of his mile-wide grin. She wasn't alone anymore. Her friend was here with her.

She glanced at Jude. 'You do your job and I'll do mine,' she said quietly as she passed him. 'That way neither of us will get in the other's way.'

'Oh don't worry,' he snarled back. 'I have no desire to get in your way, Nina.'

Maybe she was imagining it, but just for a moment Nina thought she heard an ache as great as her own in his voice.

LAURA

17 May 1882, Benevolence

It was an agonisingly slow journey back up the track to the keeper's quarters, although at least for some of the way they were sheltered from the worst of the storm. By the time they were halfway up, Laura had learned that the seaman with the broken arm was Isaac and the badly injured mate was Tom Burrows. The self-important man was Richard Jones and he didn't like any of the others, but he particularly didn't like Edmund Bailey.

'What are the chances of me being able to retrieve my luggage?' Edmund said to Laura's father as they paused.

Leo gave him a look Laura recognised. *How,* he was thinking, *could anyone be more interested in their luggage than the lives lost and maybe still to be saved?*

Mr Jones was not so tactful. 'Your luggage, sir?' he interrupted in a sneering voice.

Edmund turned to him in surprise. 'I'm sorry if I seem self-absorbed, Mr Jones, but everything I brought with me from home, from England, was in my cabin. Well ... nearly everything.' He reached into his pocket and pulled out a fob watch. When he opened the casing water dripped out. He held it to his ear and then sighed.

'A family heirloom?' Mr Jones asked, unimpressed.

'My grandfather's,' Edmund said stiffly.

It seemed as if the little man was deciding whether to lecture Edmund on his attitude or offer him advice. The latter won. 'One should always be prepared.' He patted a lump under his already bulging waistcoat. 'I too keep my most important possessions upon my person, but wrapped securely in oil skin. A man in my position can never be too careful.'

'And what *is* your position?' Edmund sounded irritated.

'I work for the government in a sensitive capacity. I prefer not to discuss the details with someone I don't trust.'

Edmund was even more irritated, and Laura thought he might continue the argument, but then his mouth twitched in a half-smile as if it had occurred to him how ridiculous it was in the circumstances to worry about a watch. His dark eyes found Laura and she could see the amusement in them, mixed with resignation.

'Of course,' he replied in a subdued voice.

'Have you no one to come to your aid, Mr Bailey?' she asked him curiously. She was sure that everyone on board the *Alvarez* had lost something—some had lost their lives—but most would have means of support elsewhere. Was this wealthy young gentleman an adventurer, then, travelling alone through the Antipodes?

'I'm sure my mother will send a bank draft when she hears of my plight, but until then I will have to rely on the kindness of strangers.' Although he spoke in a positive tone, there was something else in his voice, something that made her think he was putting on a brave face.

Laura was even more curious, but she stopped herself from asking further questions. Her curiosity, according to her father, had always been a besetting sin. This was neither the place nor the time and she should curb it, for now.

They moved on a little further before stopping again, having reached the point where every step required an extra effort. Tom

Burrows sagged between Leo and Edmund, and Isaac stumbled and gasped as he jarred his arm. Mrs Munro was silent, leaning more heavily on Laura, while Mr Jones struggled to keep up, clinging to the rope beside him with white-knuckled hands. At least they were getting closer to the quarters and blessed shelter.

'Why on earth is this island called Benevolence?' Mr Jones demanded, gasping for air.

'It's been benevolent to us, hasn't it?' Edmund reminded him. 'We're alive.'

Mr Jones glared at him, but before he could respond Mrs Munro spoke up, lifting her head with a wild-eyed stare towards the cove at what remained of the *Alvarez*.

'He's out there, I know it. I can't live without him. Not after ... not now.'

Laura thought of her own mother's tragic death, and how she and her father had struggled afterwards. Mrs Munro might think she could not go on, but she would.

'My father will go back down when we have you safe.' Laura tried to put a level of reassurance in her voice she was far from feeling. 'When the storm's passed we'll put out the boat and—'

'Why can't you put the boat out now?' She cut off Laura's words. Her hair straggled around her face, and there was a cut on her cheek that Laura had not noticed before. Blood trickled from it, diluted by the rain.

'It's too dangerous. We'd be dashed against the rocks.' She did not add that it was her father's rule that they did not risk their lives to save others when the odds were against them. Bravery was all very well, but it came at a cost, and sometimes that cost was too high to pay.

Mrs Munro clearly wanted to disagree; instead, she looked once more towards the boiling water and the sharp points of the Tiger's Teeth. The beam of the lighthouse flashed out again, and laid a track across the sea, and Laura could see pieces of wreckage littering the surface.

Mrs Munro did not seem to notice, but Laura held her breath until the beam moved on, fearful that she might see a body floating among the broken planks and rigging.

Seal ran by them and then stared back as if to say, *Come on!* Laura felt like laughing and bit her lip to suppress it as she supported Mrs Munro for another couple of steps, holding on to her as they both shook with cold. Now Laura could feel the growing tug of the wind and the sharp scatter of the rain against their faces. In a few steps' time, they would be in the thick of it, and there would be no time to rest. They would just have to battle their way forward.

'Why *is* this island called Benevolence?' It was Edmund who asked the question this time.

Leo wiped a hand across a face shiny with moisture. 'My daughter knows the history of this island better than I do. Always has her head in a book.' He chuckled fondly. 'Always asking the supply-steamer's captain to find her something or other in Hobart or Melbourne. Isn't that so, Laura? What does he call you, lassie?'

Luckily, the captain didn't mind the tasks she set him. A self-educated man himself, she rather thought he had made it his mission to pass on his knowledge to the lightkeeper's daughter. He called her Cinderella, alone in her ivory castle, which made her laugh. Not that she was going to share that with the present company. Besides, Laura was far from being a Cinderella. She did not need rescuing.

'Lass?' Her father smiled at her despite his exhaustion. 'Tell us the story of the island while we take a breather.'

Laura tried to still the chattering of her teeth. The story came easily to her; she had told it so many times. 'When Tasmania was still called Van Diemen's Land and full of convicts, there were four of them who were desperate to escape. They knew they would never be free in the colony, but perhaps if they could get to the mainland they could lose themselves there. One day, they managed to evade their guard and stole a boat and set sail. Four desperate men in a small boat, facing the horizon, dreaming of the new life they believed to be before them. It did not work out quite as they'd hoped. Their boat began to take water and ...' She paused. The story was that the boat struck the rocks just as the *Alvarez* had, so she thought it better to adjust it slightly, in the circumstances. 'Before it sank, the men spotted the island and swam ashore.'

'This was long before the lighthouse, then?' Edmund interrupted. He was watching her face intently, as if he really could picture the scene she was describing.

'Yes. At that time, the island was uninhabited. The four convicts managed to survive on fish and birds, as well as the fresh water streams all over the island. One of the men happened to be a shipwright. They discovered part of their leaky boat had come ashore in the cove, and he and the others began to repair it. There was plenty of debris washed up, too, from other vessels, and they used what they could. By now, the authorities had discovered their escape and the hunt was on. A passing ship spotted the smoke from their campfire on what was supposed to be a deserted island and word got back to Hobart Town.'

Mrs Munro had gone very still as Laura spoke. Now the woman asked, 'So, they were arrested? They didn't make their escape, after all?'

'No, they weren't arrested. By the time the authorities had organised themselves and set out for the island, the four men were gone. There was evidence they had been there, and to make it worse for the authorities, they had left an ... an irreverent note.'

Edmund laughed, and then coughed. 'I'll bet they did. And did they reach the mainland?'

'No one knows. They were never seen again. They disappeared and it became an unsolved mystery.'

'And the name of the island, lass?' her father prodded.

'For ever afterwards, it was known as Benevolence Island because it had sheltered the four men. For a little while Benevolence became famous, and people speculated on the fate of those convicts. Now I think they are mostly forgotten.'

'So, that is how Benevolence Island came to be.' Leo gave her a nod, then tightened his grip around the mate. 'Now, let's get you all into the warm. Come on.'

As they made their way towards the quarters, the calm succumbed in earnest to the gusting wind, and hard pellets of rain struck like gunshot against them. Laura felt the sting on her face and ducked her head, clinging to Mrs Munro as they forged ahead. She could smell the smoke swirling from the chimney before the solid white building appeared out of the darkness. She-oaks and melaleucas in the grove behind the cottage thrashed violently about, but at least the trees afforded some shelter. Muted light shone between the cracks in the shutters covering the windows, further sheltered by a deep verandah, and then the door was opening and Miriam stood there. She must have been keeping watch. Her round, pretty face was tight with worry, and with a cry she began to usher them inside. Her blue eyes found her husband and whatever she saw there brought the shine of tears to them. 'Leo?'

'We must get these poor souls warm, lass,' he said in the gentle voice he always used for his young wife. 'Two of them are hurt. One badly. I need to get back to the light.'

'Of course,' she said, and immediately began to direct the bewildered group. The room was warm but stuffy, still smelling of the boiled mutton they had eaten for their midday meal. The fire in the hearth had burned low, but Laura knew that with the wind outside, any more substantial blaze would mean smoke blown down the chimney to choke them. This room was large enough to double as a cooking, eating and sitting area, yet at the moment it seemed small and cluttered. It should have been a sort of paradise for the others after what they had been through, but she could tell by their faces that they were either too shocked to think so, or else they were used to better.

'Sit yourself down, ma'am.' Gently, Miriam led Mrs Munro to a chair and pressed her into it. The woman was white-faced, mouth trembling, her grief a visceral thing.

'I'll change,' Laura said, moving towards her room. 'Will I fetch something dry for Mrs Munro?'

Miriam cast a glance over her. 'I think she's more my size.'

Leo had dragged a straw mattress from one of the bedrooms, and he and Edmund lowered the mate upon it. His head lolled and he groaned, eyelids fluttering. Leo murmured something soothing as he knelt to inspect the man's head, and Laura could see that despite his time in the water, his hair was matted with blood on one side.

Laura hurried into her room and found a clean, dry dress to put on. She stripped off her wet trousers and stockings, and quickly changed. When she was done, Miriam already had water warming, and rolled bandages waiting, along with the various concoctions she collected to deal with cuts and bruises. Once when Leo had cut his hand badly on some of the lighthouse machinery, she closed the wound with neat stitches that left barely a scar.

Laura retrieved her jacket—Mrs Munro was now swaddled in a blanket—and hung it up. It would soon dry in the warm room, and she was sure once her father returned he would be keen to go down to the cove again. All she really wanted to do was sit before the fire with Mrs Munro and let Miriam fuss over her, too, but she knew her father needed her. He had gone to tend the light now—its needs were constant, and she had been his assistant all her life, and if she did not go with him to the cove then he would go alone. She could not allow that.

She hoped, one day, though she suspected it was a forlorn hope, to have her own lighthouse, but women were not given the opportunity to apply for such positions. It was an undisputed fact that many wives and daughters were more than capable of running a lighthouse. Were, in fact, unsung heroines in many situations, or famous ones in others—Grace Darling, for instance—and yet the authorities did not recognise their right to a wage and a title for the work they did. Until that day came, Laura would continue to be her father's assistant.

As if he had heard her thoughts, she felt the weight of her father's hand on her shoulder. His voice in her ear was a soft rumble. 'Lass? We need to get back. In case there're more poor souls to be saved.'

Laura nodded. As she turned she caught Edmund's gaze. There was a frown between his dark brows and he heaved himself to stand, even though it was obvious he was exhausted from his fight with the elements.

'I should come too. You will need my help, Mr Webster.'

'You've done enough for now, Mr Bailey,' her father replied evenly. 'If we need you, we'll be back for you.'

'You can help me set Isaac's arm,' Miriam added. It did not surprise Laura that she already knew the man's name. 'And poor Mr Burrows will need his wet clothes taken off and made comfortable.' She looked at Edmund with a sympathetic smile. 'You too, I think, Mr Bailey.'

Edmund hesitated before nodding. He had taken off his boots, and Laura could not help but notice again how finely they were made. Beneath his bespoke jacket, he had a jewelled pin at his throat, which was winking in the lamp light as it held his sodden neckcloth in place. Her father had called him 'fancy' and indeed he was.

'Should we stay and help first?' she asked, as Miriam followed after them to the door.

'I will manage,' Miriam said. 'I'm good at issuing orders. Almost as good as your father.' Her face tipped up to Leo's. 'Be careful,' she whispered and he drew her against him and bent to place a kiss on her curly hair. Miriam squeezed Laura's hand. 'You too,' she said. A moment later the pair of them were outside, being buffeted by the storm once more.

Laura could tell that the weather had finally begun to ease, but there were still the occasional strong gusts and she knew in her heart it remained far too dangerous to venture out in either the small dinghy they called the lifeboat, or the larger former whaleboat. She followed her father down the track to the cove, and when they reached the sand, stood with him and contemplated the wild scene. More foam had been blown up the empty beach by the waves and the tumbling roar of the sea beyond their sheltered spot mingled with the moaning of the wind above. Lifting the oil lamp, Leo swung it back and forth, and they shouted until their throats ached to anyone who could still hear them. The only response was the wail of the wind and the crash of the sea on the rocks. Laura could see that the *Alvarez* was now nothing more than a hollow shell, being battered about while its keel was pinned on the needle-sharp rocks.

'If there is anyone still alive, then they're beyond crying out for help,' Leo said. His face was ashen with fatigue.

'Poor Albert.' Laura's fingers and toes were numb. She stamped her feet and blew on her gloved hands to try to keep them functioning.

Suddenly, her father stiffened and pointed. 'There!'

Laura startled, and then ran after him along the sand. Foam blew up around her, sticking to her skirt, and she could taste it in her mouth. There was something lying at the edge of the water. A dark bundle of clothing. As they drew closer, the light of the lamp washed over the shape and she realised it was a woman. She lay facedown in the shallows, waves teasing at her long, tangled fair hair. Leo reached down and gently grasped her shoulder to roll her over.

Young, her pale, bluish-coloured skin unmarked, her lashes crusted with sand and half open over blue eyes. The ruffles of her collar were sodden and limp, and a brooch with a large orange stone held it together in place of a top button.

Leo groaned, a deep, anguished sound, and turned his back, covering his face with his hands. Shocked, Laura followed him, pulling at his arms. 'Dad? What is it? Who is she?'

He shook his head and heaved in a breath. When he lowered his hands and his eyes met hers they were dark with pain. 'I thought it was your mother, lass. Just for a minute there. The light hair and her sweet face. I thought it was your mother.'

Laura swallowed. No use reminding him that her mother had drowned many years ago.

Reluctantly, she crouched down beside the body, her hem trailing in the water. Close up, Laura saw that the woman was not as young as she'd first thought, certainly more than twenty. Her face appeared so calm, it seemed that at any moment she might open her eyes and start speaking. Just to be certain, Laura reached out and brushed her fingertips against the woman's skin. It was cold. There was no doubt that she was dead.

Leo was hovering over them, a grim set to his mouth. 'We'll get her to somewhere safe,' he murmured, and stooped down to lift her gently in his arms. He held her as if she was the most precious thing in the world, while water streamed from her clothing and her head lolled. He tightened his grip before he marched up the beach with her. There was a natural hollow in the cliff close to where the jetty was built, a shallow cave that gave shelter in the worst of the weather, and was rarely reached by the tide. Sometimes the little penguins that frequented the island nested there, but it was past nesting season now.

Her father lay down his burden, and began to remove his waterproof jacket. Underneath he wore a coat and he took that off, too, before pulling the waterproof jacket back on. 'We'll leave her here till morning,' he said over his shoulder, as Laura came to a stop behind him. 'Best not take her in with the others.'

'Yes, that's best,' she agreed, imagining the look on Mrs Munro's face.

Leo tucked his coat around the woman's body, and the care with which he did it made Laura's heart ache. He stood a moment, and then with a sigh, pulled Laura to him with one big arm. 'Let's go back,' he said. 'There's no point in staying out here any longer.'

Together they retraced their weary way to the keeper's quarters, too tired and dispirited to speak.

NINA

May 2020, Benevolence
Day One

'Everything all right?'

Paul had walked her from the beach up to the accommodation, and all the way she'd felt the eyes of the others on her. Watching, speculating and probably drawing the wrong conclusions. No doubt word of her argument with Jude Rawlins would spread like wildfire. One thing Nina knew about small groups of people in isolated places—they liked to gossip.

There was a neat-looking campsite set up in front of the cottage, something tasty simmering in a pot over the campfire and dough for bread rising nearby. Nina felt a wave of relief. At least she had chosen the right person for the job to feed everyone—Paul could create a banquet out of a few potatoes and a lamb chop.

And yet Jude's words and presence hung over her, souring the moment.

She glanced about. The generator was there, running the freezer that kept the food cold, safely lodged in a prefab hut that also held other supplies, under lock and key, and Paul and Nina's watchful eyes. Two weeks wasn't long, but one never knew. If the weather turned ugly and no aircraft could risk flying in, they might be stuck here longer—and wasn't that an awful thought. Nina's heart sank when she remembered how much she had been longing for this chance to prove herself, to atone for the stupid mistake she'd made two months ago, and now because of Jude the thought of being here for a few extra days caused her to want to scream.

Paul was giving her his most patient look. 'Nina?'

'Sorry. I'm fine. Just making a mental list of all the things I need to do.'

Paul hesitated and she knew he was going to pry. She wanted to head him off again, change the subject, but it would be no use. Paul was like a dog with a bone once he set his mind on something. She may as well get it over with.

'You and Jude ...' he began, closing the lid on the pot. Seabirds shrieked overhead, hoping for an opportunity to partake. The alfresco meals would have to move indoors if the weather deteriorated, but for now it felt perfect.

'Can we not talk about it right now, Paul.'

Paul was the only one who knew the truth. Well, some of it, anyway. She'd blurted it out in a moment of despair, after he kept trying to get her and Jude back together, but he had promised never to say anything to anyone and she trusted him. He understood the subject was closed, or at least she had thought he did. Now and again he would talk to her about it, or she would talk to him, but she tried not to rely on him too much. From the expression on his face now, though, she wondered if this was going to be one of those times.

'Nina,' he started again, facing her. 'I can imagine how awkward it is for you to have Jude here. I hope you know if you want me to tell him off for being a dickhead, then I'm your man. But it's been ten years. I have to wonder if you ever really got over what happened back then. You think you're coping, but I know you're still suffering the consequences.'

She said nothing. He had told her before that he thought she had symptoms of PTSD and needed professional help, but Nina had denied it. She told him she was managing without any of that 'claptrap'. He had given her a kind look, much like the one he was giving her now.

'What happened in March,' he went on, and then paused.

'That was bad luck,' she said. She'd been saying that since it happened, as if repeating the words would make it true. 'I apologised and they agreed it was just bad timing. It's forgotten.'

Don't stuff up this time, her boss, Kyle, had said to her as she was leaving this morning. *We're giving you one last chance. Show us you're worth it, Nina.*

Another pause. 'Then let's talk about now.'

'Let's not,' she muttered.

'You probably don't want to hear this, but Jude is suffering too.' He held up his hand when she went to angrily interrupt. 'I know he isn't suffering as much as you, but how can he understand when you never told him the truth? He hasn't had a chance to come to grips with any of it. To apologise and, well, grieve, I suppose. Maybe it's time.'

Horrified, Nina opened her mouth to tell him what she thought of that idea, but he ploughed on.

'You're both here, together. On an island. You have nowhere to go. It could be the perfect opportunity for the both of you to talk honestly and openly.'

Nina shook her head. She wanted to tell him it was a terrible idea, that even though ten years had come and gone, essentially nothing had changed. Telling Jude now would be no different to telling him then. The consequences would be the same. Worse, probably. Besides, how could she tell Jude now when she had spent all this time driving him away so they could barely be in the same space together without arguing or spitting venom? Or was she frightened? Because if she wasn't throwing barbs in his direction, then what was left?

The truth.

'I chose this path ten years ago, Paul. I'm not changing direction now. Yes, I was a little rattled to see him on the beach,' she said slowly, selecting her words so that he couldn't read too much into them. 'He hates me and I thought he'd stay well away, that he'd *want* to stay away.'

'He doesn't hate you.'

She waved a dismissive hand at him.

'Nina,' he sighed, raising a rusty-coloured eyebrow. 'This may be your best chance to put things right. If his TV series takes off, he'll be out of here and I think it's unlikely you'll be together in this way again. Not for a long time. Maybe forever.'

For a moment she felt at a loss, which was ridiculous because a forever without the prospect of bumping into Jude should be a good thing. And put things right? How could they ever be right? If she told Jude the truth, then he would hate her more because she would destroy everything he believed in. That had never been her intention. She just hadn't thought it would be so hard to push him away, or that he would keep coming back.

'You're still not over it,' Paul said. 'I don't think you ever will be until you tell him. It's all knotted up inside you. If you talk to him, then you'll begin to heal. You both deserve that, Nina.'

Paul spoke with a degree of wisdom. He had been in the army before she met him, serving in Afghanistan, and she knew he had suffered the after-effects of that tour. He had become a chef because he said that preparing and creating with food soothed him. The memories were always there for him, too, no matter how he had tried to ignore them or use a therapist to banish them, or, in the bad old days, alcohol to blur them. *Time heals* was one of his favourite sayings, *but it doesn't forget*.

'Tell him?' she answered him sharply. 'That's ridiculous. What would be the point?'

'The point? You might actually get a little peace. Or at least you'd get a decent night's sleep once in a while.'

Nina glared. She'd obviously let herself confide in Paul too much over the years.

'I won't tell anyone,' he said with a shake of his head, as if he was hurt by her suspicion that he might. 'I would never betray your confidence, Nina, and I hope you know that. But if you want to come out of these two weeks with your professionalism intact, then you're going to have to find a way to deal with Jude. There were sparks coming off you both down there on the beach and it was hard to miss.'

'I'll tone it down,' she said dryly.

'All right,' he agreed, but there was a flicker of doubt in his eyes.

'You know, I think I am just going to ignore him.' She gave a wry smile. 'Pretend he isn't here to spoil this for me. I'm going to show everyone at Island Heritage how competent I am, that I can do this job, despite Jude Rawlins.'

Paul squeezed her shoulder with his big hand. He was a big man all over, more than six feet tall and muscled like a wrestler. He used to say, when they first met, that it was a wonder the Taliban had missed him. She'd laughed, but thinking about it afterwards she'd decided there had been an undercurrent, a poignancy, to his joke. As if he really did wonder. Survivor's guilt, maybe.

'I'm glad you're here,' she added with a sideways glance. 'Despite the nagging. At least I have a friend.'

He smiled. 'Come on now. I'm your *only* friend,' he teased.

She chuckled. Glad of the change of subject, she took pleasure in observing the camp and the crew as they moved around. Some of Brian Mason's volunteers were seated in a group with mugs of tea, chatting together. The weather was good enough to sit outside as long as they were sheltered from the ubiquitous wind. When they saw her looking they smiled and waved, and she reminded herself to make introductions. In a place like this, it wouldn't take long for them all to get to know each other, and she wanted everything to go smoothly. She was good at managing, planning, but interacting with people was often difficult for her, especially on her bad days.

'I'm surprised Brian Mason got the job,' Paul said, frowning at Nina as she popped a slice of raw carrot into her mouth from the chopping board on the trestle table.

'Why? I was told he'd done this sort of thing before, and he came with glowing references. He has some family connection with the island, too. I know he has a reputation for not being always easy to work with, but that's because he's a perfectionist.' She snatched up another slice of carrot. 'He's not that bad, Paul.'

'If you say so,' he said dryly.

Nina wondered suddenly if he was right and she should have chosen someone else. Someone who could get on with everyone and yet didn't have the same fierce pride in his work as Brian Mason did. Well, it was done now, and if there were problems she would have to deal with them. Put them right.

Elle appeared, looking curiously from one to the other. 'Hi,' she said with a friendly smile in Paul's direction. 'I'm Elle.'

Nina introduced them, adding, 'We were lucky to get Elle as a last-minute replacement after Veronica couldn't make it. Poor girl had an accident, broke her leg, but she'll be fine. Just not up to island life.'

Elle smiled and switched her attention back to Nina. 'Your stuff. Where do you want it?'

Nina glanced past her and saw her bags on the ground. She'd forgotten all about them. She blamed Jude.

'Culinary emergency,' Paul murmured, sotto voce, and Elle giggled.

'I'll give you a hand.' A vaguely familiar face popped through an open door in the old lighthouse-keeper's quarters.

'Oh, thank you.'

'This is Arnie,' Paul said. 'He's a volunteer and a budding chef.'

'I'm here to learn from the master,' the younger man announced.

Was it her imagination or was Paul blushing?

Arnie grinned. He was around Elle's age, brown hair messy and his sleeves rolled up. Another of the band of eager young volunteers who had come along for the experience.

'I'll just stow my gear and then I can meet the troops. I want them to know I'm here if they have any gripes.'

'Give them a day and they'll have plenty,' muttered Paul, the voice of experience.

She smiled and turned to go, but he moved closer, lowering his voice. 'Lis Cartwright is here, too. Just so you know.'

'How did she manage that?' Nina asked sharply. She had seen the names of the volunteers and Lis hadn't been among them.

'Evidently, Jude wangled it with your boss.'

She sighed. 'Of course.' Lis, proper name Felicity, was Jude's biggest supporter. She was a friend from his school days and had hung around the beach house whenever the Rawlins family was there. Nina used to wonder if Lis was in love with him. Now she told herself she didn't care.

Besides, maybe Lis being here would keep him out of her hair. Then why the sting of jealousy? Why the empty feeling in her belly? She used to wonder if Lis had known what happened, and if she did, why hadn't she said anything? But no, she brought herself up with a jolt. She didn't want to mull over the past; she couldn't afford to. She had secrets that Jude knew nothing about. Secrets she was not going to share no matter how much Paul thought they should talk.

She collected her bags and carried them into the main cottage, the one that had belonged to the head lighthouse keeper and his family. Paul would take one room and Nina and Elle the other, while the main area could be used for dining or sheltering from the rain. There was an attic, but it was only used for storage these days. Two of the modern cottages and some bad-weather tents would house Brian Mason and the volunteers, and the single cottage to the south, once the abode of the lighthouse-keeper's assistant, was all for Jude.

Elle had already dumped her gear on one of the two beds, and although it would be rather crowded in here, Nina would only be using it for sleeping. The main area would do for any work she needed to complete, or reports she needed to write up. Elle had taken the place of Veronica, the photographer who'd had the accident—a broken leg wouldn't work on Benevolence. Elle was more than competent—Nina had seen her references. She was also permanently cheerful, which already had started to grate on Nina's nerves. Surely Elle must sleep at some point?

Almost as if she'd read her mind, Elle caught Nina's eye with a tentative smile. 'I don't snore, I promise,' she said.

Nina smiled back. 'I doubt I'll hear you even if you do. The sea air should sort us out if the work doesn't.' She didn't say she had her medication. She was prone to nightmares, and although she hadn't sleepwalked for over a year, she wasn't taking any chances. She had no intention of wandering off the edge of a cliff in the middle of the night. Something she hadn't told Kyle. *It's under control.* And she probably wouldn't have got this second chance if he knew, and she desperately needed to prove herself.

Elle followed her outside again, and Nina paused to take in the view. Until now, she had only seen the island in photographs and it was twice as spectacular in real life. She shaded her eyes, feeling the sea breeze loosen her hair and smooth back her jacket and trousers—she needed to change into the casual gear she'd brought with her. She was keeping her fingers crossed that the weather would hold out for them.

She walked up the steep incline to where the lighthouse stood, noting the signs warning about steep cliffs. To her right Thankful Cove looked serene, its beach curving around it like a white crescent moon, bracketed by rising walls of green scrub and black rock. Nesting seabirds screeched. Dangerously jagged rocks were strewn out from the bottom of the cliff on her left side. The Tiger's Teeth were the main reason the lighthouse had been built in the late 1840s, to guide ships to safety when crossing the Strait from what was then Van Diemen's Land to the Port Phillip District on the mainland. Not that it had always been successful. When the weather was bad and the clouds low, sometimes the light could not be seen, and there had been a number of wrecks over the years. What remained of them was protected, although divers had been known to apply for permission to explore when the weather was fine.

Which reminded her, as well as the maintenance on the island, she was supposed to check for unauthorised visitors. There had been reports from a number of the volunteers who had stayed here over the summer that a boat had been secretly anchored on the west side, and that a man had been seen running and hiding. The island was not open to the general public, although there were occasional visits from passing yachts and fishing boats, and Nina could understand why the guests had been a bit freaked out to have their idyll gatecrashed.

Another deep breath, feeling her shoulders relax, and she headed back to the campsite. Authorised visitors to the island were expected to keep everything shipshape, but the summer storm had caused damage beyond the capabilities of amateurs. Brian Mason would have his hands full. Island Heritage wanted everything made as safe as possible in case someone was hurt during a stay and decided to sue. They were living in a litigious world.

During a chat they'd had after he joined the team, Brian had reminded her, in his pedantic way, that one couldn't stop someone if they were determined to get their pound of flesh. 'Let's hope the volunteers are the responsible sort.'

'You'd think the brochures would give them some idea of what to expect. Unadorned living quarters and the bare minimum of comfort.'

'Definitely not Surfer's Paradise.'

His dry humour had made her smile.

'Do you think a fortnight will be long enough to finish the repairs on the buildings?'

He had tapped his pen on the desk between them, the lines in his face deepening. 'It should be. I can make it work.' He smiled thinly. 'You'd better let the volunteers know what they're in for. Hard work and more hard work.'

'The ones we've interviewed so far have been pretty keen.'

'I wonder if they realise how far away from everything the island is? It'll probably come as a shock to most of them.'

'They've been told. We have a wireless connection, but it's patchy; the weather plays a big part. No landline, although we have a satellite phone, so we're not completely out of touch. Paul is trained in first aid, but anything too serious would mean a call to head office. Let's hope it doesn't come to that.'

Brian Mason had grimaced. 'Let's hope not.'

Nina noticed the old metal bell set up on a high point on the track between the lighthouse and the campsite. It was an original and stood on a sturdy frame with a rope attached to the clapper. The sort of old-fashioned apparatus that called schoolchildren into their classrooms. It was a practical way to get everyone's attention. Wherever they were on the island, they would be able to hear it. She pondered what the lighthouse keeper and his family had used it for. Perhaps it really was a school bell, from when there were enough families with children on the island for lessons to be a regular thing.

As soon as she'd seen a photograph of the bell back in her office, she had decided it was ideal as a meeting point for the group. Not that she intended to ring it more than once a day. Mornings, she decided, after breakfast, when her team could gather together, talk over any of their issues, and messages or reminders could be passed on.

It was almost lunchtime, but Nina determined now would be a good time to test her plan and let everyone know they would be expected to meet up in a similar fashion every day.

Unhooking the thick rope, she swung it so that the bell rang loudly. The sound wasn't quite as musical as she'd hoped, but it was effective. The echoes had barely begun to die away when people were trooping towards her from the four corners of the island. Some, she noted, looked more willing to be interrupted than others.

Those she knew—Jude, Lis, Paul and the volunteer Arnie, Elle and Brian—arrived first. The rest she recognised from the photos she'd seen of them, although this was her first time meeting them all face to face. She had meant to do so before they left, but there was so much to do, and a last-minute glitch with one of their suppliers had meant she had no time whatsoever. The reason she had been working right up until the helicopter left this morning.

'Good morning,' she said brightly, when they had gathered around her. 'For those who haven't met me yet, I'm Nina Robinson.

I'm sorry to drag you up here like naughty children late for class, but I wanted to introduce myself and to let you know that I'm here if any of you need a word. At any time.'

'She's the fixer,' Paul said with a grin.

There was a ripple of laughter. *Good.*

'I'm Gemma …'

'Neil.'

'Reynash.'

The three she didn't know smiled awkwardly, held up their hands and nodded in that order. Brian Mason was frowning impatiently. 'Is this really necessary?' he asked.

'I'm afraid it is,' she replied breezily. 'And it will be happening every day after breakfast. Eightish. I know everyone is busy, but it will allow us to touch base with each other, bring up any problems, ask for help, that sort of thing.'

He grunted. Behind him, Jude stood in silence, Lis on his right— *right-hand woman?* Nina wondered slyly—and Elle was to his left. She had her camera around her neck, ready to photograph anything of interest.

'I'm sure we can manage to give up five minutes of our time each day, Brian,' Jude said calmly. People turned to look at him. They were well aware of who he was, but that wasn't the only reason. Jude had presence. He wasn't as tall as Paul, but he had charisma as well as a restless energy that used to make Nina wonder what he would do or say next. Now he was staring at her, as if waiting for her to thank him for supporting her. Well, that wasn't going to happen.

'It's not really much to ask,' she carried on, 'and I'm sure you understand why it's important. Now, do any of you have anything to say while we're here? Before I let you all get back to it.'

'Start day is officially today, isn't it?' Lis reminded her, sounding as if she had a gripe, after all.

'It is. I'm afraid there's no time to waste.' Nina looked up at the sky. 'The weather forecast is favourable for the next few days, but you never know what it might do here in Bass Strait.'

'I already know what needs to be done in the cottages,' Brian said. 'We can get started on that.' He began to walk away, only to stop and face her again. 'I take it we're finished here?'

'If no one has anything more to say?'

Apparently, no one did. Paul waved a hand. 'Lunch at twelve,' he said, heading back to his food-preparation area. The others drifted away, some of them chatting together. Elle snapped a photo of Nina with the tower of the lighthouse rearing up behind her, and with a smile, followed the rest.

Nina thought that had gone reasonably well. The sun was shining, everyone was happy, and she was finally here on Benevolence. She had a job to do and she intended to do it. And she had something to prove. The past was locked away, and she did not intend to open that door no matter what Paul said. What could possibly go wrong?

Hobart Recorder, 22 May 1882
Special Edition

The severe storm that passed through Bass Strait has left a trail of destruction. Word has come through of the *Seahorse*, a steamer, sunk with all on board, while many other vessels have been damaged or continue to remain out of communication.

Among the latter is the *Alvarez*, reported by us as carrying Mr Albert Munro and his bride to their new home in Victoria. Friends of the couple are fervently praying that they were able to take shelter before the worst of the gale struck. While the search for survivors of the *Seahorse* continues, we can only hope that the *Alvarez* makes port soon.

LAURA

17 May 1882, Benevolence

The lighthouse-keeper's quarters seemed unfamiliar and full to bursting. Strange faces were everywhere. Laura stumbled slightly, feeling dizzy. As well as the lingering scent of the mutton, there was now a cloying smell of sea water, drying clothing, antiseptic and an undertone of wet dog. Seal was lying as close to the hearth as he could get. The dog's coat was paler and longer than it had appeared when wet, and the animal was far larger than it had seemed on the beach. Long-legged and slim-bodied, with a tail that almost reached the floor. Laura had never seen its like before.

'Deerhound,' Edmund spoke, making her jump. He was right behind her, standing there in his shirtsleeves. To her surprise, she saw that he was holding Noah. He seemed so comfortable with the baby, perhaps he had one of his own.

'Sorry?' she said belatedly, clearing her throat and finding her voice.

'My dog. Seal. He's a Scottish deerhound,' he said patiently. 'I'm surprised you don't recognise the breed, being Scots yourself.'

'I don't think they live in lighthouses,' she replied, only realising how strange the words sounded after they were spoken. 'That was where I was born in Scotland. Where I grew up.'

His eyes slid over her. 'You look done in, Miss Webster. Sit down.'

Laura wanted to protest at his high-handedness, but instead she found herself swaying again. He took a firm hold of her arm, retaining the baby in the other, a frown drawing in his dark brows above his long, straight nose. He had a handsome face with even features, the sort of face she could imagine in a room full of elegant, titled gentlemen.

'Take off your coat and sit by the fire,' he ordered her in that same dictatorial way.

Laura saw her father seated in his usual chair, with Miriam busily removing his boots. Normally, he would protest his wife doing that for him, but right now he just looked dazed. The same way Laura felt.

Before she knew it, Edmund was helping her take off her wet jacket, and she was seated in a chair. She bent to untie her boots, fumbling with hands too numb with cold to unpick the knots. Edmund made an impatient sound, and as Miriam came over to them, he handed the baby back to her and bent to the task himself. Laura's wide gaze went to Miriam and caught her trying to hide a smile. She appeared charmed and Laura was not sure if that was a good thing.

'Really, you don't need to,' she said stiffly.

'Of course I do. You saved my life,' was his blunt response. 'Your feet are like ice,' he added as his hands covered her stockinged toes.

She gave a gasp, jerking them away. 'Don't!'

He leaned back, and stared at her with an eyebrow now raised. Miriam actually giggled. 'Laura hates to be fussed over,' she said in a low voice, bending confidentially towards Edmund. 'Same as her father.'

'I need to tend the light,' Leo muttered, but his eyes were already closed and seconds later his jaw went slack as he slumped back into his chair. It was probably the first time he had been able to relax since the storm began.

'I'll fetch Rorie.' Miriam's voice was fading in and out. Her father tried to argue, saying the weather was too dangerous to go out in, but Miriam pooh-poohed him, reminding him of other storms. Laura's eyelids fluttered and grew heavy. Exhaustion overwhelmed her. Even flickering images of the *Alvarez* on the Tiger's Teeth and the dead woman's pale, blue-tinted skin were unable to halt her rapid descent into sleep.

Thoughts of her mother accompanied her in her dreams. In her waking hours, Laura had forgotten what she looked like, and although there was a photograph to remind her, it was not the same. A person was more than a frozen image, which could never capture the way she had moved and smiled, the sound of her voice. Laura had been fourteen years old when her mother died while trying to save others in the wild North Sea off the east coast of Scotland. At first, her body was missing, and Laura had been able to pretend she was still alive and that soon she would come home again. And then her mother's body had washed up further along the coast, and the pain and shock of it had hit her with full force. Leo had found some solace in his work, grieving in private, and Laura had followed his lead, taking on most of the household tasks with the help of the wife of one of the lighthouse assistants.

After a year they were still bereft, and when his tenure at the lighthouse ran out, Leo decided they needed to get away entirely from the scene of their heartbreak. 'A new start,' he'd informed Laura, his eyes brighter than they had been since her mother died. The arrangements seemed to take no time at all, and soon he and Laura were on their way across the oceans of the world. He'd had so many plans, but in the end they hadn't come to anything. Lighthouse tending was what Leo knew best, and so here they were together again, manning a lighthouse, and in the midst of a tragedy.

In her dreams her mother was by her side, pale skin, tangled fair hair and blue eyes. Laura peered closer, because her face wasn't quite right. There was an orange brooch pinned to her blouse, and her mother had never had a brooch like that. Just as Laura realised that this was in fact the dead woman from the beach and not her mother at all, a voice startled her awake.

'Laura?'

Miriam was hovering over her. When she saw that Laura was conscious, she pressed a sturdy pottery mug into her hands. Hot, sweet tea. It was a little over brewed but more than welcome, and as Laura murmured her thanks and bent towards it, the steam dampened her face. She took a sip and closed her eyes. Surely nothing had ever tasted so good? Then she realised how toasty warm her feet were, and saw that she had one of Miriam's quilts tucked around her.

The clear memory of Edmund unlacing her boots and laying his hands over her cold flesh had her glancing across the room. His dog was lying by the fire, but she couldn't see Edmund, and she wasn't sure whether to be relieved or disappointed. Truthfully, she wasn't certain what to make of him. He was a gentleman, that was clear enough, but one with only the clothes he stood up in. A tragedy like this should bring everyone down to the same level, shouldn't it?

Noah cooed in his mother's arms and Laura smiled. Her father gave a soft snore, and Laura's eyes drooped again as she struggled to keep them open. Her body was telling her she had not had enough rest and she should listen to it.

'Did you find anyone?'

The voice was close to her ear, warm breath making her skin prickle. Again, Laura was brought back to wakefulness with a jump. Mrs Munro was leaning close to her, and Laura could see the gash on her cheek was covered in a neat bandage. Her light-brown eyes, the colour of tea, were fixed on Laura with an expression that should have elicited her pity but instead made her afraid. The woman looked as if she might grab hold of her and shake her if she did not answer.

'Did you find anyone?' she repeated, ignoring Miriam, who had come to try to steer her away.

'No one. I'm sorry,' Laura said, her voice husky with weariness, and wondered why she should feel the need to apologise. It was hardly her fault the schooner had come to grief on the rocks, and yet it felt as if she should have done more.

'Did you go out in your lifeboat?' Mrs Munro went on, still with that unblinking stare. 'Did you look properly?'

'The sea is still too rough to launch the lifeboat.' Miriam spoke firmly as she took hold of the woman's arm, and it was obvious to Laura that her stepmother's sympathy for Mrs Munro's grief was losing ground with her need to protect her stepdaughter.

'Where is he?' Mrs Munro asked a question that had no answer, while she twisted her hands together. 'Albert, where are you? You can't leave me alone. I'll do anything. I promise I'll do whatever you want, only don't leave me alone.'

The words were passionate, heartfelt, but before Laura could attempt a reply, Mrs Munro gave a sob and pulled away from Miriam's grip towards the window. She stood there and stared out into the darkness, as if she hoped her Albert would suddenly appear.

Miriam patted Laura's shoulder and murmured, 'She's been working up to this ever since you and Leo went out. Grief has unhinged her. She tried to wake you both up before, but I distracted her by asking her to cut up some potatoes for the casserole.'

Laura laughed softly, imagining wealthy Mrs Munro performing such a menial task. She probably had a dozen servants to do things like that. Because now Laura had remembered where she had heard the name. When the supply steamer had come last time, it had brought the latest *Hobart Recorder* and there had been a wedding notice in it. Only the nuptials of the wealthy and important were mentioned in the notices, and that was where she had seen the Munros. It explained why Mrs Munro was so distraught. Barely wed and already a widow.

Laura wriggled in the chair to get more comfortable. Her father was still sleeping soundly, but now she spotted Edmund. He was speaking to Isaac in a low voice, while once again holding Noah in his arms. Miriam followed her gaze.

'Mr Bailey is a bit of a hero in my books, Laura. He was staying with a family in Richmond with a baby that wouldn't stop crying. When it seemed to take a shine to him, he was given the job of getting it to sleep.' She sighed. 'He looks like someone you might meet at Government House. Or Buckingham Palace in London. I wonder if he's taken?' Her eyes flicked to Laura with a studied innocence, but Laura wasn't fooled.

'He's probably married with children of his own,' she retorted. 'Maybe he left them behind in England. Maybe that's why he's here in the colonies.'

Miriam frowned her disappointment and then brightened. 'I know, I'll ask him!'

'No, you won't,' Laura retorted, irritated. Edmund had been here only a couple of hours and Miriam was already planning a big romance between them. This was not the first time she had tried to match Laura with an eligible man. Whenever the supply boat arrived on the island, Miriam would cast her eye over the crew and wonder aloud whether one of them might make a suitable husband. At first Leo had laughed, until Laura had begged him to make Miriam stop.

'Doesn't she want me to live here with you both?' Laura had asked him anxiously. 'Is she trying to send me away?'

Leo had been surprised, and then he had smiled again and said, 'Lassie, she's happy and wants the same for you! Miriam doesna think a woman is complete without a husband. She's not like you. She couldn't do what you do. She's not strong in the way you are.'

Laura knew he was right. Miriam could live here on Benevolence because she had Leo and Laura, and she felt it her job to look after them, but she would struggle to do the work Laura did. Nor would she want to. Miriam's family home in Hobart had been poor yet genteel. Her father had found himself in debt, but appearances had still been more important than putting food on the table.

The first time Miriam had seen Laura in her petticoat on the beach, she had almost had hysterics. Leo had calmed her down, explaining that he would rather his daughter be comfortable with the sea, than drown like her mother. Grudgingly Miriam had accepted it, but whenever she saw Laura half-dressed on the beach or wearing her loose trousers, she would tut-tut and turn away. As if by pretending not to see helped her to cope with such unconventional, and in her eyes inappropriate, behaviour.

'We put the injured man in your bed,' Miriam said now with an apologetic grimace. 'We couldn't get him upstairs into the attic, and he was in the way on the floor in here. Seal kept trying to nudge him awake. In the morning, I can sort out more beds. And there's always Rorie's cottage.'

'Have you seen him?'

'I took him some honey for his throat and told him to tend the light. Carrot-and-stick approach always works best with him.'

'I'm glad he listens to you.' Miriam had a way of getting even the most truculent person to do her bidding. All the same, Rorie would be leaving when the steamer arrived and Laura suspected he wasn't planning on doing an awful lot of work before then. She had never liked him, and when Leo had caught him spying on her on the beach he had spoken to him in a way that made even Rorie's smirk disappear.

Seal, having heard his name, trotted over to sit beside Laura's chair. He put his long nose in her lap and rolled his eyes towards her, making her smile. She gently pulled at his ears. 'It doesn't matter about the bed. I'm so tired I could sleep anywhere right now,' she reassured Miriam, and smothered a yawn.

It was true that she desperately needed more sleep, but Miriam seemed to need to talk.

'The attic might do for the men,' she mused. Before they had arrived on the island, the attic had been divided into tiny rooms and used by the former keeper for his large family. 'And there's always the old cottage.' It was one of the original buildings, smaller and less substantial, and it stood closer to Lighthouse Hill. 'I'd need to clean it out, and there's a broken window that needs boarding up. I suppose the rain has got in and birds have probably nested inside. But who knows how long these people will be with us? The supply ship will be delayed by the storm. I suppose we can keep the invalids close in here and put the hale and hearty ones elsewhere.'

'How is the mate?' Laura said.

'Tom Burrows? Not good. He's had a considerable knock to the head and hasn't really regained his senses.'

'Even when we were climbing up from the cove and he was moving his feet one step to the next, it seemed to be a reflex action. He was barely conscious.' Edmund had come to join in the conversation, and Laura watched him a little warily as he handed Noah back to his mother, then rested a hand on Seal's back.

'At least he's comfortable and warm,' Miriam said. 'We will have to pray he recovers. There's not much more we can do.'

Laura thought of the little graveyard to the lee of the lighthouse. In it were buried the wife of one of the earlier keepers, as well as a baby and an older child. Bodies from wrecks were usually taken back to port, for their families to bury privately, but occasionally that was not possible or the victim was beyond recognition. There were two sailors in the Benevolence graveyard whom no one had claimed. Probably others, unnamed and unmissed.

'You were lucky that any of you survived,' Miriam said. 'Such a dreadful storm. I've never seen anything like it.'

'It felt pretty dreadful below deck.' Edmund gave a grimace. 'We were sent down there out of the way once the crew saw that we were off course and close to the rocks. Before they realised the hopelessness of the situation.'

Laura glanced over to Isaac the crewman, who was slumped on the floor near the hearth, his broken arm now supported by a sling that looked like one of the headscarves Miriam wore when she was cleaning.

Edmund knelt beside his dog, and his dark eyes found Laura's. 'I think he was drunk. The captain, I mean.'

Miriam put a hand to her mouth. 'Oh my dear Lord!'

Mrs Munro was back, eager to relay what she knew. 'He *was* drunk. Albert ... my husband had been informed that Captain Roberts was an experienced and trustworthy captain, but after we left Hobart Albert noticed he had been drinking. He ordered him below and asked the mate to take over. It was too late, though. We were already off course and the rocks ...'

She shuddered. 'I was in our cabin. I get terribly seasick. My maid, Elsie, was with me. I didn't see the captain after we were on board. I didn't see anyone until we were almost on the rocks. Albert came to fetch me and ... it was madness. The boat leaning to one side and the noise of the sails flapping and people shouting. The waves crashing against us and the wind roaring ... Albert told Mr Bailey to save me if he could, and then I was in the water and he was gone. Albert was gone.' She bit her trembling lips and fell silent.

No one spoke until Miriam cleared her throat and said in a rousing sort of voice, 'I have soup!'

Mrs Munro stared blankly back at her, still reliving the awfulness, but Edmund caught Laura's eyes. She could see the humour sparkling in their dark depths before he glanced down with a smile. She remembered how he had found amusement in the pompous Mr Jones, too. Perhaps Mr Bailey was the sort of man who never took anything or anyone seriously. Rather than finding favour in that, she told herself it was the sign of a man not to be relied upon.

Miriam continued, 'Nothing like a hearty bowl of soup and a thick slice of bread to lift the spirits.'

Laura agreed, and Edmund stood up with a courteous offer to help. She watched them through her lashes. He had already charmed her stepmother. Laura didn't want to be charmed too, and wondered why she was drawn to him in this inconvenient way. He was handsome and yes, he *was* charming, well spoken, clearly well educated and probably from the sort of family she would be expected to curtsey to at home in Scotland. Here too. The wealthy and privileged had brought their prejudices with them, and Edmund would not have given her a single glance in ordinary circumstances. Even Miriam would find it difficult to matchmake two such diverse people. All the same, Laura needed to keep her wits about her.

The soup *was* good, and Laura managed to finish half a bowl before her head began to nod again. When she felt someone remove the bowl from her grip she wanted to protest but she couldn't find her voice. Then there was only blissful sleep.

* * *

'Laura? Lass?'

Laura opened her eyes, blinking, disorientated. The room was barely lit now, the red glow of the coals in the hearth and the dying candlelight dancing over sleeping faces, while their bodies were huddled beneath different coverings. Miriam was nowhere to be seen, and Laura guessed she had taken Noah into her room to sleep.

'Laura?' Her father was stooped over her, his voice a soft rumble. ''Tis time to take out the lifeboat.'

It was then that she became aware that the moan of the wind had softened to a whisper and the rattle of the loose sheet of iron on the verandah roof had ceased. The storm had finally run out of puff.

Laura tried to stand up, but her body weighed a ton, while her head was light and floaty. Nevertheless, she knew she had to push through such weakness because she was needed. Folding aside the quilt, she stumbled, only just avoiding Seal, who for some reason was lying right at her feet.

Leo was already at the door, pulling on his waterproof jacket, and frowning as his busy mind catalogued what tasks lay ahead.

'Do you need help, Mr Webster?'

The voice was close and caused her to spin around too quickly, so that she had to hang on to the back of the chair to steady herself. Edmund was near enough to catch her if she fell. His dark hair was standing on end as if he too had been asleep, and there were shadows under his eyes, but it was clear his offer was not for the sake of politeness. There was unexpected determination in the line of his mouth and watchful dark eyes.

'We're taking the lifeboat out,' she said, wondering if that would put him off.

He only nodded, his voice resolute. 'Then I'll come with you.'

'Are you up to it, lad?' Leo was giving him a sceptical look. 'You've been through a bit. The storm might be gone, but there's a swell running out there. I would have thought going out in a small boat on a rough sea was the last thing you'd be wanting to do right now.'

Edmund's already familiar smile chased away his serious expression. 'I've done worse. And as I'm one of the few able-bodied chaps here, I think you could do with my help.'

Leo stared at him a moment, before he nodded and clapped him on the shoulder. 'You're right. Aye, you're right. We could do with your help. My daughter is dead on her feet.'

Laura began to protest, but her father reached out to squeeze her arm.

'Would you rather bide here?' he asked, watching her carefully.

'I'm coming,' she informed him stubbornly with a frown at Edmund, just in case he decided to argue with her.

Her father's expression was full of pride. 'I never doubted it, lass. There's a spare waterproof for you here, Mr Bailey.'

'Edmund,' he said. 'I'm Edmund here. I left Mr Bailey behind in England.'

Leo gave him a curious look. 'You're right. This is no time for social niceties, eh, lad?'

They shuffled into their wet-weather gear. Laura glanced back. Mrs Munro was asleep on the straw mattress by the window, her pale face slack, her hair wild from the dunking in the sea and the climb up from the cove. Mr Jones was seated against the wall by the hearth, head tilted to one side, his hands folded over his paunch.

Seal whined, but at a word from his master dropped back down with a mournful roll of his eyes. Edmund caught Laura's smile and returned it, before he glanced at the floor as if he was shy. It startled her to think that the fancy Mr Bailey with his bespoke boots and educated speech would be shy in her company. Ridiculous. But she had no time to consider it.

'Come on, then, the pair of you,' Leo said. 'We have work to be doing.'

NINA

May 2020, Benevolence
Day One

Lunch was eaten on the run rather than being a sit-down affair. Several of the group were already fully involved in their tasks, and Nina did not want to risk seeing Jude again so soon. *Let things settle*, she told herself. Once he got stuck into his project, he'd forget all about her; she remembered what he was like at uni. So, she took her meal away to a quiet spot, and while she ate she checked her laptop to see if there were any messages from Island Heritage.

The connectivity was awful. She'd been warned it could be patchy at best. Although she was able to slowly download an email from her boss, with several dropouts, it turned out to be just a reiteration of all they had discussed before she'd left Hobart. She read through it, anyway. Again, he mentioned the reports of a stranger being seen on the island, but also the crucial need to get the maintenance and repairs finished and ready for a time when visitors could once more stay.

You came to us with glowing reports, Nina. I'm expecting to see them fulfilled. Don't let me down this time.

This time.

It was a test, of course it was. She was aware that there had been mumblings among her colleagues about her. Did they think Kyle had been too easy on her? Nina knew it wasn't her fault that she had gone home early that night two months ago and missed the message from a wealthy donor. He had left two more messages before he decided Island Heritage was not for him, after all, and left a whopping great amount of his money to some other organisation, a rival one at that. Nina had been out of the office for two days and when she returned it was too late.

It wasn't her fault, and yet she blamed herself. She'd been working too hard and the flashback had come out of nowhere. She'd been standing alone in the kitchen at work and suddenly she was back in the beach house at Dennes Point. She'd had no choice but to leave. She was a sweating, shaking wreck. And it had taken her two days to get her head back in the right space.

Had someone found out the truth? She told anyone who asked that she was an anxious sort of person and they usually nodded and said they were too. Anxiety was a common affliction in the modern age. Though not the sort of anxiety Nina suffered from. Supposedly, everyone was okay with the disclosure of illness, mental or physical, but when it came down to it Nina knew Kyle would find a way of moving her into an area where she would be writing promotional flyers. A back office somewhere. And if he knew the real reason for her losing them the donor, he'd never have given her the Benevolence job. Not in a million years.

But there was no need to panic. It wasn't going to happen again. This time, Nina believed she had covered every eventuality. She had good people around her. It was only two weeks. A fortnight and she would be flying home with a job well done.

If it wasn't for Jude … No, she wasn't going to let him worm his way under her shiny, hard protective shell. Nor was she going to start rehashing the past, as Paul had suggested, and use this time as some sort of therapy session. There were too many dark corners she'd have to illuminate.

Packing her laptop into her backpack, and cleaning up the half-eaten lunch, Nina decided she would find Brian Mason.

He was working, making notes as he wandered around one of the two cottages that had been damaged in the storm, some rolled-up plans stuffed into his back pocket. His greying hair was fastened into a ponytail.

He looked up with a frown as she stepped into the room. Everything was covered in a thick layer of dust, or maybe it was dirt and sand, blown in through the broken window. The fireplace, no doubt once the place where pots full of meaty stew were cooked and people gathered around to warm themselves while the storms roared outside, was now full of ashes, while the wooden mantel had rotted at one side. Strings of cobwebs hung from the ceiling.

'I wondered how you were getting on,' she said. 'Do you have everything you need? It's probably too late to order in more building supplies, but I can ask.'

'I think we're okay.' He followed her perusal of the room. 'This one was built in the 1920s,' he said, as if she'd asked. 'The quarters where you're staying are a much earlier construction, and so is the assistant's cottage Rawlins is in. There was an even earlier building on the site, but it fell into disrepair and was demolished. Over the years, the population of this place ebbed and flowed, and sometimes they needed more accommodation, sometimes less.'

He had surprised her with the depth of his knowledge. 'I believe you have a personal connection with Benevolence Island?'

His expression became less friendly. 'Something like that.' She'd hoped he might enlighten her, but instead he changed the subject. 'I know we don't have long to complete this, but I'm sure we can make a good fist of it. It'll mean long days. I think I said before that I hope everyone is up for that?'

'It was explained fully when they signed on,' Nina responded, tucking her hands in the pockets of her jacket. It was chilly in here, and as well as the sense of neglect, there was a smell of salty damp. Once again, she imagined what it must have been like in days gone by. Had they felt the isolation, missing their family and the outside world? Or had they enjoyed being masters of their own little domain? She supposed you could get used to anything if you had to.

'I meant to read up about the history of the island. Did you?' she asked, as Brian took out a measure and began to check on the size of the window.

He glanced up from the note he was making on his notepad. 'I don't know a lot, no,' he spoke what she guessed was a lie. 'My wife is interested in early colonial history. She read me some pieces from a book she put in my bag before I left. I can lend it to you, if you like?'

'Thanks.' Nina said, wondering if she'd have time to read it.

Brian went on. 'There was that shipwreck here back in the 1880s. I think that was pretty well known at the time, but I'm not really aware of the details. The cemetery is not far down from the lighthouse if you want to take a look. Or you could ask Jude Rawlins.'

'Oh. Do you know him? Socially, I mean.'

Brian smiled, something she had begun to wonder if he was capable of. 'No. I'm not one for socialising, or media celebrities. I hadn't met him before last night. We arrived together and he told me some of the history of the place. To be honest, I wasn't really listening—I had enough on my mind. But he certainly seemed to know his stuff. You should ask him.'

Nina made a noncommittal noise.

Brian didn't seem to notice, continuing with his measurements.

'Well,' she said, 'if you don't need anything …?'

He made a sound suspiciously like a grunt and she left him to it.

Outside, the sun was shining but the wind was cold. Up here, she could see Bass Strait stretching far into the distance, and taste the salt on her tongue. The lighthouse tower rose to one side, facing out over the Tiger's Teeth and the sea beyond, and the white walls were stained from the years of wind and spray. It probably needed a coat of paint, but they wouldn't be doing that this visit—she'd been told the lighthouse was locked up tight and no one was allowed entry. Seabirds shrieked and she spotted nests on the cliffs. As well as a place of historical significance, Benevolence was a nature reserve.

She knew there were shearwaters here, and Cape Barren geese, but she didn't know much else. She should have done more research. Perhaps Paul would know; he'd always been interested in wildlife. Jude would definitely know, but she wasn't asking him.

Nina couldn't imagine that anyone wanting to come here for months at a time would be looking for a wild party. They would be environmentalists, or the sort of visitors who wanted some reflection time. Solitude. It was her job to make sure they were safe while they stayed. To show Island Heritage in a good and caring light.

She made her way down a stony path to the cemetery, pausing to note the various homemade crosses and piles of stones placed upon what had once been mounds of earth but were now mostly flattened. She spotted a child's name on one, and an anchor burned into the timber of another. There were some flowers laid across one of them, too, but before Nina could investigate further voices from the campsite disturbed her thoughts. Paul was standing there with Arnie, and Lis had joined them. She had seen Nina at the same time as Nina saw her, and after a moment began to walk towards her.

Nina's heart sank. Lis had never been a friend of hers. She had been to school with Jude and his sister, and when Nina and Jude became an item, Nina had often seen her around. She had been at their beach house that final time, before everything imploded. Nina had never been sure how much the other woman knew, but she had been very close with the Rawlins family. Closer than Nina could ever hope to be. Maybe in the intervening years, Lis and Jude had become more than old acquaintances? She had always known that Lis was in love with Jude. She idolised him. She'd probably do anything for him.

Awkward.

'Nina. Enjoying the peace and quiet?' Lis's smile was polite, but there was a coolness in her green eyes. As if she could see right through Nina's own polite smile.

'I was trying to imagine what it must have been like in the old days.'

Lis smirked. 'A microcosm of resentment, probably. Imagine not being able to get away from each other.'

'I suppose they could always go and sit on the beach? Or on the cliff?' Nina gestured towards the seabirds.

Lis shrugged. 'At least we're only here for two weeks.'

Nina nodded.

'I suppose you were surprised to see me here,' Lis said, just as Nina went to move away.

'Well, I've had a few surprises, but yes, I did wonder why you would want to be here.'

That was plain speaking, but Nina figured it was best to get this conversation out of the way as soon as possible.

'I hadn't planned on it,' Lis said easily enough. 'And then Jude said he was going and asked if I wanted to join him.' She smiled broadly, eyes on Nina, but there was something disagreeable about it. 'Of course I couldn't say no. You know I've always been a big fan of his.'

Nina glanced up at the sky because really she couldn't look at Lis any longer. 'Let's hope the weather holds.' If the woman was aiming to get a rise out of her, she would be disappointed. Nina would make certain of it.

'There are always storm clouds on the horizon,' Lis mocked, her sweet voice laced with venom.

Nina walked away without answering. Her shoulders felt stiff, and there was a twitchy sensation on her back, as though Lis was glaring at her. Wishing her dead, most likely. Wasn't that what she had said to her at a chance meeting about four years ago? *I wish you were dead and then Jude would not keep thinking about you.*

Yeah.

Paul waved to her, and Nina quickened her steps, glad to see his friendly face.

'Everything all right?' he asked, handing her a cracker and cheese. Nina took it, realising she was starving. 'Everything's fine,' she said firmly.

He gave her the sort of inspection he might have given his men on parade, to check whether their buttons were shined and their boots polished. She must have passed because he smiled again. 'Good. How about we take a look at the menus, and you can tell me what you think.'

'Are there fussy eaters?'

He snorted. 'No place for fussy eaters here. I have a couple of vegetarians, no problem. I think after a day's work everyone will be starving enough to eat whatever's put in front of them.'

Nina drank in the view beyond him, over the steep slope of the hillside that led down to the cove and the turquoise sea. 'It's an amazing spot. I didn't realise …' She had been too fixated on the details, too worried about doing her job properly, but now she was here, the place itself was starting to wind a spell around her. She hadn't expected that and she wasn't sure it was a good thing, not when she needed to remain focused.

'We're lucky,' Paul agreed. 'Just be careful, all right? Don't fall off a cliff.'

Nina gave a sharp laugh, more nerves than amusement. At least he hadn't said, *Don't jump off a cliff.* Oh God, had she told him about the sleepwalking as well as her insomnia?

'I'll try not to. Not without my superhero cape, anyway.'

He grinned and turned away, and relief filled her. No, he didn't know. No one did. Her secrets were still her own, and if she was careful then she could pull this off. It was her last chance and she was going to ace it.

She was safe. For now.

LAURA

18 May 1882, Benevolence

The swell was still dangerously high, but the white horses on the crests of the waves had subsided. A cold wind, full of salt spray, tugged at Laura's clothes and stung her cheeks, but it was not the furious one she remembered from earlier. Above her, the clouds were moving over a moon that hadn't been there before, round and full with a sickly pallor tinged with green.

The storm had taken the worst of its fury somewhere else and left them with the memory.

When they reached Thankful Cove, Laura's father took hold of Edmund's arm and they came to a halt. Edmund was a little startled but waited obediently to hear whatever was about to be said. They stood huddled in a group, and Laura rubbed her gloved hands together to keep them warm and stamped her feet to thaw out her toes. The tide had turned again and the beach was beginning to collect debris from what remained of the *Alvarez*, while the lighthouse sent its bright flashing light across the scene before moving on.

'My daughter and I found a body down here when we came looking for more survivors,' Leo explained. 'Didna want to say anything in front of the others. They have enough to be getting on with.'

Edmund's dark eyes narrowed as he turned from Leo to Laura. 'Do you know …?' he began and then changed it to, 'What does he look like?'

'He's a she. Youngish lass, fair hair, pretty.' Leo cleared his throat and Laura knew he was thinking again of her mother.

Edmund's expression changed to surprise. 'A woman? There were only two women on board, Mrs Munro and her maid. Could it be the maid? I never saw her. She and Mrs Munro kept to their cabin, but I saw Albert Munro when I arranged the passage to Melbourne. I knew he was travelling with his wife. I spoke to him when we were taking the air after the *Alvarez* sailed, and he said she was feeling poorly but her maid was caring for her. He told me that what ailed her was mal de mer and only a smooth passage could cure that.'

'A stowaway?' Laura suggested. 'Although, she was too well dressed for a stowaway, I would have thought,' she added, remembering the orange stone pinned to her lacy collar.

'So, this must be the maid,' Edmund said. 'Unless there *was* another woman on board, and I don't know of one, but then I'm not the captain. The mate will know.'

Leo nodded thoughtfully. 'Do you think Mrs Munro might identify her for us? Just to be sure. I need to do things properly. The Marine Board will want a full account.'

'No, Dad,' Laura murmured and shook her head. She remembered the grief in the woman's brown eyes when she spoke of finding her husband. 'Mrs Munro is in no state to do that just yet.'

Leo cleared his throat again. 'Aye, well, we could show her an item of the lass's clothing if seeing a body would be too much for her. We do need to put a name to her. Once the authorities are informed, questions will certainly be asked.'

Edmund looked around. 'Where is she? Can I see her?'

'We left her safe just over there. Above the tideline.'

They began to move in that direction. It was not until they were almost at the spot where they had left the woman's body that Leo muttered under his breath and began to run. Laura saw then that the shallow cave was empty. The tide must have swept in here, after all, although she would have thought that even if the storm had pushed the waves higher up the beach, the body would have been at the outer reaches of it. The coat her father had tucked around the woman was lying in a sodden heap, as if it had been dragged from her or tossed aside. But the body was gone.

Leo was standing, staring, as if he could bring her back by the power of wishing.

'A rogue wave?' Laura said.

He frowned. 'The water got as far as the cliff, but not into the cave. See.' He bent down and sifted the sand through his fingers. It was dry.

'Maybe she was still alive?' Edmund suggested.

Laura hesitated, contemplating whether her father's memories of her mother might have interfered with his usual clear thinking. She shook her head decisively.

'No.' That cold, bluish skin, the half-open eyes, and the long fair hair matted with sand. 'My father and I have seen the dead before. There was no mistake.'

'No mistake,' Leo repeated with grim finality.

Edmund hesitated and then said, 'Do you keep any animals on the island?'

Laura and Leo exchanged a glance. 'We have the usual farm animals,' Leo answered, 'as well as the horses and bullocks.'

'I meant native animals.'

'Wallabies, some brush-tailed possums, penguins and plenty of other seabirds. Nothing that could move a human body, if that's what you're thinking, Mr Bailey.'

'Then if the tide didn't take her, a flesh-and-blood someone did.' Edmund's voice was confident, his conclusion indisputable.

And yet, the only people currently on the island were in the quarters above, or standing here on the beach. Could one of the survivors have slipped away and taken the body despite the storm and the risks of being discovered? Perhaps. But the real question was why? And besides, how could they have known about the maid's body? Leo and Laura had not told anyone.

Laura could see by the darkening expression on her father's face that he was asking himself the same questions. Finally, he shook his head. 'We can't do anything about the poor lass now. We need to get the lifeboat out. There may be living in need of our help—the dead can wait.'

Leo picked up his coat and put it to one side, to collect on their way back. The tide had certainly moved it from its original position, but Laura wondered again if that was because of the pull of the sea or because someone had tossed it aside. *Was Edmund right?* she mused as they made their way over to the boatshed.

'How big is the island?' Edmund was gazing up at the steep hillside above the cove. 'Is there anywhere else to moor a boat?' He was obviously still exploring his theory.

'Benevolence is around five miles across and four miles long.' Leo hesitated in his stride, following Edmund's gaze. 'There's an anchorage to the south, which isn't deep enough to take vessels with more than a shallow draught, and another on the far side, sheltered by Birds Nest Island. That's only safe in calm weather. A riptide runs between the two islands and it can be treacherous. I've heard of fishermen dropping anchor there now and again, but I've never seen them. They keep to themselves.'

'Birds Nest Island?'

'It's more of a rock than an island. No one has ever climbed to the top of it, as far as I know. The cliffs are too sheer. Seabirds nest there.'

They opened the boatshed doors and secured them. Laura could see how close to the building the water had come during the height of the storm, and despite the inconsistencies, it no longer seemed impossible that the woman's body had been taken by the sea. The two boats were stowed in here, the smaller dinghy that they used as a lifeboat in waters closer to the island, and the whaleboat that was suitable for the deeper ocean.

They wheeled out the lifeboat to the beach until they reached the water's edge and were able to launch it. It was strenuous work as the lifeboat was sturdy rather than elegant, but over the years it had served them well. Leo and Laura took an oar each, and Edmund sat in the bow, holding the lamp aloft. Despite the moon, it was still difficult to see what lay in front of them, as they began the cautious task of approaching the dangerous rocks and the broken schooner.

The surge around the Tiger's Teeth was strong, and Leo made sure to keep a safe distance. As they drew closer, they could hear the groan of timbers above the wash of the waves. A word here, a dip of the oars there, they kept apart from the wreckage, eyes and ears alert for the sound of the living. Sadly, apart from the flap of a ripped canvas, there was nothing.

'Anyone there?' Her father lifted his voice. 'Is there anyone who needs our help? Call out or make some sound so that we can hear you.'

They waited, but apart from the wash of the water and the grating of timber on rock there was only silence.

'Here!' Suddenly, Edmund held up the lamp and pointed. Laura could see something floating in the water. For a moment, her heart jumped when she thought it was a swimmer, coming towards them, until she realised it was a man floating facedown on the surface.

Leo and Edmund moved to the side of the boat while Laura remained on her oar, keeping them steady. The two men leaned over the gunnel, scrabbling to grasp the sodden clothing and manoeuvre the body closer so that it could be hauled aboard. Minutes later, the body flopped into the bottom of the boat, a white hand thrown out as if in protest. Edmund grabbed the man by the shoulder and rolled him over so that they could see his face.

White flesh, like the underbelly of a fish, with a cut above his brows, and matted brown hair. His eyes were open, staring up at her, and Laura shuddered.

'Best not to look, lass,' Leo rumbled, but it was too late. Even as she turned away, Laura knew here was another image that would stay with her for a long time to come.

'Do you know him?' she whispered.

'It's Roberts,' Edmund said expressionlessly, and when she glanced at him, Laura thought he might be sick. He swallowed. 'Captain Roberts.'

They wrapped the body in the canvas sheet her father kept stowed under the stern seat, and continued on with their search. Leo called again and again, in time his voice becoming rough and scratchy from overuse, but there was no reply. At one point, they thought they might have some luck when Laura spotted the *Alvarez*'s lifeboat drifting further out. They set off for it, their boat lifting over the big rolling waves left by the storm, before sinking into the troughs. Laura's face was dripping with spray and she gritted her teeth against the cold, her arms aching from difficult rowing.

But as they neared, they could see there was no one aboard. A few boxes and bags were strewn inside, as if the boat had been hastily prepared for evacuating passengers who never came. 'Might be useful,' Leo said, as he tied the boat to their own and prepared to tow it back to shore. 'We're waiting on the steamer to bring our quarterly supplies,' he explained to Edmund. 'We're down to the last of our flour and sugar. And now that we have more mouths to feed ...'

By now, the sky was beginning to lighten with the dawn, a strip of light on the horizon spreading until the sky was a milky blue dome scattered with grey clouds. The stark scene laid out before them was even more heartbreaking.

All that was left of the *Alvarez* was a fragmented shell, her keel jammed upon the sharp rocks, while the remaining timbers, once part of the hull, had been smashed or ripped away. She was like the skeleton of a whale, beached and picked clean. The mainsail washed into the water, and there was more flotsam now, drifting with the tide. Laura knew it would end up scattered around the island, just as the dead would eventually end up there, too. Because they had to accept that there were no more survivors to save.

Leo was resting on his oar as he looked back towards the cove and the hill above it. His weary face broke into a smile and he lifted an arm in a wave. Laura followed his gaze and saw Miriam there high on the track, holding Noah, and waving back. At first, Laura thought she was alone and assumed that the others must still be sleeping, recovering from their ordeal. And then she saw a man standing to one side of her. He wore a dark sweater that she knew to be green and shabby trousers, and his beard was dark, and if she had been closer, she knew it would have been flecked with grey.

'Rorie,' Leo named him with a frown. 'Now the storm's gone, he must be feeling better,' he muttered. Leo had never liked Rorie, even before he caught him peeping on Laura. He said he was lazy and untrustworthy, two serious character faults when one lived on an island and needed to be relied upon.

As if he had felt their displeasure, Rorie slunk away.

'No point in staying out here any longer,' Leo said, abruptly brisk. 'Let's get back to shore.'

'Poor Mrs Munro.' The woman would be hoping for Albert and instead they had only bad news for her. Laura glanced down at the body wrapped in canvas. 'Although, she won't be the only one grieving.'

'It could be weeks before anyone in Hobart knows the fate of the *Alvarez*,' Leo said, as they manoeuvred the lifeboat expertly and dug the blades of their oars into the swirling water to begin their journey back to the beach.

'What about the carrier pigeons?' Laura asked.

'I thought they'd flown off to somewhere better,' Leo said.

'We still have a couple,' Laura reminded him. 'I make sure they're well fed so they're not inclined to stray.'

'They're too fat to fly, lass!'

Edmund laughed. 'Have you used pigeons before?'

'Once or twice,' Laura said, and found herself smiling at Edmund over her shoulder. 'When Noah was born and Dad was worried, and Miriam wanted a doctor. It all ended well, though, which was lucky because no one arrived to help until Noah was a month old.'

Edmund looked bemused. 'I can't imagine my mother living in these conditions. And laughing about it! Her days are structured to within the hour—she is woken at eight with hot chocolate and toast, and then she sits down to her correspondence. Luncheon is at one, and afternoon visitors are received at three in the afternoon and not a minute before. We dine at eight in the evening, and the men are always left to their cigars and port.'

His words reminded Laura how different his life must be, how privileged. She spoke the truth without thinking. 'I couldn't live a life where my every moment was regulated. There is much to do here, but apart from tending the light, I make my own decisions. I value my freedom.'

'Is it freedom? You live on an island far away from the rest of the world. Many people would see that as effectively a prison. Aren't you lonely? Bored?' Although his questions might be considered impertinent, she could see he did not mean them to be. He was trying to understand.

'Not lonely, no. And not bored. And definitely not in prison.'

'My daughter is a great reader,' Leo said into the ensuing silence.

'Don't you want to see other places, meet other people?'

Laura thought about it. 'I'm not sure I do,' she decided. 'Whatever its inconveniences, this is my home. I would miss it. Don't you miss your home, Mr Bailey?'

His expression darkened and he looked away, watching as a gull flew low across the water. 'I have no home,' he said. 'I have been cut loose, Miss Webster, and told to make my own way in the world.' There was a tightness to his mouth and jaw, as if his situation did not please him.

'But … why?'

Leo grumbled a warning, 'Laura,' but Edmund answered her, anyway.

'I was considered a bad egg. More trouble than I was worth. I have an elder brother to inherit, and I was surplus to needs. I was sent to the colonies to make something of myself. To find a new life.'

'And have you?' Laura asked curiously, despite her father's glare.

'Not yet,' Edmund admitted, his gaze sliding from Leo to Laura. 'I don't seem to be trained for much despite my expensive education and charming manners.' This time his smile was wry.

'So, you are a bad egg with charming manners?'

'Laura,' Leo sighed, but she ignored him and so did Edmund.

'A bad egg should always have charming manners,' he explained, that teasing note in his voice. 'It allows him to get what he wants when other means fail. Not that it helped me after that business with …' He glanced at Leo and whatever he saw there seemed to recall him to his audience. 'Well, I won't go into details, but it was not my finest hour and my father suggested I go to the Antipodes and learn to be a man and not a damned … dashed wastrel. My sisters wept and my mother, too, but they did not beg him to let me stay, so I can only assume they agreed with him. At twenty-one, I was aboard a ship for Hobart, where a distant cousin has a property, and everything I now owned in a single trunk. A year later, I am on an island in the middle of nowhere with nothing.'

Laura tried to think of something sympathetic to say to that unloading of emotion. Because he was obviously feeling hard done by, despite the undercurrent of dry humour in his voice. Feeling sorry for himself and trying to keep a stiff upper lip.

She remembered then what Edmund had said last night, the words that had upset Mr Jones. 'Is that why you were asking about your trunk? Because all you have is in it?'

He grimaced. 'All my worldly goods sunk to the bottom of the sea.'

'It might yet wash ashore, lad,' Leo said kindly.

Edmund did not seem convinced. Laura glanced surreptitiously at him. He could not be such a bad egg, could he? If he was willing to sooth Noah for Miriam, and help Laura remove her wet boots, or drag the body of a dead man into their lifeboat? Surely, a lost cause wouldn't put himself out like that?

Suddenly, she was too tired and cold to think anymore. Sad too. This had been a dreadful night and the day was not the end of it. A moment later, the keel of the lifeboat slid through the shallows and wearily she climbed out to help haul it up the beach.

NINA

May 2020, Benevolence
Day One

It turned out to be a long day. In the afternoon, Nina had spent some time answering questions from the volunteers about Island Heritage and how the organisation worked. Most of them seemed keen to do this all over again, if they had the chance, or even spend three months caretaking. Brian soon took over the conversation, explaining how he had mapped out the areas in most need of repairs and decided that all of the cottages could do with painting. There was some joking about the colour scheme, but Brian was firmly on the side of white. They had the tools and equipment they required—most of it was already stored here. And really, this wasn't Nina's area of expertise. That was Brian's call, and she stayed silent, not about to step over the line. When he announced his team would start work at six am the next day and only return for breakfast after putting in a few hours, she expected a few grumbles, but no one said a word.

Although Nina felt as if she'd had a good day, ticking off the items on her team-leader list, there was still more to do. Kyle had informed her this morning before she left that he wanted to hear from her via the satellite phone at the end of the day. She felt a spike in her heartrate as she waited for the connection, but after asking her some pointed questions, he seemed satisfied with her answers. 'Well done, Nina,' he said. 'I knew you could do it.' As if she was five years old and had just won the egg-and-spoon race. Then he went on to tell her that he would be away for a few days—'My wife's mother has had a fall'—and she tried to sound sympathetic and not relieved.

'I'll give you a call when I get back,' he said. 'I'll expect a full report then. You might want to ask Jude Rawlins if he needs anything from our end. There's been plenty of interest from the media. An interview, maybe?'

'I'll do that,' Nina lied. 'I hope your mother-in-law recovers quickly, Kyle.'

She set down the handset. By the time Kyle rang her again, she hoped to have plenty of good news to tell him. With any luck, he'd forget about the lost donation and start seeing her as integral to the organisation.

As the evening drew on, they watched the light changing over the sea. The air grew chillier, and despite their sheltered position there was a nasty little breeze, but it was nothing that a couple of extra layers of clothing couldn't fix. Elle had been taking photos, no doubt capturing the sense of camaraderie—she was focused and serious when she was working. Reynash had found a bike from somewhere and bumped over the rough ground, carrying messages from one part of their campsite to another. He made a comical sight, and the tired faces around the campfire were full of laughter.

Darkness had fallen now, the velvet sky clear of clouds and awash with stars. While they had eaten their dinner, there had been plenty of talk, but now the conversation was intermittent at best, and yet no one seemed to want to retire. There was something almost cosy here in their sheltered spot. Arnie brought out a guitar and was playing it softly, his voice low, and the sound washed pleasantly over Nina. It was almost as if the ghosts of the past had gathered around them, eager for company. Which was ridiculous. She didn't believe in ghosts.

Only the living could hurt you.

She hadn't seen Jude after their meeting at the bell. Paul mentioned that he had asked for some sandwiches and taken them with him back to his cottage. No doubt he had scripts to write and video to film. Just like her, he had a lot riding on his time on the island. Fame and fortune awaited him, but then it always had. Jude had been destined to be famous, it had just taken a bit longer than they all expected.

Paul was chuckling at something Arnie said, and Nina smiled. Paul deserved some happiness. His last relationship had ended in tears—she'd taken him out on the town to drown his sorrows. Maybe he and Arnie would strike up something more than friendship. Elle was with the younger volunteers, nodding at something one of them was saying, her expression engaged. Finally Brian Mason yawned and stood up, murmuring a goodnight, and after that the others began to drift away to their beds.

Nina followed. She was so tired she expected to go out like a light. Instead, she tossed and turned in her sleeping bag on the narrow, creaky bed, trying not to wake Elle, who breathed softly nearby. The sea washed against the cliffs, as if it too was breathing. Deep and regular. The wind got up as the night went on, and an occasional gust moaned around the verandah outside her window.

She hadn't done much research on the island, but she had seen some black-and-white photographs, with the various lighthouse keepers standing proudly before the tower, their wives and children gathered around them. It had been a different age, when the only help for those in need was to flag down a passing ship. Time had moved more slowly and those who lived here had to learn to be resilient and self-sufficient. And in the end, both those things were likely not enough, as evidenced by the crosses in the graveyard.

She remembered the flowers then, and wondered again for whom they had been laid. They were wilted, the sort of eclectic bunch you could buy at a 7-Eleven rather than a florist. Someone on the island had done that. Brian? He had ties to the island but hadn't wanted to discuss them with her.

The window rattled. Something ran along the stone-flagged verandah, light steps. An animal. Were there possums on Benevolence? Or more likely rodents of some sort, living on the birdlife. She knew there were no foxes or rabbits, as both had been eradicated by Island Heritage before they could declare the island a nature reserve.

Uncomfortably, that was when she remembered the reports of a stranger on the island, wandering at will and hiding himself from the visitors staying here. Someone had seen a boat moored on the west side, in the shelter of the small, uninhabited island that lay off the rocky coast. There was always the possibility that Benevolence was being used as a meeting place by criminals. Drugs or guns came to mind.

Nina stopped her imagination before it could run riot. She told herself that whoever had been lurking was probably long gone, and if not then surely the arrival of her team would have sent them running. Or sailing. They were perfectly safe.

She heard another sound, and this time the approaching footsteps were heavier. Definitely human. They paused just beyond her window, and stood a moment in silence, listening, just as Nina was listening. There was a scratch, the flick of a lighter perhaps, and then the distinctive smell of cigarette smoke.

Her heart began to pound. She froze, unable to get up to see who was outside wandering around in the dark. Fear swamped her even as she heard the steps leave the verandah and crunch over dry leaves and twigs, climbing the steep incline that led to the upper track and the lighthouse, before they were lost in the wash of the sea and the moan of the wind.

Nina struggled to overcome her panic, breathing evenly, telling herself everything was perfectly all right. But despite her heart rate slowly returning to normal, she knew it was too late. Already the past was wrapping its arms around her, squeezing, and it was inevitable she would dream of it.

NINA

Summer 2010, the Beach House, Dennes Point, Bruny Island

The beach house had been in Jude's family long before he was born. It was more of a shack, and he'd told her that more generations than anyone could remember had lived there. These days, it was a meeting place for cousins and siblings. It was relaxed and far enough away from Hobart for you to feel as if you were in another country.

Relatively new to the Rawlins family, Nina had only been there a few times, usually when it was someone's birthday or on other special occasions. Now, it was the summer holidays and the perfect time to relax at the beach.

Jude and his brother were messing around, pretend-fighting, and Nina laughed with the others. When Murray gave Jude a shove and he fell off the little jetty and into the water, their mother finally spoke up.

'Boys! For God's sake, behave.'

Mrs Rawlins, a thin woman, drawn and ill-looking, was seated in her deck chair under the shade of an umbrella. Her daughter, Mandy, sat beside her, headphones on as she listened to her music.

Nina knew that Jude's mother suffered from a serious heart condition and her children were all very protective of her. She'd had to give up her job with the public service last year, and now they were relying on their paternal uncle Colin's help, along with some government payouts.

Jude had dreams of being a journalist, and Nina knew he worried those dreams might never come to fruition. If the family needed him to earn money now, then he would have to do it, even if it meant giving up his future. Murray was training to be a qualified solicitor and barrister, and had a job lined up in his uncle's firm, while Mandy was still at school.

The Rawlinses were the sort of family who planned years ahead, and now that Angela was ill, everything seemed on the verge of heading off course. It was causing them a lot of stress. Lucky that Colin had stepped in, although Nina sometimes wondered how much of his help was to do with family feeling and how much was because it suited him. There was a coldness in his eyes, a pragmatic air about him, that she didn't quite trust.

She knew that Jude's dad had left them when Mandy was very young. He'd run off with another woman, leaving his wife to support all three children. Colin had stepped into the picture then, angry with his brother, agreeing to pay for the children's education. But ... there was always a 'but' with Colin. He expected them to do as they were told, and Murray was going to be the heir to childless Colin's law practice. Colin had big plans for him, it seemed.

Jude was wading out of the water, trying to avoid a group of kids with boogie boards. One of them must have said something, because he laughed and then pretended to lose his balance and fall backwards into the waves. Lis went to help him, flapping her hands like a worried duck. She got on his nerves, Nina knew, and wasn't surprised when he caught her and tossed her into the water. Lis squealed, and when she climbed out, shivering, went straight to Mrs Rawlins, who gave her a towel and a hug. Nina watched as the two of them sat close together, whispering. Lis was the daughter of a friend of the family, and Mrs Rawlins had taken her under her wing when it became obvious that the friend was more interested in her own life—late nights and partying—than caring for her daughter. Nina knew Mrs Rawlins liked Lis and didn't like her, it was obvious from her suspicious stares, but Nina didn't really let it bother her because all that mattered was whom Jude liked. And that was Nina.

Nina's family wasn't anything like the Rawlinses. No one would have expected her to give up her dreams if one of her parents fell ill. Anyway, they were comfortably off and she was an only child. They held liberal views about her living her own life and they theirs, but she had thought they were reasonably close until she met Jude's family. They were so close it was almost stifling. No one had any secrets, and every decision was argued over and discussed at length. She would hate to live like that, and sometimes she thought about how she would manage if she and Jude stayed together. How she would juggle her feelings for him, which grew deeper every day, with her ambivalence for his family.

'Lazy bones.' Jude sat down beside her, shaking his wet hair like a dog and chuckling when she flinched away. His dark eyes slid appreciatively over her pink bikini and she couldn't help but feel a warm blush of pleasure. From the first moment they'd met at the canteen at Hobart University, there'd been a connection between them. A definite spark, as if someone had struck a match, which was still burning. These days they were inseparable, or would be if she didn't fight to put some distance between them. And that was only because she thought it wasn't healthy to be in each other's pockets all the time. And yes, his family didn't like them pairing off so emphatically. No doubt Colin had some nice, perfect girl lined up for Jude.

Well, too bad.

Jude had told her that he wanted them to travel when they'd finished uni. Take a year off before they found jobs. Of course that was dependent on his mother, Nina knew, so she wasn't committing herself to his plan. Eventually, he wanted to get into travel writing. Nina's future was more conservative. Find a job, possibly in administration. She was good at planning and organising people. She and Jude were very different when it came to their personalities, and maybe that was a good thing. She liked to think she reined him in, while he freed her.

Uncle Colin came and stood over them, throwing a shadow as he lit up another cigarette and blew out a cloud of acrid smoke. He was a big man, his hair greying, his blue eyes piercing. Nina found he intimidated her more than she wanted to admit. He was a barrister and she could imagine him in court, putting the fear of the law into the witnesses for the prosecution. He would have liked to be a QC, but that honour had eluded him.

'I have a place for you in the firm, Jude, if you change your mind. Scribbling is all very well, but there's no money in it.' It sounded as if he was picking up a conversation they had had earlier.

Jude shrugged. 'I know. I still want to give it a go.' He looked up, wary. Nina felt the tension in his bare shoulder as it pressed against hers. 'Besides, isn't Murray going to be the QC in the family? I wouldn't want to take the gloss off him.'

Murray, sitting opposite, raised his beer. 'Too right,' he said with a smirk. Lis cuddled in beside him, and he put an arm around her, but his gaze was on Jude and Nina. These days it always was.

Mrs Rawlins called out to her brother-in-law and he moved away, and Nina sighed in relief. Jude reached for her hand and squeezed it. His breath was warm against her ear. 'Let's get out of here after dinner,' he said. 'I need some alone time with you.'

She smiled, ignoring Lis's jealous glare and Murray's smirk. 'Sounds good,' she whispered back.

* * *

Nina's eyelids moved as she dreamed. The past she tried so hard to bury was there in brilliant technicolour and there was nothing she could do about it.

Outside, the sea whispered and the wind moaned and the island slept while the lighthouse watched on.

Hobart Recorder, 5 April 1882

Rumours currently abound in Hobart. Our readers will remember that in January three ships of the Imperial Russian Navy were in port. Although their visit was friendly, it brought into stark focus the current lack of protection against attack from foreign forces in our fair state. Forts and batteries from the early days have fallen into utter disrepair. Now gossip has begun to circulate that the visit in January was a precursor to a further, far more hostile, visit by these foreign forces. Our state is unprotected, and despite reassurance from the Tasmanian Government, fear has reached fever pitch.

LAURA

18 May 1882, Benevolence

Rorie was standing at the back of the room, beside Mrs Munro, and Laura saw he had his hand on the woman's shoulder. As unlikely as it seemed, he appeared to be comforting her. As soon as his eyes met Laura's, he dropped his hand to his side and his fingers clenched nervously.

Eagerly, Mrs Munro moved forward as Leo and Edmund joined Laura inside, their waterproofs dripping. The gust of wind that blew in behind them made the lamp flicker.

'Did you find anyone?' she asked, her voice seeming to vibrate with hope.

Rorie had followed behind Mrs Munro, his eyes bright with curiosity disguised as concern. Rorie was always interested in other people's business. 'Mrs Munro here has been telling me her husband is missing,' he went on, as if he was in the woman's confidence. Laura wondered why Mrs Munro would be confiding in Rorie, but before she could consider it further there was another interruption.

Mr Jones had bustled towards them in that very important manner Laura was already beginning to recognise. And dread.

'Mr Webster, I need to get to Melbourne. I have information to place before the Victorian Government.'

'Mr Jones,' Leo began wearily.

'I cannot impress upon you enough just how important this is.' He puffed out his cheeks, impatiently. 'Really, there must be some way. What if someone on the island is ill? Doesn't a ship come to you then? Well, this is far more urgent than that.'

'We have carrier pigeons,' Miriam said, 'but they fly south to Hobart.'

Mr Jones gave another huff. 'Really, this is intolerable.'

'Do be quiet!' Mrs Munro was glaring furiously at him. 'Who cares about you, you silly little man.' She gasped and wiped at her eyes as Jones stiffened indignantly. 'Did you find anyone?' she asked again, only just holding herself together.

'We found the captain,' Laura said. 'I'm sorry to say he was dead.'

Miriam made a sympathetic noise.

'He was a drunk in dereliction of his duty,' Mrs Munro responded coldly. 'He lost lives. I cannot feel sorry for him. He got what he deserved.'

Laura understood her feelings, and yet to hear her spout such heartless words was still a shock. There was a silence, as if the others were just as surprised by the outburst.

Leo cleared his throat. On the way back to the quarters, they had spoken about the dead woman and what to say regarding the missing body. Laura still wondered whether she had been washed away by a freak wave, despite her father being adamant the tide could not have reached her. Despite that, they had decided that something must be said if they were to identify the poor lassie. Mrs Munro was their best hope.

'Earlier I found a woman's body, Mrs Munro,' Leo said, his voice a weary rumble. 'I think it was your maid. Unless there was another woman aboard the schooner?'

'My maid?' Mrs Munro swayed, suddenly seeming much more fragile. Rorie moved quickly to support her. Her eyelids fluttered as if she was about to faint. But before the others could react, she seemed to steady and then pulled away from Rorie almost violently.

'Mrs Munro, I'm sorry, but I have to ask you some questions,' Leo began, as Miriam set a chair for the woman. She sat down rather clumsily, her hands clasped together, twisting, wringing. 'What was the lass's name? And what did she look like?'

She was silent a moment and Laura saw her swallow. 'Fair hair. She had a—a sweet face.' She swallowed again and shook her head. 'An innocent.' The expression in her eyes seemed rather lost. 'Her name was Elsie. Elsie Wright.'

'Was she wearing a cairngorm?' Leo asked after a pause.

Mrs Munro shook her head. 'A what?'

'An orange stone brooch,' he explained. 'Pinned here.' He pointed to his throat.

'I remember that brooch,' Rorie spoke up. 'Poor girl. She loved it so.'

Now they all turned to him. 'You remember the lassie?' Leo demanded in amazement. 'How can that be?'

Enjoying their attention, Rorie gave a smug smile. 'Mrs Munro and I are acquainted. I worked for her father, Colonel Fernley. That was before Mrs Munro here was wed.' He stopped and his smile broadened, reminding Laura unpleasantly of a shark.

Leo's expression hardened. 'You knew Elsie Wright, Rorie?'

'As I said, the orange stone brooch was a favourite of hers. Pretty girl. A little giddy, as my old ma used to say. She drowned, did she?'

Mrs Munro gasped, and Miriam shot Rorie an angry glance before putting a soothing arm around the woman's trembling shoulders and murmuring, 'There, there.'

'Since you're here, Rorie,' Leo said sternly, 'you can come up to the lantern room and help me top up the fuel.'

Laura knew Rorie hated his job and he looked as if he would have liked to protest. He must have seen by Leo's face that a refusal was out of the question, because he reluctantly stomped out after him.

Edmund had watched them go, before he flicked his gaze to meet Laura's. Was his mind travelling in a similar direction to her own? When they had discussed the matter of the missing body on their way back from the beach, Edmund had again speculated whether someone else had been involved in the dead girl's disappearance, but Leo had refused to countenance that. The thought of a stranger prowling his island and stealing bodies was probably too much right now. Laura had not argued, but with Rorie's confession that he knew Mrs Munro and Elsie Wright, there seemed to be a strong possibility that he was involved.

Had he been watching when Laura and her father found the body? Had he gone down after the beach was empty? But why would he? He could not possibly know the body was that of a woman he recognised. It made no sense. However, if he was simply being curious, sneaking around where he had no right to be, as he often did, and then realised he knew the woman ... *That* made sense.

'How is Tom?' Edmund asked Miriam. 'Any better?'

'He is still unconscious,' she said. 'Isaac is in there with him now. We thought he might be thirsty and tried to trickle some water down his throat. Without much success, I'm afraid,' she added sadly. 'Maybe you can persuade him to drink, Mr Bailey?'

'I'll see what I can do.'

After Edmund had made his way into the other room, Mrs Munro spoke again. She sounded frightened, diminished, as if the idea of a life without Albert, and now Elsie, was unbearable for her.

'Colonel ... that is my father told that man to leave. Rorie, I mean. He was stealing. He was told to leave and he was gone by the next morning. I'd forgotten all about him until now.'

Miriam tut-tutted but said, 'I'm not surprised. He has been a sad disappointment to my husband. Not many men applied for the position of assistant keeper, and at the time he seemed the best of a bad lot. We've since discovered that Rorie is very good at saying what people want to hear, but not so good at living up to their expectations. Besides which, he's a sneak.' She glanced at Laura, clearly remembering the time Leo caught Rorie spying on her from the clifftop. 'He'll be leaving on the next steamer.'

'Speaking of which!' Mr Jones had been hovering, just waiting for a chance to return to his favourite subject.

'Mr Jones,' Miriam said with her special brand of purpose and determination, 'I think it might be a good idea if you compose a note. For the carrier pigeon. I can't promise it will reach Hobart, but it can't hurt to try.'

He stared at her, his expression hovering between hope and uncertainty, and then he nodded decisively and went to find a pen and paper.

'Laura?' Miriam nudged her and beckoned, and she followed her into the bedroom.

With the door closed, it was peaceful in here. Noah lay fast asleep in his crib, and with his soft, fair hair and smooth, fine skin, he looked so sweet that Laura smiled despite her dragging weariness. Her baby brother was a joy to her, something she had not expected when he was born. She was used to her position as only child, which brought with it the pleasure and burden of being her father's assistant, as she had been from an early age. Was she ever cossetted like Noah? Perhaps her mother had cooed to her when she was a babe in arms, but Laura did not remember it. Her first memories were of the wild sea and the howling wind, and her parents struggling to keep their lamp alight, so that the coastal trading vessels would not strike the rocks.

Now she was so smitten she knew she would do anything for one of Noah's smiles. She thought of teaching him the skills her parents had taught her, and it warmed her heart, even though she suspected Miriam did not want her son to follow in his father's footsteps. Her stepmother would be dreaming of a landlubber's life ashore, safe from storms.

'How long do you think composing a note will take Mr Jones?' she asked, and then yawned at the very sight of Miriam's handsewn quilt on the comfortable bed. The once bright colours had faded to restful pastels over time. Miriam had told her that she made the quilt for her glory box, and then asked what Laura had in hers. She had then to explain to Laura what a glory box was. It was not the first time the two women realised what wildly different lives they had led.

'I'm hoping he's a slow writer. I want to get Mrs Munro settled by the fire,' Miriam said with a sigh. 'The woman hasn't slept more than a few minutes at a time. Always jumping up, asking if we have any news, or staring out of the window. What did you think about Rorie and her?'

Laura shook her head. 'Apart from it being a coincidence I would not have expected? I don't know. She doesn't seem to like him very much.'

'And who can blame her if he was stealing from her father? I wonder why they didn't have him locked up.'

'It sounds like he ran off before they could do so. He and Elsie Wright seemed close, or at least they were, as he tells it.'

Miriam shrugged and sat down on the bed, giving Laura a quizzical look. 'Did you really not find anyone else from the *Alvarez*? I thought Leo seemed to be holding something back.'

'Apart from the captain, we didn't find anyone,' Laura said. 'We put him in the boathouse. He'll be safe there.' But her stepmother was watching her as if she knew there was more, and knowing how relentless she was in her pursuit of a secret, Laura blurted out the story of the missing maid.

Miriam's eyes grew rounder. She was silent for a moment when Laura finished, a frown wrinkling her usually smooth forehead. 'That doesn't make sense.'

'No,' Laura said, 'it doesn't.' She almost went on to mention her reflections on Rorie making off with the body, only to change her mind. It was all rather grim and it would worry Miriam, and Miriam had enough to worry about. 'She was probably washed out to sea again. I wouldn't be surprised if she turns up with the next tide. And there'll be others. They'll wash ashore over the next few days. That's what happens,' she went on. 'We found their lifeboat, too, and towed it ashore. It seemed as if they'd prepared it and were abandoning ship, but by then it was too late.'

Miriam sighed, resigned. 'Then they've all drowned.' Her gaze sharpened on Laura. 'You look done in, love. Climb into bed and get some sleep.'

'I should have gone with Dad,' she grumbled.

'He probably wanted a private word with Rorie,' Miriam said. 'Best if you weren't there to hear that. The language may have been a little colourful. Now lie down, my love, and sleep. I should think there will be plenty more to do when you wake up.'

Laura did as she was told. Once again, her vivid memories of the storm and the dead bodies were dulled by exhaustion and she was grateful for that. She preferred they did not haunt her dreams. Soon her eyes were closing and she was sinking into the wonderful embrace of the bed. Her body went limp and the last thing she heard was Noah snuffling and Miriam's soft voice crooning to him by the cradle.

NINA

May 2020, Benevolence
Day Two

The sound of voices woke her, followed by the dull thud of a hammer from the cottages at the rear of hers. Nina searched frantically for her watch, and peered at the digital readout with bleary eyes. Nearly eight! Everyone had been up for hours, except for her. She'd slept in on her very first morning.

Wildly, she grabbed some clothing, knocking things over in her rush to dress. Her heart pounded as she struggled into shorts, shirt and hoodie, before she sat down to pull on her shoes. *No time to do anything more*, she thought, as she ran her hands through her hair, just as the meeting bell began to ring. Loudly. She saw Lis Cartwright through the door of the quarters, busily swinging the rope. Even from this distance, she could tell how smug Lis looked at getting one up on her old enemy.

Just great.

She waved with false cheer, and with a muttered swear word ducked back into her room to collect her notebook and sunglasses. She needed to brush her teeth, too, but that could wait until after she'd had some coffee. Taking a deep breath, she set off for the growing group of people.

They didn't seem too concerned as they chatted amongst themselves, although silence fell as she approached. Nina told herself that this wasn't a black mark against her. That she could laugh it off. That it wouldn't even be remembered in an hour. All the same, she was very aware of her flushed cheeks and pasted-on smile. She hated to be made to look incompetent, or worse, foolish, and right now it was especially important she appear to be the sort of employee Island Heritage valued if she was going to keep her job.

'Slept in?' Lis said with wide-eyed innocence, as if she wasn't trying to sabotage Nina's career.

'Unfamiliar bed,' she replied, when all she really wanted to do was punch her on the nose. 'How is everything? Everyone raring to go?'

'We've all been "going" for hours,' Arnie said with a friendly teasing grin.

Lis snorted in a not-so-friendly way.

There was an awkward silence, and then Paul spoke up. 'Nina has been putting in the big yards for months, so I suppose we can give her the benefit of a few hours' extra sleep. As long as she doesn't do it again,' he added, wagging his finger at her in a mock-serious way. This time there were some laughs. Nina reminded herself to ask for a bonus for him.

'I promise not to do it again.' She gave them the Scout's-honour sign.

'There is one problem.' Brian's grave voice drew her attention. His eyes were tired and his grey hair was loose and more rumpled than hers, as if he had been running his hands through it, and he was as far from smiling as it was possible to be. 'The satellite phone isn't working.'

That *was* a problem. As their emergency link with the outside world, the phone was essential.

'I had to call in to the office, check on something,' Brian went on, as if he thought she might ask him why he was using the phone at all. 'The wireless internet is down. Something to do with emergency upgrades. I thought I'd use the phone, instead.'

'Okay.'

'I asked Paul and he said it was fine,' he added, frowning, as if Nina had accused him of breaking the rules. The phone was locked up with everything else in the prefab hut, out of bounds unless the key was borrowed from Paul or Nina.

'That okay?' Paul asked now, rocking back on his heels.

'Of course. So what was the problem, Brian?'

'It's not working,' he repeated, more than a little impatiently.

'I used it last night, so it was working then.' His frown deepened, and she hurried on, in case he thought she was accusing him of damaging the damned phone. 'Sometimes the weather interferes with the satellite connection. Or so I've been told.'

'I understand that, but I don't think that is the problem.'

'Okay, I'll check it out. Will it matter if you can't reach the office right now?'

'No, I don't think so. Just a nuisance. It was a personal matter,' he added awkwardly, folding his arms. 'In my opinion, we should expect to be out of contact most of the time we're on the island, anyway. Learning to make do is a valuable lesson. All the same,' he gave her an intent look, 'we should have a reliable backup system if the phone isn't working.'

'A marine radio would have been useful.' It was Jude. She hadn't realised he was there, but now he was standing beside Lis.

A marine radio? Why had no one suggested that to her?

'If this had been a working lighthouse, we'd probably have had one,' he continued on with his lecture. 'To contact passing ships and for them to contact us.'

'Right.' She wrote that down on her notepad, her hands shaking so much it was illegible. 'I'll examine the phone.' She forced another smile. 'Are there any more problems? Questions?'

No one had any of either, and after a pause, the group broke up. Paul called out that breakfast was ready, so most of them headed over there. He stood next to her, appearing concerned.

'Do you want to see the phone now?' he said. 'Might be better to let the rush die down first.' If you could call ten people a rush.

'I'll wait.'

'Maybe Brian did something to stuff it up,' he murmured, leaning in closer.

'God, I hope so.'

He huffed a laugh and patted her shoulder before returning to the breakfast table.

Nina walked further along the track that led down the hillside, enjoying the view, wishing after all that she had collected a coffee first. The water in the cove was smooth, with barely a wave, but further out the green-grey surface was tipped with white horses. She drew the salty air into her lungs. Voices drifted back from the cook's tent, interspersed with laughter. There was nothing like a hearty breakfast to cheer people up.

It was fine, she told herself. *It was fine, it was fine.* She took a deep breath, and felt her determinedly cheerful bubble burst. How the hell was she going to fix the phone? She wasn't a Telstra technician.

'You look like you need this.'

Elle was behind her holding a mug of steaming goodness. She seemed wary and somewhat apologetic.

'Sorry, I should have woken you, but you were curled up fast asleep. I wasn't sure you'd slept much? I heard you moving around most of the night.'

Nina took the mug and sipped, then sighed into the steam. 'You're right, I didn't sleep much, but you should have woken me. Next time shake me until I'm conscious, okay?' She smiled to take away the sting. This wasn't Elle's fault, it was Nina's.

'You've got it,' Elle said chirpily.

Nina expected her to go back to the others, rather than linger while Nina took another sip of her coffee.

'What's with you and the hot travel writer?'

Nina opened her mouth and closed it again. That was one way of putting it, she supposed. Elle laughed and shook her head. 'Sorry, that was a bit blunt. I'm only asking because there's an atmosphere around the two of you, and Lis, is it? She isn't too happy and has been telling anyone who listens that you should never have got the job in the first place. That you only got it because you lie and use people, and then throw them away when you're done with them.'

Nina groaned. Lis was causing trouble, but was it for her own warped pleasure or in support of Jude? Nina didn't know and nor did she care. She would have to put a stop to it, talk to Lis, but she wasn't about to explain the tangled situation to Elle.

'We have a bit of a past,' she said, playing it down. 'Just the usual silly stuff. Lis likes to hold a grudge. If she says anything else let me know, but in the meantime I'll talk to her.'

Elle nodded, watching her carefully. 'Right. So, nothing to see here.' Her eyebrow lifted ironically.

'I've known them both since uni. I knew the family and … It wasn't a very happy time,' Nina explained reluctantly. 'Long story short, absolutely nothing to worry about.'

Elle shrugged. 'It's none of my business, I just thought you should know. Stuff like that can easily get out of hand.'

She was right, and Nina needed to put a stop to it as soon as possible. 'If Lis isn't happy she can come to me, although it's probably a bit late for her to bail out.'

Elle chuckled. 'Maybe we can build her a raft?'

Nina didn't go there, even if the thought of Lis paddling off into the sunset was a good one. She finished her coffee and felt better for it.

'How are you going with the photographs?'

'Good, I think. Not that I can download them at the moment—the internet is crap. I'm heading up to the cottages in a minute, to take some of the team at work.'

Nina nodded. 'Okay. I'll see you later, then.'

She watched Elle walk off. The breakfast rush looked to have finished and Paul was packing up. Her gaze lifted to the lighthouse, high above her. The light was glinting off the windows in the lantern room and just then she had the strangest feeling that she was being watched, and froze. But such a thing was plainly ridiculous. The lighthouse was locked and no one was allowed inside. It was just an empty shell.

Deliberately, Nina turned away and ran a hand through her hair to hold it as a gust of wind caught the fair strands, blowing them into her eyes. She was procrastinating. Time to do what she was being paid for and fight fires. The phone first, and then Lis.

LAURA

18 May 1882, Benevolence

Laura woke suddenly, disorientated and confused. Beyond the window the sky was light, with strips of weak sunshine shining through the shutters. There was the sound of a bird's frantic singing from one of the trees outside and the low hum of voices through the closed door. Laura stretched, her fair hair loose and tangled around her. She pushed it out of her eyes and wished she could push aside the fog in her brain as easily. Noah was no longer in his crib. He must have woken and Miriam had come in to collect him while Laura was dead to the world.

Had Miriam managed to get any sleep for herself? More likely she had spent the night tending to the needs of the others. And what of her father? She hoped that Rorie had taken over the watch so that Leo could get some rest. Almost at once, her thoughts returned to the lifeboat and their earlier, desperate search for survivors. Perhaps this morning there would be bodies on the beach? She hoped that one of them was the missing maid. At least then they would know it was the tide that had taken her, and awful as that was, it was better than the alternative, where Rorie or some unknown person had carried away Elsie Wright's lifeless body and hidden it.

Laura lingered in the bed a moment more, tempted to stay and nap, and then with a soft groan threw back the quilt. Her body ached, but she was young and strong, and she knew she would soon overcome the effects of her labours. There was much to do and Laura had never been one to shirk her duties.

She glanced in the mirror and splashed some cold water from the jug on the stand over her face, before patting her skin dry with a towel. There, at least that ensured she was properly awake. She needed to be alert to deal with whatever confronted her today. Rorie and Mrs Munro, and Tom the mate, as well as Edmund.

A bad egg with charming manners.

She remembered their conversation, her father grumbling as she asked impertinent questions, and Edmund marvelling at her strange and isolated life. He seemed interested in her in a way that was flattering and simultaneously a little alarming. She told herself it was probably just his fascination with an existence that was so far removed from his own. The two of them had been thrown together in a way that could never have happened in normal circumstances. If they had been in Hobart, Edmund and Laura would never have met; they would have moved in such different social circles. Once the steamer arrived he would be gone, and no doubt glad of it, too, and she could settle back down to the familiar daily routine on Benevolence. Forget all about him.

And yet ... Laura wondered if she would forget him. He was young and handsome and unlike anyone she had ever met before. More to the point, he had brought with him a strange sort of restlessness. An odd sense of discontent. She had lived in lighthouses since she was born, apart from that short time when she first came to Australia. It was her life, and she was comfortable with the hard work and loneliness. There was a freedom in it, and she was content with her solitary ways. She had never thought to expect something more until he looked at her with such puzzled amazement.

Was he right? Should she want more?

Laura read a great deal. She read about other places and people. Other lives. She read about adventures in foreign parts—it was a way of travelling without leaving the island. If she felt unsettled, then she quickly quashed such feelings. Best not to let them free, best not to give any resentment the chance to fester. She was happy, mostly. But Edmund had brought those wayward emotions to the surface and she did not like it. He forced her to ask questions of herself that she could not answer. Was she missing out, as he seemed to be suggesting? Would she regret it if she did not experience life outside of her island? Was she somehow less of a person if she lived and died in isolation?

At the same time, the thought of striking out on her own, of leaving her father and Miriam, of taking part in those adventures, alarmed her. She recalled being in London, before they had embarked on their ship, and all the hustle and bustle. Buildings blocking out the sun and the feel of the wind on her face. She had felt bemused and a little frightened. Hobart was not much better. When they had arrived on Benevolence it had been as if she'd come home. The lighthouse, with its familiarity, her life ordered and meaningful. She had felt set free. She had told Edmund all this, but she wasn't sure he had understood how one could be captive to a small island and yet completely free.

Well, it was no use in mulling over those questions now, Laura decided, impatient with herself. Who knew what awaited her this morning? There was no time to imagine herself into a different future when her wits needed to be firmly in the here and now.

Laura smoothed down her crumpled clothing. She desperately needed to change, but her room was being used as a sickroom and she would feel awkward if she intruded on Tom Burrows and whoever was keeping an eye on him. She glanced about at Miriam's room, but she and her stepmother were not the same size—Miriam was a petite thing and Laura was tall and strong-limbed like her father. It was doubtful she would find anything to fit her here. With a resigned sigh, she shook out her skirts, buttoning the bodice up to her throat and brushing down her sleeves, before she pulled on her stockings and boots. She plaited her untidy hair and coiled it up with a few pins to secure it. Then with a deep breath, she opened the door.

Miriam stood with Noah in her arms, speaking in a soft and serious voice to Isaac. His craggy face looked more rested this morning and he was wearing one of Leo's shirts. Edmund Bailey was sprawled in a chair by the fireplace, his long legs stretched out and his ankles crossed. His fine clothing was dry but as rumpled as Laura's. Seal lay beside him, one eye fixed watchfully on the room's occupants. Her father inhabited the opposite chair, his chin sunk deep onto his chest. They were both asleep.

'I saved you some porridge.' Miriam had come up beside her. 'You must be famished. It's nearly noon, Laura.'

Noon? Laura was shocked. She never slept so late. Miriam anticipated her next questions.

'Don't worry, last night Rorie tended to the light. And earlier your father and Mr Bailey went down to the cove to search, but there was no sign of any more survivors. Or anything else for that matter,' she added, at Laura's questioning look. 'Certainly not Albert. Mrs Munro was understandably distraught but seems to be holding up better than yesterday. I'm not sure she has come to terms with her loss yet, poor woman, but she will in time. She must, I fear. I sent her to sit with Tom. I thought it would benefit her to be with someone worse off than herself.'

Laura considered if it would. Mrs Munro seemed completely obsessed with her own ill fortune, and who could blame her? 'How is he?'

'He still hasn't regained his senses, not properly, but he has woken briefly a number of times. He took some soup, which I think is a good sign.'

'Does he remember what happened?'

'I don't think so. He seemed to be having trouble understanding where he was. Although, he did recognise Isaac before he drifted off again, so perhaps in time he will begin to regain more of his senses.

I asked Mrs Munro to read aloud to him, but she said she preferred not to.'

Laura could tell it was a source of irritation to Miriam that Mrs Munro did so little to help. As another woman, Miriam would have expected her to prepare some of the meals, or join in with the other domestic tasks. Edmund, a gentleman one would think unused to such chores, and Isaac, a seaman, had been of more use to her than Mrs Munro.

'Mr Jones is busy writing letters.' Miriam nodded to the corner where the desk was poked into a small space, the little man hunched over it. 'I don't look forward to telling him that even our strongest pigeon would struggle to fly with such a hefty weight to carry.'

Laura smiled. 'At least it's keeping him quiet,' she said softly. 'What can be so urgent that he needs to get word to Melbourne, anyway?'

'No doubt something of great import.' Miriam sounded tired and irritated. 'Never mind that someone else is cooking his food and keeping him warm and dry while he scribbles.'

'Do you need help cleaning the old cottage?' They both suspected the survivors would not be rescued anytime soon, and until then they would need shelter. Being crammed up in here would soon begin to tell on their nerves, if it wasn't already. Besides, Laura wanted her room back.

'Later perhaps. For now, you must eat up.' Miriam pressed the bowl of porridge into her hands. 'Your father mentioned searching the perimeter of the island. There will likely be nothing to see, but he said he needed to be sure.'

Isaac approached them, carrying a mug of tea in his good hand. 'I thought Mrs Munro could do with this.' He gave Miriam a bashful smile.

Miriam beamed at him and he blushed, almost spilling the tea. Her stepmother tended to have that effect on men, and wasn't adverse to using it.

Isaac slipped past, and after knocking, went inside her room. Laura stared longingly at the closed door. Everything she owned was in there, including her collection of newspaper cuttings, and she was sure she had kept something from the *Hobart Recorder* that mentioned the Munros. She did not keep everything she read, only the bits and pieces that caught her eye, and she rather thought the Munros had.

With a sigh she set about eating her breakfast, only realising after the first spoonful just how famished she was. Apart from the soup last night, she had not eaten for many hours, and now her body was crying out for sustenance.

Miriam was busy with a fussing Noah, and Mr Jones was still crouched over the desk composing his important letter. By the time Laura had finished the porridge, Edmund had begun to stir, stretching his arms above his head. Next moment, his eyes blinked open and found her.

'Good morning, Miss Webster.' His voice was husky and he gave her a sleepy smile which was far more attractive than she wanted to admit. Disorientated, she felt as if she had been caught in a breaking wave, her body tumbling, helpless, her heart thudding, her lungs aching for air.

She did not smile back. 'Good afternoon, Mr Bailey.'

He broke out into a grin, as if her reserve amused him. Then he sat up, rubbing his hands briskly over his unshaven face. Leo was also waking up. Laura could see that the lines on her father's face were more deeply etched than usual, and his big, strong body seemed folded in on itself. Vulnerable. He was exhausted and now she felt guilty, remembering her earlier thoughts of escaping the island to see the world.

'We should search the cliffs and the inlets,' Leo echoed Miriam's words. 'The tidal surge could have taken debris from the *Alvarez* around the island.'

Miriam drew closer, her gaze fixed on Laura in a meaningful way. 'Laura can do that. She can take Mr Bailey.'

Leo frowned, looking at his wife and then his daughter. Laura could see he knew they were ganging up on him and wanted to protest—and she was willing him to do so—but perhaps he was feeling the effects of the long night more than he wanted to admit, because he abruptly gave in.

'Lass? Can you manage that? As long as Mr Bailey doesn't wander too close to the edge of the cliff and fall over.' He was half joking, Laura could see, by the twinkle in his tired eyes. He and Edmund already seemed to have reached a place in their association where such teasing was not impolite.

As if to prove it, Edmund snorted a laugh instead of being affronted. 'Mr Bailey will be certain not to fall off any cliffs.'

'Laura's dog blew off once in a gale,' Miriam said with a sigh, reaching to pat Laura's hand. 'Poor thing.'

Edmund's dark eyes warmed with sympathy when they met Laura's, but she pretended not to notice. Before he could speak she hurried after her father, leaving him to follow. It was only as she went to close the door that she realised Seal had bounded after them. The dog wagged its tail, clearly eager for adventure.

Once on the track to Lighthouse Hill, Leo took out his spyglass, raising it to his eye and gazing out past the Tiger's Teeth and what little remained of the *Alvarez*, to the heaving grey-green sea. Eventually, he folded the glass and slipped it into his pocket, while the wind gusted, tossing at his greying hair.

'I should go and check if all is well with the light,' he said. 'Rorie has been up there since last night and I wouldn't put it past him to have forgotten to replenish the oil. He's done it before. Are you sure you'll be all right, lass?'

'Of course,' she said, surprised. Laura was more than capable of searching the island for anything washed up from the storm and Leo knew that. It must be Edmund, then. She noticed Leo's quick glance at the other man, who had bent down to pet his dog.

'Maybe you'll find Elsie.' Leo lowered his voice, regret in his tone, as if her disappearance was a personal failing on his part.

'I'll check on the animals, too,' she said.

Her father smiled. 'Aye, give the horses a rub from me.' With a nod to them both, he began the climb to the lighthouse, which rose like a red-and-white needle against the blue sky. He did not look back, his thoughts already on other matters. *Rorie and his many failings, probably*, Laura thought.

Laura led the way along the upper walking track. This one would take them above the head-keeper's cottage, around Thankful Cove, the trolley rails and the whim, and on to Rorie's cottage. The southern part of the island was more sheltered, and the soil was more productive than the stony stuff found around Lighthouse Hill, or the sandy ground near the cove. There was a paddock for the horses and any other animals needing enclosure. The bullocks were tethered nearby, while the sheep and cattle were allowed to range further afield, and as well there was a coop for poultry. Laura planned to spend some time making sure all was well there before she continued on her circuit of the island.

She noticed that Edmund had stopped and was staring out to sea, as if fascinated by the sight of so much water in front of him and no land. Her father always said there were two sorts of people when it came to islands—those who settled in and enjoyed the solitude, or those who loathed every moment of it and simply marked time until they could be off into the world again.

She imagined Edmund was of the latter.

Just then Seal raced past her, gave a woof as if to ask her what was taking her so long, and with a smile Laura set off again. *Edmund could follow or he could stay*, she told herself, *that was entirely up to him*. Better he did not follow, better for her peace of mind and turbulent thoughts. But she must have wanted him to follow, after all, because when she heard his steps hurrying in her wake, she felt a warm rush of relief.

They walked on in silence, and she took note of the damage the storm had done to the vegetation here. There were branches from scrubby trees torn off by the wind scattered everywhere, and tussocks of grass flattened by the rain. A wallaby went bounding away and Seal set off in pursuit, only to be recalled by Edmund.

'What's over there?' It was not until he asked the question that she realised how far they had come. Edmund was pointing at the white cottage half hidden by a granite boulder.

'Rorie, most of the time,' she said dryly. 'That cottage was built for the assistant keeper, when we can get one. The assistant before him drank himself into a stupor most days and nights, and before that there was a married couple whose children were always ill. In the old days, it was the convicts or ex-convicts who manned the lighthouses. Perhaps they were glad of the work, or the solitude. Now it's a struggle to find anyone who will stay longer than three months. They say they do not enjoy the life.'

'Ah.'

She glanced at him, wondering what that meant, but decided not to ask. They had reached the rise with the boulder, before the land sloped down to the cottage and the barns and pens. Laura was relieved to see the two horses had been taken from the paddock and placed safely in their yard. Ted, the bay gelding, came at once to the fence to see her, while Nelly, the chestnut mare, took her time. The cow and calf were lowing at her. They would need to be fed and their water trough checked—although with all the rain they had had, she did not think it had run dry. Some of the sheep had come to the paddock—the gate was wide open, she noticed—and the chickens were eager to be released from their coop.

'I need to take care of the animals before we go any further,' she explained to Edmund as she slipped through the railings and into the yard.

The work would take some time and Laura did not expect Edmund to help her, so she was surprised when he ordered Seal to stay put and followed her in.

'These two rotate the whim that pulls the trolley up the rails from the jetty?' he asked, but it was not really a question. Her father must have told him. 'How did you get them out here?' He reached to stroke Nelly, his hands sure and confident as he murmured praise. Obviously, he was used to being around horses and knew what he was doing, but then, as a gentleman who no doubt had horses of his own, he would. Laura refused to be charmed.

'They came by boat,' Laura said as she set about her work. 'Everything comes by boat or we have to do without. You get used to doing without.'

'Since I turned eighteen, I've spent most of my time in London,' Edmund said. 'I'd forgotten how much I loved being in the country, at our house there. I thought, when I came to Tasmania, that I would enjoy farming.'

'You didn't?'

He shook his head. 'I was bored. Just as I was in London.'

'When I am bored I read my books,' she told him. 'Or look at the sea. It changes all the time. It never gets boring.'

He didn't answer her, and when she glanced at him she could see he was working up to something. 'Do you know what they call a man like me?' he asked suddenly. And, when she shook her head, 'I'm a Remittance Man. Someone who is sent to the colonies and paid an income to stay away. My family do not want me to come home. I'm an embarrassment to them, Miss Webster. At home I was thought of as a rascal, wasting my father's money and bringing my family name into disrepute. In Tasmania, I was thought of as over-privileged, useless and unnecessary. My cousin made certain none of the females in his household were alone with me, despite my assurance that I would never harm them or their reputations. I may be a rascal, but I am not a cad. I could tell he was glad to see the back of me. I belong nowhere.'

Laura wondered if she should be sorry for him, and yet he didn't sound as if he wanted that. He was merely stating the truth as he saw it. 'You need to find your place in the world,' she said. 'Everyone has a place, and you just haven't found yours yet.'

'You make it sound simple.'

She heard the underlying pain beneath the derision in his voice and wanted to ask him about the dreadful things he had done, but could not quite find the words. For a time they worked in silence, apart from soft praise for the animals.

'You're not worried about being here alone with me?' he asked her curiously at last. 'I could see Mr Webster had his doubts. He must trust you not to be taken in by my charms.'

That made her laugh. 'You may think that living on an island makes me naïve and foolish, but I assure you, Mr Bailey, I can take care of myself,' she informed him confidently.

He nodded. 'I do believe you can, Miss Webster.'

It was well into the afternoon by the time they had finished. Laura knew they still needed to walk the track around the island, but all the same, she felt happier now that the animals had been dealt with. She would have to make sure Rorie put the chickens back in their coop before nightfall. There were no predators like foxes on Benevolence, but sometimes she saw seahawks circling.

'What's that?'

Edmund had climbed up onto a rocky outcrop on the edge of the cliff, which overlooked the south side of the island. There was an inlet here, but it was rarely used, the bottom being too shallow for most boats. But she followed him up and stood beside him, leaning forward to stare at where he was pointing, while the brisk breeze tugged at their clothing and hair.

Her heart jumped. She could see something white tangled among the rocks and heaving up and down with the wash of the sea. After a moment, she breathed a sigh of relief.

'Just part of the sail,' she said. 'But we can take a boat around there later, to make sure.'

Edmund nodded, looking a little deflated.

'We still have a lot of ground to cover,' she reminded him, and they set off again, with Seal trotting beside them.

The air was fresh, and she gazed out over the island as it lay bathed in the sunlight. Above them, the sky was alive with birdlife—parrots and cuckoo-shrikes with their red wattles, as well as the small birds who lived in the shrubby bushes. 'Whenever we have a storm, no matter how terrible it is, the world seems cleaner afterwards. Washed clean and ready to start again.' She spoke awkwardly, aware of him listening in silence. When he said nothing she went on.

'Perhaps we all need to go through struggle to remember how precious life is. You say you are bored, Mr Bailey, but I think you are unhappy. You survived the storm and you should celebrate that. Put the past behind you. When you find the place in this world where you are meant to be, then I think you will know it. And when you know it you will find happiness.'

He was watching her, she could feel his gaze, but Laura stared ahead along the track.

'You are the most extraordinary girl,' he said at last, softly.

This time when she looked he was smiling, and she couldn't help returning his smile.

NINA

May 2020, Benevolence
Day Two

A satellite phone was not much different to a mobile phone. It was a little chunkier perhaps, and Nina had been told that because it relied on a link to satellites circling the Earth, there might be problems. The satellite might be out of range, or the weather might cause interference. All the same, it should work most of the time, and it *wasn't* working now.

Nina fiddled around with it, not really knowing what she was doing, and it was only when she took off the casing that she saw the problem.

Some of the wires were burned out, as if there had been a small fire, enough to short them. She frowned down at the mess, trying not to panic. Surely they'd packed spare parts in case of a situation like this?

Nina was crouched down over the phone, which was situated in the prefab hut, usually locked up for security reasons. The cost of using the phone was steep and Kyle hadn't wanted just anyone calling on it. Calls to check on boyfriends or girlfriends and the like. Unexpectedly, the light that streamed in through the door diminished and startled her into spinning around.

'Everything okay?' Paul was standing behind her. She hadn't even heard him come in.

'Did we get some spares for this thing?' She waved a hand at the phone.

Paul came closer. 'I don't know. There's a box in the corner. Do you want me to have a look?'

Nina shook her head. 'You have enough to do feeding the masses. I'll look.'

'Do you think you can fix it?' Paul added. 'I mean … we don't need it right now, but you never know, and we're a long way from help if we do need it.'

'Should have gone with the carrier pigeons,' she said, and saw his hazel eyes sparkle with laughter before his sombre expression returned.

'Arnie seems to know a bit about electrical systems. Well, he's changed a few fuses, anyway. I'll ask him.'

Nina nodded, and he left her. Paul was right, it was serious, but only if they couldn't fix it and there was a situation that meant they needed to use it urgently. And how likely was that? She really had no reason to think things wouldn't be perfectly all right, so why did she have this niggling sense of unease?

She wished she was one of those women who could just breeze through life, who never seemed to run into trouble. Nina's brain seemed to shoot off in all sorts of directions. Catastrophising, her doctor called it.

A symptom of your illness. Try meditation. Relax more. Go on holiday.

Easy for some.

Nina stood up. Where was Arnie? Maybe this was something simply fixed, and nothing to worry about, after all.

* * *

According to Reynash, Arnie was at the assistant-keeper's cottage where Jude was staying. Nina hesitated, and misinterpreting her expression, Reynash grinned and offered to dink her on his bicycle. She laughed and waved him off, but as she found her way to the upper track that ran above Thankful Cove, she told herself she wasn't nervous about seeing Jude. Of course not. She was going to be polite. Professional. Golden Boy Jude would have nothing to complain to Kyle about, as far as she was concerned.

She paused to look out over the water, fascinated with the play of light over the waves and the constantly changing shades of blue and green and grey. Nina had been more of a dreamer in her younger days. There had been plenty of time to dream then, but now she was always busy. Always needing to get things finished, to show a professional front to her colleagues. To hide the truth. If Kyle found out about her flashbacks and her nightmares, her debilitating insomnia, he would have less faith in her ability to keep it together. Well, he wouldn't. She'd make certain of it. These days she was far more driven than before, pushing herself ever onward, trying to prove that she was better than the rest. Because deep in her heart she was afraid that she really wasn't, and if they found out the truth then they would know it, too.

She took a breath and then another, rolling her shoulders and shaking the tension out of her arms. *Don't look back*, she reminded herself, her own special mantra. *Always look forward.*

The track took her on, past the headland on the far side of Thankful Cove, where there were still the remains of the whim, and along the coastline in a southerly direction. The land here was gentler, the vegetation lusher. Evidently in the early days, sheep and cattle, which were kept to feed the lighthouse station, had roamed freely.

The white cottage lay at the head of a valley.

As she neared it, she noted the walled garden needed weeding, something that was on the list of tasks for the team to complete while they were here. Volunteer caretakers were expected to grow their own vegetables if possible, but it seemed that the storm that had damaged the cottages had also flattened the little greenhouse.

Her gaze moved on to the cluster of old sheds and the falling-down remains of post and rail fences that had once kept animals secured. There must have been horses to turn the whim that hoisted the supplies and fuel oil up the tracks from jetty to hilltop. Horses or bullocks to pull the cart that took everything on to the cottages and the lighthouse itself. It must have been hard work.

There were no animals now. As a nature reserve, the island did not allow any introduced animals that might be destructive to the environment. There were strict guidelines in place, and even pets were banned from landing.

Just then Arnie's voice rose in laughter, and she peered around a wooden lean-to that looked as if it were about to lean itself into oblivion.

He was standing in the yard, holding up a brick. 'How old are they?' he asked someone out of Nina's sight.

She took a step to the side and saw Jude. He was bending over a neatly stacked pile of the same bricks. 'Pretty old, I reckon. Convict maybe,' he said, before he straightened, stretched his back and pushed at the dark hair that had fallen into his eyes. It was longer than it used to be, or maybe he hadn't had time for a haircut before he arrived. COVID probably had something to do with that.

'Were there convicts here on the island?' Arnie asked curiously.

'Convicts manned most of the lighthouses in Tasmania in the early days. There's a story about a group of them who escaped from Hobart and tried to sail to the mainland. They ended up here on Benevolence and it was a while before the authorities realised. By the time the boat arrived to arrest them, they were gone. Left a cheeky note behind.'

Arnie chuckled. 'What did it say?'

'The accounts I read considered it too lewd to repeat, so unless it's been preserved nobody knows.'

'Might be worth researching.'

'I thought about it. You never know what you might find in the archives. Plenty of trash, but plenty of treasure, too.'

Arnie grinned as he threw down the brick and wiped his hands. Then he noticed Nina. He cleared his throat and said, with a quick glance at Jude, 'Hi, boss. Were you looking for me?'

'I was, Arnie.' Nina picked her way carefully through the long grass. She had been told there were no venomous snakes on the island, but one could never be too sure. She noticed that Jude had his arms crossed over his chest in a defensive pose, or maybe he was just bored. She cleared her throat. *Professional*, she reminded herself. 'How is the cottage?'

'Comfortable.' He watched her, letting the silence stretch.

'I'm here for Arnie. You might have heard Brian this morning saying that the satellite phone isn't working. I had a look at it and a fuse or something seems to have burned out. I'm no expert, but we have a box of spare parts and I'm hoping there's something in there that will get it working again. Paul said you're the man for the job, Arnie.'

Arnie pulled a wry face. 'I don't know about that. I used to work in a Telstra shop, but that was mostly selling, not much repairing. I'll give it my best shot. Can't promise, though. Give me a break from brick stacking. I'm not sure why Brian thinks that's a good idea.'

'He's planning to use them outside the cottages. Create paths and a patio.' The familiar voice had come from the shadows near the cottage and Lis stepped out. 'So we can sit and sip martinis in the evenings.' She smirked.

'Or watch the stars. They're brighter here, have you noticed?' Jude was watching Nina.

'I've been too busy,' she admitted. 'I'll make a point of it tonight.'

Lis had come up beside him, giving Nina a narrow-eyed glare. Her shorts were short and tight, but she could carry them off. She'd always been a beautiful girl, on the outside, anyway, and Nina couldn't really blame Jude for liking her company, although she wished he'd chosen someone less vicious. Which reminded her, she needed to have that talk with Lis about her rumour-mongering.

'Do you want to come for a swim?' Lis asked, ignoring Nina and speaking to Jude. 'I went in earlier. Water's glorious.'

'As good as the beach at Dennes Point?' The words were out before Nina could stop herself.

Lis snorted a mocking laugh, but Jude said nothing, staring at her, lines on his forehead that didn't used to be there appearing prominent.

Arnie was glancing between them with interest, and Nina decided she had what she'd come for. Lis could wait. She gave the volunteer a smile she hoped didn't appear too forced. 'Come on,' she said. 'Let's see if we can fix the phone.'

On the way back, she asked Arnie if Lis had been sent over with him by Brian for the bricks. He shook his head. 'No idea,' he said. 'She was there when I got to the cottage.'

Lis was supposed to be a volunteer helping with the maintenance of the island. She wasn't Jude's personal secretary or whatever role she was playing these days. Nina ground her teeth. Something else she was going to have to confront sooner rather than later.

None of the spare parts that Arnie needed were there. He examined the damage and shook his head. 'I don't think I can fix it,' he said.

'Can you give it a try? Rig something up?' Nina attempted not to let her desperation show.

'I'll do my best. But won't they realise something is wrong when you don't call in? Send the copter out?'

'The helicopter costs money. Besides, they won't do anything at first. My boss is away for a few days and he's not expecting me to call.' She was on the verge of asking him about improving the wireless reception, or how long he thought the 'upgrade' might take, when Arnie pointed at the burnt wiring.

'This looks like it was done deliberately.' He said it almost reluctantly, as if he felt a little foolish for mentioning it.

'What?' She gaped at him. 'What do you mean "deliberately"?'

He scratched the back of his neck and shook his head. 'I don't know. It just strikes me as wrong. If there was a fire it wouldn't start here. It's as if someone set it deliberately so that we couldn't call out.'

'That seems ...' she began, at a loss for words.

'Weird? Yeah, it does. I mean, why would anyone do that?'

Nina wanted to dismiss his suggestion out of hand. Why *would* anyone do that? It made no sense that someone on the island would vandalise such a vital piece of equipment. More likely, it was an unfortunate accident. Arnie must have realised he was being a bit dramatic because he didn't say any more, setting to work to try to mend the phone.

She stood and watched him, not really seeing him, her thoughts turning and twisting like snakes in a pit. The prefab hut was kept locked. She had a key and so did Paul, but no one else. Her key had been safely in her room, and was now in the hut door. Perhaps Paul had lent his out to someone other than Brian? She would ask him when Arnie was done here. But even so, it came back to the same question. Why would anyone destroy the phone, their line to head office, and more importantly, to help if they needed it?

With a final grimace, Arnie huffed, 'Sorry, it's a bit beyond my skill set.'

She told him it was all right, thanked him and sent him on his way. But after he had gone she stood there, telling herself that it must be a freak accident and not deliberate sabotage. There was no other possible explanation. Nothing that made sense, anyway.

When she locked up the hut after her, everyone seemed to have vanished. She could hear laughter and whooping coming from below in the cove and went to stand on the track that led down to it, shading her eyes with her hand.

The water sparkled as if diamonds lay on its surface, glittering in the noon sunshine. Her team were diving into the water, splashing each other, acting like kids. She supposed some of them were barely more than that, and it *was* their lunchbreak.

Lis gave a particularly loud shriek as she kicked water at Jude. He scooped up a bath-load in his arms and sent it back at her. She fell backwards, losing her balance, face going under, and came up spluttering and gasping. Jude laughed uproariously.

I won't look, she told herself, but she kept on doing just that. Couldn't help it. His back was broad and muscled, and his board shorts hung low on his hips. He could have been the boy she loved all those years ago. The one she had hoped to spend the rest of her life with.

Fault lines appeared and that hard kernel inside Nina threatened to crack wide open. She struggled to hold it together, perspiration making her shirt stick to her in a way that had nothing to do with the sun.

Once, when they were at the beach house, Jude had taken her to Cape Bruny Lighthouse. They stayed until sunset, huddled together to keep warm, while the light changed over the rugged coastline and the vast expanses of the wild Southern Ocean. It was as if they were on the edge of the world, just the two of them. She hadn't thought about it for a long time, but now it was as clear to her as yesterday. Clearer, probably. He said his great-something-grandparents had kept the light here, and he often thought about that. Perhaps genetics had coloured his own dreams of visiting wild and distant places. She had listened to his hopes and told him hers, and it had felt like they would be together forever.

'Nice for some.'

She jumped. Brian had come up behind her without her noticing. She hoped he hadn't seen her nervous response. She shoved her hands in the pockets of her shorts so he wouldn't see them shaking, but he seemed more interested in frowning with disapproval. She guessed he wanted her to shout out, call them all back to work like a headmistress at a reformatory school.

'It's their break,' she reminded him.

'As long as they don't slack off this afternoon. Plenty to do.'

She nodded, and with another glance at the beach, followed him back to the cottages. She also had plenty to do. She quashed the strange longing in her heart, the ache in her stomach. That was all in the past, she reminded herself. Over and done. Jude and Lis might want to re-create the easy life of their summer at Dennes Point, but Nina knew that beneath the pleasant, poignant sepia memories lay rocks as jagged as those stretching out from the island. And just as dangerous.

Hobart Recorder, **20 September 1881**

The funeral of the late Colonel Eldred Fernley Esq. will be held at St David's Cathedral on the 25th of September. Colonel Fernley was well known and respected in this state and there are expected to be a great many mourners attending. He had been resident in Tasmania for forty years, after arriving to take up land in New Norfolk, where he lived on his property, Mallowmede, with his wife until she passed away nearly ten years ago. Before he arrived on our shores, he served with the British army in India and Ceylon. He often spoke of his time there, and had a great appreciation for the beauties to be found in those countries.

He leaves behind an only child and the sole heir to his considerable fortune, Miss Rochelle Fernley, to grieve his passing. After the funeral, Colonel Eldred Fernley will be laid to his final rest beside his wife.

LAURA

18 May 1882, Benevolence

Laura and Edmund continued along the track, following it around the south side of the island towards the rocky escarpments of Birds Nest Island. Here the granite cliffs were even more rugged, dropping straight down to the sea, while the seabirds nesting in them screeched and wheeled. Pigface clung to the rocky soil with its fleshy leaves and pink flowers. It was almost as if the storm had never been, although the sea still rose and fell with a sizeable swell and she was not sure she would like to be out there in a small boat. The blue of the sky was intense, seemingly more so after the gloom of the past few days, and Laura shaded her eyes with her hand. As she had said to Edmund, the world had been washed clean.

Birds Nest Island lay just off shore, rising steeply from the waves, the narrow gap between it and Benevolence a cauldron of white water. There was an indent in the coast here, but it wasn't a safe anchorage like Thankful Cove. At the moment, any craft that attempted it would be dashed to pieces, although when the weather was fair boats had been known to drop anchor for the night. It had happened a few times that Laura knew of, and probably others that she did not. Once, a fisherman had crossed the island to the keeper's quarters and asked for food, but most of them slipped away again and vanished without a word. It seemed unlikely that anyone had taken shelter here during the storm because it was far too dangerous. If they needed a safe haven, they would have found it in Thankful Cove.

Laura and Edmund stood in awestruck silence, being buffeted by the wind and looking down into the churning cavern between the islands. There was no wreckage from the *Alvarez* to be seen in the turbulent waters, and if there were bodies then they were impossible to see. Birds were using the air currents to lift themselves up, up, until they were nothing but tiny white specks above. Two wallabies bounded away when they spotted Seal, before they vanished into some scrappy undergrowth. Apart from them, and the birds, there was no sign of a living creature.

'What a solitary life this is,' Edmund said. 'The only way to leave this island is by boat or to swim.'

'I've never considered swimming to the mainland,' Laura said.

His eyebrows rose in that way that was becoming familiar. '*Can* you swim?'

'Like a fish.'

He laughed softly. 'I can imagine it.'

Once again, he was looking at her as if she was a creature completely beyond his realm, and yet there was also admiration in his gaze. Slightly nervous now, Laura kept talking.

'I have few womanly accomplishments. I do not sew beyond mending and I do not paint or draw or play an instrument. Miriam did all of those things when she was in Hobart, before she married my father. She thinks I am a savage, although she would never say it to my face. She wants me to learn to be a lady. I think it is too late.'

'Far too late, and it's a good thing,' Edmund agreed, and there was a warmth to his smile that made her feel a little giddy. 'I always wondered what the point was of educating young ladies to be nothing but ornaments. It must be terribly tedious. My brother and I got to have all the fun while my sisters were sweating over their needlework.'

He had surprised her. Again.

'Where were you before Benevolence?' he went on, openly curious now.

'In Scotland. My parents had a lighthouse posting there, but my mother died when I was fourteen. She drowned while trying to save passengers from a sinking ship in a storm. Much like the one we have just lived through. Mrs Munro might not understand why we did not go out in the lifeboat earlier and risk our lives, but my father does not take those risks. Not anymore.'

Edmund was sombre now, all laughter gone from his eyes. 'I see that. It is not your job to risk your lives, anyway, although I am most grateful that you did.'

'You saved two other lives as well. Mrs Munro and Tom Burrows. Without you, they both would have drowned. You said before that your family do not believe you worthy—a bad egg—but I think if they knew about the *Alvarez*, they would be proud.' Miriam often accused her of being too blunt, but as the two of them stood here together, there was a sense of intimacy, of camaraderie, that gave her permission to speak her mind.

He glanced down at his feet with a wry smile, and when he looked up his eyes were watchful. 'You have not asked me what I did that made my family send me away.'

'No. I'm not sure it matters. You don't seem like a bad person, Mr Bailey. You were eager to help my father when he needed it, you were kind to Noah and Miriam, and you warmed my feet.' She bit her lip and did not respond to his sharp laugh. 'That all points to you being a good man.'

'Or an extremely devious one,' he countered.

She wondered why he wanted her to think the worst of him. 'Your parents must miss you,' she said gently.

He shrugged almost angrily. 'They have another son, a better son.'

'Now you're just being pitiable!'

That made him laugh again. 'I am attempting to be honest, Miss Webster.'

'Perhaps when they learn about the *Alvarez* they will ask you to come home.'

He shrugged as if he did not care, but she could see he was affected as he struggled to take a breath. 'It would be pleasant to believe that, but experience tells me otherwise.'

Before she could ask more, or delve into his life in a manner Miriam would tell her was just plain rude, he changed the subject.

'How long is your father contracted to remain on Benevolence?'

Laura let him have his way. 'He has another three years on his contract. After that, I don't know what he will do. I think Miriam wants to go home to Hobart, so that Noah can attend school. She misses her family, too.'

'And you?'

Laura tucked a strand of her hair behind her ear. 'They will ask me to live with them, I'm sure. To be honest, Mr Bailey, I don't know what I will do. This has been my home for nine years now and I will miss it, a great deal.'

She knew it was true. She tried not to think about leaving because of the pain it gave her, but Laura was too practical to pretend it would not happen. She needed to consider her future, and Edmund was pushing her to do just that.

'Your father said you are a great reader,' he said. 'That is not the same as experiencing the world firsthand.'

'I am not a fool, Mr Bailey.'

'Far from it,' he said promptly. 'I had a thought ... a very silly one, no doubt. I'm not sure I should even speak it aloud, but I feel as if I should. I am a man alone, without a clear future, but with plenty of experience of the world, and you are a woman alone, without a clear future, and with little experience of the world beyond this island. It seems as if we can help each other, Laura.'

He had called her by her first name, something she rarely heard from those outside her family. Her head was spinning because what he was saying, what she thought he was suggesting … Well, what *was* he suggesting? She had opened her mouth to ask him when …

'Great God,' he blurted out.

Laura followed his startled gaze. There was a man stumbling towards them, perilously close to the edge of the cliffs. Just as they started forward, he fell to his hands and knees and for a moment remained like that, his head bowed, as if the struggle to go on was just too much. Now she was closer, she could see that his clothing was in disarray, with rips to his trousers, and his jacket was gone, while his shirtsleeves were smeared with watery trails of blood.

The man collapsed when they reached him, rolling over with an effort so that he lay on his back. He threw his arm up to cover his face with a groan, as if the sunshine hurt his eyes, and Laura saw that his fingers were torn and bloodied, the nail of one completely gone in a mess of gore.

Edmund knelt and put a hand on the man's shoulder. The man groaned again. 'It's Mr Munro,' he said in wonder.

Munro's hair was tangled and encrusted with salt, and when he let his arm fall back onto the ground, his skin was chalky with deep dark shadows under his eyes. He tried to speak and then licked at lips that were dry and cracked.

'Are you real?' His voice was a hoarse croak. 'Is it … can it be Mr Bailey?'

'Sir, are you badly hurt?'

Mr Munro struggled to focus on his face. 'Is that you, Bailey?' His face lit up as he tried to sit, only to fall back with a cry, his hand pressed to his ribs. He gasped. 'My–my wife. Is she? My *wife*, Bailey? Did you save her as I asked you? Please tell me that you did!'

'I did, Mr Munro. Indeed I did.'

Tears filled the man's eyes and spilled over, making tracks down his dirty cheeks. Laura felt the sting in her own. Munro gave a sob, his chest heaving, only to freeze and groan again with pain. Were his ribs broken or was it worse? Before Laura could ask, there was barking from nearby. Seal had returned from whatever exploration he had been on, and he sounded seriously upset.

'Hoi there! What have you found?'

It was Rorie, stomping along the track towards them. Until now, she had not realised how late it was in the afternoon. The shadows were beginning to stretch out across the ocean, and the sun was lower on the horizon, although with still enough power to warm her skin.

'Your father sent me to see what was keeping you,' Rorie went on, but now his gaze was fixed on the man on the ground. 'Is that …?'

'It's Mr Munro!' Laura could not contain her excitement.

Edmund was assisting Mr Munro to sit up, while keeping Seal away. Laura moved to help, avoiding the man's ribs.

'Mr Munro?' Rorie repeated, sounding shocked. 'We thought you were drowned, sir.' His shadow fell over them as he stood staring down.

'I was swept off the ship,' Mr Munro said, and stopped with a painful grimace, before he continued. 'There was nothing before me but steep rocky cliffs, and I began to climb. God knows how I did it. A dozen times I was certain I would fall and be dashed to pieces. And yet I clung on and kept climbing, and when I reached the top I think I fainted. I'm not sure how long I have lain here in the elements before I heard your voices.'

Rorie moved, so he was no longer in silhouette, and Mr Munro seemed to see him for the first time. He startled and almost fell back, but saved himself by clutching onto Edmund and Laura. She was certain the two men recognised each other. She supposed it made sense that they would, if Rorie had once worked for Mrs Munro's father. The strange thing was, neither of them acknowledged it.

'We need to get you back to the quarters,' Laura said. She gave a nod to Edmund, and they awkwardly heaved the man to his feet. He whimpered in pain.

'I think my ribs are broken,' he said. Together they supported Munro as he walked between them, staggering more from exhaustion than any injury to his feet and legs. Rorie did not help but watched on, a hand on Seal to keep him from joining in and knocking them all over. They made their way slowly along the track, Rorie's eyes on them the whole time.

Instead of following their original route, they went eastwards over the middle of the island, where the track cut across the rocky, stony ground and through tufts of grass and scrub. This way was rougher but so much shorter that it seemed worth the trouble.

At one point Munro asked to stop, and stood staring at the wild scenery and sunset-streaked sea. His attention was caught by the tower of the lighthouse painted in the regulation colours—red at the top and white at the bottom. It stood tall and grand in front of them, and for a moment he seemed incapable of speech, as if he could not believe he had survived the wreck and the storm. Once he had known that his wife was living, he hadn't asked about anyone else, so perhaps that was enough for him to take in.

'Only a little further,' Laura urged gently.

Seal ran before them, barking, and by the time they reached the quarters, Miriam and Leo had come outside to see what the fuss was about. Rorie loped towards them, shouting the news, and then Laura's father was heading over. It seemed barely any time later that Mr Munro was being helped inside the cottage.

Mrs Munro was seated at the desk Mr Jones usually occupied. As soon as they entered, she looked up and gave a wordless cry. Stumbling to her feet, spilling paper and pen behind her, she flung herself at her husband. His arms went around her, weak but as desperate as she was, and they clung together.

He was whispering something in her ear and she was shuddering with deep, wrenching sobs. He spoke again, more urgently, and his wife nodded in a jerky fashion. Laura wondered what he was saying. Words of love? Gratitude? Or promises for their future. It was a moving moment, one she was sure those who watched on would never forget.

Eventually, Munro lifted his head and seemed to notice their audience. 'Thank you,' he croaked. 'We will be forever grateful.'

'You were brave,' Leo said. 'And lucky. A good combination, Mr Munro.'

'Perhaps. But if there is anything I can do … anything. I am happy to pay any reward now I am reunited with my beloved wife.'

It was a generous offer, made in the midst of so much emotion. But Laura was not surprised by her father's emphatic refusal, and Miriam's tearful one. Except for Rorie. He was smiling and it was not a nice smile. As if he had every intention of taking up Mr Munro on his offer.

NINA

May 2020, Benevolence
Day Two

Paul had produced a delicious meal for dinner and everyone oohed and aahed before they tucked in. Appetites had increased after the day of physical labour, and the team agreed that the smorgasbord set out on trestle tables at the front of the lighthouse head-keeper's historic cottage looked mouth-wateringly good.

Nina could imagine the old bricks Brian had been collecting laid here, creating the patio that Lis had sneered at. A place to sit when the weather was good, with perhaps a brick wall to one side, to offer more shelter when it wasn't.

Elle was busy with her camera, taking candid shots of the gathering. The resulting media would be used by Island Heritage to promote the project with captions like: *Volunteers enjoying island life during the pandemic! A satisfying end to a busy day!*

Nina bit into her enchilada and tried not to moan. Some of the group were clustered together on deckchairs, chatting and laughing, already forming a bond. Paul and Arnie were talking in low voices, their expressions more serious, and Jude was standing with Lis beside him while she spoke, waving her hands around expressively. But he wasn't listening to her; his gaze was fixed on Nina.

Was he remembering their romantic trip to Cape Bruny Lighthouse?

She managed not to spill anything, turning away as if to add more cheese to her tortilla. Seagulls screeched overhead, wanting to join in the feast, while the lighthouse looked solemnly on, the last of the light reflecting in the thick glass windows of the lantern room.

Being here with Jude hadn't been something she'd contemplated when she was chosen to run this project. There was stress enough in knowing she was being watched by head office, in being aware of her own shortcomings and in the endless planning she had had to do before they'd even left for the island. But that was what she was good at, planning, fitting the pieces together to make a seamless whole. She put her head down and worked hard. The emotional stuff—the feelings, the pain in the pit of her stomach—that was the difficult part. Her medication was meant to help her get past that, and most days it did. She knew that any extra stress, anything that pulled her out of her routine, wasn't good for her, but here, now, there was nothing she could do about it.

Get through it. Move forward.

She needed to talk to Lis, and she knew she couldn't leave it too much longer, but she'd be damned if she did it while Jude was standing there listening. Ready to intervene for his childhood friend in a way he had never done for her.

Nina brought herself up short. That wasn't fair, was it? He hadn't intervened for her because she had never told him the truth. He had been desperate, that night he came to see her, begging for an explanation, tears in his eyes, wanting things to go back to the way they had been before. Only they couldn't, and when she had told him coldly that she had changed her mind and it was over, his bewilderment had morphed to anger. He'd said she wasn't the woman he had thought she was, that he'd been a fool, that Lis had been right about her. That she had just been using him until something better came along.

That had hurt. After he'd gone, slamming the door, she'd curled up in a ball on the sofa and wept until there were no more tears to cry. She'd known that was the end then and he would never come back. She had cut the ties between them with her cruelty and indifference, when inside her heart was broken in two.

No, she didn't want to talk to Lis in front of him.

Instead, she went to chat with Neil, Gemma and Reynash, asking them questions about their studies and their hopes for future employment. Their idealism shone so brightly it made her feel tarnished and old. She had been like that once, but now she struggled to connect with that girl. It wasn't just because she had become jaded and cynical. The Nina of ten years ago seemed like a different person, as if the two women were separated by a chasm that could never be bridged. The happy, confident Nina, the Nina who had been excited for her future, and the Nina she was now. Head down, working hard, hiding in plain sight.

Was Paul right? Was the only way forward to go back? To face the past and admit to it, to bring it out into the open? Yet that was impossible. Not just because she had been concealing the facts for so long, but because the reasons for her actions were still as relevant today as they had been then. Too many people would be hurt besides herself, and despite all she'd suffered, she couldn't do it.

Nina set aside her meal, no longer hungry. She made herself a cup of Earl Grey, taking her time with it, being 'present' as she went through the process. While she was concentrating on the here and now, she could hold the past at bay. But of course it couldn't last.

Brian sought her out. She didn't realise at first that he *was* seeking her out, because some of the others joined them. He waited and fiddled with the cups, rearranging them, moving the teaspoons back and forth. He put a teabag in a mug, took it out again. When they were alone, he leaned in closer—she could smell sawdust and paint from his clothes and skin.

'I'd like a word in private, if you don't mind,' he said in the sort of voice a policeman might use when he came to arrest you.

Her heart sank at his serious tone. What else could have gone wrong? At dinner, she had explained to them all about the satellite phone, playing it down, letting them think it was an accident. No one was inclined to take it too seriously, and they soon moved on to other subjects, and she was glad of that. The phone wasn't working, yes, but she hoped it would not become an issue.

'I don't mind,' she said.

'Not here.' He glanced around at the others, although no one was watching them. 'Up at the lighthouse.'

Nina hesitated and then nodded. 'All right. Let me finish my tea and I'll meet you there.'

He agreed, and she watched him walk quickly away, out into the fading light. Nina caught Paul's eyes over the heads of the others and his mouth kicked up in a faint smile. He ambled over to join her, Arnie following in his wake.

'I'd say you've outdone yourself,' she said. 'But you're always amazing.'

Paul snorted a laugh, while Arnie patted him on the back. 'Super chef,' he said fondly.

Nina cleared her throat to regain his attention. 'I know I'm probably worrying about nothing, but with the phone not working ... We do have enough supplies to last until the fourteen days are up?'

'You *are* worrying about nothing. We have plenty. The freezer is stocked. We could hold out for a month if it became necessary. Tonight's spread was special, to celebrate our first full day of work on the island, but it won't always be like this. And if necessary, I can eke things out with rice and pasta.'

'Us growing boys need our carbs,' Arnie said, a teasing note in his voice. He was flirting and Paul was loving it. Nina left them to it.

It was time to find Brian and discover what was too hush-hush to discuss in front of the others.

The sky was transforming into all sorts of extraordinary colours as the sun went down behind her. Crimsons and oranges and golds reflected off the ocean surface, while the shadows of the cliffs stretched far out over the sea. The weather had been so perfect since they arrived that she couldn't imagine how it must be in the midst of a gale. Pretty terrifying, she supposed. As she headed up to the lighthouse, she passed the graveyard. The flowers were still there, though looking a little worse for wear. She'd mentioned them casually tonight, but no one had admitted to laying them on a grave. Maybe whoever had done it felt self-conscious, and if that was the case then she could hardly force the issue. Or maybe it was a simple act of respect, to remember the dead. And what did it matter, anyway?

It was just … curious. She was curious.

Brian was waiting. He came to meet her as she neared the tower, the white surface seeming to reflect the fiery sunset. Brian's face appeared even craggier in the shadows, and she could read the real worry in his eyes.

'I think somebody is playing games with us,' he blurted out as soon as she was close enough. He shook his head. 'I thought about not saying anything, but … It feels wrong.'

Her stomach gave a lurch. 'Do you mean the phone?' she said. 'Has Arnie spoken to you?'

'No. Why?' His heavy brows came down and his gaze drilled into hers.

A gust of wind moaned around the lighthouse and something loose rattled above, perhaps the railing on the balcony that encircled the lantern room. Suddenly, she felt exposed up here where anyone could see them and wonder what was so secret they could not discuss it at the campsite. It had been a mistake.

'Let's go down a bit,' she said, and led the way back along the track to the cove, Brian following her with an impatient sigh.

From above the beach appeared empty, the tide on its way in, the cove peaceful and inviting. A picture postcard symbolising tranquillity and beauty. There was still plenty of light for them to see their way, and without speaking they began to descend together. There was railing to the side of some steeper parts of the track, probably to help those less spry than her team. On the way, Brian pointed out the sections that needed to be repaired. 'Not safe to put your weight on this bit,' he warned, giving the wood a good shake. Nina winced. 'Everything rots eventually in the sea air. I'm actually surprised no one's fallen through. I've told the others to be careful until we start repairs here. I want to finish the cottages first. There's more to do than I thought, so ...'

His voice droned on and Nina tuned him out. When they reached the beach, she took off her shoes and enjoyed the sensation of the sand squishing up between her toes. How long was it since she'd stood barefoot like this, with the salty air caressing her skin and the wash of the waves soothing her racing thoughts? She knew how long, and the disturbing realisation jolted her out of the moment.

She discovered that her heart was racing, her palms sweaty, and she thought she was going to have to make an excuse and leave him. He'd know there was something wrong with her, if he didn't already, and she couldn't let that happen. If she was at work, she could have locked herself in the bathroom, or pretended she had to run an errand just to get away from watching eyes, but here on the beach there was nowhere to hide. 'Give me a minute,' she muttered, then began walking to the edge of the water. She stood facing away from him and took deep breaths, steadying herself, and gradually the symptoms of an impending panic attack began to fade. Finally, she turned to him.

As she had suspected, Brian was standing a short distance from her, watching with a frown. He hadn't taken off his shoes, she noticed, and he didn't look particularly pleased with her. He'd make a complaint probably, when they returned to Hobart.

'Sorry,' she said with a feeble smile. 'It's been a long day.'

He jumped straight back into their previous conversation. 'What did you mean about me talking to Arnie? What does he know about the tools?'

'Tools?' she repeated, puzzled. 'No, I meant the satellite phone. When he looked at it earlier he wasn't sure whether or not it *had* been a malfunction.'

'You said just now that it was,' he said, sounding accusing. 'You told everyone there was nothing to worry about.'

'Yes, I did. I thought it best not to speculate. Arnie did think it might have been deliberate, but he couldn't say for certain. I didn't want to put ideas in people's heads.'

Brian stared at her in silence, the darkness falling rapidly so that now his features were barely visible, and she found herself blathering on nervously, unable to stop. 'I mean, what possible reason could there be for anyone to do that? Destroy our best means of communication? It *must* have been a malfunction.'

'Well, I have something else to add to that mystery.' He sounded angry. 'You know they keep some tools here on the island for any repairs that need doing when the caretaker is here?'

'Yes, of course.' She knew because after making extensive lists of the equipment they would need, she'd discovered a lot of it was already here. It had saved time and money. The equipment was stored in a shed to one side of the cottage.

'We've been working on refitting the glass in the broken window. I needed some putty and went to get it before dinner so I could get straight to it tomorrow morning. While I was there, I remembered I needed a couple of other things. That was when I noticed that there were tools missing. A pick and a crowbar. A shovel. Probably more—I didn't have time to make a list. At first I thought someone had removed them for work purposes, but when I asked no one would admit to it. I searched the cottages we've been working in, as well as the general area, but I couldn't find the missing items.'

Nina stared back at him, at a loss.

'I mean, they're not imperative to the work we're doing, we can make do, but it's annoying. And worrying. Don't you think?'

'Yes.' She tried to come up with a reason why this was happening, but her mind was blank. 'You're sure they were there in the first place? Perhaps whoever was staying on the island before lockdown took them or lost them or—' *Threw them into the sea.*

'I have an inventory made by the last person on the island. I checked over it. They were there when we arrived. Now they're gone.'

'You looked everywhere?' She knew it was ridiculous to keep prodding at him, but what was she to say or think? It seemed an unimportant detail, and yet he was right. It was worrying.

'As much as I was able. If someone hid them on the island somewhere … But I have to ask myself why.'

'A joke?'

He didn't even bother to answer that. 'As I said, they could be on the island somewhere. And then there's the lighthouse itself. Are they in there? I know it's supposed to be locked up. A no-go zone. Do you have a key?'

She met his eyes, puzzled by his change in direction. 'No.'

He huffed a sour laugh. 'Well, Rawlins does. He was boasting about it yesterday. Plans to do some filming in there.'

Jude had the key to the lighthouse? She had been told that no one was allowed in there, because a few years ago there had been an accident; a visitor had fallen down the inside stairs and been badly injured. There had been an emergency evacuation, an expensive operation, and the cost had been borne by Island Heritage. Kyle wasn't keen for a repeat, and so no one was to go inside under any circumstances. As Nina had not planned to do so, she hadn't given it another thought. Until now.

Jude had the key. She was in charge and yet they had given the key to Jude without her knowledge. What did that say about her position as team leader, or the confidence Kyle had in her to do her job? She felt anger begin a slow burn inside her.

She needed to talk to Jude.

'Okay,' she said. 'Leave it with me for now, Brian.'

'You do believe me?' he demanded, and she wondered why he would think she doubted him.

'Yes, I believe you.'

'I'm not saying it's anything sinister. Things go missing all the time on job sites. But here,' he raised his arms as if to encompass their isolation. 'We're all supposed to be working for the good of Island Heritage, for the island. You heard them talking tonight, all those moral high grounds. Stealing tools just doesn't seem to fit in with this lot. To be honest, I can't understand it.'

Nina shivered and wrapped her arms about herself. Brian had inadvertently brought up something she hadn't really wanted to consider. That there was someone else on the island. A stranger. Watching them, stealing from them.

'It is worrying,' she agreed, struggling to make her voice confident and soothing. 'I'll get to the bottom of it, Brian.'

He eyed her a moment more, as if wondering whether he could believe her, or trust her. Then he gave a hefty sigh and walked off towards the track. Nina watched him go before she turned back to the tide line. A wave washed up, covering her feet, the water icy cold, but she hardly noticed.

How was she going to uncover what was happening here? Speaking to Kyle wasn't an option. Was there some connection between the missing tools and the broken phone? It seemed unlikely, and yet ...

When the voice spoke behind her she gave a violent jump and spun around, only just saving herself from falling.

'So, what do you think is going on?'

Jude. He couldn't have crept up on her from the track, he would have run into Brian. He must have been here all along. Hidden by the deep shadows of the hillside, maybe lurking near the old boatshed by the jetty.

'Did you have to frighten me like that?' she demanded, her voice shaking. Her heart seemed to have lodged in her throat.

'Sorry. I would have spoken up earlier, but Brian seemed wound up and I didn't want to interrupt.'

'Or you wanted to eavesdrop.'

'That too.' There was a smile in his voice, and it was so familiar. Here in the dark, she could almost pretend they were back at the beach house, the two of them as they used to be. The thought made her feel dizzy, untethered. She pushed it away.

'You heard him. What do *you* think is happening?' She crossed her arms. Another rogue wave washed up, this one soaking her to the knees. She stepped back. The tide was coming in fast and soon it would be too dark to see anything. She glanced towards the hilltop. The comforting glow of light from the cottages and the campsite seemed a long way away.

'I don't know,' he said at last. 'I suppose one of your volunteers could be playing silly games. Thinking it was funny or maybe they'd prefer not to work too hard. Although, Brian's right when he says none of them seem the type.'

'Unless it's someone else.' She said it before she could stop herself.

'You mean someone on the island that we don't know about?' he asked curiously. 'Why would you think that?'

He sounded interested, intrigued, and suddenly she wanted to tell him. She had to tell someone, and at least Jude wasn't immediately embroiled with all of this. His connection with Island Heritage was recent, and he was not intimately involved with the team. Well, apart from Lis. He would have an outsider's view.

'There have been reports of a trespasser on the island. The last lot of caretakers saw someone, but they could never get close enough to bail them up. The person always ran away or hid. It upset them. They felt ... unsafe.'

'No one found out who it was?'

'Not at the time. I'm supposed to follow up while we're here, although I'm not sure how I'm going to do that.'

'Look for litter?' he said, and she wasn't sure whether he was serious or mocking her. She ignored him.

'I'm guessing that whoever it was must be long gone. You'd think. But what if they're not? What if they're still here on the island and they want us to leave?'

Putting the thought into words chilled her, and she moved further away from the rising tide, glancing once more at the lights above.

'How did they get onto the island?' Jude mused. 'The only other anchorage, apart from the cove, is pretty unsafe. I'm talking about Birds Nest Island. Although, I suppose in this weather it would be okay. They could anchor there and use a dinghy to reach Benevolence. There are ways and means.'

'That's all very well, but the real question is *why*. Why come here in the first place?'

'There is that.'

'I'll go over there tomorrow.'

'No. Don't.' He said it quickly, a warning.

Surprised, she looked over at him, trying to read his face in the darkness.

'I have something better,' he said, and there was the sound of that smile again. 'A drone. I brought it with me to take some aerial shots of the island for the television series. It runs a video camera with a link to my laptop. Real time. If there's anyone here who shouldn't be, then I can capture them on film.'

'Of course you can.' She knew she sounded snarky, but all the same Nina was relieved not to be wandering around the island where there was a possibility someone was hiding. Someone whose agenda was a mystery to them.

'Jude?'

The call came from further up the track. It was Lis. She was peering down into the cove and couldn't see them. Nina waited for Jude to respond, but he didn't. After hesitating, Lis returned to the camp.

'She asked to come and I agreed,' he said. 'I thought it would do her good. She's been through a pretty tough time, recently.'

'Lis always suffered a lot more than anyone else.'

'You never liked her,' Jude retorted.

'She never liked me.'

He said nothing for a moment, and then headed towards the track. 'Come on,' he said. 'Let's get back.' He took a torch out of his pocket and flicked it on, illuminating the rough ground.

Nina followed him, silent now, deep in thought. The drone was a good idea, and it would mean they could search more thoroughly and without putting anyone in danger. Because if there was someone else on the island, then they obviously didn't want to be found.

By the time they reached the place where the track divided between the camp and the lighthouse, she was panting, her leg muscles aching. 'There was something else. The lighthouse. Brian said you have the key.' She sounded resentful and he noticed.

'It was a last-minute thing. I asked to film in there and was granted permission.'

'Right.'

'You're still the boss, Nina.'

She bit her lip to stop herself from snapping at him. 'Wouldn't the lighthouse be the perfect place for someone to hide?' she said.

He paused, staring ahead, and then nodded in agreement. 'We can look tomorrow,' he said. 'I don't fancy stumbling around in there in the dark. I'm told it's in dire need of repairs.'

Nina had planned to do just that, but even as she opened her mouth to argue, she knew he was right. Tomorrow would be soon enough to begin their search.

They began to separate. Jude needed to take the high track to get to his accommodation, and yet he had only taken one step when he stopped and turned around to face her. 'Do you remember that time we went to the Bruny Lighthouse? I was thinking about it before. Strange that we've ended up together at another one.'

'Tasmania is known for its lighthouses, and we both work for Island Heritage,' she reminded him evenly. 'Not really so strange.'

'Well, it feels strange to me,' he retorted. For a beat he was silent, and then he spoke again, awkwardly, not his usual self at all. 'You know, just now we've spoken like normal human beings. For the first time in years. Does this mean you've called a truce?'

She didn't know what to say, so she said nothing. She could see him now in the glow of the torch he held down at his side. His expression was grave, his eyes fixed on her. Waiting.

'What happened to you back then, Nina?' he said at last.

When again she didn't answer, couldn't answer, he shook his head and walked away. Nina could only watch him. Above on the highest point of the island, the lighthouse was a dark needle. She stared up at it, wondering what she would do if she saw movement or a flicker of light. Put it down to a ghost? But when there was nothing, she made her way to bed.

As she climbed into her sleeping bag, she tried with all her might not to allow her thoughts to drift into the past. In her head she began to tick off her tasks for the following day, but even as she closed her eyes, she could feel herself slipping back to that time.

NINA

Summer 2010, the Beach House, Dennes Point, Bruny Island

Despite it being nearly midnight, the beach had retained the warmth of the hot summer sun. Nina could hear the wash of the water a few metres away and smell the balmy salt air. It was perfect, really. The others had all gone to bed, although Lis had lingered and pouted until Colin told her to get inside and leave the 'lovebirds' alone.

Jude stroked her arm, his fingers warm and slightly roughened from digging in his mother's garden. This summer, Mrs Rawlins had decided she wanted a change and her children had obliged. Colourful petunias were arranged in pots along the verandah, the flowers already drooping. Nina wondered why they had bothered, but really she knew. Angela Rawlins had been abandoned by her husband, and now she was sick and her family would do anything to make her happy. Even Nina had been affected by the warm smile on the woman's tired face when she saw the effort her two sons and daughter had put in. There was no doubting she loved them back.

'I think we should stop at Tahiti,' Jude said, interrupting her thoughts.

'Why Tahiti?'

'I like the thought of treading in the footsteps of Captain Bligh and Fletcher Christian.'

Jude had always been interested in history. He liked odd facts and out-of-the-way places. If he hadn't decided on journalism, then he might have been a teacher.

'And after that?'

'Well, there's Pitcairn, of course.'

'Of course.'

'I wonder if we can land on Easter Island?'

Nina laughed. 'At this rate, we'll never come home again.'

She wasn't sure how the subject had started—sailing across the Pacific in their own boat. She didn't know anything about boats and she wasn't sure Jude did either, but it was a dream, a fantasy, they enjoyed embellishing whenever they were together like this. The one time they had mentioned it to Colin he had stared at them as if they were insane. *That* wasn't in his plans for his nephew at all.

'Maybe we shouldn't come home. We can keep going, all the way around the world.'

She leaned back into his shoulder with a sigh. This was nice. The sense that they had plenty of time, years and years together. While other people were rushing to work on trains and buses, they were still in the throes of choosing their path. Nina suspected that without Jude she might be one of those rushers—she was inclined to panic if she didn't get her assignments in on time, or she wasn't ten minutes early for an appointment. He centred her, calmed her, allowed her to breathe.

'I think we should find an island,' she said. 'Live on it. Just the two of us.'

He laughed. 'We're on an island,' he reminded her.

'I meant an island with just the two of us.'

'Sounds perfect.'

'Somehow, I doubt your family would think so. They wouldn't want to let you go.'

'I'm not sure that's true,' he said. 'Murray is the eldest, so that gives me the option to slack off. No one cares what I do.'

After his mother became too ill to work, the family had all stepped up. Colin had big plans for Murray, but sometimes Nina suspected Murray wasn't completely on board. He talked the talk, yet there were moments when she noticed he'd go quiet, a look almost of despair on his face. Surely Murray had dreams of his own? Then again, she didn't know him all that well. Maybe he did want to be a QC, drive a posh car and wear bespoke suits? All she did know was that he watched her and Jude as if he was jealous of their future, and his intent gaze made her uncomfortable when it fixed on her.

'Do you think Murray will stay the course?' she said, before she could stop herself. 'Colin has put a lot of weight on his shoulders, hasn't he?'

Jude peered down into her face with a frown. 'What do you mean?' he said sharply.

Nina thought about back-pedalling, but she'd come this far and it seemed important to put the possibility out there.

'Um, well, I suppose I mean if he changes his mind and … I don't know, if he decides he doesn't want the pressure. He is under a lot of pressure, Jude. I know Colin is helping you all out, but he seems to want a lot in return. What if Murray just says "no" and heads off on the boat instead of us, and you have to take over? I just …'

He was still frowning and she knew he didn't want to talk about that happening, let alone think about it. Jude was lucky he had some freedom to do as he wanted, but that freedom could be taken away if Murray changed his mind. She was right and he knew it, and it frightened him.

'Sorry,' she whispered, wrapping her arms around his neck. 'Don't listen to me. You know what I'm like. Glass half empty.'

The stiffness in his shoulders began to ease and he leaned in to kiss her. The kisses grew more intense, and with a groan he stood up and held out his hand. 'Come to bed?' he whispered.

Nina smiled and was about to follow him inside when there was a shout. A light came on in the beach house, footsteps pounding. A door slammed. Jude took off, leaping up onto the verandah, Nina at his heels.

The kitchen light was on, and Angela had collapsed on the floor and was gasping for air. Her face was as white as the tiles on the walls, and her lips blue. By the time Nina got there, her sons were leaning over her, Murray holding her hand, Jude speaking softly, while Mandy sobbed to one side. Lis huddled in the corner.

Jude looked up, his dark eyes wild, fixing on Nina. 'Ring for a bloody ambulance!' he snapped.

Hands shaking, Nina reached for her phone.

Hobart Recorder, 2 May 1882

Once again, rumours are circulating about foreign ships in the waters of Bass Strait. You may remember our story from earlier in the year when tales about the invasion of our fair shores caused a panic in the population. Recently, our source inside the government had a conversation with this reporter, and although he would not confirm the whispers, he did say that they were taking matters seriously.

Seriously enough, in fact, to send one of their men posthaste to Melbourne, where decisions will be made as to how to tackle the escalating situation.

LAURA

18 May 1882, Benevolence

Munro sank into a chair. His wife had made frantic cries for help as he began to sag in her grasp, and the others had come to her rescue. Now he sat close by the hearth, his face grey with exhaustion and pain. Miriam went to fetch the injured man some water and her medicine box, while Mrs Munro sat at her husband's feet, pressed against him, staring up at him in dumbfounded joy. Her hands plucked at the torn cloth on his knees, stroking him as if she could not bear not to touch him, as if she could not believe he was really here.

Laura understood. In his fight for survival, Mr Munro could have drowned any number of times, or been dashed to pieces on the rocks. He had been inspired to survive and reunite with his beloved wife, and so he had scaled a cliff no one would have believed was possible to climb—his torn fingers and hands bore testament to that. She had read that people could perform incredible feats to save their lives, or the lives of others, miraculous rescues that defied belief, and this seemed to be one of them.

When Miriam returned, she began to carefully inspect Munro's torn hands, tut-tutting over the state of them. Gently, she helped him off with his blood-stained shirt, but even so he hissed and groaned at every movement. Once he was bare from the waist up, the cuts and bruising were plain to see. Miriam carefully ran her hands over his ribs, feeling for breaks.

'What happened to you?' Leo said. 'Mr Bailey has told us how you asked him to save your wife. What happened after that?'

Munro fleetingly closed his eyes, gathering his strength, before he began his tale.

'I was swept from the ship by a wave and I thought that was the end of me. There was a piece of timber from the *Alvarez*, and when it washed past me I clung on to it and let it take me. It was so dark, apart from the light from the lighthouse, and that wasn't always visible. I seemed to be drifting further and further out to sea, and I began to wonder if I was going to vanish over the horizon. It was a very lonely time for me. I prayed that my wife was safe, but I did not want to leave her. Not when we had our whole lives before us.'

'Albert,' Mrs Munro whispered, lips trembling.

He touched her cheek and winced in pain. Then he spoke again.

'The tide began to turn and I realised I was drifting back towards the island. The lighthouse was getting closer, but my excitement soon changed once more to despair. I could see the light from your cottages, and yet I wasn't near enough to the little beach. No matter how I kicked and paddled, I couldn't seem to get any closer, and then I was swept around the cliffs. The sea here was rougher, and I was very cold by now. I didn't know whether I could hang on much longer, and feared that I would drown, after all. It is possible I fell asleep, or lost consciousness. When I awoke, I could see a channel before me, between the larger island and a smaller one. It was horrific, full of white water and pounding waves, and I knew if I drifted into that place I could not possibly survive.'

'Albert,' his wife said.

He gave a laugh that could have been a sob. 'By now I was sure I was going to die, but I did not want to die like that.'

'You need not go on if you don't want to,' Miriam said. 'I must dress your wounds.'

But Albert shook his head. 'I want to go on.' He swallowed. 'Perhaps it was sheer luck, but suddenly I was near enough to fling myself against the cliffs. I was pushed higher by the waves and each time I hung on, not caring if I was cut or hurt, just knowing I must not let go.' He gulped at the memory, eyes closing as he fought for composure.

'My love, you don't have to ...' his wife murmured.

He seemed not to hear her, lost in his own dreadful memories. 'I don't remember climbing. I think for a time I stayed where I was, not sure what to do, but the only way to survive was by climbing up, so I did. It was like a dream. A nightmare. I didn't quite believe it when I reached the top.' He touched his wife's face again, a radiant expression on his own. 'It was you who saved me,' he said. 'I could hear your voice in my head, urging me on, begging me to live. Telling me we had so much ahead of us.'

Laura exchanged a glance with Miriam, and they moved away, taking the others with them and leaving the emotional couple alone.

'I'll fetch him some soup,' Miriam said, 'and when I have dressed his wounds he must rest. He'll need a change of clothes. He cannot stay in those wet and torn trousers.' Her brow wrinkled as she considered the problem of finding more spare clothing.

By the time Albert had finished the soup, with his wife's help, Miriam had found a pair of Leo's trousers and a shirt. Mrs Munro had already removed her husband's boots and stockings, and because of their protection, his feet were not as badly damaged. The meal seemed to have revived him somewhat, and he spoke again as she bathed his hands.

'Was anything able to be saved from the *Alvarez*?' Albert peered around the room, his gaze fastening on Edmund.

'Nothing of consequence. The lifeboat had been hastily stocked ready for us to abandon ship, but there wasn't time.'

'Mr Bailey has lost everything he owned,' Laura said, and then felt her cheeks flush as Edmund gave her a smile.

'That's true,' he agreed. 'I have nothing to my name, but I count myself lucky to be alive.'

Behind him, Mr Jones huffed.

Albert nodded his agreement and then asked, belatedly, 'Who else survived? Apart from you, Mr Bailey, and my dear wife, and Mr Jones there.'

'Tom Burrows, the mate—' Edmund began.

'Tom's alive?' He seemed startled, and then shook his head and explained, 'He went below. I did not see him after that. I assumed he had been hurt, or trapped.'

'He was lying half unconscious on the deck,' Edmund said. 'Your wife and I helped him to shore.'

'He was very lucky,' Mrs Munro said.

'Is he able to ... Where is he?'

'In my daughter's room,' Miriam said. 'He is delirious most of the time, and in a great deal of pain. I don't know if he will recover.'

'I sat with him earlier,' Mrs Munro went on. 'He's in a very bad way, Albert.'

'This will hurt, Mr Munro.' Miriam glanced at him. 'Can you bear it?'

'I rather think I can bear anything right now,' he said, and despite the pallor of his face and his obvious distress, there was almost a twinkle in his eyes. He gritted his teeth and waited until Miriam was done before he spoke again. 'And the others aboard the *Alvarez*? Did they all drown?'

Miriam answered him and then went on to say, 'Isaac has a broken arm, but he will mend. He's sitting with Tom, now. I hope he will pull through. He *has* been waking for longer and longer periods, and he even recognised Isaac earlier.' She brightened at the memory. 'There is hope for him, as you yourself have proved, Mr Munro, by surviving against such terrible odds.'

'What of Captain Roberts?' Albert asked.

'We found his body,' Edmund said. 'As well as your wife's maid.'

Munro jolted, his gaze wide as he reached for his wife's hand. 'Elsie?'

'She drowned,' Mrs Munro confirmed and carefully squeezed his damaged hand. 'Mr Webster and his daughter have seen her.'

'I don't know if it is of any comfort, sir,' Leo spoke, 'but she looked very peaceful.'

There was a respectful silence and Laura wondered when her father was going to tell them about the missing body.

'And there's Seal,' Laura reminded them, with a glance to where Edmund's dog was stretched out against the wall.

'Ah, Seal.' Albert smiled with relief at the lightening of the moment. 'I remember Seal. Where did you say you found him again, Bailey? On the road to Richmond?'

'Lost and abandoned on the highway,' Edmund said. 'Such an elegant dog to be tossed aside. I felt a kinship with him, and he decided he was mine and has been ever since.'

Mr Jones stepped forward to take centrestage, evidently thinking it was once again time for him to put forward his case. 'I need to get to Melbourne,' he announced, as if it were that easy. 'You are a man of means, Munro. You must be able to help.'

Albert gave him a bewildered look before he asked the others, 'Is there a vessel large enough to take us all?'

Again, it was explained to Albert about the supply steamer that was due soon, and the possibility of rowing out and flagging down a passing ship. 'I would not risk it yet, the sea is still too rough,' Leo added. 'And we don't know how much damage the storm has wrought. If there were more ships lost, then the authorities will be busy.'

'There is a lifeboat,' Mrs Munro said. 'They went out in it yesterday.'

'Can it be sailed to the mainland?' Albert asked.

'You can see the Victorian coast from here,' Mr Jones piped up, clearly excited at this prospect. 'I cannot believe it is not possible to—'

'The lifeboat is a dinghy,' Leo interrupted, 'and taking that out into the Strait would be far too risky. A small boat in such dangerous waters? No. The whaleboat is another matter, but I still wouldn't risk it right now. Besides, I don't see the need. The supply steamer will be here, eventually. We must wait and be patient.'

'But surely an experienced sailor—' Mr Jones would not give up.

'Mr Jones!' Miriam said in the sort of voice not to be argued with. 'My husband is a fine sailor, but he is needed here. You must accept that we are all confined to the island for now.'

The little man flushed angrily and looked as if he might continue to protest, before heaving a huge sigh as he stomped off.

Leo gave his wife an amused grin. 'Speaking of being needed here, I have to go and tend the light.'

'I thought Rorie was supposed to be taking the first watch?'

'I sent him down to the boatshed to check on Captain Roberts. We canna wait much longer to bury him, lass. Tomorrow morning, I reckon.' There was an uncomfortable silence. 'When Rorie comes back send him up to me.'

After he had gone, Miriam gathered her medical supplies. 'If the others will give us some privacy, Mr Munro, I have a change of clothing for you. When you are done I want you to sleep. Perhaps Mr Bailey can help Laura bring the other straw pallet down from the attic. You can rest in here and your wife can watch over you.'

Indeed, Laura thought, *it was unlikely they would be able to prise Mrs Munro from his side.* She and Edmund lay the straw pallet under the window where Mrs Munro had kept watch since the first night, and it was only then that Laura realised it was close to full dark.

She remembered the chickens then and that she had meant to ask Rorie to secure them for the night. Too late now, she'd have to do it herself. But to her surprise, when she stepped around the side of the cottage, ready to make the climb to the upper track, Rorie was standing on the verandah. At first, all she saw was a shadow against the light from the shuttered window, but the light inside brightened as Miriam lit a lamp, and she could see it was indeed he. He had not heard her approach and she had a chance to observe him.

His eyes were closed and his chin was down on his chest, as if he was sleeping on his feet. But he was not asleep. Had he been listening to the conversation inside? She could see by the curve of his mouth that he was smiling at some private inner joke. There was something about him then that raised her hackles. She did not trust him, she had never trusted him, and right now she could tell he was up to no good.

He must have felt her presence because he straightened abruptly, his eyes widening, before he plastered that familiar smirk on his face. 'Laura,' he said in a sing-song voice he would never have dared to use if her father was standing here. 'I was just thinking ... Seems like some people get all the good luck, don't they?'

She frowned, not understanding him. 'Good luck?'

'Aye. Albert Munro, I mean. Saved by a miracle from certain drowning when anyone else in the same spot would have perished. And then his wife ... Well, he's one lucky bugger.'

Laura supposed he was right, but the way he said it niggled at her, as if he was jealous somehow of the other man's good fortune. 'You know him, don't you? I could see that he recognised you.'

'I know him all right. I know them both.' Rorie's smirk broadened. 'I think I'll ask him for a job. Something easy that pays well.'

'Why would he do that?' Laura said before she could stop herself. 'After you stole from Mrs Munro's father?'

Rorie's smile dropped away. 'Is that what she said?'

Laura did not respond, she simply watched him.

'You shouldn't believe everything you hear, Laura,' he mocked. 'Awful lot of liars out there.'

Laura wanted nothing so much as to walk away, but she needed him if she did not want to go all the way to the assistant's cottage and back again, in the dark. Miriam needed her help more than Rorie.

'Dad says you were checking on Captain Roberts.'

'That's right. Haven't done it yet. I don't think the captain'll care if I'm a bit late. Unless he's disappeared, of course.'

His words threw her. Did he know about Elsie, is that why he'd said that? She almost asked him, but he spoke before she could do so.

'We're putting him in the ground tomorrow. At least the rain softened it up. Break our backs digging, otherwise.'

That was true enough. The only part of the island where the soil was any good was near Rorie's cottage, which was why the garden had been laid out there. Which reminded her. 'I let the chickens out before,' she said. 'Can you put them back in their coop? I wouldn't want to lose any of them.' When he began to object she added cunningly, 'And I know how much you like eggs for breakfast.'

He snorted a laugh. 'Clever girl. Very well, I'll lock them up good and tight. Can't be too careful, can we? You never know what's out there, waiting, in the dark.'

She did not like the way he spoke, or the look he gave her, but she stayed silent as he tipped a finger to an imaginary cap and walked away.

* * *

Despite the short time they had all been together, everyone had fallen into a routine. Miriam bustled about preparing a meal, with Laura's help, and Mrs Munro sat with her husband while he slept on. Isaac had watched over Tom until Mr Jones took over. By then, Leo had returned from the lighthouse and was asking for Rorie.

'I saw him just after you left,' Laura said. 'He was going to check on Captain Roberts and put the chickens back in the coop. Perhaps he's asleep in his cottage?'

Leo looked as if he would like to go and drag the man from his bed, but then Edmund offered to take the watch with him. They set off, their heads together as if they had known each other for years.

Her father seemed to have taken the younger man under his wing, despite his earlier distrust of him. Laura suspected it was because Edmund was willing to do whatever was asked of him without complaint. And even when he was not asked, he had a way of stepping in and helping out. He also seemed interested in the island life, which was probably because it was so novel to him.

He would soon get sick of it, she told herself, *and like Rorie be longing to leave.*

I am a man alone, without a clear future, but with plenty of experience of the world, and you are a woman alone, without a clear future, and with no experience of the world beyond this island. It seems as if we can help each other, Laura.

What had he been about to ask her when they stood on the cliff top, before they found Mr Munro? He had not approached her again. Perhaps he had had second thoughts? And yet, she wished she knew what he had meant. That tumbling feeling inside her warned her that she was getting too invested in him, but she could not seem to help it. Like a shearwater flying before a gale, she had no choice other than to let it take her.

After they had eaten, Miriam came with her to collect some of her belongings from the room where Tom lay. They were as quiet as possible, but he must have heard them or sensed them because he stirred, muttering, and then groaned when Miriam placed her hand to his brow. Laura took what she came for and left her stepmother instructing a surly Mr Jones on how to bathe the poor man and reduce his fever.

Noah was already down in his cot, sleeping like an angel, and Laura moved about the bedroom, preparing for bed. Miriam would be sharing with her tonight, while Leo and Edmund took turns in the lantern room. By the time she had undressed and washed, then climbed beneath the covers, she was more than ready for sleep.

Laura felt as if she had hardly closed her eyes when she was awoken. At first she didn't know why, but as she lay there she could hear the sound of whispering. She glanced at Miriam, only to find her sleeping peacefully by her side. There was the soft patter of rain and she almost drifted off again, until a noise came from outside and she lifted her head to stare at the shuttered window. It must be very late, or very early. Apart from the rain, everything was so still, the wind having dropped. The world felt hushed in expectation, ready for another dawn.

'Has he said anything.'

That was clear enough, but the voice was too low for her to recognise who had spoken, or even to tell if it was a man or a woman. There was a soft bump, as if whoever was out there had knocked against the wall near the window.

Another person answered, but she could not understand any of it. They must be sheltering under the verandah.

'You know we'll have to stop him.'

Goosebumps ran up her arms. There was something very ominous about those words, something threatening. Something wrong. The other person spoke again, and despite the lack of words, Laura thought they were protesting.

And then, 'You know we have no choice.'

Seal began to bark. The footsteps moved quickly away. Laura rose and walked on bare feet to the window, bending so that she could peer through the crack in the shutters. It was not as dark out there as she'd thought. The moon was up, giving the scene a soft glow. Seal was bounding around, waving his tail, and then Edmund moved into sight, bending to scratch the dog's head. He straightened and looked over his shoulder, away from the cottage, as if he had heard something in the grove of she-oaks and melaleucas. And then he and his dog were gone.

Had he been one of the whisperers just now? She shivered, hugging her arms about herself in her flannel nightgown. If it had been Edmund, then who was the other person? But she did not think it had been him. Laura shivered again. She needed to be careful. Something was not right and she needed to protect herself and her family.

NINA

May 2020, Benevolence
Day Three

'Nina?' A male voice, forcing its way through chemically-induced sleep. The sound of her name was accompanied by gentle shaking. She thought for a second, as she came out of her dream, that she was back on the beach at Dennes Point, and that she had fallen asleep there. Lying warm in the sand with Jude's arms around her. But no, that wasn't right, was it? Angela Rawlins had collapsed. Everyone was scared she was going to die, and Nina needed to ring an ambulance. She needed … she …

'Nina, wake up!' The shaking was no longer gentle.

Had she drunk too much? There had been a time afterwards when nothing seemed to help. She couldn't sleep, she couldn't stop remembering, and the only choice had been to drink herself into oblivion. She'd wake up, mouth dry and nasty, head pounding. Going in to the office and pretending she was all right, ignoring the looks from her work colleagues. She'd managed to wean herself off the dangerous drinking, found a doctor to whom she told parts of the truth, and was given some medications that helped. Most of the time, anyway.

'Nina?' It was Elle's voice this time, but it wasn't Elle's big hand shaking her. 'Has she taken something?' Elle whispered. 'She seems pretty out of it.'

Had she? Nina remembered then. She had swallowed a couple of her pills, to try to sleep, after it was obvious she wasn't going to. The conversation on the beach with Jude, the past intruding on the present, her mind had been full of it, whirling sickeningly as if she was on a showground carousel. The pills hadn't stopped the flashback, but at least she'd slept through it rather than waking screaming, or walking off a cliff.

'Nina,' Paul said urgently. 'I need you up and awake.'

She finally fought off the heaviest tendrils of the drug. It was dark, not morning as she'd thought. She hadn't slept in this time.

'What is it?' She could hear the slur in her voice and wished it wasn't there.

The bed shifted as Paul sat down, trapping her in her sleeping bag. 'Someone tipped out the diesel for the generator. It's all over the ground, stinking to high heaven. When I got up, I could smell it.'

'If someone threw a lit match in it ...' Elle began, eyes wide.

'It's not as flammable as petrol,' Paul said quickly, 'but it could still burn.'

Nina was awake now. She wriggled around and Paul stood up to let her struggle out from inside her sleeping bag with a groan. 'Why would anyone do that?' she said, looking from Elle to Paul in the darkness, lit only by the faint light of Paul's torch, set facedown on the floor.

'Why would someone mess with the satellite phone?' Paul asked with a grim note, as she followed him out of her room.

And remove some of the tools, Nina remembered now. She hadn't said anything about that yet, but she needed to. The phone, the tools and the generator. The three things must be linked.

Outside the sky was awash with stars, and the sea a dark mass glittering beneath, spangled with reflections. As Paul led her over to his makeshift kitchen, she could smell the fuel. The stink of it caught in her throat and made her choke.

'Who did this?' She was not really expecting an answer.

'I don't know,' Paul said. 'But we need to clean it up.'

'We need to ring head office,' Nina responded, wiping her hands on the legs of her sweat pants, over and over again.

'The phone,' Paul said abruptly. 'Does someone want us to be cut off? Are they trying to isolate us?'

Elle's eyes were huge in the torchlight, and Nina wanted to reassure her, but she didn't know how. Because that was exactly how it looked. Someone was trying to cut them off from help. She wished she could speak to Kyle, run this by him, because declaring an emergency evacuation was well above her pay grade, even if it was possible.

'There's nothing else you noticed?' she said to Paul.

Paul swept his torch around. 'Not really. Just went to wake you up.' He picked his way over to the trestle tables, cursing when he stepped in a puddle of diesel. 'I'll have to wait until daylight to have a good look,' he said. Then, 'I don't understand. Why would anyone do this?'

'We still have solar, and gas,' Nina said. They would have hot water at least and cooking facilities. The lights would still go on.

'But it's the generator that runs the fridge and freezer, and without it the food spoils. I'm not saying we're going to starve, but it's inconvenient. If whoever's doing this is a practical joker, I can't see the funny side.'

Unless it wasn't one of them at all.

Would a stranger be more willing to put their lives in danger? To frighten and unsettle them for reasons as yet unknown. That made more sense. She wished now that she'd searched the lighthouse last night, as it was the obvious place. Like the trojan horse of old, the enemy could be situated right in the middle of their safe place.

Paul was busying himself cleaning up the fuel and she jumped in to help him. Elle was biting her nails, watching them, her eyes shining in the lights Paul had switched on.

'What will this mean?' she asked. 'If we can't run the generator, I mean. What can we do?'

Paul glanced at her. 'I still have the diesel already in there, so it will run for a while, but not for long. It was low and I was going to fill it up today.'

As grim as their situation was, it wasn't as dire as it would have been in the old days, Nina thought wearily. It would have been worse when the lighthouse keeper was reliant on the supply ship arriving, and if it was late, then survival became all the more difficult. Disaster was only a bad storm away and each day the clamour of hungry mouths would grow greater.

Elle was still watching them, as if trying to understand what was happening.

Good luck with that. Suddenly, Nina didn't want to discuss this in front of her.

'Go back to bed,' Nina told her. 'Paul and I have got this. Get another hour of sleep.'

The girl didn't argue, just gave a jerky nod and set off. By the time Nina and Paul were finished with the clean-up, the sun was just peeping over the horizon behind them. The air was still, the birds waking to squawk their morning songs.

As they worked, Nina had told Paul about the missing tools and Brian's concerns that someone had stolen them. He listened, tired face creased in a frown. 'I can't imagine one of these kids thinking that would be funny. The phone and the diesel. It's malicious, Nina.' He was breathing fast. Angry.

'Jude has a key to the lighthouse,' she said once he'd finished.

'I thought we weren't allowed in there.'

'We aren't. He got it from Island Heritage, said he was going to film inside, and they caved in.'

Paul looked beyond her at the white column rising into the pale-blue sky. The sun reflected back from the windows of the lantern room, dazzlingly bright, making it impossible to see if anyone was staring back. Something about the place made her uneasy, and right or wrong, she had a sense that they were being watched.

'What are you thinking, Nina?' he asked her quietly.

'I heard someone outside the first night,' Nina said. 'I thought it was just one of us, but …'

Paul's gaze sharpened. 'You think there's someone else hiding on the island? But where?'

'The lighthouse? There was a trespasser on the island a few months ago. Maybe they're still here? Maybe they think the island belongs to them? Maybe they want to drive us away?'

'Funny way of doing it,' Paul responded. 'They've messed up our phone so we can't call for the helicopter to collect us.'

He was right. Could whoever was doing this not want them to leave at all, but instead plan to keep them here, trapped, prisoners. That was even more disturbing and she pushed the idea away before she could begin to panic. 'I'm going to get dressed and then I need Jude's key.'

'Did you ever think that maybe this is his doing? Jude's? Ramp up the drama. Be good for his profile, wouldn't it? I'm surprised it didn't occur to you, Nina.'

'You think Jude is behind this?' she said, shocked, and yet trying it on for size.

'You're not his biggest fan, what do you think?'

She stared at him, her thoughts whirling. 'I can't believe it,' she said at last. 'And why would he put himself at risk as well as the rest of us? It seems a step too far if he wants publicity for his new show.'

'Unless he isn't at risk. How do you know he hasn't got another phone we don't know about? He might be planning to save the day.'

He was right, Jude could have another phone in his cottage. It was possible, although she was still struggling to believe he was so dangerously ambitious that he would put people's lives in danger.

'I don't know,' she said at last, 'but I'm going to find out.'

'Everything all right?' It was Arnie.

Paul murmured a response as she walked quickly back to the cottage.

Nina dressed, pulling on her hiking boots, and tugging on a puffer jacket over her jeans and sweater. The air was cold and there was a stiff breeze now, keeping the sun's warmth at bay. Elle wasn't in bed, and Nina wondered where she was. Telling the others, she suspected, being the bearer of bad news. Perhaps she was the sort of person who enjoyed that type of thing. Well, it was too late to stop her now, and what was the point in keeping everyone in the dark, anyway? They'd have to be told at some point that the food may not last for the whole of their stay. Paul would be the best one to explain about rationing it.

As she left the cottage, she could smell coffee and hesitated, wondering if she should make a cup to go. But she needed to get that key, and so she climbed up to the higher track and set off briskly along it.

The day had started in earnest now, and despite her tumultuous thoughts, she couldn't help but be distracted by the beauty of the cove and the sea stretching out before her. Far on the horizon, a tanker was moving steadily past. The chilly air had her digging her hands into the pockets of her jeans and hunching her shoulders. She felt a little light-headed—the lingering effects of the medication, or lack of sleep. Both probably. Soon she had reached the drop into the valley, and was overlooking the old animal pens and the white cottage, Jude's current accommodation. There was a trickle of smoke rising from its chimney.

Nina paused to gather her thoughts. She couldn't rush in there and demand the key, no matter how much she wanted to. She would have to explain to him what had happened, get him on side, and after years of being enemies that might not be an easy thing to do. All the same, she could not believe Jude wouldn't respond to the urgency of the situation. Surely he hadn't changed that much?

With a sigh, she began making her way down towards the cottage, and that was when someone stepped out in front of her.

Lis.

Nina stared back at her. It felt like a rerun of yesterday, and she couldn't help the same unwelcome and unwanted question entering her mind: *Had she spent the night here?* Lis resembled a guard dog protecting its bone, the shadows under her green eyes and the drawn look on her face adding to her fierceness. Something was wrong, and although she had never liked Lis, and Lis had certainly never liked her, Nina felt a prickle of concern. Last night, Jude had said the other woman was going through a tough time, and Nina had dismissed it. Now she wondered just what those words meant.

'What do you want?' Lis demanded in a voice that was even more belligerent than usual.

'I need to see Jude.' Nina spoke calmly, refusing to be baited.

'I'll bet.' Lis folded her arms. 'Are you planning to ruin his life again? It took him years to get over you. Did you enjoy doing that to him? I don't know who the hell you think you are, but that's not happening. I'm not letting you—'

'I need the key to the lighthouse,' Nina cut her short, already feeling sick from the confrontation. This was why she hadn't spoken to Lis yet. The other woman wouldn't shy away from making a scene, and to Nina scenes meant a spike in the level of her anxiety, probably nightmares, flashbacks and the sense that her world was spiralling out of her control.

Lis had been staring suspiciously, and now she repeated, 'The key?'

The cottage door opened and Jude stepped out onto the verandah. He looked as if he'd just woken up, with his hair standing on end, and yet somehow he was still his handsome and charismatic self. And the shadows under his eyes were almost as dark as Lis's, and probably Nina's own.

'What's going on?' he asked.

Nina made up her mind then. If she had to have it out with Lis, then why not right here, right now? And maybe Jude would finally see what kind of woman he had been sticking up for all these years.

'I need a word while I have you here, Lis,' Nina began, doing her best to ignore her pounding heart and sweaty palms. 'I want you to stop spreading untrue lies about me to the others. You volunteered to be part of the Island Heritage team, not working your own sick agenda. We're here to help each other, not undermine each other. If you didn't come here to comply with those conditions, then you need to leave.'

Although she couldn't, that was the trouble.

Lis huffed a cynical laugh. 'Undermining you?' she sneered, and took a step towards Jude, as if aligning him with her. 'I was giving them a heads up about you. In case they didn't already know what an incompetent waste of space you are, Nina.'

'Lis.' Jude's voice was sharp, his shock apparent. 'I said what is going on? Nina?'

She swallowed. 'I need the key to the lighthouse,' she said. 'That's why *I'm* here.' She looked pointedly at Lis.

'I'm here with Jude,' the other woman said.

Jude shook his head at her. 'Lis,' he said, but there was a touch of despair in his voice, a fondness that he had never lost for this girl.

It made Nina angry that he could never see just what a destructive wrecker, what a nasty piece of work Lis was. It was the same with all of the Rawlins family, they were equally as blind. And Lis had always been part of that family. 'A second daughter,' Angela had called her once. Unlike Nina, the incomer, the woman who threatened their close-knit happiness, the cuckoo to be driven out. And driven her out they had.

Lis held up her arms in angry surrender. 'All right, all right. I'm on breakfast duty, anyway. Better get over to the camp before I get my pay docked. Oh, that's right, I don't get paid, do I?'

As she walked past Nina, she gave her a glare, and then she was striding up the rise and over the top and gone.

Jude moved to hold open the door. 'Come in, Nina,' he said wearily. 'I'll get you the key.'

He made it sound as if she was a burden, just like Lis. Nina was so furious and upset she could barely reply. How dare he speak to her like that!

'I don't want to come in,' she gritted. 'I need the key to the lighthouse. Last night someone tipped out the diesel from the generator, and I've just finished helping Paul clean it up. Without the generator, we won't be able to keep the freezer or fridge running. I don't know who did it, but I think it would be a good idea to search the lighthouse. And I need to do that now.'

He was staring at her, astonished, and then he nodded slowly, his expression closing down. 'All right,' he said. 'I'll get the key.'

He had left the door open, but Nina stood outside and waited. There was no way she was going inside. She didn't want to see evidence of Jude and Lis's cosy life on Benevolence. And she was hardly going to search the cottage in case Jude had another way of communicating with head office—another satellite phone—because he would have it well hidden. As she stood in the shadow of the verandah, in the silence, Nina felt very much alone. Her parents had always been more interested in each other than their daughter, and seemed relieved when she had left home to navigate her own future. It gave them the opportunity to travel to the places they had always dreamed of, and she had never told them about her trauma. Would they have come home to support her? Probably, but she wasn't sure she wanted them to. It would have been like living with strangers. She had friends, Paul was one of them, but when it came down to it, since Jude, there had been no one she was intimately close to. A couple of temporary lovers—it was better to keep things superficial, and then if they started asking too many questions she could end things—but no one who had meant to her what Jude had meant all those years ago.

If she was a romantic she might say he had been the love of her life. Or the destroyer of it.

Hobart Recorder, **18 May 1882**

There has been no word yet in regard to the missing schooner, *Alvarez*. As you will remember, recently married couple Mr and Mrs Albert Munro set out on the *Alvarez* to begin their new life in Victoria. Also on board were Mr Edmund Bailey, a visitor from England and relative of the Marquess of Albury, and Mr Richard Jones, a government man. Captain Roberts was well respected among the maritime community, and his mate, Tom Burrows, leaves behind a wife and eight children. Funds are now being raised by friends for the support of their families, although where the little schooner could be is still a mystery. That she did not reach Melbourne after the terrible storm that ripped through Bass Strait is a certainty, and there has been no word of her taking shelter along the Tasmanian coast. Prayers for the safety of all on board will be offered on Sunday at St David's Cathedral.

LAURA

19 May 1882, Benevolence

Next morning, two bodies had washed up in Thankful Cove. Albert Munro made his way carefully down the track to the beach, his wife clinging to his arm, to see if he recognised either of them.

Time in the sea had marked the poor souls, unlike the seemingly untouched body of Elsie Wright when Laura first saw her. Mrs Munro hung back while her husband went over to where Leo and Edmund had laid out the corpses on the sand. Laura stood with her, having no wish to see the corpses, either. Mrs Munro had been attached to Albert's side since he had made his remarkable escape from death. Understandably, it was as if she was afraid to take her eyes or hands off him in case he vanished. Now Laura could feel her trembling, her breath coming quickly, and took her hand, meaning to comfort her.

'Oh.' Mrs Munro startled at the contact, but before Laura could withdraw, her fingers clung tightly. 'I wish …' she said, and then bit her lip and began again. 'Why couldn't everything have turned out as we planned? I just wish …'

'They were seamen on the *Alvarez*,' they could hear Albert's sombre voice. 'Captain Roberts' men. God rest them.'

'Elsie?' Mrs Munro said. 'You said you saw her. Where is she now?'

'She was washed out to sea again,' Laura said. It was the story her father had decided upon. 'We thought she was safe, but the tide took her, Mrs Munro.'

Mrs Munro searched her face as if seeking a lie. At last she nodded. 'Perhaps that was for the best. She loved the sea. Couldn't wait to visit Hobart to go down to the harbour and see the ships sail in. She always hoped to see someone she knew. A familiar face.' She laughed oddly.

'Elsie didn't suffer from seasickness like you?' Laura remembered that that was why Elsie had stayed below in the cabin with Mrs Munro, to keep her company in her affliction.

Mrs Munro's gaze was fixed on her husband, where he stood with the others. When she spoke her voice was soft and a little dreamy. 'Elsie knew she could never go home even had she wanted to. There was nothing for her there. She missed it, though. Missed her family and the places she loved. She always hoped that one day ...' She bit her lip.

'Sometimes I miss the place I came from,' Laura said. 'But only because my mother is buried there and I know I will never see her grave again.'

Mrs Munro's eyes filled with tears. 'Exactly,' she said. 'All those ties broken. It was a relief when she met ... That is ...' She stumbled to a stop.

'You must have been close?'

'Close? She was a servant.' She blinked, as if she had remembered where she was. Then her husband was standing before them, frowning slightly.

'My love?' He took her arm in his, and Laura could see the way his bandaged fingers dug into her. He looked concerned, but more than that. He seemed eager to keep Laura from seeing the full extent of his wife's trauma. 'My wife is very tired,' he said. 'This has been a terrible time for her. Come and rest, Rochelle.'

Rochelle Munro gave Laura a forced smile. 'I *am* tired,' she agreed, her cheeks flushing with embarrassment. 'I think … I think I was talking nonsense. I do apologise, Miss Webster.'

She had been, but it was understandable, and so Laura said. As they walked away, she wondered if the wonderful new life the Munros had planned would ever be quite what they hoped, or would memories of the shipwreck hang over them forever more. While Mrs Munro was grieving her husband, before he was found, she had seemed unbalanced, but Laura had thought she would soon recover now he was reunited with her. Perhaps she was wrong, perhaps that damage would take far longer to repair.

Later in the morning, they held the burial service for Captain Roberts and the two men who had sailed alongside him. The island graveyard was situated above the cove and below the lighthouse, in a section of ground that gave solitude to those interred there as well as those who came to mourn them. The former burials on Benevolence were an eclectic group and included a lighthouse keeper from the 1850s and his wife and child, who had died when a ship brought typhoid to the island, as well as the child of a later keeper and several unknown souls who had washed ashore and were unclaimed. Those were the graves that had been marked by wooden crosses or small cairns of stones. No doubt there were unmarked graves, too, those hastily buried with no thought given to marking the spot.

When it came to digging the graves, Laura's father sent Isaac to fetch Rorie from his cottage, only for him to return to say the assistant keeper was not there. He also mentioned that the chickens were running free. Leo muttered that was typical and he would be glad when the other man was gone. Without being asked, Edmund took one of the shovels and Leo the pick and the two of them dug down through the hard earth. Laura took over when her father needed a break, and Isaac did what he could with one arm.

Mr Jones had wandered away when it looked as if he might be called upon to perform any physical labour, and Leo protested when Miriam made an attempt to take the pick from him.

'Good God, woman,' he huffed. 'I'm not ready to hang up my boots yet.'

She smiled at him. 'Oh I know that, but even a man of your stamina needs to sleep.'

'I need to tend the light first.'

Leo had been up all night with Edmund, doing a double watch when Rorie did not appear. Last time Laura had seen him had been outside the cottage, with that horrible smirk on his face.

Albert Munro interrupted her thoughts. A chair had been placed for him a little way from the graveside, and he looked pale and shaky. As usual his wife was by his side, his bandaged hand clasped in hers.

'I wonder if you could show me around your lighthouse, Mr Webster? If it isn't too much trouble. I'd be interested to know the workings of it.'

Leo's eyes brightened with pleasure. 'No trouble at all, Mr Munro,' he said. 'As soon as we are done here. The spiral staircase is very steep,' he added.

'Do you think you can climb so many stairs?' Mrs Munro asked him anxiously. 'It is so tall.' She squinted up at the lantern on top of the tower, shading her eyes. 'Should I come with you, Albert?'

'I'm sure I can manage. Don't worry, my love, I will take my time.'

They exchanged a look and she nodded, dropping her gaze back to the grave.

'Let's hope we don't have to dig another one for poor Tom Burrows,' Isaac said matter-of-factly.

Grim silence followed this, but Laura knew they were all wondering if the mate would pull through.

After the burial service—Mr Munro spoke a few solemn words and Leo offered a prayer—Laura set off to Rorie's cottage to repair his neglect. And to give him a piece of her mind. She should never have trusted him to do as she asked, and she would not put it past him to have refused her request from sheer vindictiveness.

She was so immersed in her angry thoughts, it was not until Seal ran past at full gallop that she realised Edmund had followed her.

'I don't need any help,' she called back. 'You should sleep, too.'

'I slept more than your father,' he responded, confirming her suspicions that Leo would not have left an inexperienced man alone with his precious lamp. 'And I want to see you give Rorie a good telling off.' He was slightly breathless when he reached her. Dark eyes examined her as if he found her endlessly fascinating. 'I'm not trying to take your place, you know,' he said evenly. 'I'm only trying to help. At home ... no one much wants my help, or needs it. When I was with my cousin in Richmond, he seemed to prefer I stay out of the way. I am enjoying the unique feeling of being useful, Laura.'

Now Laura felt guilty for behaving like a sullen child. She should be glad of his help for her own sake as well as her father's. 'Of course,' she said briskly. 'We're all grateful for your help, Mr Bailey.'

He smiled at his feet—he seemed to do that often—and then shook his head as if he did not believe her. They walked on a little way in silence, and she was tempted to ask him whom he had been meeting with last night. She was not positive that he was one of the conspirators whispering outside her window, far from it, but perhaps she could trick him into giving himself away. Eventually she said, 'Did you stay up in the lighthouse all night?'

'Yes. Apart from taking Seal out for a walk,' he said easily, as if he had no trouble confessing to it. 'The sea was quite beautiful. I could see phosphorescence in the waves. I stood and watched them for some time. I never thought I would find solitude so addictive.'

'I imagine you didn't get much solitude at home,' she said when he fell silent.

He grimaced. 'None at all. Part of that was my own fault, I suppose. I grew up thinking I must fill every moment with pointless activity. There are always horse races and card games, drinking with others in my position. A gentleman's son does not work. It is not the done thing, you see. Until I was sent out here, I was not encouraged to do anything but be idle, while upholding my position and avoiding scandal.'

'Did you? Uphold your position and avoid scandal?'

He stared at the ground. 'I think you know the answer to that question. Up in the lighthouse, last night, it was as if I could hear my thoughts for the first time.'

'And what were they telling you?'

He gave her a look that was almost awkward. 'If you don't mind, that's between my thoughts and me. To be frank, I felt a little out of my depth. I do not usually delve into my inner workings.' Then, as if her previous question had only just struck a chord with him, he asked, 'Why? Did Seal wake you?'

Again, it was on the tip of her tongue to tell him about the voices outside her window. She had planned to tell her father, but with the burials and his tired face she had kept it back. The whispers last night had worried her, though, in a way she could not remember being worried before. Laura was used to physical challenges; she lived a difficult life on an island where the weather was bad to very bad, and self-reliance kept her alive. But this seemed something more. Last night, when she had climbed back into bed beside Miriam, she had found it difficult to sleep. Over the years, Laura had learned to trust that niggling doubt when it told her something was wrong and to take care, and now the niggle had turned into a frantic scream.

'No, Seal didn't wake me. I was already awake. I got up and looked through the shutters and saw you and Seal outside. I wondered ... Were you alone?'

He frowned at her. 'I was, but now you ask me that, I did think I heard someone else. In the trees behind the cottage. I couldn't see anyone. Is that what you mean? Was there someone outside besides me? Did you see them?'

'No. I didn't see anyone, but ...'

'But?' He was not going to give up, and suddenly Laura was tired of prevaricating.

'There *was* someone else. Before you and Seal arrived, I heard them talking, although their voices were so low I couldn't understand much of what they said. But it sounded … it was as if they were worried about someone on the island. "Him," they said. They were worried about "him" knowing something he shouldn't know. And that they'd have to stop him.'

Edmund stared at her. 'Stop him?' he repeated sharply. 'I don't like the sound of that. Have you told your father?'

'Not yet.'

'What exactly did you hear, Laura?' he asked her.

She recited the words as best she could remember, feeling a little foolish as she did so. Perhaps it meant nothing, perhaps she was imagining a desperate situation when there was none. Perhaps the voice in her head was wrong. But she knew it was not.

When she'd finished, they continued to walk in silence and she could see he was turning over her words because his frown was back. Laura decided she did feel better for having told him. There was still a small doubt in her mind concerning him, but she couldn't think of anyone Edmund would be meeting with in the dark, or whom he might want to 'stop'. He had been a passenger on the *Alvarez* without companions. Whom could he be conspiring with? No, strange as it felt to admit it, if there was anyone she trusted besides her family, then it was Edmund Bailey.

The assistant-keeper's cottage appeared to be empty. No smoke rose from the chimney, which was strange as Rorie always had a fire going, no matter the weather. He said he felt the cold on this godforsaken lump of rock. There was washing hanging on a line strung up under the verandah. The place was generally untidy and uncared for, and Laura knew her father would not be happy. He was the sort of head keeper who insisted his light station be shipshape.

The two horses had spotted her and Ted crowded towards the fence, Nelly not far behind. She could see that Rorie had not filled their water troughs or given them fresh oats. Despite his lack of enthusiasm for work in the lighthouse, he was fond of the horses and could usually be relied upon to care for them. It looked as if he had done nothing. And Isaac was right, the chickens were still running free. Angry now, she stepped up onto the verandah and thudded her fist against the door.

'Rorie! Come out here right now! Rorie!'

The door creaked open. It had not even been closed properly.

Silence greeted her. No sound of the occupant scuttling off to hide. She stepped inside, Edmund breathing at her back. As she had expected, the fire was out. There was a feeling of emptiness about the place, too. She already knew there was no one here.

'Rorie?' Edmund called. He moved around her and went towards the closed door of Rorie's bedroom. Laura hoped she was wrong and he would find the man asleep in there, but Edmund shook his head.

They proceeded to search the cottage from top to bottom, to no avail. A pot of stew sat on the stove, and a dirty bowl on the table. Last night's supper, but nothing to show Rorie had eaten breakfast this morning. Had he left in the night, and if so why? Laura took another look around the room, and something in the fireplace caught her eye. A pale gleam. Proof that there had been a fire yesterday and Rorie was yet to clear it out. Approaching the hearth, she knelt and snatched up the poker, stirring the pile of ashes.

A scrap of creamy-coloured cloth. It was not completely destroyed, although it was shrivelled at the edges. Laura touched the undamaged section with her fingertip and it felt silky and soft. A fancy frill, half burned, had been torn almost completely off, and there was a button. It must have been the button that caught her eye.

She knew at once that this was part of the blouse Elsie Wright had been wearing when they found her washed up on the beach. Laura had leaned over the woman's body, felt her cold skin, and she knew she was not mistaken.

Edmund was standing behind her. 'What is it?' he asked, puzzled, glancing from the remnant to Laura.

'Elsie, Mrs Munro's maid. This is her blouse. A piece of it, anyway.'

He crouched down beside her, taking the poker from her hand, and used it to push the piece of cloth out of the ashes and onto the hearth. 'Odd,' he said. 'Wasn't there a brooch that she was fond of? Wasn't it pinned to her blouse? Is that there, too?'

The orange-coloured stone. A cairngorm, her father had called it. Laura and Edmund searched carefully through the ashes, sifting them from one side to the other, but the brooch was not there.

'Would it have burned in the fire? Although I think if it had, if it melted, then there would be signs of it.'

'Yes.'

Edmund watched her, waiting for more, and she knew he was thinking the same as she was.

'Rorie must have taken Elsie,' Laura said it aloud, shocked and yet she was not surprised. 'Was that him last night, whispering outside the window? But who was with him?' As far as she knew, Rorie did not make friends easily and there was no one on the island he was close to. Apart from Mrs Munro. She remembered how he had comforted her, stayed close to her, spoke of his past and of knowing her and Elsie. Was it Rorie and Mrs Munro plotting outside her window?

Edmund spoke before she could put her thoughts into words.

'If he took Elsie's body and stole her brooch, then where is she now?'

Laura remembered the overgrown garden and the general disarray of the cottage and its surrounds. Surely, if there was a grave she would be able to see it? The thought led her outside and she shaded her eyes, whirling around slowly to survey the area. The vegetable patch was undisturbed and grass grew thick elsewhere. There was nothing to suggest someone had been buried here, recently.

'Do you think that's where he is now?' Edmund said. 'Burying the poor woman's body?'

'He would have done it last night. It's odd. I know Rorie is not to be trusted, and I can't say I like him much, but for him to have gone out and not come back? It doesn't feel right.'

When Edmund looked at her, she could see he felt the same. 'We should finish up here and then tell your father,' he decided. 'We might need to start a search of the island. He can't have gone far, can he?'

She shook her head. The only way off Benevolence was by boat and Rorie was no sailor. The last time he had gone with her father in the lifeboat he had been sick as a dog, and the water had not even been very rough. He would not take the risk.

Meanwhile, the animals still had to be taken care of, and she set to feeding and watering them, and counted the chickens to see if any were missing. Apart from being disgruntled from their night out of their comfortable coop, they appeared not to have suffered anything worse. Edmund helped her without being asked, but she could tell his thoughts were as engaged as hers on the question of Rorie.

'He's probably hiding under a rock somewhere,' she said, pulling a face. 'He'll come out when the steamer arrives.'

Something else niggled at her then. Seasickness. Mrs Munro's dreamy voice at the graveyard, and Mr Munro's protective hold on her. But at that moment Seal ran up to them, panting and demanding attention, and the question was lost.

NINA

May 2020, Benevolence
Day Three

The first thing Nina noticed when she stepped inside the lighthouse was the smell of tobacco. Cigarettes.

A wave of dizziness washed over her, and she clung to the wooden rack just inside the door. She searched for a distraction. Her fingers tightened on the rack and she focused on it more closely. Once upon a time, wet-weather gear and overcoats must have hung here, ready for the keeper and his assistants to pull them on before they stepped out into the wind and rain.

'What?' Jude said, and lifted his hand as if to steady her. They hadn't spoken much on the walk from his cottage. He'd asked a few questions, clarifying the situation, and she had answered briefly. The key he had been given was new, bright and shiny. Evidently, the old one had gone missing during a previous visit to the island. 'Probably souvenired,' he'd said.

'Are you all right?' he asked now.

'I'm fine,' she snapped. She wasn't about to tell him about the footsteps outside her room that first night on the island, the unknown person who had lit a cigarette. That as far as she knew, no one in their team smoked. She could imagine the expression on his face. *Crazy Nina. It's all in your head.* Over the years, she'd leaned to be extremely careful with her words, knowing how easily she could be destroyed.

'If you say so.' He gave her an impatient frown and turned away. She was sorry then, but it was too late to soften her response. And much too late to explain herself.

Inside the tower it was gloomy. Daylight seeped through the five windows set in a vertical line up the white-painted granite wall, their glass thick and smeary. A spiral staircase twirled its way aloft to the lantern room, but otherwise the space appeared abandoned. Empty.

Jude clicked on his torch and the beam shone off the metal caging as he swung it around. Nina could see the area they were in now was being used for storage. A stack of broken furniture and old fuel tins, empty barrels and some piles of moth-eaten bedding. She could not see Brian's missing tools. There was a pickaxe with a broken handle, but she couldn't imagine Brian letting anything he was in charge of fall into such a state of disrepair.

'Hello!' Jude called. No one jumped out and nothing moved. Nina told herself that the smell of cigarettes might be just a lingering memory from the habit of a long-ago keeper. 'Anyone here?'

Silence, apart from the sounds drifting in from outside.

Jude began to climb the metal stairs, his steps creaking and echoing around them. Nina followed, hand on the railing. It felt gritty and grimy, and there were rusty patches where the frame had been bolted together. The place was badly in need of Brian's maintenance, but it wasn't going to get it this visit.

There was a closed-in space below the lantern room, and Nina could see an old single bed without a mattress, the metal framework and springs speckled with more rust. 'Probably the watch room,' Jude said. Nina tried to imagine the lighthouse keeper and his assistants sitting in here during their shifts tending to the light. There was a small kerosene stove, too, with a single burner, and an old coffee pot that had seen better days, as well as some chipped enamel mugs. It was obvious the place hadn't been used for a very long time.

The lantern room was reached by a smaller staircase fastened to the wall of the tower. These thickly glassed windows filled the place with so much radiance that Nina found herself squinting, adjusting after the gloom below. The smell of kerosene replaced the faint sting of cigarettes, mingled with dust and the sea.

'This used to be a Wilkins lantern room,' Jude said. As if he was giving a tour, she thought wearily. Although, at the same time, she found herself listening, interested in what he had to say and drawn in by the familiar sound of his voice. 'It was replaced later on. The groups of smaller lamps and their reflectors were time intensive, expensive to run and to keep in good working order, so they were replaced too. In the 1930s, from memory. You can see there is a single lamp here now, and a Fresnel lens. Instead of whale oil they used kerosene, and later electricity. The generator was run from the old fuel store near the base of the tower.'

'You've done your research.'

'It's an interest. Those summers on Bruny Island, the lighthouse on Cape Bruny ... I suppose they stuck with me.'

That summer had coloured her life, too, and it hadn't all been bad. There were good memories, it was just that she seemed to only concentrate on the bad.

The lens that must once have been pristine and gleaming was dirty, and the windows were coated with salt and splatters of bird droppings, giving them a milky look. The lamp stood blackened and forgotten when once it must have shone bright, humming with power as it was reflected into the lens and then out into the dark night.

Nina walked over to the windows. She was so high, with the sea below her, and the island's cliffs stretching out on either side. It was breathtaking. Despite the mist that softened the horizon, she felt as if she could see forever.

'I believe on a clear day you can see the Victorian coast,' she said. At least she knew that much.

A bird soared past, and then dived down towards the water. White caps broke on the waves around the Tiger's Teeth, the oily black rocks barely showing now that it was high tide. Nina moved around the tower until she was spying on their campsite. She watched Brian pointing to some lengths of wood, his minions scurrying to obey his instructions. Lis was helping Paul with lunch, the two of them chatting easily, while Arnie watched on. Reynash was back on his bicycle, bumping down the track.

Her gaze lifted beyond, over to the western side of the island, and any signs of activity. The contours were more obvious here—the island was not a flat piece of rock—and she could see across to the sharp rocky bulk of Birds Nest Island. She knew there was a chasm between the smaller island and the larger Benevolence, but she couldn't see that. Or the hidden, sheltered spot where a vessel might be moored.

'We can go out on the balcony if you like.' Jude was at the door, giving her a half-smile. 'The engineers did a structural check last time they were here. I was told it's safe, as long as it's not too blowy. We should be okay if we hang on.'

'Sounds encouraging,' she murmured as she followed him out.

There was a safety railing around the balcony, but all the same she imagined in bad weather it would be dangerous up there, with water to slip on and lashing winds to blind you and tear you off the flimsy railing and fling you into oblivion. What a precarious life it must have been.

'A wild and lonely life, with a heavy load of responsibility.'

It wasn't until Jude had answered that Nina realised she'd spoken aloud. They stood a moment, looking down towards the sea as it boiled around the cliffs. No wonder they had needed a lighthouse here in the days of sail.

'How many wrecks have there been?' She should have read up on it, but there hadn't been time. There was never time. Nina was always working all hours, struggling to prove herself. During instances like these she wondered why, what was the point? She was broken, wasn't she?

The sudden acknowledgement shocked her, and she bit her lip and turned her face away, in case he saw her despair.

'Not as many wrecks as you might think. Lis copied some of the records and newspaper reports for me. She's more often than not in the archives section of the state library in Hobart. She's an independent researcher, and a good one. I brought them with me. I can share if you like.'

Lis was an archivist? She wouldn't have pictured that. 'Brian has a book on the island. He's going to lend it to me.'

'Is that the one by Halpin? He was the last keeper here. I'm still waiting for my copy.'

'I'm sorry, I really don't know. He told me his wife got it for him. He has some connection to the island.'

'I think his grandfather was an assistant keeper in the thirties or forties. Drank himself out of a job.'

'Well, that explains why he didn't want to talk about it.'

'He's ashamed, I think. Brian would never do something like that.'

'No, he wouldn't.'

'There was a child who died here. Brian brought flowers. His wife's idea.'

The explanation was simple, after all. 'I saw them. I wondered who ...'

They were having a conversation. It felt slightly clunky and a bit fragile. As if she was walking on thin glass that might crack and shatter at any moment, and yet ... If also felt strangely good. The situation they found themselves in seemed to have created a bridge between them. She had forgotten how comfortable she used to feel with Jude, or maybe she had just pushed it out of her head. Tucked it away out of sight like an inconvenient truth. What was the point in remembering things like that? Because the past was not something she could change or mend or return to without causing immense damage.

Her hair whipped into her face and she tucked it back, holding it at her nape. He was watching her, his gaze sliding over her cheek, as if he was remembering those times he would touch her skin, trace the curve of her ear. She swallowed the lump in her throat.

Jude cleared his throat and spoke again. 'I've been reading about Leo Webster. He was the longest-serving keeper here in the eighteen seventies and eighties. He had his wife and daughter with him. It was his daughter who acted as his assistant. She was his right-hand man, if you like.' He laughed at himself. 'Woman. During their time, the island had one of its more famous wrecks, a schooner called the *Alvarez*. It capsized when it struck the rocks down there. Six people were saved, which was pretty remarkable when you remember they were caught up in what was later called one of the worst storms of the century.'

Another bird flew up close, as if curious, floating on the air currents briefly before diving away again. Nina held her breath as she watched it sink effortlessly until it was just a dot above the waves. She had never been a fan of heights, but there was something stomach-sinkingly fascinating about being up here. Her fingers clenched white on the top of the metal railing as Jude continued.

'I thought I might talk about Leo and his daughter, Laura, on my show. It really is one of the amazing untold stories of the island's history. If they'll let me.'

Nina looked at him in surprise. 'Can't you do whatever you want? You're the star, aren't you?'

'Is that what you think?' He sounded surprised. 'Yes, when I was making my own shows for YouTube, I did as I liked. And I made them on a shoestring budget. Now there's big money at stake and everyone wants a say. I need to negotiate every step, and if the producers don't like what I'm doing, they tell me to change it. I'm not my own boss anymore. True I'm the supposed face of the series, but I can be replaced. There are plenty of more amusing and better-looking presenters just itching for this job, especially if the series takes off. If I make things difficult, they'll dump me just like any other employee.'

Nina hadn't thought of it like that. Jude had created the idea, but that didn't mean he was going to be part of it long term. It seemed unfair, and she felt outraged on his behalf. 'You could go back to your own stuff,' she said. 'If you had to, I mean.'

He shrugged. 'Not sure it would feel the same. The pressure has ramped up. Mum is already calling me the next Michael Palin. Around Tasmania in ninety days,' he added with a smile, referencing the travel show that Michael did years ago. Since then, there had been any number of travelogues with famous and not-so-famous faces to head them. Jude was right, he was replaceable.

'Your mother must be proud of you,' was all she said.

Nina had thought she'd hidden the bitter note in her voice until he gave her a sharp look. He was reading her too well.

'How is Angela?' she added quickly, paddling away from dangerous waters. She didn't want to end up like the *Alvarez*, on the rocks.

'She's in a care home these days. It got too much for Mandy and it wasn't fair for her to be Mum's carer and put her career on hold. We all got together for a meeting and found Mum a nice place, where the nursing is top notch. She still struggles some days, but at least we know she's safe and being taken care of.'

Nina nodded, trying not to remember that night when Angela Rawlins collapsed in the kitchen. The panic on her children's faces, as if it was the end of their worlds. It had certainly been the end of hers.

'You should drop in and see her,' Jude went on, eyes on her face.

Nina made her expression as blank as possible. 'I doubt I'd be welcome.'

He didn't dispute it, and she could imagine what his mother had said after their relationship had ended so abruptly. Seeing Jude hurt, in pain, Angela would have protected him by tearing Nina to pieces.

'What's Mandy doing now?'

He smiled. 'She's studying medicine. She was always bright. She has a partner, no kids yet. She says she's too busy.'

'And you?' Nina asked, trying to keep her voice steady. Pretending they were like normal friends catching up. It felt surreal. Her last question echoed in her head and she wondered if she should take it back. But that was what friends did, wasn't it? Asked about personal matters?

'Me ... what? Do I have someone special?' He looked away, staring out at the misty horizon as if the answer was to be found there. 'No. I'm single, busy with work, which I love, most of the time. Sometimes I miss having someone to ...' He cleared his throat and didn't finish. 'Well, I keep busy. And you, Nina? You keep yourself very private. I've been nosy enough to ask around when your name is mentioned, but no one seems to know much about you. And I wouldn't ask Paul. Not that he would tell me, anyway. If he wasn't gay I might think you and he were a couple.'

He'd asked about her? That surprised her. She thought he would hate her too much to want to know if she was happily ensconced with a new man. She and Jude had been deeply in love, the sort of love that should have lasted a lifetime. She had always known there would never be anyone else for her, not like that. Was it possible he felt the same? Was it possible that despite everything, he still wanted her back?

The thought made her dizzy, shaky. 'I keep busy, too,' she said quickly, not willing to delve into those dangerous waters. 'My parents are living in Queensland now, and I haven't seen them for a while, but we catch up on Skype.'

He laughed softly. 'We used to talk about sailing around the world, remember?'

Nina didn't reply. Of course she remembered, but it definitely wasn't something she wanted to talk about now. It hurt. It still hurt so much.

Another gust of wind caught her hair, tugged at her clothing, and abruptly she felt far too exposed up here.

'What about Murray?' she said recklessly. 'You haven't mentioned him. I thought he was going to be the first QC in the Rawlins family? Or at least, he would have been if Colin had his way.'

Something in Jude's face made her heart begin to beat in that rough, painful way that meant trouble ahead. 'Yes, that was the plan, wasn't it? He did start work in Uncle Colin's chambers. A rising star. We all thought …' He shrugged irritably. 'It didn't work out. He's moved on. Well, Uncle Colin let him go. He wasn't happy about it, but in the end he felt he had no choice. He …' Jude sighed, and looked at her as if he'd decided to lay all his cards on the table, and just for a moment she thought he knew. Her hands were damp with sweat, clinging to the railing, and her heart threatened to jump out of her chest.

'What?' she said in a soft, quivering voice. 'What about Murray?'

'Christ, you're as white as a sheet. He's not dead, if that's what you think. He might as well be, though, for all the resemblance he has to the brother I remember. He moved to Sydney and he now has a raft of dodgy clients after joining a practice that specialises in getting the Mister Bigs off. You name anything illegal and we're pretty sure Murray is into it. I know he gambles … eye-watering amounts. Mum still sees him, and Mandy calls him up. These days I prefer to keep my distance.'

Nina tried to take that in. She had the advantage over Jude, knowing what really lay under Murray's pleasant smile. All the same, hearing what had become of him was a shock. He'd gone off the rails in a big way. She remembered the look on his face that day at the beach house when maybe it sank in that everyone was depending on him, the weight of expectation on his shoulders, and no way out. It sounded as if he'd done everything he could to throw off those expectations, and to transform himself into someone else.

But then how did she know? Murray might always have been the man he now was. Dangerous and evil, a destroyer. He'd just hidden it until he no longer could.

'Nina.'

It was the tone of his voice that made her turn, rather than the word. She shook off the past, and saw that Jude was staring back through the window. The lens was grouped in the centre, around the lamp, but she could see past it to the other side of the lantern room.

'What is that?' He pointed and then opened the door. She followed him in. Something loose above her head rattled. Jude was moving quickly now, and an instant later she was standing beside him, staring at the object that lay at his feet. It was tucked out of the way, behind the landing where the staircase led up from the watch area, and yet she was amazed she hadn't seen it before. She had been distracted by the view, she supposed.

A sleeping bag. Not old and musty, it seemed almost brand new, and there was an empty packet of cigarettes on the floor beside it.

Their eyes met. 'You were right,' he admitted, his dark eyes bright. 'There's been someone living in here.'

'Recently, do you think?' A water bottle lay on its side near the top of the bag, and the crinkly, shiny wrapper from a chocolate bar. Both appeared to be recent, although she supposed they could be days old.

'Just because someone was here doesn't mean they are now,' Jude said. 'Maybe they realised the game was up.'

Nina raised her eyebrows at him. 'You sound like an Agatha Christie novel.'

'I was hoping I was right,' he said.

'Instead I was right,' she retorted.

Impulsively, she bent down to straighten out the bag and run her hand over the cloth, wondering if there was something inside.

There was.

With a glance at Jude, she unzipped the top and reached between the two layers, carefully, fingers searching. She caught hold of a plastic bag and drew it out. It was half full of small pills of varying colours. They resembled children's sweets, only she was certain no child should ingest these.

'Drugs?' Jude said, leaning closer. 'Do you think it's someone's private stash?'

'I don't know.'

'Wasn't that what Kyle was afraid of when he heard about the trespasser on the island? Someone using this place to transfer narcotics?'

'Yes. It makes sense. A safe place to transfer drugs and money. As long as no one else was here to get in the way.'

'And then we arrived.'

She told herself she should be searching the island, she should be ringing the bell and calling a meeting. Warning everyone of her fears. Yet she stood here feeling paralysed and confused, overwhelmed by the position she found herself in.

There was something else in the sleeping bag. Compact, hard. Even before Nina drew it out, she knew what it was.

Light weight, a series of cylinders secured together ... A gun.

With a gasp, Nina dropped it back on the sleeping bag.

'God!' she whispered. 'This gets worse and worse.'

'Looks homemade,' Jude said with interest, leaning in. Then, catching her eye, 'This isn't good, is it?'

'Drugs and a gun, no, it isn't good.'

'Whoever has been staying here isn't harmless. We need to find them.'

They did. 'Why leave this here?' she said. 'Why were they in such a hurry?' She waved her hand at the plastic bag of pills and the weapon.

'They realised we were on to them.' Jude bent to pick up the items, cautiously. 'We need to give these to Paul. He can keep them safe. They're evidence.'

'Yes.' She peered around her. 'Whoever this was ... they've been hiding in plain sight. Watching us.' The thought made her shiver.

'And they have a key. The lock was intact. Maybe they have the original one that went missing? You need to ask Kyle.'

'No satellite phone,' she muttered. 'For now, we're on our own. Unless you have some way of communicating that you haven't told us about?' She raised her eyebrows.

'Is that what you think?' He seemed offended. 'That this was all a publicity stunt for my new show?' He shook his head. 'I wish I did have another satellite phone tucked away,' he said. 'But I don't.'

So, they really were on their own.

'I need to talk to the others,' Nina said. 'See if anyone knows about the sleeping bag. Maybe there's a perfectly reasonable explanation.' Although, that didn't feel like the case. 'And we need to search the island.'

He nodded. 'I'll use the drone for that.'

He went to follow her down the stairs, but she stopped and looked back over her shoulder at their intruder's home away from home. Someone was watching them, spying, playing games. It wasn't personal, probably some drug trafficker way down the food chain, and yet … it felt personal.

Jude put his hand on her shoulder, the warm strength comforting. 'We'll make sure no one can get back into the lighthouse. If they're hiding on the island and we take away their shelter, then they'll have to come out at some point.'

'Unless they have a boat.'

'Well, if they do we'll know soon enough,' he said.

They would. Nina felt a tingle in her fingertips, an ache in her stomach. She knew it was possible their trespasser was no longer on the island, but she had that niggling sensation again. That feeling that they were being watched. And it didn't bode well. They were in danger, and it was up to her to protect them all from that danger.

When Nina wasn't even sure she could protect herself.

LAURA

19 May 1882, Benevolence

They did not find Rorie. They searched until it was fully dark, but there was no sign of him and nor did he answer their calls. Either he did not want to be found, or there was something very wrong.

Laura had brought the piece of burnt cloth from Rorie's cottage back with her, and when he saw it, Leo was at first angry and then just as puzzled as she and Edmund were.

'He wanted the brooch,' her father echoed Edmund's thoughts. 'He was a thief. Do you remember whenever something in our food store went missing? Miriam always blamed him.'

They were inside the main room of the quarters, eating their supper. Miriam had made another filling meal to satisfy everyone's hunger, but Laura wondered how long they could go on before their rations ran out. If the supply steamer did not get here soon, they would be in trouble.

Mrs Munro had been asked to examine the scrap of material in case she could add any information. The woman was holding a mug of tea and her hands were clenched around it, her brown eyes growing wide as she bent closer. She did not seem to want to touch it, shaking her head wildly when Laura offered it to her.

'I'm sure this was what Elsie was wearing,' she said. 'I gave the blouse to her. It was one of mine. She was particular about her apparel. Fussy.' And then, 'Rorie was always sweet on her. I told her to watch out for him, but she believed the best in everyone, always. She wasn't used to attention like that, and I think her head was turned.' She swallowed and her eyes brimmed with tears. 'Was it the brooch? Was that why he …?'

'It seems likely,' Leo answered her. 'Was it worth anything? I thought it was a cairngorm. Pretty but not valuable.'

'No, cairngorms aren't valuable,' Mrs Munro said firmly. 'It seems so unkind of him. To take that from her when she was … defenceless. So cruel.' She glanced towards her husband, where he was asleep on the straw pallet. The walk with Leo around the lighthouse had tired him out and Miriam said he was moving painfully when he returned. 'Elsie could be naïve when it came to the world and the evil in it, but she didn't deserve to be treated with such disrespect by a man who pretended to be her friend.'

'Do you think it was a keepsake to him, then?' Laura asked. 'Rather than something he could sell for money?' Rorie had never struck her as a sentimental man. Had he really cared for the poor young woman, or was it just another of his self-seeking plans to get whatever he could to make his life easier?

Mrs Munro gave her a helpless look.

'We need to find him,' Leo said with quiet seriousness.

'If he's out there he'll have to show himself at some point,' Miriam said, reassuring everyone as usual. 'He'll get hungry. Rorie's stomach will bring him out soon enough.'

Leo gave a jaw-breaking yawn and Edmund offered to take his watch when it was light-up time. 'I feel confident I can hold the fort, Mr Webster. You are an excellent teacher. And if I have any problems I will come and fetch you immediately.'

Laura's father hesitated briefly but then agreed, which surprised her and also showed how much he had grown to trust the younger man.

'You can sleep in your bed tonight,' Miriam added a further temptation.

Laura jumped in. 'You deserve a few hours off, Dad. Mr Bailey will watch the light, and as he said, he can always come and get you if he needs to. I'll watch over Tom so that Miriam can rest too.'

Again, Leo seemed as if he wanted to argue, but he was so tired that in the end he just nodded and lumbered off to bed. Edmund went outside with Seal and Mrs Munro returned to her husband's side.

Miriam gave Laura a grateful smile, squeezing her hand affectionately. 'Tom may wake up off and on, but you can doze in between,' she said. She dropped her voice. 'Mrs Munro has already promised to take over at dawn. It's taken longer than I hoped, but she seems to have developed some empathy. Anyway, if she changes her mind, the rest will be up and about by then, and one of us can take her place.'

Laura finished her supper, only then noticing that Edmund was back. It was almost time to light the lamp, but he was looking at her as if he wanted a private word first. Even as she thought it, he caught her eye and gestured with his head towards the door. Miriam was busy with Noah and had not noticed, so she followed him out.

'Why do you think Rorie is in hiding?' was the first thing he said when they were alone.

'Whenever Rorie has hidden before it's because he's done something wrong and he's afraid of getting into trouble.' They stood close together, their voices low, and it reminded her of last night and her overheard conversation. She asked herself again if one of those whispering conspirators was Rorie, but somehow it just did not fit. Rorie was a coward and a loner, not a conspirator. He was far more likely to run away and take cover than take charge of a situation.

'And the brooch,' Edmund went on. 'Why would he take that when it's worth nothing?'

'A keepsake? If he was sweet on the girl, as Mrs Munro said. Although somehow, that doesn't ring true to me. I can't imagine

Rorie mooning over a brooch, weeping for love lost. He'd more likely sell it and pocket the money.'

She had amused him. 'You don't think much of him, do you?' He did not wait for her to answer and his smile faded. 'I didn't see the girl when she was on the beach. Can you describe the brooch to me, Laura? Humour me,' he added when she gave him a questioning look.

Laura took herself back to that time on the beach. She closed her eyes and that seemed to help, or maybe that was because Edmund was a distraction. 'It was as big as a small egg, and set in an oval ... frame, I suppose you would call it? There was some decoration around the edges. Filigree, is it? That was gold, or gold coloured, because it wouldn't have been real gold, surely? The stone itself was orange. Although ...'

'What?' He was watching her with interest.

'It was orange, but in the light of our lamp, I could see so many other colours deep inside it. Orange and gold and yellow. Like ... like ...' She paused and an image came to her. 'I saw a glass blower once, in Hobart, creating an object out of molten glass, and it was a little like that. Beautiful. I was only able to look for a moment—there were other things to be done—but I remember how mesmerising it was.'

He seemed to understand. 'It doesn't sound like a cairngorm,' he said at last. 'It sounds like something far more valuable. But I don't understand how Elsie could have been wearing a precious stone. Unless someone gave it to her.' But even as the thought occurred he shook his head. 'There's a mystery here, I think. We will have to leave it for now, though, because I have to go tend the light, Laura.' He stared back at her for what seemed ages, and she wondered what he was going to say. But in the end all he said was, 'Be careful. There is something about this we don't understand. I wouldn't want my extraordinary girl to be hurt.'

'Rorie wouldn't hurt me,' she said quickly, because his words stirred feelings inside her she did not want to examine, not now. 'He's a sneak, but I don't think he is physically dangerous.'

'Anyone can be dangerous if they're cornered.'

As Edmund walked away, she found herself remembering how Rorie had spied on her, and wondering if he had spied on Elsie, too, when he worked for Mr Fernley. Mrs Munro had called Elsie innocent, a lamb to the wolves. Had Rorie charmed her into falling in love with him and then abandoned her when he was accused of stealing? Again, that seemed rather fanciful. Was Rorie the sort of man to turn a young woman's head, even one as naïve as Elsie? They might be friends, but lovers? No, Rorie was no Edmund Bailey.

Because Edmund was a gentleman, handsome and charismatic. The sort of man she would never have been thrown together with in normal circumstances. She did not think her head had been turned, she was no Elsie, but she knew she was on the verge of falling for him. Falling in love? It seemed ridiculously soon for that. Falling into enchantment, perhaps. He might call her an extraordinary girl, and she confessed it quickened her pulse, but she knew better than to lose her heart to him. Edmund was only here for a short while whatever he said, and when he left their very different worlds would never collide again. It would be foolish of her to let herself believe. To hope.

Very foolish indeed.

* * *

When Laura relieved Isaac of his watch over Tom Burrows, she found him more restless than usual. Isaac warned her that the mate seemed caught up in a nightmare he could not awaken from. Indeed, the poor man tossed restlessly, throwing off his covers despite the cool night, and then lying there shivering until she covered him again. Laura was kept busy doing her best to sooth him, or diligently trickling some of the water Miriam had set beside his bed past his parched lips. He drank a little, and Miriam had said he had taken some soup earlier. He was no worse, at least.

Noah's soft cries drifted through the wall from the other bedroom, followed by Miriam's soothing voice. She was singing him a lullaby, but it was as if the little boy had picked up on Tom's restlessness. Or perhaps it was Laura's unease after her conversation with Edmund earlier. Eventually, Noah settled again and silence fell over the cottage.

She *was* uneasy. There were too many questions that she found impossible to answer with certainty. The missing woman, the missing brooch, and now Rorie had disappeared. She felt as if the safety and security of her home had been invaded. She was longing for the supply steamer to come and take away these strangers, and she was also dreading it. Because Edmund would go too, and he had unsettled her the most with his talk of her needing to experience a world she was not sure she wished to live in, reminding her of the end of her time on her beloved island. Despite that, she thought she would remember him every day for the rest of her life.

Tom was finally sleeping deeply and peacefully. *Poor man.* Isaac had told them that the Burrows family consisted of eight children. How would they be fed with their father gone? Isaac had taken passage on the *Alvarez* at the last moment, planning to visit his brother in Melbourne, so he did not know the other seamen. What he did know had been imparted to him by Tom, a gregarious man with a generous heart.

Laura looked over at the old trunk against the far wall of her room. It had come with her from Scotland all those years ago, full of her belongings, her memories, and it was still with her. These days it had become a handy place to store things that interested her, including illustrated books and magazines, and the newspaper snippets she saved from those the captain on the steamer brought her every three months. The words written in newsprint were like a bridge to the outside world. Whenever she was handed something new, she devoured it ravenously and kept the cuttings she thought she might want to read again. She had quite a selection now in her trunk of memories.

Perhaps Edmund is right.

The thought was a worrying one. Did she need to spend time living the sort of normal life others did? Was her collection a cry for help from a lonely woman? She knew Miriam would love nothing more than to show her what she was missing. They had only three years left on Benevolence and then things would change dramatically for them all.

With an effort, she put those difficult thoughts from her mind. She had been longing to search through her newspapers ever since she heard of the Munros, certain that she had kept something that related to them, and now that Tom was resting, she had the time to do so.

The lid had her initials burned into the timber. Soundlessly, she rested the lid back against the wall and began to unpack the collection, skimming through each bundle. Some of them had been damaged by their journey to the island, stained with seawater or the print smudged, but it was not one of those she was looking for.

Tom groaned and shuffled around, muttering broken sentences. His bandaged head twisted from side to side on the pillow. 'No! Please … don't … don't!' Laura waited as his voice faded and he settled again, before resuming her task.

When she found it, it wasn't the Munro wedding, after all. This was an earlier story concerning their engagement. Probably the report of the wedding would come with the next ship, but she could already see that this notice was long. Rochelle Fernley, belonging to a family of some importance, received a great deal more attention than every other couple's obligatory two lines. Laura sat back, leaning against her trunk, one eye on Tom, and read through the closely printed paragraphs.

January 22 1882—The engagement of Miss Rochelle Fernley and Mr Albert Munro has been announced to much rejoicing. The pair have been inseparable since Miss Fernley's father, Colonel Fernley, passed away last year. Miss Fernley plans to sell the property that her father left to her, and she and Mr Munro will be relocating to Victoria, to make a new life there. Mr Munro is one of our most capable and ambitious young men, so it is no surprise he wants to move on to greener fields. Miss Fernley is a much-loved member of New Norfolk society, and her sweet and generous nature will be greatly missed. We do hope the happy couple will not forget their friends and well-wishers in Tasmania.

For the sake of the many ladies who will be interested in the engagement, I can report that Miss Rochelle Fernley forewent full mourning for a grey pastel silk dress with a cluster of flowers in her hair intertwined with a jaunty blue ribbon, the exact match of her eyes. Miss Fernley wore her father's gift to her, pinned at her throat. She informed me that it was the same gift he gave to her mother after he retired from the British army in Ceylon. It is a most striking piece of jewellery.

When this journalist informed Miss Fernley this was his first job with the Recorder, *she insisted he be fetched a plate of canapes and a flute of champagne. She was kindness itself and I can declare absolutely that her eyes were the bluest I have ever seen.*

Goosebumps prickled Laura's skin. The engagement party had come to life in her head, the kind and sweet Miss Fernley with the jewel pinned at her throat, and her smiling blue eyes. Juxtaposed with it was the memory of an intense Mrs Munro, deranged with grief, refusing to leave her husband's side. Her blue eyes reddened from weeping. But no, none of that fitted. It was wrong. Not just the change in personality, but because Laura had looked into Mrs Munro's eyes numerous times since the *Alvarez* had capsized, most recently during tonight's supper, when those eyes had filled with tears over her maid's tragic end. And Laura knew they were not blue. They were most definitely brown.

Was it possible the reporter had got it wrong? And yet ... The blue ribbon matching her blue eyes—why would he make mention of that fact if it were not true? It did not seem like a mistake, not at all.

She tried to still her wild thoughts and began to calmly consider this new information from all angles. But she kept coming back to the blue eyes. And the jewel pinned to Rochelle's throat. The gift from her father, the 'striking jewel'. Laura remembered the brooch, its orange colours seeming to draw her in, catching the light of the lamp, swirling like molten glass. It was not a cairngorm. As Edmund had said, this was something far more valuable, a jewel that belonged to a wealthy woman and not a servant girl.

The story of the brooch, that Elsie had been so fond of it she wore it everywhere, was one that Rorie had told. Mrs Munro had stumbled in her agreement, watching him as a rabbit might a snake. Rorie knew and he had collaborated with Mrs Munro. He had seen a chance to make some money, or an easy life, and he had taken it. Yes, that was the sort of man Rorie was. He had not been half in love with Elsie, but he had known what the brooch was worth, and when he saw the body on the beach he had taken his opportunity.

Hardly knowing what she was doing, Laura began to return the newspapers to the trunk, putting them in all topsy-turvy. She closed the lid but kept out the cutting of the engagement, clutching it in her hand. She wanted to show it to Edmund before she acted. She wanted to see if his conclusions matched her own.

The brooch worn by Elsie. Elsie's dead body on the beach. Mrs Munro wailing for Albert. Mrs Munro's brown eyes. There was only one explanation, it was just that she did not want to accept it. Mrs Munro was Elsie. Rochelle Fernley was dead, her body washed up onto the beach in Thankful Cove, and Elsie had taken her place. But she was not on her own. She could never have done such a thing without Albert Munro's full knowledge and support.

There was a sound. The door to the bedroom began to open.

Laura had been so engrossed in her thoughts that she had not realised that dawn's light was creeping through the shutters. It was morning and Mrs Munro was coming to relieve her.

Laura looked up, and in her shock at seeing the very woman she had just been speculating about, she gave herself away. She tried to blank her expression, but putting the newspaper behind her as if it was a secret only made matters worse. Mrs Munro's brown eyes narrowed as she stepped inside the room.

'You know,' she said at once, her voice trembling.

Laura shook her head to deny it, but her mouth had other ideas. 'You're Elsie.'

The other woman contemplated her for a moment, and Laura could see the dismay in her face. But there was calculation, too, and a sort of cold-hearted shrewdness. Before Laura could think to do anything, she was calling out, 'Albert! Come in here.'

Laura backed away. 'Father!' she responded, making Tom startle.

Albert was in the room now, gaze going from one to the other. Laura could hear stirring from next door. Voices. Her father's low grumble and Noah's wail.

'She knows,' Elsie said as Albert came to stand beside her. If anything could have convinced Laura she was right, then it was that simple act of solidarity.

Albert stared at her, mouth tight, jaw tensed. 'How do you know?'

Elsie took a step towards Laura, crowding her, and snatched at her arm, forcing her to show her hands. The woman had always seemed a little unhinged, something Laura had put down to grief, but she had never been violent. Now Laura felt the bruising strength of her grip, and saw the fiercely determined expression on her face.

The clipping tore as Elsie pulled it from Laura's fingers. She frowned at it and then pushed it to Albert. Laura realised then that Elsie couldn't read, and remembered how she had refused Miriam's suggestion that she read aloud to Tom.

'It's the engagement notice,' Albert said. 'You said that she wrapped that foolish young reporter around her little finger. He was half in love with her by the time he left.' He frowned. 'Blue eyes,' he murmured, and they exchanged a glance.

Laura swallowed. The two of them weren't even pretending now and that felt bad. Very bad.

'Laura?' The door was flung back and her father strode inside. Big and safe. Leo had always looked out for her, and despite the odds they faced, she believed he would now. Miriam was behind him, her eyes wide as she took in the others. *Everything would be all right now,* Laura told herself as she moved towards them. Only to have Miriam cry and cling to Leo's arm. Mr Munro had a pistol. He lifted it carefully in his bandaged hands, aiming at Laura. Until then, she had not realised it was possible to feel so afraid.

Because everything was not all right and even Leo could not make it so. They were at the mercy of two desperate and dangerous people.

'Now,' Albert said in the sort of voice that brooked no argument. 'This is what is going to happen next.'

NINA

May 2020, Benevolence
Day Three

It was late morning when Jude and Nina left the lighthouse. By now, there were clouds moving in to cover the sun, making it seem a very different sort of day from those that had come before. The air was cold, and Nina was glad of her padded jacket. She wished she'd worn a few more layers underneath it, but there was no time for that. She started to ring the bell, calling the team together.

People began to appear. Brian came out of the cottage he was working on, a frown on his face, his tool belt low on his hips. Reynash and Gemma were behind him, muttering together. Paul and Arnie, obviously interrupted in their lunch preparations. Elle came to join Nina, her camera secure around her neck, looking pale and worried, and not at all her usually bubbly self.

'What is it?' she asked. 'Is it about the generator? Do you know who did it?' Her voice sounded strained and she waited impatiently for Nina's answer.

'No. Well, not entirely. There's been someone living on the island. We found a sleeping bag in the lighthouse, along with some other things.'

Elle frowned. 'What other things?'

'Nina?' Paul was beside her. 'I saw you up in the lighthouse. What happened?'

Everyone was there now, waiting and watching.

Jude held out the plastic bag and the gun. Someone gasped. Paul's gaze sharpened. 'These will be safer with you,' Jude told Paul. 'We found them up in the lighthouse with a sleeping bag. Someone has been dossing there.'

Nina spoke then, going over the spilled diesel episode this morning, reminding them of the satellite phone and then Brian's missing equipment. She tried to keep a close watch on their faces, thinking that maybe if one of the team knew more than they were saying, she could catch them out. But they all seemed naturally concerned and shocked, which was nothing out of the ordinary. When she finished there was silence followed by a few exchanged glances, as everyone took it in.

'Is whoever this is still here on the island?' Brian sounded outraged. 'What on earth is going on? Why would they want to steal from us, destroy our equipment? What good will that do them? If they're using the island as a place to traffic drugs, why didn't Island Heritage know about it?'

'It could be someone gone rogue,' Paul said. 'Someone who now considers the island their territory.'

'We don't know that.' Jude was standing with his hands in his pockets. 'We don't know what their agenda is. What if it's just someone with a few issues who wants their solitude?'

'More likely a drug-running crazy,' Paul muttered.

Arnie snorted a laugh and then, when Brian glared at him, held up his hands in apology.

'So, what's next?' Brian asked.

'I have a drone,' Jude said. 'I'm going to send it over the island. Whoever this person is, they can't hide forever. If they're still here then we'll find them.'

'Is that a good thing?' Paul said. 'Cornering a dangerous person, trapping them, making them feel desperate?'

'Wouldn't it be better to know what or who we're dealing with?' Jude retorted.

Paul nodded reluctant agreement. 'Just be careful,' he said, turning the weapon over in his hand. 'This might look like a kid's toy, but it's real.'

'Dangerous,' Elle said and then seemed to realise she'd spoken aloud. 'I did some freelance work for one of the newspapers. Too many of these weapons are getting into the country. In the wrong hands ...'

'Are there any right hands?' Nina asked.

Another silence ensued, broken by Brian. He sounded fed up. 'And in the meantime? I vote we just get on with things. That's what we're here for, isn't it? What else are we going to do? Come on, folks, let's get back to work.' And he began walking towards the cottage he was repairing. A few of his volunteers trailed after him, while others went to resume whatever they had been doing before Nina rang the bell.

'Just ... be careful!' Nina called.

There were a few murmurs, a few raised hands, but no one responded.

'For once, I think he's right,' Paul said. 'We should just get on with it. That's what we're here for. Whoever this is seems to want to frighten us, and I never respond well to bullying.'

Arnie gave her a wink over Paul's shoulder and Nina smiled. With Paul's size and military training, it would take a brave man to bully him.

'I was wondering if Elle could take some photos of this lot,' Paul held up the gun, 'and inside the lighthouse. Document the evidence. It might be useful later on.'

'That's a good idea,' she agreed. 'Can you do that, Elle?'

Elle looked reluctant.

'You can take someone with you.'

Arnie said he'd go, and Jude handed over the key. Lis followed them, and Nina was tempted to tell her not to, but then she changed her mind. There was safety in numbers.

'Let's get started with the drone,' Jude said.

'Good luck!' Paul called to them.

Nina saw the question in her friend's eyes. She gave him a quick thumbs up and hurried towards Jude, heading along to the upper track and the assistant-keeper's cottage.

* * *

Jude worked at setting up the drone, a frown of concentration on his face. 'The camera sends images to my laptop, so we should be able to watch in real time. Might as well get it to fly right over the island before we start poking around the cliffs. We can check the anchorage near Birds Nest Island. If there's a boat there, we'll see it.'

'Okay.'

He met her eyes with a wry grin. 'That's what's supposed to happen, anyway. I've had a few lessons, but I'm still a novice. They would have sent a film crew with me, until the restrictions put paid to that. Can't say I'm sorry,' he added, with another glance at her. 'I didn't want them looking over my shoulder. I'm a bit of a loner, always was.'

He used to be. She remembered how Jude would go off somewhere in his own mind, drifting in dreams, and she would laugh and kiss his cheek, and ask him where he'd been this time. More recently, he'd seemed far more extroverted, surrounded by admirers. Different. Or at least that's what she had thought, but perhaps he wasn't different at all. Perhaps, like her, he was simply hiding behind a mask.

They took the drone outside and Jude stood back, controls in hand. Nina watched as it rose several metres into the cloudy sky, barely making a sound, before it began moving away, towards the western part of the island. The wind had risen and it struggled a bit under the buffeting, but it kept flying until it was out of sight. Nina was still staring at the spot where it had been when Jude called to her.

'I have the controls set for FVP, so I can guide the drone using the images I'm seeing. Come on. We'll take a look at the camera feed.'

He had placed his laptop on a table in the shelter of the verandah, and she sat beside him, tugging her sweater over her hands to keep them warm. As he had said earlier, the pictures on the screen were being transmitted from the camera attached to the flying drone. It was rather like being in the helicopter when she had first arrived, only not so high up, and things on the ground weren't being blown about by the force of the rotor blades. There was also no audio, so everything was recorded in silence.

At first, they could only see the vegetation that covered much of the island, scrubby bushes and tufts of native grasses, with an occasional group of trees. She-oaks and tea-tree mainly, nothing very tall. Some wallabies bounded off, as if sensing the unfamiliar, and a group of Cape Barren geese was huddled belligerently together on their piece of territory, obviously squabbling with a newcomer. They strutted off angrily as the drone sailed over.

In no time the machine was approaching the cliffs, and now there were seabirds squawking silently, and flying so close that Nina was worried they might knock the drone out of the sky.

And then the land fell away, dizzyingly, to the sea below. Bright-pink pigface grew in the crevices, along with the tougher grasses. There were birds everywhere, too many to count; Birds Nest Island was well named. Nina could see the chasm that separated the two islands now, situated between inhospitable rocky faces and overhanging ledges. She noticed some shallow caverns and crevices in the cliff faces, but they were certainly not the sort of places anyone could hide in, even if they could manage to climb up to them. The sea was empty, too, a vast heaving mass with not a boat in sight.

'I'll move to the other side of Birds Nest,' Jude said. 'I doubt a boat would get much shelter there, but it would be well hidden from anyone on Benevolence.'

'Whoever it was could have already sailed away.'

'Maybe,' he agreed, concentrating on the controls, 'but I don't think so. If whoever was in the lighthouse left in such a hurry that they forgot their prized belongings, they'd hardly have had time to sail away.'

The drone moved over the top of Birds Nest Island, capturing film of the seabirds that made it their home. Nina could only imagine the noise they were making. And then they were on the far side.

They both exclaimed at the same time. Nina leaned in, her shoulder pressed to Jude's as they stared at the screen.

Because there *was* a boat anchored there. A white yacht that swung gently on its chain, rolling in the swell. 'We need to get closer.' Jude sounded excited as he deftly moved the controls. 'See if there's anyone on board.'

The drone came down over the yacht and now they could see the empty deck. No sign of anyone. 'They could be below,' Nina said. Even to her untrained eyes the yacht seemed untidy, ropes thrown about instead of tied off, and one of the sails was bundled up in the cockpit rather than being properly stowed away. Abruptly, the yacht swung on its anchor and Jude hurriedly took the drone back up to a safe distance.

'Does it have a name?' Nina had noticed the writing in black along the white hull, but it was a fancy, curly type, difficult to read at this distance.

Jude edged the drone in once more, closer and then closer again, hovering beside the name. 'What is it?' he said. 'Can you read it? What's wrong with Times Roman, for God's sake.'

Nina laughed despite herself. The curly script really was difficult to read, but a moment later she had it. '*Mermaid Dream*? No, *Mermaid's Dream*.'

Jude stared, and she could feel the tension in him, but before she could question it, he said, 'I think you're right.'

'Well, we can check that out,' Nina went on, excitedly. 'There would be a register somewhere, wouldn't there? An owner?'

'I guess so. Unless it's hired, or on loan.' He was watching her face, that strange tension still there. 'I need to think,' he said.

'Whoever's yacht it is must be on the island. Can you do a search?'

He hesitated and then nodded brusquely. The drone responded to his commands, hovering a little before it began to rise and move steadily back over Birds Nest Island and the wild water of the chasm, to Benevolence.

'We should check the southern edge of the island first,' Jude said. 'There's an inlet there, but the draft is too shallow for larger boats.' He had rotated the drone in that direction as he spoke, when suddenly he stopped and backtracked.

'Look.' He pointed at the screen.

At first she couldn't see anything, and then she picked out a flash of colour, a movement. Someone was crouched amongst the grass tussocks, trying to hide. She could see dark hair and the back of a jacket, and a white hand. Jude manoeuvred the drone so that it flew lower, just as the person glanced up.

A pale, blurry face. Another adjustment and the picture came into sharp focus. It was Elle. Nina could see the photographer's pretty features and short hair as she huddled on the ground. Her eyes were wide and staring, and she appeared frightened.

'Wasn't she supposed to be in the lighthouse?' Nina said, not knowing what to think. Why was Elle out here? And whom was she hiding from, because it certainly seemed like she was hiding from someone.

'Yes,' Jude said. 'She was with Lis and Arnie.'

As they watched, Elle leaped to her feet and began to move swiftly away. They saw her glance back over her shoulder at the drone, which was now following her, and then her gaze went beyond it. Her mouth opened as if she was yelling out to someone, and then she waved her arms. Was she trying to tell them something?

'What's she doing?' Jude said. 'Is she running away from someone?'

Just then, Elle put her hands over her ears and sank down to the ground. The image on the laptop began to break up. It pixelated, froze, and then the camera feed cut out altogether. They were staring at a blank screen.

'What's happened?' Nina asked, but Jude shook his head with a frown.

'I don't know. Something's happened to the drone.' He fiddled with the controls. 'Whatever's wrong is beyond fixing from this end.'

'Do you think she's hurt?' Nina went to stand up. She felt rattled, and more than a little afraid. 'We should go and find her.'

He held her arm. 'Wait, Nina. Let's just think about this.'

'I'm in charge, not you, I need to—' Panic was making her irrational. She took a deep breath and tried to steady herself. How could things have gone so very wrong?

'What was Elle doing out there?' Jude said. 'You're assuming she is in danger, Nina, but what if she and this unknown person in the lighthouse are in this together.' He looked grim.

Nina stilled, considering. 'You mean she was going to the yacht? But how?' It would be impossible for Elle to climb down those cliffs, and what, swim out to the boat?' She shook her head, rejecting the idea.

'The owner of the yacht must have a dinghy. An inflatable. It's probably tucked away safely further around the coast. That inlet I mentioned, with the shallow draft. Elle could be going there.'

'But why?' Nina demanded. 'We're missing something, Jude. How could Elle be involved in this? This is her first time on the island. She was a last-minute replacement for someone else.'

Jude gave her a furtive sideways glance. 'Um, there's something I need to tell you. I probably should have mentioned it before, but … Well, we haven't exactly been sharing, and I really didn't think it was important until now.'

Nina stilled. He'd recognised something. She could see it in his face, in the uneasy movement of his body. Was it the boat? Before she could ask her questions he stood up. They were close together, and she half recognised how tempting he was, how familiar. The feelings that had never gone away. She took a step back, to give herself some distance.

'Tell me now,' she said in a cold, hard voice.

Jude seemed to be considering his words carefully. 'Okay, here's the thing. Lis works as an archivist, I did tell you that. She's often in the state library and she happened to see Elle a few months ago.

She didn't know who she was then, of course, but it stuck in her memory, and when she saw her again here on the island she remembered. I said it probably meant nothing. A coincidence.'

Nina still didn't get it. 'Why would seeing Elle in the archives seem strange? She's a photographer. She could have been following up a story.'

'The reason it was strange was because Elle wasn't alone.' He hesitated, as if he really didn't want to tell her. There was an expression in his dark eyes that resembled panic, and it was so strange to see it again after all these years that Nina felt her own fear levels begin to rise. The warning quickening of her pulse, the flash of heat over her skin, that sick twist in her stomach.

'Come on, Jude, spit it out,' she said. 'What aren't you telling me.'

He rubbed a hand over his eyes as if he was tired. And then he blurted, 'She was with Murray. She was in the archives with Murray, and Lis said they looked like friends.'

Murray and Elle. Murray was here? But no, that was ridiculous. Why would he be? Then she remembered that weird tension she'd felt in Jude.

'The boat,' she whispered through stiff lips. 'You recognised it, didn't you?'

'Yes,' Jude admitted. 'If it's the one I'm thinking of then it belongs to Murray.'

Murray's yacht, Murray's friend, Murray with his dangerous clients and out-of-control behaviour. Murray in the lighthouse, staring down at her, watching her, all this time. Murray ...

Jude was still speaking, but Nina had stopped listening.

The air around her began to hum, and the scene in front of her began to sway back and forth, around and around. A wave of heat washed over her, her head pounded, and her throat was dry. She tried to take a step, but her legs were like jelly, her hands shaking violently as they clung to the verandah post.

She shook her head, but there was no stopping it. The flashback. She was going back.

**'The Jewel Box Affair' by Harald Jensen
(Article in An Interesting History of Precious
Stone Mining in Ceylon, published 1880)
Book held in the Hobart State Library**

Ceylon has long been famous for its amazing array of precious stones, many of them adorning the crowns and regalia of the royal heads of Europe. At one time, the sapphires, emeralds and diamonds to be found in the streams of Ceylon were much sought after.

In 1860, Theodore Braglia, a little-known but promising and enterprising jeweller in Europe, arranged for a box of Ceylon's finest stones to be sent to him. He planned to create beautiful pieces for the wealthy aristocrats of Europe, in opposition to some of the better-known names of the day. It was a tremendous outlay, and a tremendous gamble. The jewels were placed in a small locked box, ready to be shipped. However, when it came time to carry the box to its transport, it was nowhere to be found.

One rumour was that it had been stolen by a member of the native population, as part of their struggle against colonial rule. Another rumour suggested that Braglia's competitors did not wish him to succeed, and so ruined him. The poor man ended his life rather than face bankruptcy. A final solution to the mystery was that one of the British military officers in the household of the Colonial Governor had taken the jewel box and shared it amongst his fellows. Later, it was said that several of the jewels were seen adorning the necks of the rich and famous. A large and especially beautiful yellow sapphire was said to have made an appearance in the island of Tasmania, in the hands of one Colonel Fernley, a former officer in the Ceylon household. However, the jewel has not been examined by an expert, so no comment can be made on this speculation.

How these stones were stolen and where they ended up remains a mystery to this day.

LAURA

20 May 1882, Benevolence

Once more, they were gathered together in the main room of the head-keeper's quarters. It could have been a meeting between friends, apart from the fact that Albert Munro stood with a pistol in his bandaged hand, his eyes cold and watchful. His wife … although Laura knew now that she was not and had never been … stood behind him, her face pale and set. The graze on her cheek had scabbed over, and seeing Laura's stare, she self-consciously put up a hand to cover it.

The two of them had admitted that they were already lovers, and that once the *Alvarez* had foundered, Elsie had taken her drowned mistress's place. 'A crime of convenience,' Albert had declared, as if there was nothing wrong in replacing one's dead wife with her maid.

'As the *Alvarez* began to sink, I handed Mr Bailey my most precious possession. It isn't my fault he believed Elsie was my wife. Once the mistake had been made, Elsie was unable to correct it.'

'Unable or unwilling,' Leo said with disgust. He had read the now crumpled and torn engagement notice from the *Hobart Recorder*, and listened as Laura pointed out the discrepancies in it. His gaze moved to Elsie, and she lifted her chin, refusing to look away.

Albert moved closer to her, sliding his free arm about her waist. 'I fell in love,' he said simply. '*We* fell in love. I found a woman who was my other half, and she was clever and strong and willing. Yes, we were conducting an affair. Through no fault of her own, she was mistaken for my wife, and when my wife was found dead ... Well, where was the harm in continuing the deception? She hoped I was still alive, but in the event I was dead, she knew I would want her cared for. As my widow, she would receive that care. Is that a crime? I don't think so.' He smiled at the woman by his side. 'My clever girl.' Elsie smiled back, a besotted expression on her face.

Laura felt a chill deep in her bones. Albert spoke so matter-of-factly, as if what he said made perfect sense, and the trouble was, it did make a sort of sense.

'But Rorie knew you,' Laura reminded them. 'He recognised Elsie, and tried to use that knowledge for his own gain. Where is he? Have you hurt him?'

Albert gave a snort of laughter. 'Rorie has gone to ground because he's a lily-livered coward. He'll turn up when he believes it's safe to do so.'

'And will you confess to the authorities?' Leo said. 'Will you tell the truth now you are discovered?'

'No,' Albert said quietly, 'I will not.'

'You are determined to carry on with it?' Miriam asked in amazement. 'But we know, Mr Munro!'

'Yes,' he agreed, 'so you do.'

The chill in Laura's bones lodged in her heart, as if a ball of ice had formed there. Would Albert hurt them to stop them from giving away his secret? Her father and Miriam, and dear little Noah? She could see the calculation in the man's cool gaze and it frightened her more than Elsie's instability.

'Monstrous,' Mr Jones declared, while Isaac shifted uneasily. The two men had been ordered to stand by the wall, while Laura, Leo and Miriam were seated at the table, Noah on his mother's knee.

'How so?' Albert retorted.

'What would you know, you silly little man?' Elsie spoke over him, glaring at Mr Jones. 'You are a fool who has probably never loved or been loved. What Albert and I have is beyond your comprehension.'

Her eyes were blazing, her cheeks flushed. There was no going back for her, and Laura was beginning to realise she would do anything to make her dream of bliss with Albert come true.

'But ... surely you did not expect such a thing to go unnoticed?' Miriam asked, squeezing Laura's hand rather painfully.

'Why not? No one will know us in our new home. They will accept the truth I give them.' Albert sounded so confident, so arrogant.

'And what will you do when the steamer comes? You can't expect us to remain silent.' Laura lifted her chin, telling herself to be brave when she was feeling rather sick. Were the pair of them quite sane?

Noah grizzled, rubbing his eyes, and Miriam held him protectively close. 'You cannot mean to hurt us?' she whispered.

'I am on a very important mission,' Mr Jones interrupted, sounding breathless. 'If you try to stop me from completing it then you will be brought to book and—' He fell silent when Albert turned on him.

'I don't care about you or your mission, you fool.' His bandaged hand tightened on the pistol and that must have hurt because he winced. 'And to answer your questions, I know you cannot remain silent, I would not expect it, but I will not hurt any of you. Not if you all do as I say.'

'How can we believe you?' Leo retorted. 'You're a liar, why should anyone believe you?'

'I assure you, I do mean what I say.' Again that confident swagger of arrogance. Albert was the sort of man who could face danger and coolly find a way through. 'And I must thank you, Mr Webster, for showing me the gun case in your lighthouse. It was the work of a moment to distract you and steal a pistol.'

Leo's face darkened. 'You can't escape, you coward.'

Miriam tried to hush him, anxious of the consequences, but again Albert did not seem overly perturbed.

'Why can't I?' he mocked. Laura wondered if he was beyond fear now, so set was he on his path that he was convinced of the rightness of the action he and Elsie had taken.

The sun was shining weakly through the window, and she remembered that Edmund was still up in the lighthouse, oblivious to what was happening. His watch was over and he would be wondering why Leo had not come to relieve him.

She tried to remember exactly what Edmund had said to her on the beach the night he and Elsie helped Tom to safety. Had he simply assumed Elsie was Mrs Munro? Or had Albert told him so, as he handed her over to him? Before she had a chance to mull it over, her father spoke in an angry voice.

'If you're planning to lock us up then I warn you, it will be noticed that no one is manning the light. What if another ship founders on the rocks? Are you willing to risk more lives for your own selfish ends? And what of the supply steamer? The captain won't take you aboard without my agreement. Questions will be asked. Or do you intend to kidnap the crew of that ship, as well? Where will this madness end, sir!'

Albert smirked and shook his head at Leo, as if he was an innocent. 'Come now, Mr Webster, I doubt any of that is possible. I am only one man with one pistol, even if I am an exemplary shot. No, what is going to happen is that you are going to sail Elsie and me to the mainland.'

Leo exploded, 'Me?' While Miriam and Laura protested equally loudly.

Patiently, Albert waited until the noise had died down. 'Of course,' he said. 'You have a boat. You are a capable sailor. If you do as I ask then no one here will be harmed. Once we reach the mainland and set foot on dry land, we will disappear, and you will let us. Then you can return to your island or do whatever you please. You can send the authorities after us if that will make you feel better, although I can assure you they won't catch us. But that's hardly the point, is it? If you do as I ask then you can be satisfied that you have protected your nearest and dearest, and given a sop to your conscience.'

Leo ignored his taunt and looked at Miriam, and then Laura. She could see his mind working. 'The only boat we have is the lifeboat,' he said. 'It's a dinghy and hardly a seaworthy vessel.' He was trying to give himself time to decide what to do.

'Nonsense,' Albert retorted. 'You were boasting to me only yesterday that you had two boats. You said the whaleboat was strong and able to go to sea. I am willing to risk it.'

'The lamps need refuelling every hour or so, and the clockwork machine needs rewinding every eight. Who will do that?'

'Your wife? Your daughter? They both seem competent.'

Leo was quiet, then seemed to make up his mind. 'You are asking a great deal.'

'You cannot go!' Miriam cried out. 'Leo, please!'

Laura's voice was softer, and when no one heard her above the cacophony she said it again, louder, and stood up at the same time. 'I'll do it. I'll sail you to the mainland.'

There was another explosion of sound, a mixture of her father's anger and Miriam's fear, accompanied by fresh wails from Noah. And then in the middle of it all, Edmund came through the door, his startled eyes questioningly searching the room.

Albert Munro spun around and lifted his pistol, pointing it directly at him. 'Get inside,' he warned. 'Over there with the others, Mr Bailey.'

Astonished, Edmund moved over to Laura's side and she felt his shoulder bump against hers. 'What is this?' he asked, his shocked voice gravelly from a long night with little sleep.

'I can see why you would not want to leave your island in charge of a man like this,' Albert said nastily. 'A useless gentleman, hardly a man at all, a *boy* whose family has sent him to the colonies to be rid of him.'

Edmund flushed. 'Not so useless,' he said. 'I saved your wife, remember?'

'She isn't his wife,' Laura said. 'She's the maid, Elsie.' Quickly, she explained the situation to a bemused Edmund, adding, 'Now they want to run off together.'

Albert bared his teeth. 'Well?' he demanded. 'Who is it to be? I really haven't time to waste until you make up your minds.'

'My father can't leave,' Laura said before Leo could speak. 'He has to stay, he's the only one who knows the lamp well enough to make repairs if they're needed. And then there's Miriam and Noah. I'll take you. Besides,' she gave her father a beseeching glance, 'I'm the better sailor and he knows it.' It was the truth and she hoped he would acknowledge it now and accept they had no option.

Leo stared at her and then he dropped his head onto his chest with a sigh. Slowly and reluctantly, he nodded. 'I do know it, lass. I taught you well.'

'How many days will it take to get to the mainland from here?' Albert had fixed his gaze on her, and Laura forced away her unease, answering the question honestly.

'Two days, if we're lucky with the winds. *If* the weather holds.' Which was never certain in Bass Strait.

Albert and Elsie put their heads together and spoke too low for anyone else to hear. Two days in a small, open boat was nothing to look forward to and they must know that, but they were also desperate to get away before the steamer arrived. Like Laura, they had no choice. She could take them to this new life they wanted so desperately, and in return, well, she could be assured that everyone she loved would be safe.

'My daughter is right,' impatiently, Leo broke into their tete-a-tete. 'She can get you to the mainland. But before I agree to any of this, I need to know she will not be harmed when you get there. That matters to me more than your new start,' he added with a hard stare.

'I will go with her.' Edmund's statement ended with a surprised silence.

'You don't know anything about boats!' Laura cried.

His dark eyes widened, as if he was astonished at his own daring. 'Maybe not, but I can follow orders. I will do what you tell me without argument. You cannot go alone, not with these two,' he added. Before she could argue he leaned closer, speaking for her alone, a determined note in his voice. 'Albert might promise not to harm you, but once you reach the coast, who knows what they might do to keep their secret? Neither of them is to be trusted. If I'm there I can even up the odds.'

Laura opened her mouth, closed it again. Edmund was right. If she had to do this then she needed an ally.

Leo fixed Albert with a look that made most men quake. 'Very well. The lass and Edmund will sail you to the mainland and you will not harm a hair on their heads. Do I have your word?'

It was Elsie who answered. 'I swear they will not be hurt if they do what Albert says,' she said, gaze moving from Leo to Laura and Edmund. 'I do swear it,' she repeated, while Albert stood silent beside her, keeping his own counsel.

* * *

The whaleboat was at the water's edge, washed by the calm waters of Thankful Cove, and ready to set out on its voyage. It was of lighter construction than the dinghy they used as a lifeboat closer to shore, and could take four oars if necessary. In this case, they would only need enough for Laura and Edmund, and they would be using the sails. The boat was fitted with a mainsail and a boom, and a small sail for the bowsprit. Laura hoped to use both if possible to enable them to reach their destination faster.

The wind was more southerly than usual, a good sign, Leo said, and she should use it while she could. But she should also expect the wind to return to the northerly or westerly, more common at this time of year, and that would mean a rough crossing.

'I hope neither of them get seasick, lass,' he added with a smile that said the opposite.

'It was Rochelle Munro who had the mal de mer,' she said. She remembered Elsie telling her about the maid going down to the harbour, about her longing to meet someone she knew from home. Instead, she had met Albert and thrown in her lot with him.

By the time they had everything prepared, it was almost noon. Beneath Albert's watchful eye and his steady hand on the pistol, they had stowed away enough food and water for several days, just in case. Laura was wearing her thickest sweater, her trousers, and her waterproof jacket, while Edmund was clothed entirely in Leo's warmest clothing. They were too big for him but more sensible than his own fashionable attire. He was also wearing one of Miriam's knitted hats, pulled down over his hair, and he was rumpled and in need of a shave. He looked a far cry from the young gentleman she had come to know.

Although Edmund had been cast off by his family, for whatever reason, they had seriously misjudged him. He was no villain. He was kind and generous, willing to learn and help, and to get his hands dirty. Now he had agreed to trust his life to Laura and a small boat, all to protect her from Albert and Elsie. He was a man to be proud of, and she found herself aching to tell that to the world.

She was determined that whatever happened after this was over, whether she never saw him again, she would make him understand he was worth so much more than the sum of the choices he had been given.

They were as ready as they would ever be, and there was nothing else to keep them. Leo took Laura by the shoulders, his fingers unknowingly painful, as if he did not want to let her go. 'You're as brave as your mother, lass, but you're not reckless. You have my caution. Use it well.' He spoke the familiar words.

'I will. I promise. I'll keep us safe.'

He nodded, eyes bright with tears, and then pulled her into a fierce hug. Then Miriam was hugging her, too, her cheeks wet with tears. Laura kissed Noah's soft hair. Mr Jones blundered into their tender moment, oblivious to anyone but himself. 'Take these,' he ordered, and handed over a waterproof package of papers. 'Give them to the authorities as soon as you reach land. Tell them the matter is urgent.'

Edmund retrieved the parcel and slipped it inside his jacket with a nod to Mr Jones, who closed his eyes in obvious relief at the completion of his mission.

Seal leaped around them, eager to go too, but Edmund caught his hairy face and said sternly, 'You stay here and I'll be back for you.'

Miriam gave him a watery smile. 'We'll take care of him,' she promised. 'Make sure you take care of Laura.'

'I think she will be taking care of me,' Edmund replied, looking a little overwhelmed.

'I trust you, lad.' Leo clasped Edmund's hand in his own. It was his highest accolade. 'I reckon you can do anything you put your mind to.'

Edmund did not seem to know what to say to that. Perhaps no one before in his life had ever expressed their faith in him. He swallowed and nodded at the ground, and then it was time to go.

Once the whaleboat was out far enough, Laura and Edmund took an oar each and pushed past the growing swell. Beyond the Tiger's Teeth, they would set their sails. She had the sun, the stars and her compass to keep her on course. She told herself it was all she needed. Leo had spoken to her at length, and they had discussed how she should act under a variety of circumstances, although she thought that was reassurance for himself rather than her. One never knew what the weather might do in this part of the world.

She turned to look at the little group on the beach. *Please let me see them again.* Panic twisted her stomach, but she refused to allow herself to believe she would not return. A warm hand covered her own and Edmund was leaning close. 'You'll be back before you know it,' he murmured. He might not know much about sailing, but he seemed to be an expert when it came to reassuring her. She met his eyes and nodded. She trusted him. They would do this together.

Albert and Elsie were huddled closely in the bow, no doubt reliving their last moments aboard the *Alvarez*. There was still flotsam from the schooner visible from here, and probably bodies beneath the green-grey sea with its rolling swell. Laura put all of that from her mind and began to consider her next step on this dangerous journey.

From now on, their fate was in her hands.

NINA

Summer 2010, the Beach House, Dennes Point, Bruny Island

The ambulance had taken nearly an hour to arrive. There was no bridge over to the island, only the car ferry, and that had taken forty minutes, and add that to the journey from the hospital ... It felt interminable. During that time, Angela had stopped breathing. Twice. It was Jude who had brought her back, giving her CPR, compressing her chest, while everyone else had stood around white-faced. When Angela began to breathe again for the second time, Mandy broke down and sobbed into her uncle's shoulder. Lis hung on to Murray, who had stared down at his mother as if he was in shock.

Well, they were all in shock.

Although Nina had known Angela was ill, it was one thing to know a fact and another to actually watch someone die in front of your eyes. Twice.

When the ambulance arrived with sirens wailing, and the paramedics jumped out and went into action, Nina found herself standing beside Murray. He looked so shattered that she took his hand and gave it a squeeze.

'She'll be all right,' she murmured the words she did not know were true.

He nodded slowly, staring at the scene before them, as if he was struggling to process it.

'At least Jude was here,' she went on. 'He took that first-aid course last year.'

'I said it was a waste of time. Shows how much I know.' Murray gave a laugh that was rough and grating.

'He's a hero,' Nina said gently. 'I heard one of the paramedics say that if it wasn't for him … Well, they may not have got here in time.'

Murray looked at her then, and something in his eyes seemed odd. Different. As if he was a stranger. Before she could react, he smiled and was back to being Murray again. 'He *is* a hero,' he agreed, his hand squeezing hers so tight it hurt.

Once Angela was stabilised, the ambulance began its return journey to the hospital. The family followed. Nina had tried to bail out, saying she would be in the way, but Jude wouldn't hear of it. Shaken, wild-eyed, he'd insisted she get in the car with him, and she couldn't say no. Not when he needed her. He might be a hero, but he was still Jude, the man she loved. In the waiting room, he clung to her hand, his knee jiggling, while Murray sat across from them, staring into space, and sometimes at Nina. Mandy sobbed on Colin's chest, until she eventually fell asleep. Lis's mother had come to collect her, and despite her protests, the girl had been led away. As the wait continued, Nina went in search of teas and coffees, and packets of plastic-wrapped sandwiches. They didn't want them, but at least it made her feel useful.

When finally the doctor came to speak to them, Mandy was awake again. It was the moment they had been waiting for and dreading at the same time, but the news was far better than they had hoped. Angela was resting comfortably, although she would not be leaving the hospital anytime soon. Two members of her family could visit her right now, and the rest would have to come back in the morning. By then, they should know a lot more about her condition, and the specialist would be available to talk about her ongoing treatment. But the consensus was that Angela had had an extremely lucky escape.

The relief in the room was palpable. Nina squeezed Jude's hand. He bent his head and kissed her temple, eyes tightly shut. 'Thank God,' he whispered against her skin. Then he had let her go, and was exchanging hugs with the others.

It was decided that Mandy and Jude would be the two to go into the room and see their mother. Colin had his car and would wait at the hospital until the siblings were ready to come home. On the way, he wanted to call into his office and get some of the files he needed for tomorrow—he had already decided he'd be working at home until they knew more about Angela. Jude and Mandy would stay at Colin's place to avoid the drive back to Bruny. Murray would take Nina to the beach house in Jude's car. Jude had asked her to sort out some of Angela's clothes and personal items, and she could bring them to the hospital in the morning.

After more hugs and a few tears, of relief this time, they all went their separate ways.

It was quiet in the car on the drive to Dennes Point. Nina felt Murray glancing across at her as he drove, but she was too tired to make conversation. There was no one else on the vehicular ferry, and by the time they docked on Bruny, her body was craving sleep. She could hardly keep her eyes open. When they arrived at the house, the place was still lit up. No one had thought to turn off the lights when they left for the hospital. Wearily, Nina waited for Murray to unlock the door and then followed him inside. Unfortunately, that was when he seemed to get his second wind.

'I'll make us some toasties,' he said, striding into the kitchen. 'Come on, sit down, Nina.' Next thing she knew, he was pouring them both a glass of wine.

Murray wouldn't stop talking. There was a glitter in his eyes and a manic edge to his laughter. The Murray she knew was self-contained, although there were times when he got a little overexcited, but didn't everyone? Right now, it was as if that overexcited version had taken over. Understandable, she supposed, after what had happened, but she would have preferred him to crash and sleep it off. Instead the wine kept coming, and she felt obliged to sit with him, and listen, even after she had refused to let him refill her glass.

His words washed over her while she tried to make sense of them. He told her about Colin's plans for his future career, how he never did anything for nothing, and that he wanted Murray to repay the money he'd spent on the Rawlinses' education by lifting the profile of his practice and becoming a QC. Colin hadn't made it that far in his own career, although it wasn't from lack of trying, but Murray showed a great deal of promise. And once Murray reached those dizzy heights, then Colin would partake of the glory.

'It's my father's fault,' he said sullenly. 'If he had kept it in his pants and not run off with that tart, we wouldn't have had to ask Colin for help. He was furious with his brother, said he had an obligation to fulfil, but Colin doesn't do anything for nothing,' he repeated. 'Now we're in hock to him. He wants his pound of flesh. My flesh.'

Murray told her how the thought of what lay ahead made him want to run into the sea and just keep swimming towards the horizon. That the pressure Colin was already putting on him was like a monster wave, pulling him under. Surprised by his desperation, Nina tried to think of a solution.

'Can't you tell him you will work for him for a certain length of time? Until you pay him back. Wouldn't he accept that?'

Murray snorted a bitter laugh. 'He won't accept anything but complete capitulation. I never wanted to be a barrister, anyway. Wearing a suit and tie makes me feel like I'm choking. I tried to pretend I could do it, I told myself I could, that I *had* to, but this summer's made me see just how much I'm going to hate it.'

'What would you do, then, if you could change things?'

He laughed. 'I want to travel the world and surf on all the famous beaches. I could pick up jobs to pay my way, enough to make ends meet. I don't need much. I want to be free. I can't handle the sort of responsibility Colin is laying on me. I don't want to be the sacrificial lamb. I don't want all of those expectations weighing me down. I was going to tell Uncle Colin this summer, I was building up my courage, but now with Mum sick ... How can I? There's no chance of escape. I can feel the noose around my neck tightening, Nina. I can't breathe!'

'Tell them,' she said, hearing her voice slurring. 'Tell them, Murray, before it's too late. Jude will—'

'Understand?' he mocked. At some point she had reached out her hand to him, and now his grip was making her fingers numb. 'Jude the hero. Jude the one everyone loves. He doesn't want the responsibility, either. Do you really think he's going to step in and take my place?'

'They love you, too,' she protested, but she knew he was right. Jude didn't want Colin's ambitions weighing him down.

'Jude's a lucky bastard,' Murray spat.

'Do you really think he won't listen to you if you tell him how you feel? You can face Colin together, explain ...'

Wildly, he shook his head at her. 'You don't understand, do you? You've never had to shelve your dreams. Nina, spoilt little girl, not a care in the world. Jude's crazy about you, do you know that? He gets the job he wants as well as the girl. Hardly seems fair, does it?'

The way he was looking at her wasn't the Murray she knew. This stranger with his hate-filled eyes. Nina stood up, stumbling, and clung on to the chair back. 'I'm going to bed,' she said in a voice that struggled to be calm. 'You should too. If you're not going to follow the script, if you're going to tell them what you really want to do with your life, then you need to be sober. I'll help. Jude and I will stand by you.'

He laughed roughly, in a way that was close to screaming, or crying. She felt so sorry for him then, and almost stayed, but she was drunk and tired, so she made her way to bed.

Sleep took her under quickly, but it was the sort of restless sleep that came with too much alcohol. She tossed and turned, reliving all that had happened, before finally falling into a more comfortable state. It must have been nearly dawn when she woke. Suddenly. The light was just creeping through the curtains. And she knew something was very wrong.

Murray's face was really close to hers, and his heavy weight was on top of her. She was naked and so was he, his sweaty skin sticking to hers, the smell of sour wine strong enough to make her want to vomit. Then came the shocking realisation that he wasn't just on top of her, he was inside her, pushing and grunting, and she was pinned down, held, unable to stop him. Unable to do a thing.

She must have told him to stop. She must have struggled and told him to get off. Afterwards, she could never remember clearly. The next thing she knew for certain was that he was standing by the bed, Jude's bed, and staring down at her.

'I'll follow the script,' he said. His bare chest was rising and falling heavily, sweat standing out on a face that looked pallid and greenish in the dawn light. 'I'll let Jude go off and do his thing. But I deserved this, Nina. I've always wanted you and he owes me.'

Nina couldn't speak; she wasn't sure she was capable of it.

Murray had his back to her. 'I need to get Mum's stuff to take to the hospital,' he said. 'I don't expect you to come with me.' And he walked away.

Nina wasn't sure how long she lay there. Eventually she got up, her body hurting, tears long since dried on her cheeks. She was violently sick, retching even when there was nothing left in her stomach, and then took a shower and dressed. It was as if she was caught in a nightmare. How could the man she had thought of as a friend, the brother of the man she loved, have raped her?

What did he expect her to do? Put it behind her? What had he said? *He owes me.* As if Jude would be okay with it, would turn a blind eye if it meant he could carry on with his own dreams while Murray set his aside for the good of the family.

She knew she should call the police, but the thought of telling them what had happened, of reliving it, of being poked and prodded ... No, she couldn't. Not yet. She just wanted to go home and lock herself in her room and sleep and pretend it never happened. *Later*, she thought. She'd think about what to do later.

The taxi finally arrived and she climbed in and closed her eyes. Perhaps it *had* been a dream and when she woke up everything would be all right. Jude would be waiting for her and they could carry on with their lives. Carry on with their happy-ever-after.

NINA

May 2020, Benevolence
Day Three

'Nina? Nina?' Someone was calling her name. She felt strong, warm arms around her, a huff of breath against her ear. A hoarse, worried voice. 'Nina, what's wrong, please, please … Sweetheart …'

She blinked, trying to orientate herself. The flashback had been so powerful. She had been there, back in the past, held captive by the same emotions she had felt then. For how long? She wasn't sure. She only knew that her heart was beating violently, her clothing was damp with perspiration, and there was a headache thumping behind her eyes.

The assistant-keeper's cottage, that was where she was. And Jude. He was with her. He shifted beneath her, and she realised he was holding her, and they were on the couch. She was sitting on his lap, almost enveloped. There was a red mark on his jaw, as if someone had hit him. She had hit him during her struggles with Murray. She had hit Jude.

She was sick of this. Sick of feeling this way, of reliving the past, of being broken. She pulled away.

'No.'

He let her go. He looked shaken, ill. Was he remembering the night his mother had collapsed? When Angela had died twice and he'd brought her back? Well, Nina wasn't going to die. At that moment, she was full of conviction. No matter what Murray did to her next, she was going to survive and grow stronger. She was going to live.

She stared accusingly down at him. 'You already knew it was Murray's yacht. Why didn't you tell me?'

'I'm sorry,' he said carefully, watching her. She didn't blame him for sounding like he was trying to pacify a tiger. Flashbacks were frightening for her, but they must be terrifying for innocent bystanders. She tended to lose all contact with the present as she lived out the trauma of the past. Fighting, screaming, sobbing. She didn't see or hear the people around her. It had only happened once or twice at work, and she'd managed to lock herself in the bathroom until she had talked herself down. Being here, knowing about Murray, had changed matters, escalated them. Jude must have thought she'd gone insane.

'So, Murray is on the island? Your brother is here?' She needed him to confirm it.

He cleared his throat. He seemed to have decided to go along with her and pretend what he had just seen hadn't happened. 'I think he must be. I know he has a yacht and I'm sure that's its name. I've never been on it. I don't have much to do with him anymore. I told you he's got himself in with a dangerous crowd. He's not the man you knew—'

Nina closed her eyes and turned away from him. 'I know Murray better than you think.' Her voice sounded rough. Her throat hurt. She stood in the doorway as the effects of the flashback faded. She was shaky and nauseous, and she needed to lie down and take some of her medication, but there was no time for that now. She swung around to face him again. He was still watching her like an unexploded bomb.

'You said, before, that Lis saw Murray and Elle together in the archives.'

'Yes.' He got up and moved across to a table which was stacked with files and loose papers. 'She saw them and she hid. She and Murray ... well, the bad time I told you she was having, it was to do with him. She knew he was addicted to gambling, and drugs, too. He boasted to her that he could get hold of anything she wanted—cocaine, MDMA, the lot. She thought she could help him, but he let her know her help wasn't wanted, so she threatened to go to the police. She thought that might change his mind, shock him into a realisation of what was happening to him. Unfortunately, it had the opposite effect. Murray sent a couple of thugs around to scare her off.'

Nina folded her arms, feeling cold. The sweat was drying. She needed a hot shower. It would have to wait.

'Did they hurt her?'

'A few bruises. Mostly, they just frightened the shit out of her.' He was watching her carefully. 'Nina, what just happened?'

She shook her head, stopping him before he could start. 'What were they doing? In the archives, I mean. Murray and Elle.'

'Lis wondered about that, too. She waited until they'd gone and tracked down the papers they'd photocopied.' He handed her a file, the contents inside neatly marked. 'She thought it might interest me. When she heard I was coming here to Benevolence, she wanted to come too. I organised it, even though I knew you wouldn't be happy, but you didn't understand what was going on, Nina. And you wouldn't let me talk to you about it. About anything.'

He was right, but she couldn't discuss that now. There was too much to take in. Murray was on the island. Her mind was reeling from that fact. And it wasn't Murray the quiet boy who had laughed with her on the beach and calmly agreed to the future Colin had laid before him. No, this was the Murray she remembered from that night ten years ago, the stranger, the man with the savage laughter and the hard hands. The man who had destroyed her life because he thought he was owed.

'Nina,' Jude said wearily. 'Listen to me. I'm going to make us some coffee, and then we're going to talk. I'm not taking no for an answer this time.' He turned to the kerosene stove.

Nina opened the folder. There were pages from the *Hobart Recorder*, a newspaper now defunct, as well as several other sources. She took them over to the window, where the light was better, and tried to read. The words bobbed before her eyes, meaningless; she couldn't take them in.

'Jude?'

The sound of his name brought both their heads up. Lis was standing in the doorway. 'There were some more drugs tucked under the sleeping bag. White powder, this time. I gave it to Paul.' She shot Nina a dirty glare as she strode into the cottage.

Jude added a third cup to the two he had lined up. Then, as if remembering whose drugs they might be, his face lost all trace of colour. 'Christ,' he whispered, his gaze catching Nina's. It was a long time since she had seen him look that shattered, as if his world was coming apart, and it gave her no pleasure.

Lis was over by the open laptop, staring at the screen. Jude must have brought it inside when Nina was out of it. 'Any luck with the drone?' she asked.

'Yes.' Jude hesitated. 'I was just about to tell Nina about the documents you found. The letter.'

'Why tell her?' Lis snapped.

'Because Murray's yacht is anchored just off Birds Nest Island,' Jude said gravely. 'We think he's here, Lis. He's been here all along, and Elle must know it.'

Lis digested that, scowling, but it was all pretence. She sat down clumsily on the couch and Nina could see she was terrified. 'Bloody Murray,' Lis gulped. 'Well, Elle's gone off somewhere. She was supposed to go up into the lighthouse with Arnie and me, but she said she had to get her other camera, and then she didn't come back.'

Nina remembered Elle's frightened face staring up at the drone. If she was in partnership with Murray, then she probably had a bit to be frightened about.

'As for that,' Lis nodded at the papers in Nina's hands, 'I found out Elle was doing a thesis. Some obscure jewellery robbery in the nineteenth century with connections to Tasmania. God knows how she discovered it. Anyway, she found a letter from a man called Roderick McNeil written on his deathbed. If Murray's here, then that letter's the reason why. He's in debt to some very dangerous people. He can't pay them back, he's broke. He needs a bargaining chip, a circuit breaker. I think this is it. His way of getting them off his back until he can come up with a better plan.'

'A letter?' Nina sat down beside her on the worn couch, and began to search through the folder.

Lis made an impatient sound and snatched it off her, and leafed through it. She drew out a photocopy and handed it back. 'The letter,' she said.

'Lis,' Jude sounded a warning.

'Do I really need to read this now?' Nina asked. 'Shouldn't we be looking for Murray and Elle? I feel as if we should be doing something, not—'

'You need to read it to understand what Murray is doing here,' Jude replied, and set down her coffee on the arm of the couch. 'Read it, Nina. Please.'

She met his eyes and felt something inside her shift. Here they were, she and Jude, and there was so much water under the bridge and yet ... It felt as if some things were just as they had been ten years ago. She loved him, had never stopped loving him, and that was going to be a problem. But right now it felt like a blessing.

Nina cleared her throat, deciding to put away those thoughts for later, and focused on the letter. It took a little while for her brain to begin to concentrate properly; it was still struggling with the after-effects of the flashback. Halfway down the page, she began to have a clearer understanding of what she was reading, and went back to the beginning to start again, ignoring Lis's impatient groan.

When she had finished, and before she could open her mouth, Lis handed her another photocopy. 'Read this,' she demanded.

Nina read it. She read about Albert Munro and Elsie Wright, who had run off together after Albert's wife, Rochelle, was drowned in a shipwreck. She read about Rochelle's yellow sapphire, which was actually orange and worth a fortune, and which she wore in the form of a brooch. How Rochelle's body was washed onto the beach at Thankful Cove, and how Roderick McNeil had found her there.

She looked up, but before she could speak, Jude said gently, 'Drink your coffee, Nina.'

Nina thought about arguing, but in the end it seemed easier just to do as he said. The coffee was good and she wasn't sure what to say. They were trapped here on an island with no way of contacting the authorities, and it was possible the man they were trapped with was the one who once had raped her.

She suspected Jude might already have an inkling that something wasn't right—the flashback would have been a clue—but he couldn't know the whole story. And soon she was going to have to tell him.

Letter written for Roderick McNeil on his deathbed, penned by Father James Jackson, visitor.

I, Rorie McNeil, am a miserable sinner who is destined for the fires of hell. Once I thought I would live forever. Who thinks about death when you're hale and hearty? But now I am old, and as the days pass, I know that soon I will be dead. I am afraid, and Father Jackson has promised that if I confess to my sins and repent of them, then I can be spared. Those sins are too numerous to be written of here, and Father Jackson has promised we will have time to talk about them. But there is one sin more heinous than the rest, and I need to confess it here and now.

In the year 1882 on Benevolence Island, I committed a vile offence. After the tragic shipwreck of the schooner *Alvarez*, I found the body of a woman on the beach. She was wearing a brooch that I recognised, just as I recognised the woman as Rochelle Fernley. I once was employed by her father and the brooch was well known to me. I knew it was valuable and I wanted to sell it.

I carried her body up to my cottage on the island, where I was the assistant lighthouse keeper, and removed the brooch. I stripped her and burned her clothing and wrapped her in a blanket, and then I took her to a narrow fissure on the south side of the island and threw her down into it. I covered the entrance to the fissure with branches and grass, so she was well hidden. She has lain there all this time without the benefit of a Christian burial.

Albert Munro, Rochelle's husband, had survived the wreck, as well as the maid Elsie Wright. Elsie was pretending to be Rochelle, and I knew they were lying. I feared for my life, so I hid myself around the cliffs of the island, waiting for the supply ship to arrive. I was hungry and thought to steal some food from the head keeper and his wife, but I was caught in the act.

The head keeper, Mr Webster, locked me up in the fuel hut until the ship arrived. I was taken back to Hobart, but I lied my way out of trouble and I was soon let go.

The brooch was left behind. If I had been caught with it I would have gone to gaol, so before I went into hiding, I put it in Captain Roberts' pocket. He was one of the dead from the *Alvarez*, and his body was in the boathouse, awaiting burial. He was buried shortly afterwards, and as far as I know the jewel is still there, buried with him in his grave.

I am a miserable sinner and may God have mercy on my soul.

Signed: Rorie McNeil (His X mark), 3 March 1911.

LAURA

20–22 May 1882, At Sea

They made some good headway before a brisk wind, until it died away almost entirely. Calm weather and fitful breezes made progress difficult. When there was a reasonable gust Laura had to tack constantly, an exhausting process, although Edmund soon picked up the procedure, and working together they forged ahead.

Leo had suggested they set up a tarpaulin over the bow of the boat, for shelter, and that was where Albert and Elsie lay, when they were not eating or drinking. Albert still had his pistol at his side. But Laura's hope that he would fall asleep and she could take it away was short-lived when she noticed the two of them were taking it in turns to watch and sleep.

She would have been happier with the gun in her hands, but she could not let it distract her. She needed to concentrate on getting them all safely to the mainland. Time enough then to seek help.

As darkness fell the wind dropped altogether, and she and Edmund dozed, one of them with a hand on the tiller, the small oil lamp they had brought with them offering some light. They had met no other craft, and the sea around them appeared endless and enormous. The waves were still larger than normal after the storm, rolling the whaleboat in an uncomfortable motion. Neither Albert nor Elsie seemed to suffer from it, although both looked pale and tired. Laura did not think she was much better, and Edmund had dark circles under his eyes, while his whiskers had begun to grow into a beard.

By dawn the wind had picked up again, and they made better headway. There was still plenty of food and water, but she made sure to ration both, just in case the journey took longer than they hoped. She had heard enough stories of sailors lost at sea to be wary of ever taking the elements for granted. And she had to wonder, if things were to go awry, whether Albert and Elsie would be willing to sacrifice Laura and Edmund so that they could survive for a little longer. They had not shown themselves to be compassionate souls, and the only thing that currently gave Laura and Edmund value was their ability to sail the boat.

The good voyaging weather did not last. By afternoon, the wind had dropped again and a fog closed in, making it impossible to see for any distance. Without the ability to plot a course, Laura was worried they would lose their way beyond her capacity to find it again. Soft rain began to fall steadily, and the air held a distinct chill, adding to their misery. Laura and Edmund were glad of their waterproofs, while the other couple huddled together and sheltered as best they could.

It was eerie in the damp, misty silence. Their voices were muffled, and the occasional sound of waves was impossible to pinpoint. For a time, no one said anything. Laura had noticed Edmund glancing at the pair cuddled together beneath their covering, as if he was considering a question. Eventually, whatever was bothering him became too much, and he spoke.

'How do you expect to get away with it? Passing off your wife's servant as your wife?'

Albert looked surprised, and then impatiently cleared his throat. Elsie moved even closer to him with an uneasy glance. 'All one needs is a brave heart and a confident manner and one can get away with most things.'

His arrogance was astounding, but the awful thing was, he was probably right.

'And if the *Alvarez* hadn't foundered? Would you and Elsie have continued your affair in secret? Under your wife's nose?'

'My wife was indifferent to me.'

'That's not how it sounded in the engagement notice.'

Albert shifted tetchily, and yet he seemed keen to make himself understood. 'Rochelle was an heiress. Her father doted on her, left her everything, and she would have just frittered it away. She was always finding some poor deserving cause to give to. People knew she was soft-hearted, and they played upon it. The bankrupt store-owner, the deserted wife, the old friend who needed a loan. They all loved her, but when I told her their love was coloured by her wealth she wouldn't listen.' His laugh was a sneer. 'I have a nice little property, but it's only a start. I wanted to buy more land, put down roots. We argued and she agreed to come with me, but only for a year. She didn't like the isolation. She said she preferred town life. I knew she would have upped and left me long before that year was over. She said she loved me, but she was spoiled and selfish, and—'

'You killed her, didn't you?' Edmund's accusing voice echoed oddly around them in the fog. 'It wasn't a spur-of-the-moment decision of Elsie's to switch identities, was it? The two of you planned it and carried it out.'

'It's as Albert says,' Elsie burst out. 'It made sense for us to-to ...'

'To take what was not yours?' Edmund said coldly. 'I'm no saint, but even on my worst day I didn't consider murder the solution to my problems.'

'How do you know what you would do until the time arrives?' Albert said. He turned to Laura, his eyes alight with malice. 'I've seen the way you look at Miss Webster. What would your parents think if you brought her home as your bride? You cannot tell me they would be pleased and welcome her with open arms. What if you had to make a choice between love and the wealth you felt entitled to. What would you do to bring about the ending you desired, Mr Bailey? If a way to have it all was offered to you?'

Laura wanted to tell Albert he was wrong, but Edmund reached out and covered her hand on the tiller with his, and she stayed silent. 'That's where we differ,' he said softly. 'I would live my life as I saw fit, but without harm to others.'

'You can't know what it was like!' Elsie protested. The woman looked unsettled, eager to tell her side of the story. And Laura wanted to hear it, the truth at last.

'Why don't you tell us, then?' she said.

'I—' Elsie began, but perhaps Albert did not trust her as much as he would have them believe, because he took over the conversation once more.

'Elsie and I were lovers. We fell in love. But it wasn't enough. I knew that we could have more. I didn't want to marry one woman only to have to hide and lie to spend time with the woman I truly wanted as my wife. I had already begun to court Rochelle before her father fell ill. When Colonel Fernley died, I made myself indispensable to his daughter. In some ways she was absurdly trusting and generous, and we married much sooner than I had hoped.'

'So, it was greed,' Laura said in disgust. 'You pretended to love Rochelle so that you could get your hands on her money.'

Albert shrugged. 'If you like. That is not uncommon. I'm not ashamed for marrying for money. And why not have it all? Elsie did not want me to marry Rochelle, but I persuaded her to accept it, for a little while. I told her my plan and she agreed it was perfect. Rochelle and I intended to travel to Victoria to make a new life, and at some point on the way there I would see to it that she disappeared. Elsie would take Rochelle's place as my wife. No one would be the wiser because where we were going no one knew us. We could leave our old lives behind. Or that was the plan, before the *Alvarez* foundered.'

Elsie interrupted. It was as if she needed to talk, to explain how clever they were, or perhaps it was a confession. Albert did not seem to feel any guilt, but Laura was sure Elsie did.

'Rochelle and I were in the cabin.' Her voice trembled. 'She was suffering from seasickness—she was always sick on the water—so we stayed below. It was better that way, because no one would see us and be able to describe who was the mistress and who the maid. We didn't plan to do anything yet, not until we reached Victoria. That was when Rochelle would disappear and I would take her place, so that when we arrived at Albert's property it would be as if she ... she had never existed.'

Elsie could not help but see the horrified disgust on the faces of her audience, and it seemed to affect her. Albert must have seen that, too, because once again he took over the story.

'When we were told to abandon ship, it seemed logical to act. No one knew Rochelle or Elsie apart from myself, no one could identify either of them. It would be a tragic accident. I went below, but I found Elsie and Rochelle were in the midst of a disagreement. Rochelle had guessed what Elsie was to me, and she was upset. Elsie was trying to calm her, but without much success. Rochelle kept saying that she would stop us, that she would tell people, and ... I couldn't allow that.' He pulled a face. 'I stepped in and acted immediately, and her life was extinguished.'

He sounded as if he was pleased with his prompt action. Albert had murdered his wife and he was proud of it. Laura could only stare at him in shocked horror.

'I had planned to dispose of her body over the side of the boat, or else leave it in the cabin when we abandoned ship. Unfortunately, at that moment the mate opened the cabin door to send us up on deck. And he knew. I could see at once from his expression that he knew. Before he could act, Elsie pushed him, and when he fell against the bunk I struck him. Hard on the head. I thought the blow was fatal, so I left him there while we hurried up on deck. I had forgotten Rochelle's brooch in the rush, a bad mistake. Once on deck, I could see just how grave matters were. Our chances of surviving were slim, so I asked Mr Bailey to save Elsie. It was appalling. Everything was about to fall apart. At least Elsie had a chance, I told myself. I even considered whether she might be better off without me.'

'Oh no, my love!' Elsie cried out. 'Never!'

Albert patted her hand. 'I decided to entrust my life to the sea. I jumped into the water. And as you can see,' he smiled in his superior way, 'the sea rewarded me. I survived. *We* survived.'

'It was you,' Laura said, as the truth suddenly occurred to her. 'Both of you. Outside the window. Plotting to kill someone. I thought you wanted to get rid of Rorie, but it was Tom Burrows, wasn't it?'

Elsie did not deny it. 'We could never have known Rorie was here on the island. It was a horrible coincidence. He knew me at once, of course, and I knew he would ask for money for silence. He always admired me, but I wasn't fooled by his sugary words. I wasn't an innocent fool like Rochelle. I let Rorie think I would agree to anything he said, but all I could really think about was Albert, out there in the water. If Albert didn't survive, then I had told myself that whatever happened to me no longer mattered.'

'Were you going to kill Tom?' Laura could hear the furious indignation in her voice. 'Was that why you became so concerned about him, sitting by his bedside and stroking his brow? You are a wicked woman!'

'Laura.' Edmund had one cautious eye on Albert.

Elsie put a hand to her mouth with a sob, and Albert put his free arm around her, drawing her even closer to his side. 'Don't you see? We had to get rid of him. If he recovered he could give us away before we escaped. Rorie was easily manipulated, but the mate would not be so easily persuaded to stay silent.'

Such evil spoken in such an offhand manner.

After that there was silence. Laura slept a little, only waking when there was a rattle and a gust of wind flapped the mainsail. Another gust and the sail began to fill. Laura leaped up, moving to make the most of this miracle. The whaleboat moved forward, Edmund steering while Laura managed the sails, adjusting them as the wind shifted and grew stronger. Soon they had sailed out of the fog and above them the sun, previously nothing but a misty ball of light, shone out.

Relieved, she turned to Edmund.

'Are we on course?' Edmund asked.

'As far as I can tell. I can't be sure where we will land, but I'm hoping somewhere along the coast west of the entrance to Port Phillip Bay.'

They grinned at each other. They were taking on the elements and winning, and it felt good.

Once Laura was back in the stern, and sat beside him, Edmund leaned in closer and murmured to her, 'When we near the shore we must watch them even more closely. I don't trust either of them, but particularly not Albert. He would kill his grandmother if it gained him a penny.'

Laura thought a moment. 'He says this is all for love, but I don't believe it. Love is not like that.'

He reached out and brushed her cheek with his gloved fingertip, his gaze lingering on her lips before locking with hers. 'No,' he said. 'Love is not like that.'

'Edmund,' she whispered.

'I want to tell you why I was sent to the colonies,' he said, his face set and determined. 'There was a woman, older than me, a friend of my mother's. I thought I loved her. There was a scandal and her husband demanded I be dealt with.' He made a savage sound. 'Dealt with, like a cur. I thought she would stand with me, explain, but she let me take the blame. In return for their silence, my father sent me away and told me not to come back.'

Laura stared at him, not sure what to say. It sounded unfair, but far from the terrible scandal she had expected. 'You were young and foolish,' she said. 'And in love.'

He shook his head. 'Young and foolish certainly, but not in love. I know that now.'

She thought that was probably true. Edmund might be a gentleman's son, but he was younger than the woman involved. She had been married, experienced, and she had stolen his heart. Beneath his polish and sophistication, Edmund was a gentle soul. She could imagine his hurt.

'I was bitter and angry. I hated my father for sending me away, and my mother for allowing it. Now, I wonder if they haven't done me a favour.'

Laura wanted to ask more, but the boat needed her attention, and the conversation lapsed.

They made good progress, and soon the coast was visible before them. At first it was just a patchwork of misty colours on the horizon, but eventually the colours took shape and became cliffs and sand hills and trees. Just as the fog closed in again, she realised they must be close to the Rip, the notorious entrance to Port Phillip Bay and thence to Melbourne. Not quite two miles wide, the narrow aperture was made even narrower by reefs and rocks. It was at its most dangerous when the tide was on the turn and large volumes of water were forced in and out of the bay.

'Best to avoid the Rip,' her father had said, when they were discussing her voyage. 'Too many ships have gone to their grave there.'

The warning words sent a bolt of panic through her, and Laura tried to steer the boat away, but it was already too late. They were caught in the strong tidal surge, tugged forward as if by unseen hands, and she had no option but to allow them to be taken.

It was made worse by the mist, pressing upon them like cold breath, and the distant, mournful sound of a fog horn. A wave broke over the bow, and she heard Elsie squeal. Then another. The whaleboat rose up and down at an alarming rate, and in between larger waves the water was choppy and muddled. Laura and Edmund did their best by using the oars to keep her steady, but there was the real risk of being swamped. They were already taking on water, too quickly to use the bailer or the pump.

The fog shifted again and Laura could see a beach away to their left, the sand pale, and hills rising above. The water beneath them now was dark and deep, and she remembered something her father had said, about the Rip being even more dangerous because of the alternate deep and shallow seabed depths within it. An eddy caught them, twisting them, and then a big wave washed over them.

Laura shook the water from her eyes, anxiously looking about for Edmund. He was still there, hands clinging to the gunnels. Elsie and Albert were in the bottom of the boat at the bow, water swirling about them. Most of the supplies had been washed overboard.

By now she was beyond exhaustion, but when an area of slack water opened before them, Laura headed for it. A moment later the larger waves returned, but now they were sending the whaleboat towards the beach, and she heard Edmund give a whoop. The feel of their keel dragging across sand was the sweetest sensation Laura could remember.

Somehow, she and Edmund dragged the whaleboat up onto the beach, stumbling and falling, fingers numb and legs shaky. Once they were on dry land Albert climbed out, holding his hand out to Elsie. The four of them stood, clothes and hair sodden, chilled to the bone and barely alive, warily eyeing each other. Laura had just saved their lives, but if she had thought that would make Albert think kindlier of her, then she was mistaken.

He lifted his pistol.

He was going to kill them, she knew it. The beach was empty, no one else in sight. He was going to shoot them dead and leave their bodies here for the gulls. Edmund's cold hand reached for hers—they had both lost their gloves by now—and she felt the press of his fingers. There was comfort in his touch, a sense that they could have been more. She wanted to argue and fight, even to plead although her pride made that difficult, but she had no strength left.

Then Elsie spoke. 'It isn't true, what you said, Miss Webster. We will keep our word. Won't we, Albert? We will let them go.'

Albert hesitated, obviously reluctant to agree. The fog horn sounded again, but the air was clearing. Somewhere above them birds were singing.

'Get some rope from the boat,' he said. 'I'm not having the police on my tail before we're well away from here.'

The next few moments were almost a relief. Laura and Edmund's hands were tied behind their backs, the two of them then tied together, back to back. When Albert was satisfied, he spun around, and with barely a glance, walked away. Elsie followed after him. When she reached the crest of a low sandhill she turned, her hand half raised before it dropped again. And she was gone.

'I thought …' Laura tried not to sob, but she was too tired to stop the sound, too broken to stop her emotions pouring out now that they were safe. Edmund's hands fumbled for hers, and she felt his warm breath on her cheek as he leaned back.

'It's all right,' he said. 'We're alive. Hush, Laura. I wish I could kiss you.'

That made her laugh, and eventually she was able to pull herself together.

We are alive, she thought. *We did it. What happens now?*

NINA

May 2020, Benevolence
Day Three

Nina and Jude made their way across the top of the island towards Birds Nest. The weather had changed, a fog rolling in over the island bringing with it cold, dripping rain. The tussocky grass was now so long it made the track they were following almost invisible. Mowing it was to have been part of their maintenance work, but Nina wasn't even certain that was going to happen now. She wasn't certain of anything.

Kyle needed to know what was going on, but there was no way to contact him. Was he expecting her to call? It was probably too soon.

Jude strode in front of her, using a sturdy stick he'd found to knock aside the grass. Nina reminded herself that there were no venomous snakes on Benevolence, which was one good thing about the place. Although right now, she wasn't sure what was worse, a tiger snake or Murray Rawlins.

When they'd returned to the camp with Lis, to fill the others in on their news, Paul had been furious. He knew what Murray had done to her, and she could see that he'd like nothing better than to tear the man in two. Before she and Jude set off to look for Murray and Elle, Nina had persuaded him to stay at the campsite and keep an eye on things. He was the best person to protect the others, she reminded him, and Jude was Murray's brother. He would hardly hurt him, even if he was flying high on whatever cocktail of drugs he might have taken.

She wasn't sure if she really believed it. She wasn't sure Paul did either, but he took his role seriously and reluctantly agreed. Brian was continuing to work on the cottages, muttering about it being pointless to down tools and sit around, wringing their hands, when there was still so much to do.

Nina had agreed. The younger members of her team needed to be kept occupied. After Brian had led them away, she, Paul, Jude and Lis had had an intense conversation.

'If Elle is involved, then she could have taken the key to the hut,' Paul said. 'She was sharing a room with Nina and Nina had a copy. Easy for Elle to steal the key, deal with the satellite phone and put it back. You were pretty out of it at night.'

Nina wanted to argue, but she knew it was true. She avoided Jude's quick frown, adding, 'And Murray could have broken into the toolshed. We don't know when that happened.'

'He must have the original key to the lighthouse,' Jude said. 'That was stolen on the last visit by Island Heritage, so he must have already been here then.'

'He was the man seen running away by the caretakers,' Nina surmised. 'I wonder how long he's been coming here?'

'Six months at least,' Jude replied grimly. 'That was when Lis saw them together in the library.'

'He could have been working for some of the Mister Bigs,' Lis said. 'He owed them so much he had to do whatever they asked. This island is probably a safe place to transfer drugs, guns, whatever else they're into. I think they enjoyed telling him what to do, making him their errand boy. Murray Rawlins, big-time barrister, bowing and scraping.' She looked pale, subdued, lacking her usual combative air. 'He told me some of it, and I found out the rest. He left me alone in his apartment one day and I went through his stuff.' She lifted her chin, refusing to be embarrassed. 'I know that was wrong, but I wanted to help him.'

Nina found she could understand that. She could even sympathise.

They stood in a huddle, coming to grips with the situation. Then Jude shook his head in disgust. 'I'd like to say I understood his thinking, but I don't. I don't even know who he is anymore.'

Nina had surprised herself by reaching out and giving his arm a squeeze.

They had been walking now for forty-five minutes. Nina bent her head against the gusting wind, eyes narrowed as she followed Jude's boots along the almost invisible track to the west of the island. They hadn't said much so far, both deep in their own thoughts, and Nina was grateful he hadn't asked her any questions about her flashback, although she knew he would. Right now, they just needed to find out what had happened to the drone. And Elle.

Jude's boots stopped, and then turned around to face her. Nina lifted her head. His dark hair was a wild mess and there was rain trickling down his face. His dark eyes were on hers.

'Do you think Murray's already found the sapphire?' he said. 'I mean, he's had plenty of time.'

'If he had found it, you'd think he'd be gone. Maybe he's still searching. Is Captain Roberts' grave marked? How does he know which one it is?'

'Good point.' He blew on his hands to warm them. 'I can't remember seeing any plans for the cemetery. Has he been digging up every grave? Christ.' He shook his head, and then looked over his shoulder and pointed. 'Birds Nest Island,' he said.

The weather had closed in so much since their walk began that she couldn't see the island, just a darker shadow in the fog. A few sharp drops of rain fell, striking their jackets with a rattle. It was colder now, too, the sky a gloomy mass of grey, pressing down on their heads.

Was this weather good for Murray? If he was planning to get back on board the yacht and sail off, then the fog would hamper him, but if he was still on the island then he could stay hidden.

More rain fell around them and Jude yelled, 'Come on!' and grabbed her hand. His fingers were strong and warm and she clung to them as he tugged her along after him. The ground beneath them was getting wet and slippery, and he stopped well back from the cliff edge and turned around.

'I think we saw Elle over this way.'

'Jude, she's probably long gone.'

'Maybe. I want to find the drone,' he said. 'It was around here when it went down. Shouldn't be too hard to see.'

It took fifty long miserable minutes before Nina spotted the machine, upended in a straggly bush. When he reached in and lifted it out, the cause of the crash became obvious. The body of the drone had a hole in it, the camera mangled, and there were blackened streaks across the fuselage.

'Is that—'

'Someone shot it out of the sky.'

'Murray has another gun?' Nina wasn't sure why she should be shocked. He was involved with some dangerous people, so of course he would have more than one gun. All the same, the thought made her look nervously over her shoulder.

'Stupid idiot.' Jude said it to himself, anger and pain clear in his voice and expression.

'Would he …? Do you think he would use it on any of us?' Murray with a gun could only mean bad things for everyone. And for her, especially. After all these years of keeping her secret, she had a horrible feeling that he was going to enjoy threatening her, maybe even hurting her. She reminded herself she had friends here, people who would stand by her. Murray was only one man.

Jude was watching her face. 'Let's get under shelter,' he said. 'I don't fancy walking back to camp in this.'

During their search for the drone, they'd found the ruins of what must once have been another hut. Time and the weather had left half a brick wall—the same bricks Brian was planning to use—and it offered some protection at least.

Jude settled along the ground, back close against the wall, and Nina sat beside him. It was dry here, but the rain still dripped onto them. With a grimace, he shrugged out of his jacket, and shuffling closer to her, he tucked it over both their heads, making a waterproof umbrella.

Nina could feel the warmth of his body through his clothes, the comfort of being close. This was Jude, she reminded herself, the man she had driven away and tried to keep at a distance for ten years. But they were past that. They had reached a new place, not the same one they had inhabited ten years ago—it never could be—but something new. The tentative beginnings of an understanding.

'I don't know what happened to Murray,' Jude said after a moment. 'I thought I knew him, but it turned out I didn't. He resented doing what Colin wanted, I suppose, but I didn't know that until it was too late. I wish he'd said something earlier.'

Was he really that blind? 'Maybe you just didn't want to listen.'

He looked at her with surprise and a touch of anger. 'What does that mean?'

'It means you were focused on your own future, which is fine. I'm not saying there's anything wrong with that. It's normal. Come on, did you really want to step into his shoes? We were talking about sailing around the world, and next thing you're wearing a suit and tie and working in Colin's office? Marching to his very exacting drum? Was that something you would have agreed to without a fight?'

'You know nothing about it.' The fog gave his face a green tinge, and his dark eyes blazed. She was used to him being pissed off with her, but this was different. As if she had stepped into a space where she had no right to be. She remembered then how protective the Rawlinses were of each other. Cut one of them and the others bled.

'He told me,' she said, her voice scratchy. She wasn't going to let him intimidate her, but she had never enjoyed confrontation, even less so these days.

He went silent.

Nina swallowed, knowing that she was circling the truth she had kept from him for so long. 'He had dreams, Jude. He wanted to surf at all the famous beaches. He wanted to teach others to enjoy the waves. He wanted to earn just enough to keep moving from place to place. A free spirit. And suddenly, his future was decided for him and he felt trapped.'

She had had a lot of time to think about Murray's state of mind. Not that it made her hate him any less, or want to forgive him, but understanding was part of forgiving herself. Over the years, she had learned that victims often did that, blamed themselves.

'Unhappiness and discontent can be a dangerous combination. Eventually, he was either going to turn those feelings on himself, or on others.'

'When did he tell you?' The anger was gone from his voice, and other emotions had taken over. Pain and regret and guilt. She felt his warm breath on her freezing skin and concentrated on her own breathing. *In and out*, calming, deep breaths.

'The night your mother collapsed. When you were at the hospital.'

'Why are you telling me now, Nina? After all this time.'

'I should have said something before,' she conceded. 'You don't know how ... That time was so confusing ... I was in a bad place. But I should have told you what he said to me that night. I let myself be persuaded not to.'

Her mouth trembled, and a tear ran down her cheek. She wiped it away impatiently. As if she wasn't damp enough from the rain.

He seemed to be thinking over her words. 'Who persuaded you not to, Nina?' And before she could answer, 'What happened before at the cottage ... When you ... zoned out? Was that to do with Murray? Because it was after that night everything changed between us, and you would never talk to me about it, Nina.'

She glanced at him and found him staring back at her. There were the stirrings of understanding in his face. The beginnings of a shocked realisation that made her want to squirm and pull away, but there was also a sense of relief. If she could lay down this secret now, unwrap it in front of him, then perhaps she could begin to heal.

It was time.

'It's called a flashback,' she said at last, the words easier to say than she'd expected. 'People who have experienced trauma get them. I was re-experiencing something that happened to me. Paul says I need to get help, he says I have a form of PTSD. He's right, Jude. I've tried to keep all of this inside for so long, but I can't do it anymore. I can't.'

'Nina,' he whispered, and then reached to take her in his arms. When she stiffened, he said, 'Is this all right? Sorry. Maybe I shouldn't ...'

'Yes,' she said. 'It's all right. You haven't held me for a long time, and I just ... It's nice, Jude.'

She felt him chuckle. 'It is nice. I missed you, Nina.'

She began to cry. 'I missed you, too.'

He kissed her cheek. 'I loved you. So much. You broke my heart.'

'I know. I'm sorry.'

'I think it's I who should say that,' he said, and she heard the shakiness in his voice. 'I need you to tell me what happened. Will you do that? Please?'

She gave a shudder. 'Yes. I want to.'

It took a while. Her voice dipped and wavered, strong at some points, dropping to a whisper at others. He listened in silence, his arms warm around her, his head bent to hers. At one point, she felt his tears splash against her skin and the sound of his sobs. When she was finished they wept together.

'I just want to hold you, Nina. Is that all right?' he murmured. 'I don't want to talk anymore. I don't know what to say. I don't ... I can't ...'

'Yes,' she whispered. 'It's all right, Jude.'

The fog began to shift around them, a strengthening breeze stirring the tendrils, and the world began to come back into focus. Nina closed her eyes. This was good. She let herself enjoy the closeness. Jude was on her side, and the amazing thing was, the thing she had not let herself remember all these years ... He always had been.

LAURA

24 May 1882, Queenscliff, Victoria

Major Ellsworth's wife fussed over her, twitching a sleeve here, smoothing a flounce there. The dress Laura was now wearing belonged to Major Ellsworth's daughter, and although Laura was a little taller they were mostly the same size. It was a beautiful dress, far more beautiful than anything she had ever worn before. There was a lace panel on the bodice, and she brushed her fingertips carefully over it, worried her roughened skin would catch on the fine decoration. A lighthouse-keeper's daughter was not used to garments made only for display. Her clothing was practical and long-wearing, and she was not quite sure how to stand or move in this borrowed finery when she was used to striding along rough tracks and rowing boats.

Laura and Edmund had not waited long for help. Some fishermen from a nearby cottage had found them, and after kindly offering to take care of the whaleboat, had pointed them in the direction of the authorities.

They were wet and cold and dirty, but there was no time to waste. As they walked, Edmund had smoothed his fingers over the marks on her wrists from the ropes, as if he wanted to make them go away. Laura thought there was something rather wonderful about that.

Retired Major Ellsworth, who had made his home in Queenscliff, was at first sceptical as they told their story, and then he was amazed. Laura noticed that the elderly military gentleman took more note of what Edmund said. Despite Edmund's insistence, he seemed to find it particularly difficult to believe that a young woman could have sailed a boat so well and so accurately. Eventually, they were told to wait and a police inspector came to question them in the presence of another military officer, who was not retired.

They listened intently to the story of Albert Munro and Elsie Wright, frowning and directing a lowly constable to take notes. But Laura could see they were more interested in the parcel of papers sent by Mr Jones.

'Do you see that building there?' the military man asked, nodding to the window. Laura was so tired she had forgotten his name, but dutifully she turned towards the high walls of a military fort. The man went on. 'This fort was built during the Crimean War, to stop the Russians from invading our country. It has been allowed to fall into disrepair, but now we are rebuilding and enlarging it. Making it a veritable fortress,' he added with satisfaction.

Laura and Edmund exchanged a puzzled look. All she really wanted to do was lie down and sleep, but it seemed as if nobody cared about that.

'The papers Mr Jones sent ...?' Edmund politely filled the silence.

'Mr Jones has sent us some valuable information. Statements, do you see. Confirmation of what we feared.'

'So, the Russians do intend to invade?' Edmund said, eyebrows raised. 'We are a long way from Russia, sir.'

'Nevertheless, that is what the rumours suggest. We must be prepared.'

His self-important manner reminded Laura uncomfortably of Mr Jones.

'We urgently need to find Albert Munro,' she reminded him. 'He murdered his wife and would have put to death another man if he had had the chance. You need to send a boat to Benevolence Island where that badly injured man is, and other survivors who are waiting to be rescued.'

'Yes, yes. All of that is in hand,' he dismissed. 'Do not concern yourselves.'

After that it was a blur. Mrs Ellsworth took them under her wing, sending Edmund off with her husband's valet and deciding Laura needed a hot bath before she tucked her up in bed.

'Sleep well,' Laura heard her say as she drifted into sleep. 'Then I have some good news for you both!'

It wasn't until the next day that Laura learned the 'good news'. There was to be a reception held in her honour at one of the grander hotels in Queenscliff.

'A reception,' Laura repeated dubiously. 'For me? No, really, I don't think ...'

'Indeed, you cannot refuse! Mr Bailey, tell Miss Webster we will not take no for an answer. And, sir, I believe you are related to the Marquess of Albury?'

Edmund, who had arrived for breakfast, smiled politely and stared at the ground. 'A distant relative,' he said.

'Well, even so, it is a privilege.'

Laura wasn't sure where to look. The Edmund from their voyage across Bass Strait, the scruffy man who had held her hand and spoken of his past, was changing before her eyes. She told herself she had always known this would be the way of it, and that she would have to let him go, but it hurt. It hurt a great deal.

Mrs Ellsworth's voice interrupted Laura's memories of the past few hours. It felt as if she was caught once more in the tidal streams of the Rip. She had been bullied in a very polite way by the Ellsworths, and now she was wearing their daughter's dress.

'Your deportment needs a little work,' Mrs Ellsworth muttered to herself, a keen eye on Laura. 'But no one could dispute you are a lovely girl, Miss Webster. I am sure the gentlemen here tonight will be taken with you. I wouldn't be surprised if we don't get some calling on us tomorrow, just so they can see you again.'

Laura did not know what to say to that. She wanted to fiddle and twitch, but she had been told to stand still as the maid finished dressing her hair. A circlet of flowers had been woven through the fair tresses on her crown, while the length was now up above her nape in a heavy sort of bun, held in place by a multitude of pins.

She stared at herself in the mirror and decided she looked like someone else. A stranger. Certainly not the Laura Webster she was used to. She did not know what to think. She tried to tell herself that she was experiencing the life that Edmund had told her she needed to experience. This was what she had been missing. Then why wasn't she more excited at the prospect of attending her first ball?

'You are a heroine, Miss Webster. Everyone here tonight will know it.' Mrs Ellsworth stood back now and clasped her hands to her bosom in a rather dramatic manner, although Laura noticed her eyes were calculating. As if she was already planning Laura's wedding.

And was she a heroine? Like Grace Darling, or some of those other lighthouse women, saving shipwrecked folk from the waves, or trying to. Her mother had been a heroine, but Laura did not think she was in the same league. She had simply done what was asked of her, and what she was good at. And besides, Albert and Elsie had got away. Surely, if she was a true heroine, she would have managed to prevent their escape?

When Mrs Ellsworth led Laura into the ballroom, she grew more uneasy. There were a great many people crammed into it. How could they breathe? Laura was certainly finding it difficult. She had been forced into a corset and it was laced up so tightly she wondered if she would ever breathe again. Evidently, that was not a concern, though. It was one's outward appearance that mattered.

There were many introductions, and she did her best to respond. Glances were sent her way, excited and knowing, and everyone seemed to want to speak with her. And touch her. A squeeze of the hand, a brush of fingers, a firm hold on her arm. It was as if she had become a talisman, and to touch her was good luck.

Laura began to feel slightly sick.

At first she searched for Edmund. Over the past days, she had become used to his shy smiles and admiring looks. But soon she saw that he was similarly engaged with the major's guests. Especially women, and there seemed to be rather a lot of them surrounding him. Pretty girls with gay laughs, waving their fans in front of their faces, eyes wide and flirtatious.

He might be a black sheep, but he was related to a marquess, and not even the fact that he had been sent off by his family to the colonies could disguise his London polish and sophistication. He fit this setting far more eloquently than Laura, and she felt her foolish heart sink.

Well, now you know, she told herself, accepting the proffered glass of champagne. It was nasty stuff, but she sipped it, just so she could tell Miriam she had. Her stepmother would be agog when she heard about all of this, would want to know all the details, so Laura did her best to take them in, although her head felt full to bursting with the noise and the swirling colours and the strangeness of it all. She longed to be standing on the cliffs of Benevolence, gazing out at the far horizon. At nothing. Just her and the elements and her own thoughts.

'You look exquisite.'

And there was Edmund, standing at her side. She noticed again his dark evening wear, the crisp white shirt beneath his jacket and the high collar. His hair had been trimmed, and his face shaven, and he was very handsome. He had always been handsome, of course, but she could not help thinking he had looked better with her in the lifeboat, the woollen hat pulled down over his hair, his eyes squinting at the horizon, and his hand on hers on the tiller.

She did not know this man before her now. He frightened her a little. He was a stranger.

'Borrowed clothes,' she said. 'I'm not sure I am myself in them.'

He leaned down closer, conspiratorially. 'I know. I am used to it and even I find it odd. I have only been on Benevolence for a short while and solitude seems to have entered my bloodstream.'

She did not believe him. He was being kind, trying to make her feel better. It was the way Edmund was.

Another man bowed to her, interrupting them. 'Miss Webster, may I have this dance?'

'Yes, yes, thank you.' She smiled awkwardly, glanced at Edmund as he stepped back, and was whirled away. At least Miriam had taught her to dance. Now she was grateful for those lessons in the large room at the cottage, ignoring her father's laughter and applause, watching her steps. She still had to concentrate on those steps, but was confident she would not disgrace herself.

There was a break in the dancing while supper was served, the dishes so numerous and strange, Laura found it difficult to decide which to eat. Not that they were not delicious. A creamy concoction with raspberry jam and sponge was so delectable that if she was not being watched by all these people, she would have gone back for more.

The speech that came afterwards made her feel sick again. The major stood up and lauded her bravery, recounting her voyage from Benevolence to the mainland in great detail, using words like *astounding* and *remarkable*, and *our very own Grace Darling*. He spoke darkly about the ambitions of foreign powers and how lucky they were to have been warned in time. It was as if Albert and Elsie did not exist, and that Laura had made her dash from the island simply to deliver Mr Jones's papers. The major ended by saying she deserved a medal and he intended to start a petition to get her one.

There was thunderous applause.

Laura was asked to respond, but all she could do was stumble through a thankyou, and then smile until her face ached as everyone applauded again. It was awful and she hated it. She wanted to walk out. She wanted desperately to go home.

There was more dancing after all of that. She saw Edmund dancing too, but he did not ask her. She saw him making men and woman laugh, being his charming self, completely in his element. Perhaps, she thought, his mother would hear of this and send him the money for his passage home? That would be a good thing. He could resume his role in the society he was born to inhabit. Like the hero in one of the novels Laura liked to read, all would be forgiven and a happy ending would wrap up the story nicely.

Eventually, it became too much. A singer began to warble her way through a popular song, and Laura chose that moment to slip away. Retired Major Ellsworth and his wife lived behind one of the grand hotels that graced Queenscliff's harbour frontage. It was not far from where the ball had been held, and although she had come by carriage, Laura decided she would much rather walk.

She suspected if anyone saw her they would think her actions scandalous, but there was no one about, and besides, she simply no longer cared. Too bad if her borrowed slippers were so thin that she felt every stone on the footpath, and the breeze was chilly against her bare shoulders. She wanted solitude and quiet, and as the gentle sound of the sea filled up the emptiness inside her, she began to feel more herself.

'Laura! Miss Webster!'

The sound of her name being called brought her to a stop. At once, she wished she had ignored it and continued walking. Now there would be questions she did not want to answer. But the gentleman was moving swiftly closer, and as she suspected, it was Edmund.

'Aren't you enjoying yourself?' he asked her with a frown. The night about them was soft velvet, the stars distant silver buttons, and the smell of the sea was so welcome, tears pricked her eyes. Or perhaps it was Edmund being here that did that because soon he would be gone.

'I ... I don't know. It was interesting. Perhaps I would learn to enjoy it?' She had not meant to make it a question.

He laughed. '*Would* you learn to enjoy it?'

She could not lie, so she sighed and said, 'No.'

'Where are you going?' he said curiously.

'Back to my room.'

His gaze slid over her finery and the humour in his eyes was very familiar. 'So, you thought you'd walk?'

'I didn't want a fuss.'

He took her hand, placed it carefully on his and then began to walk with her. 'Tell me what you are really thinking, Miss Webster. You have never bothered to prevaricate with me before. Your honesty is one of the things that I like most about you.'

Was it? Laura walked a little in silence, gathering her thoughts. If he wanted honesty, then she would give it to him.

'From the moment we met, I could tell you were surprised by the life I lead on Benevolence. The solitary life. You told me about your sisters, and your mother, and how you could not imagine them in my place. You said I needed to experience the world outside of my island. That I may find I liked it.'

He was staring at the ground, his head bowed. His shoulders seemed rather stiff, as if he was struggling with some thoughts of his own. 'I did say that, didn't I? Should I apologise?'

'No. I don't want you to apologise. You meant well, and what you said made sense. I know my father will be leaving the island in three years, and Miriam will want to stay in Hobart. I told you that. I have decisions to make and you were right when you said I had never really lived a life other than that of a lighthouse-keeper's daughter.'

'I don't think the brief glimpse you have had tonight should put you off, Laura. This has been rather excessive.'

She smiled. 'It has, hasn't it? But you seemed to enjoy it. Why couldn't I? Honestly, Mr Bailey, I don't think I am made for social engagements and chitchat and ... and dancing. Well, not this sort of dancing, anyway. I didn't mind dancing with Miriam, laughing at our missteps, feeling comfortable. I didn't feel comfortable tonight.'

'No, I could see that.'

'You didn't dance with me.'

She had not meant to blurt it out, and he turned to her, surprised. 'I wasn't sure you would want me to. Besides, I thought you should learn what it's like to be in demand, sought after. I thought you might like it.'

'Not really. I would have liked to dance with you.'

'I wish I had, then. I wanted to.'

'You are related to a marquess.' She hadn't meant to say that, either.

'I don't care about that.'

'But others do.'

He shook his head and they carried on walking, more slowly now, as if making the most of these last moments.

'Major Ellsworth has arranged for a boat to sail to Benevolence tomorrow,' she said. 'They will bring poor Tom back with them, as well as Mr Jones and Isaac. I'll make sure Seal is aboard, too.'

'Thank you.'

'I'm sure Mr Jones will be over the moon.'

'He'll expect a medal as well, you wait and see.'

She huffed. 'I think it is all a storm in a teacup, the Russians, but I may be wrong.'

'It seems unlikely they would be interested in us,' he agreed. 'Will you be on the boat?'

'Yes. I have to get back. My father needs me, and I miss everyone. It's my home.'

'Then this is goodbye.' He was watching her, his face in shadow.

Laura nodded, refusing to let the mood become solemn. 'I suppose it is. I wish you well, Mr Bailey. I'm sure that one day you will find out what makes you happy.'

He paused and then he lifted her hand to his lips. 'I'll never forget you, Laura.'

'No, and I won't forget you.' Her throat ached and her eyes were full. Who would have thought that when she first met Edmund Bailey that saying goodbye to him would be so difficult?

'Will you be all right?' she asked him tentatively. 'I mean, you said you were destitute.'

He grinned wryly. 'Turns out I do have a friend of the family here, and he is happy to put me up until I find my feet. I'm sure he will write to my father, and perhaps he will feel guilty enough to send for me. I am not holding my breath, however.' He didn't look excited at the prospect, rather he looked resigned.

They did not say any more, and then she was at her destination, and he bowed a farewell as she went inside. And that was it. Over. Was it a romance? She thought it might be, or could have been. Her first romance, then. Something to ponder in the years ahead.

It was odd, though, and uncomfortable. She had not thought her heart would ache so, or she would feel like weeping at the thought of never seeing him again. The conversations they had had, the smiles they had shared ... She would miss him. She rather thought she would miss him every day for the rest of her life.

* * *

It was morning in Queenscliff, and she stood on the deck of the boat that was to take her back to Benevolence. She was not sorry to be leaving Major Ellsworth and his wife, kind as they were. They had not been very happy with her for leaving the ball on her own and so early, but she had made up her mind. She was stubborn when it came to making her own choices, not the malleable girl Mrs Ellsworth had hoped her to be. Perhaps she wouldn't get that medal, after all.

Someone leaned on the railing at her side. Laura wished they would leave her alone. The captain and several of his officers had come to speak to her since she had boarded the ship, and although she had been polite, she really wished they wouldn't. She stared towards the grand hotels of Queenscliff and waited for this one to say his piece.

Miss Webster, will you tell me about ... Miss Webster, is it true ... Miss Webster, I wish you would ...

Instead, the voice beside her was one she was very familiar with. 'I thought I might come and stay for a while.'

She seemed to have lost her ability to speak, and the use of her eyes. They blurred, forcing her to blink hard, her hands tight on the railing.

'I've decided I rather like solitude. I thought we might be able to enjoy it together. If that is acceptable to you?'

He was staring down into the water, wearing the woollen hat and her father's jacket, as if he had rejected the man from last night in his handsome evening clothes, with his polite chitchat.

'There was a moment, on the island,' he went on, when she said nothing. 'I don't know if you remember.'

I am a man alone, without a clear future, but with plenty of experience of the world, and you are a woman alone, without a clear future, and with little experience of the world beyond this island. It seems as if we can help each other, Laura.

'I do remember.'

'I thought ... I believe we could deal well together. Different as we are, we fit very well. We could try, at least.'

'Are you sure that is what you want?' she said. 'I think you could have so much more if you stayed. You could have your old life back, Edmund. Not many men would want to give that up.'

'I could. Maybe. But I wouldn't be happy.' There was sincerity and hope in his expression. 'I think I am just beginning to understand what real happiness means. It would feel like defeat if I walked away now.'

Laura gave that some thought. If he was willing to take this chance, then she should let him. 'Will you be staying long?' she asked tentatively.

He smiled, and she could see she had pleased him. 'As long as you. If your father allows it.'

Whatever he saw in her face made him bolder. He slipped an arm about her shoulders and tugged her in against his chest. 'Laura,' he whispered into her hair. 'My extraordinary girl.'

NINA

May 2020, Benevolence
Day Four

They hadn't meant to fall asleep—there was still the fear of what Murray was up to and where Elle had disappeared to—but the revelations of the previous day caught up with them. Snug together, sheltered and warm, Nina did not wake until just before dawn. It was the wind that woke her, strong gusts coming in from the west, moaning around the brick wall, rattling the timbers that once had made up the cottage. When Nina peered blearily out from their shelter, she saw that the fog was gone. Birds Nest Island loomed beyond the cliff, the birds surprisingly quiet, and the sky appeared ominous.

There was a storm coming.

Jude's stomach rumbled and she glanced at him with a smile. He grimaced. 'I'm starving,' he admitted. 'I need a Paul breakfast. How are you feeling?'

'Hungry,' she agreed, sidestepping a deeper answer. The emotions from yesterday were still raw and she thought they might bleed if scratched. Best to let things settle. She stretched out a hand and he took it, hauling himself to his feet with a groan. He looked tired, but something had changed between them; a new sense of calm, despite all that was yet to be resolved. Nina felt better than she had for a very long time.

More blasts of wind pushed against their backs as they began to make their way to the camp on the other side of the island. She hoped Paul hadn't been worried—he'd probably expected them to wait out the fog. She thought he trusted her enough to know she could take care of herself.

Jude called out something, but his words were whipped away by the increasing strength of the wind. There was a special scale which was used when reporting wind gusts, and Nina had intended to learn about it before she came. Of course, there had been no time. But she wondered now what these gusts were on that scale, because they seemed worthy of a number.

Next time she lifted her head, it was to see the white tower of the lighthouse rearing up before her, like a symbol of hope against the dark clouds of the coming gale. Was that what ships long ago had thought as they approached the dreadful Tiger's Teeth? But more likely it would have been night-time, wouldn't it? Darkness and pounding seas and screaming winds, and nothing to save them but the beam of the lighthouse.

Was Jude her lighthouse? It seemed trite and yet she felt as if him knowing the truth, him being here with her, gave her a sense of hope she had been lacking for so long. He had loved her, he'd told her so. She couldn't let herself believe he still did, not in the same way he had before, it was too painful. Because Nina still loved Jude and that was something she had no intention of telling him.

Sunrise was blanketed by clouds, but the light was increasing as they neared the camp. It was a new day. Nina felt headachy—she probably needed her medication—but she'd think of that later. She was going through a list in her mind, ticking off all she needed to do, when the fireworks started.

Stunned, she stopped, and then Jude was shouting, and she understood. It wasn't fireworks she was hearing, it was gunfire. Someone was shooting.

A moment later she heard a scream.

And then they were running. She could feel the heavy pounding of her heart, the sick sensation in her stomach. Jude's face was white and strained, and she recognised his fear. She knew she must look the same. She needed to get to her team—now.

The track they were on ran high behind the campsite and the keeper's cottages, with the grove of she-oaks and tea-tree between them and the buildings. Jude stopped, taking her hand in his. 'We can't just rush in and save everyone,' he said. 'I know you want to, Nina, but we have to think this through.'

Nina was already thinking. Ahead of them the track branched, one part going on to the lighthouse, the other dropping down towards the cove and the cottages. They would be visible if they went on. Here, where they were now, there was some protection from the trees.

'This way, then,' she said, tugging him forward down the steep slope. They scrambled over the stony ground, their steps causing some smaller stones to rattle down into the trees. Nina was petrified that would give them away, but no one shouted or came to look. In fact, it was ominously still when they reached the rear of the 1920s cottages Brian had been repairing. One of them was directly behind the keeper's cottage where Nina was staying, but the other was slightly to the side with no obstructions in front of it.

Nina could hear voices now, and a woman sobbing. Cautiously, she and Jude peered around the corner of the far cottage. Because it had been built further up the slope, it was on higher ground, overlooking the old head-keeper's cottage, and the campsite Island Heritage had set up. Normally, Paul would be down there cooking breakfast. Not today. She could see that because of the foul weather, he had been in the process of moving his operation inside, but he'd been interrupted. Some of the tables and chairs were still scattered around, with uncooked food on plates. A loaf of bread lay on the ground, its slices spread out like a pack of cards.

Reynash's bike was on its side, as if abandoned mid-flight. Canvas was flapping wildly, and she noticed that one of the tents had come loose. The side was lifting and the wind had scooped out the contents, sending loose papers fluttering and dancing down the hillside towards the cove.

'Where are they?' Jude said.

Nina shifted again, easing further around the corner of the white granite wall, so that now she could see beyond the campsite, where the lower track branched off to the steep climb to the lighthouse, or the more meandering descent to the cove.

'There,' she whispered. 'By the bell.' Had she rung it only yesterday? Now the members of her team were standing beside it, as if summoned. Well, most of them were standing, but there was someone on the ground.

It was Paul.

Shocked, Nina stumbled, wanting to run out to him. Her vision blurred, her heart rate picked up, but Jude's grip on her hand steadied her. When she could see again, she realised Lis and Arnie were huddled close beside Paul, who had blood on his shoulder and was grimacing in pain.

'He's alive, at least he's alive,' she whispered. It was something to hold on to.

'They look bloody terrified,' Jude muttered.

He was right. They seemed frozen in place. The group had their backs to her, apart from Paul, and she could see how stiff and angry Brian appeared. There was a man holding a gun, waving it around, and Elle was at his side. The girl turned then, and she appeared shaken. Their voices were loud enough to hear despite the wind and the rattle of the rain.

'You never said you had another gun.' Elle folded her arms tightly around her waist, as if she was holding herself together. 'You're in no state to be—'

'I don't tell you everything,' her companion said, his voice alive with frustration and rage. Rage at the world, at himself, at his own situation. 'We need to find the sapphire and they are going to dig up every grave until we do.'

It was Murray. Of course it was. Nina wanted to curl up in a ball and hide, but she couldn't do that. She wouldn't. Because Murray had hurt her friend, and he would hurt the others if she let him.

She wanted to be brave, but at the same time she could feel herself beginning to spiral. She had to prevent it. It was dangerous enough to be here, within metres of the man who had destroyed her life, but if she had a flashback ... lost control ... was no longer able to protect herself or the others, and all because of what Murray had done to her all those years ago ... No, she couldn't let that happen. She wouldn't.

Her fingers squeezed Jude's and his gaze met hers. 'Do you think he'll take the jewel and go?'

'I'll dig it up myself if he agrees to that.'

'But we've seen him. We know him. He can't get away for long.'

'I don't know if he even cares right now,' Jude said. 'He's out of his head on something. Probably thinks it's a clear and sunny day.'

The wind gusted again, tugging at their hair and clothing, picking up a container of utensils and sending them clattering over the ground. Murray was still waving his gun, issuing instructions, and Arnie picked up a shovel that Nina saw was lying with other tools in a pile on the ground. Reynash bent to retrieve a pick. They were going to dig up the graves in the cemetery while a gale was blowing and a man threatened them with a rifle.

They needed help. She turned to Jude.

'Stay here,' he said, in typical macho style, and before she could argue, he had stepped out from the shelter of the cottage and begun to walk towards the others.

* * *

'Murray!'

Jude had to raise his voice to be heard now. The gale was getting worse. Murray swung around, gun raised, eyes wild, and Nina saw him properly for the first time.

He had aged more than ten years. His hair was longer, his body leaner and harder, and his face lined in a way that spoke of excess and unhappiness. Then in a flash he was grinning, his mood completely changed.

'Jude! I wondered where you'd got to. I knew you wouldn't have gone far. It is an island, after all.' He chuckled at his own joke.

'What are you doing?' Jude sounded eerily calm. 'Why are you here?'

'Didn't Lis tell you?' He was still grinning, but his tone had turned nasty. 'She tells me she knows everything. Clever old Lis, too bad she chose the wrong side.'

Lis's pretty face twisted. 'I hate you,' she hissed.

Murray laughed. 'It was always Jude, wasn't it? Good old Saint Jude. Well, that's just too bad.' He leaned forward with a vicious expression on his face. 'All those wasted years, hey?'

Lis began to cry, and suddenly Nina remembered her doing that at the beach house, cuddled up against Angela Rawlins, seeking comfort. Right now, Lis looked broken.

'What is *wrong* with you?' she sobbed. 'Why are you like this?'

Murray's smile vanished. 'You should ask Nina about that. Nina, where are you?' he went on in a sing-song voice. 'I know you're here somewhere. I've been watching you.'

Nina leaned hard into the cottage wall, pressing her forehead to the rough stone until she thought it would bruise. Fear washed over her, making her body sweaty and shaky, and she struggled to keep it at bay.

'She's back at my cottage.' That was Jude answering, sounding completely plausible to anyone who didn't know him well. But Murray had known him for thirty-two years.

'You're lying. Nina always had an overdeveloped sense of right and wrong. For all her slutty ways—and yeah, I used to hear her moaning all the way down the passage from your bedroom—she always liked to take the moral high ground. She's right here, probably hiding behind the cottage over there, thinking she'll talk me into handing over my gun and saying I'm sorry. Isn't that right, Nina?'

Her nails bit into the soft flesh of her palms. The past was roaring towards her no matter how she tried to hold it back. Murray's voice, his taunts, the taste of him on her lips, the press of him on her body. Too much. It was all too much.

'Do you know what she did for you,' Murray was still talking. 'Do you know, Jude? How about I tell you. And feel free to jump in any time, Nina,' he added, louder, mocking.

She tried to move, whether to confront him or run away, she wasn't sure. But it was too late. She was already spiralling, the world fading, as she stepped back into the worst moments of her life.

NINA

Summer 2010, Hobart

Nina had locked herself in her room at the university and refused to answer the door when Jude came knocking and calling. He'd become increasingly frustrated. Her phone had blown up with messages, pleading at first, then confused, and finally angry. She didn't have the strength to answer any of them.

She should go to the police, she knew that. And yet she felt paralysed with pain. Not physical pain, that had soon dissipated, but heart and soul pain. Betrayal, disbelief, shock. The memories circled around and around in her head until she could neither sleep nor bear to be awake.

Sometime afterwards, a key turned in her lock and the door swung open. At first she thought it was Jude, that he had talked the supervisor into handing over her key, but then she recognised Colin. He switched on the light and she flinched, and then he came over to where she was sitting huddled in her one good armchair and stood staring down at her. As usual, he stank of cigarettes. He was twisting the door key in his fingers, flipping it back and forth.

'I know what happened,' he said. 'Murray confessed to his mother. Have you been to the police?'

She didn't know what she was expecting, but his face showed no sympathy or anger on her behalf, no commiseration for the traumatic experience she had undergone. When she shook her head, she saw Colin's shoulders relax and his hand tighten on the key, his knuckles white. He was relieved.

'Angela wants to talk to you,' he said. 'Come with me to the hospital. We'll sort this out. Come on, Nina, get dressed. It'll be all right.' For a moment he looked at her with distaste, and she realised she was still in her dressing gown, hair a mess, face pale and swollen with crying.

She did as he said. He even helped her tie up her shoes. She didn't seem to have any will of her own, as if the strong and decisive girl she knew had been taken from her, and this other pitiful creature stood in her place.

Once they got to the hospital, Colin took her arm and led her into Angela's private room. Until then, Nina had forgotten that one of her children might be in there with her. Jude, or worse, Murray. But there was no one else. Of course not. Colin would have made certain of it.

Angela was sitting up in her bed, her face white and drawn, while her eyes, dark eyes like Jude's and Murray's, were red with weeping.

'Nina,' was all she said.

Colin pulled out a chair and Nina heard his low voice say, 'She hasn't been to the police.'

Angela burst into tears, hands covering her face. Nina didn't know what to say, what to do, so she waited.

'We need to talk to you, Nina,' Colin said at last.

What was there to talk about? Surely the facts spoke for themselves, and they had to see that Murray couldn't expect to get away with what he had done. That wouldn't be fair, would it?

Colin leaned against the wall beside the bed in the small room. Outside, staff and trolleys moved up and down the corridor, machines beeped, the air filled with business. Angela was attached to a monitor, Nina noticed belatedly. The line on it was moving in steep curves and she wondered how far it could go before an alarm sounded. Colin must have wondered too, because he was the one who began the conversation, his voice unruffled. Composed. His courtroom voice.

'Murray wants you to know how sorry he is. He never meant to hurt you. He can't even remember how it started, whose fault it was. I hope you will be generous and agree that to take this further, to apportion blame, would be cruel and unnecessary.'

Nina blinked. She tried to laugh but couldn't get the sound past the lump in her throat. 'Whose *fault* it was?' she forced the words out. 'Whose *fault*? He raped me.'

Angela gave a wail which Colin ignored.

'He says you encouraged him to think—'

Nina wasn't having this, she wasn't. 'He raped me,' she said furiously. Almost immediately, her anger gave way and she was weeping again, her head in her arms on the hospital bed.

There was movement, and then she felt Angela's hand close on her arm. Her fingers were cold and damp. 'Don't send my son to jail,' she whispered brokenly. 'Please, please, Nina.'

The alarm on the monitor went off then. In no time, there were nurses with worried faces in the room, and Nina was asked to leave. Colin took her arm and led her out.

There was a waiting room just down the corridor, and after checking that it was empty, he showed her in and closed the door. Nina could still hear the alarm sounding, but then it stopped. She wasn't sure what that meant, but Colin didn't seem to be too worried. Angela must have been stabilised.

'If Murray goes to jail she'll die.'

Nina stared up at him. 'Then Murray should have thought of that.'

Her flash of spirit seemed to surprise him. 'Yes, I suppose he should have. You can go to the police, Nina, I'm not stopping you. Have him charged, taken to court. I'll defend him. We can go through the whole process. Though to be honest, I'm not sure Angela will survive to hear the verdict.'

She knew it was true. Weak, ailing Angela would have another episode and that would be it. Nina already knew what he was going to say next.

'What do you think her family will say when she dies? When it was your actions that killed her?'

'He should be punished,' she said.

'Well, I will argue otherwise, but let's just suppose you win and Murray goes to prison. What will happen then, do you think? Angela might survive, that is possible, but she'll need care. Mandy is still at school. Jude is still at university with all his dreams, and I'm willing to pay for him to finish his course. But he'll have to take Murray's place in the firm, that's only fair. What do you think he will feel about that? You know him as well as I do. He'll be bitter and unhappy, and he'll be looking for someone to blame. You, Nina, he'll blame you.'

'How can it be my fault?' she croaked. 'Murray—'

'Can't you see that's how he will view it? Especially when I tell him what Murray said. That you led him on. That you have been leading him on for months now. Sitting on the beach in that skimpy bikini, smiling at him, reeling him in like a fish on a line. Who do you think Jude will believe? His family or you?'

Nina blinked. Was this really happening? She shook her head in disbelief. 'I have never felt like that about Murray,' she said. 'I love Jude.'

'Then prove it.'

She tried to use reason against him, stand strong, refuse his ridiculous demands. In response, he pummelled her with words, drawing pictures of her day in court, the worst kind of scenarios. The family shattered, Angela dead or dying, the blame laid squarely at her door. Jude walking away from her in disgust. Nina didn't even remember agreeing, but she must have.

Later, she would see how thoroughly he had worked her using a combination of moral blackmail and her love for Jude. He'd played on her weaknesses, browbeating her into agreeing to something she never should have agreed to, but by then it was too late. It was done and there was no going back.

Colin drove her home.

'You're doing the right thing,' he assured her, giving her shoulder a fatherly pat. 'Now, I'm going to offer you some advice, Nina. Forget about Murray. I'll tell Jude you've decided you need some time to think about your future. He won't be happy at first, but he'll get over you and move on. You've given him the best chance he'll ever have to make his dreams come true. And you're a clever, beautiful girl. I have every confidence you will make a success of your life.'

And that was it.

Even if Colin hadn't cut her loose, she knew she could never see Jude or any of the Rawlins family again. She could not be in the same room with him or Murray, with any of them. She had agreed to lie for the man she loved and her reward was that she could never be with him again.

So she withdrew. No explanation, no excuses. She withdrew and gradually Jude stopped calling her phone or knocking on her door, or asking to see her. Perhaps Angela or Colin made up some story, but by then Nina was just glad that he had stopped and she did not have to pretend anymore to an indifference she did not feel. Her life was shattered, over, and she would never truly recover.

She hadn't known that then, of course. She'd thought that, someday, she would be herself again. That as Colin had said, she would be able to move on and make a new life. A better one.

But she never had, and lately it had got worse. The past overwhelmed her sometimes, sucking her down into its maw. Medication, alcohol, working all the hours she could, none of it seemed to help. With a sense of despair, she knew that the only thing that would make it stop was to tell the truth.

NINA

May 2020, Benevolence
Day Four

Nina stepped out from the side of the cottage, her hand still resting hard against the wall. It was meant to appear casual, although it was actually a necessity if she was going to stay upright. Her legs were shaking so badly she thought she might fall down anyway, but her pride demanded she show him he couldn't stop her.

'Murray,' she said. 'What a surprise.'

His head came up sharply. He seemed nonplussed, but it didn't last. He gave her that wild, slightly unhinged grin. '*There* you are,' he said, as if they'd been friends for years. 'The last time I saw you, you weren't at your best. You don't look too good now, actually.' He made a moue of concern.

'I'm much better, thank you. I'm more worried about you, Murray. Do you want to put the gun down so that we can talk?'

He laughed. 'Does Jude know what you did to save him and the family? I think we should tell him, don't you? How you suffered in silence all these years to keep the status quo. Not that you suffered as much as I did, mind you. I thought Colin would let me go, but instead I dug myself an even deeper hole. He held what I'd done over me and made me toe the line. Threats if I showed any sign I might refuse.'

'Poor you.'

His face grew cruel. 'And you're a liar. That night ... I like to think you enjoyed every moment of it.'

Nina felt the hard stone sink from her chest to her stomach, the ache so painful she wanted to howl, but she wasn't going to give him the satisfaction. 'You are a vile person, Murray. You always were. You've just proved it.'

Oh, he was angry now. Jude, who had been looking back and forth between them, moved in front of her as if to protect her. That only made Murray angrier.

'Get out of my way, Jude.'

He was in Jude's face now, the rifle gripped in white-knuckled hands. Behind him, Nina could see that Paul was speaking urgently to Brian and the others. Elle put a stop to any plan they'd come up with.

'Stay put,' she said sharply. 'Murray, you'd better get your act together if we're going to get out of here.'

'You bastard,' Jude said. 'You hurt her.'

He sounded shattered, but Murray shrugged impatiently, as if he didn't have time for this. 'You had everything. And then Nina came along and you had her, too. You owed me—I took what I was due.'

Jude struck. The gun clattered to the ground, but the two men were more focused on each other, struggling and rolling, fists flying.

'Get the gun!' Paul shouted.

Nina and Elle headed towards it at the same time. Nina ran to get there first. Lis tripped Elle and she went flying, and Arnie dived at her, sitting on top of her while she screamed and swore and struggled. Nina picked up the rifle.

It felt surprisingly light in her hands, light as air but deadly. She took aim at Murray's back—he was on top of Jude now, while Jude clawed at his face.

'Stop it!' she commanded. 'I'll shoot you if you don't.'

The two men halted, and Murray looked at her, his chest rising and falling crazily. His expression was a mixture of anger and sadness now.

'Why didn't you fight like this before?' he asked her. 'Why didn't you stand up to Colin? I could have gone to prison, but it would have been better … better than …'

Nina gaped at him in amazement. 'You're telling me it was all a cry for help? To get you out of working for Colin? Because you were too pathetic to stand up to him by yourself?'

'Fuck you,' he growled, and struggled to his feet. Just as he did, a violent wind gust came through. The half-collapsed tent Nina had noticed before broke up and went flying. The sheet of canvas hit Murray, but so did the pole, and he stumbled a few steps away and then went down. And didn't get up.

The shock froze everyone just for a moment, and then Jude got painfully to his feet. His nose was bleeding and he wiped it on his sleeve with a grimace. Paul stood up with Lis's help, and Nina handed him the gun. By then, Jude was kneeling beside his brother.

He'd removed the sheet of canvas from him, but when Nina got close enough to stand beside him, it was obvious to her that some serious damage had been done. A jagged piece of metal that had been attached to the pole had cut his neck, and there was a fast-growing pool of blood around Murray's head.

Jude was trying to staunch it, using his hands, but it wasn't stopping. Nina ran to get some towels and they both pressed them to Murray's neck. His face was a terrible colour, and he didn't seem to be conscious.

'Jesus.' Brian stared, while one of the others turned away to vomit.

There was a sound coming from the water. Lis called out, 'There's a police boat out there!' and then they heard the helicopter.

'For God's sake, let me up,' Elle said through gritted teeth. 'I'm an undercover officer. Get off!'

Arnie, looking rather stunned, got off. Elle shook herself like an angry cat. The bubbly photographer was gone, as was the angry girlfriend. This was someone else, someone serious and professional.

Nina thought Elle was going to head down the track that led to the cove, to meet up with her colleagues, but instead she came over to Nina.

'I'm sorry,' she said. 'I took the key to the hut. I needed to disable the satellite phone so none of you could put out a call for help. Murray would have tried to escape and we had everything in place. Even your boss, Kyle, knew what was going on, and the woman I replaced—Veronica.'

'So, you were playing a part? It was all a lie?'

'I had to get onto the island with Murray. We needed to push him into a corner. His yacht's full of contraband. He'll have to give us names now.' And then, with an assessing glance at Murray, 'I'll get the medic.'

* * *

Nina couldn't get warm. The air temperature had dropped dramatically and the fog was back. At least the wind had calmed so that the helicopter could make an emergency flight to Flinders Island. The fire in the big hearth inside the cottage was roaring, but there was more smoke inside than going up the chimney. Brian had been eying it as if he'd like to get a brush and climb in there.

Nina kept seeing Murray's face, the blood, and then the police gathered around him. Jude had been sitting, hands loose between his knees, blood all over them. He was too shaken to say anything, and Lis had taken him back to his cottage to clean up. Paul had been cared for, his wound tended to while Arnie hung over him. Meanwhile, Elle had been everywhere. Nina was still having trouble believing that she had been playing a part all along. Well, two parts.

Now they were all gathered in the lighthouse-keeper's cottage, and the police officer who seemed to be in charge, and whose name Nina had already forgotten, was answering questions.

'We'd been watching Mr Rawlins for some time. He's in deep with some very dangerous people, and he was reckless enough for us to hope he'd help us bring them down. Not intentionally,' he added, when he saw the question in Jude's eyes. And the hope that his brother, like Elle, might have been on the side of good, after all.

'He had gambling debts, drug debts, and he couldn't pay any of them. We found out through an informant that his creditors had learned about the sapphire from one of the archivists, a woman with criminal contacts. It was a bizarre enough prize to capture their imagination. And Murray was desperate to get himself out of the mess he was in, so when they told him the price he needed to pay—get us the sapphire and we'll wipe the slate clean—he agreed.'

'So the sapphire is real?' Lis said, looking at Elle.

Elle glanced at her superior and he nodded for her to go ahead. 'It is real. The same archivist who had contacted the criminals made inquiries about the legality of digging up graves, and that raised a red flag with us. Once we knew what was going on, it seemed the ideal way to draw Murray and his criminal friends into our net. I was set up in the archivist's place and Murray made contact with me, unaware that I was undercover. Murray ... Mr Rawlins was fascinated by the story. He couldn't stay away from the island. I'd begun to wonder if he planned to keep the sapphire if he found it, which would have caused us problems and probably got him killed.'

'But he didn't find it,' Jude guessed. 'Had it already been removed?'

'No. As far as we know, it's still here. Somewhere. Short of digging up every grave in the place, I think it's going to remain lost.'

Arnie had cooked up a substantial breakfast, enough to feed everyone. Now he was handing out hot drinks. Paul had gone in the helicopter to Flinders Island. Murray, still alive but only just, had gone too. They would be given treatment there and then transferred to Hobart. 'I won't be happy until I see Paul again,' Arnie had said to Nina. 'I don't think he's as indestructible as he thinks he is.'

'Unless the letter was full of lies,' Jude suggested now. He had changed and washed, but his eyes had shadows under them and his face was haggard.

'Rorie was supposed to be confessing his sins so he wouldn't burn in hell,' Lis said. 'Maybe he was telling tales to the priest. Maybe he thought God wouldn't notice.'

Lis had spoken to Nina earlier. They hadn't had much to say, but Lis had offered an apology and Nina had accepted. The other woman had been through a lot more than Nina had realised. Murray had hurt them both. Maybe in time they could find more than that in common.

Elle spoke again. 'Mr Rawlins was spiralling out of control. The diesel... there was no point to that. I knew then I was losing any hold I might have had on him. I radioed my superiors that the time had come to end the operation.'

There was a silence.

'If that's all ...?' The police officer looked around the room. 'We'll arrange for you to fly back to Hobart by fixed-wing aircraft when the weather improves. Probably tomorrow.' He gave a curt nod and Elle followed him out of the room. Nina thought she might glance back, make some acknowledgement, but she didn't. And then she was gone.

Kyle would have heard the news by now. The police had been in contact with him before they arrived on the island—a matter of courtesy, evidently. Nina wouldn't be surprised if he blamed her for the whole mess. Jude? Well, he was the golden boy, no one was going to blame him.

'Nina?'

She glanced up, bleary-eyed, to see Jude standing in front of her. He gave her a wry smile. She could only stare at him. Dark hair curling around his ears, stubble on his jaw, the lines at the corners of his eyes. He was still the boy she had loved. Had never stopped loving.

'Can we talk?'

'Sit next to me.' She shifted over on the couch, making room, and he dropped down beside her. 'Have you heard how Murray is?'

'Only that he's still hanging in there. Not sure if that's a good thing or not.'

Nina found his hand and squeezed. 'It's got to be a good thing, Jude. You want him to live, don't you? So you can tell him what an idiot he's been.'

He looked at her as if wondering how to say what he wanted to say. 'You must hate us. First Murray, and then Colin and then me.'

'You didn't do anything wrong.'

'But if it hadn't been for me, you wouldn't have let Murray get away with it.' He threw his head back against the couch with a soft groan before leaning forward again. This time his gaze was intense. 'I think I knew something had gone on. I knew, but when I tried to find out what, no one would tell me. Then Colin spun me a story about you sleeping with Murray, and how you were too ashamed to admit it. He said it was for the best if I let you go.'

Nina glared at him. 'You believed him.'

'I didn't want to. I wanted to talk to *you*, but you wouldn't talk to me. Murray was acting odd too, guilty, but more than that. I should have tried harder. I'm so sorry.'

'I'm going to make a statement,' Nina said, when she had control of the tremble in her voice. 'I don't know if it's too late. Paul has been telling me all along I should do it, but I was pretending it had never happened, or I was strong enough to get past it. Only I wasn't.'

'I wish …' He blew out a breath. 'Nina, I wish you'd told me. I wish you'd trusted me. I would never have wanted you to do that. And do you know, it made no difference. Murray couldn't be the man Colin wanted him to be. He fell apart. We all did.'

Nina wanted to say 'good', but she restrained herself. They sat in silence for a time, hands clasped. She was even beginning to doze off when Jude spoke again.

'Can I come and see you? After this is over?'

She blinked at him.

'You look like a sleepy possum,' he said tenderly.

Perhaps there was something in her expression, but he cleared his throat and straightened up, his voice losing that intimate quality.

'I don't want to lose what we've found. I want to be friends again. If … if you'll let me?'

'Jude …'

'Don't answer now. I know it's too soon to think about any of that. It's been a crazy few days.'

Nina stared at the smoky fire, not sure what to feel. She knew she should say 'no', because this was ridiculous, wasn't it? That after all that had happened—and the fallout from Murray was going to be huge—they could be friends.

They had always fitted so well together, Jude and Nina. She reined him in and he freed her. Perhaps it would be possible, one day, but there was something he didn't know. She still loved him and that could get awkward, painful, and she wasn't going to live a life of secrets and lies. She was done with that.

'I'll have to think about it.'

He smiled and seemed content with that, then closed his eyes.

After a moment Nina closed hers, too.

LAURA

1890, Bruny Island, Tasmania

The sea roared against the cliffs below her, the salty spray stinging her eyes and coating her lips. She shifted her feet, making sure that her balance was evenly distributed because it was not quite as it used to be. There had been a storm through a few days ago, but thankfully there had been no wrecks to worry about, nothing like that fateful night in 1882.

It had been five years since her father and Miriam had moved to Devonport, where Leo had bought himself a small fishing boat and Miriam had opened a little shop. They were happy, Laura was sure, despite the way Leo sometimes looked longingly out to sea. Noah had a sister now, and Laura missed seeing the children.

She missed Benevolence, too, and often thought about that time, and the people they had saved from the sea. She liked to keep track of them in the newspapers that were delivered via the supply steamers every three months.

Despite widespread consternation over Mr Jones's papers, and the rebuilding of forts and batteries up and down the coast, the invasion had yet to come.

Tom Burrows had recovered against all expectations, although he would never be the same again. He did not remember the Munros or the *Alvarez*, those memories wiped from his injured brain, so their fear had been misplaced. It did not matter that he forgot things; his eight children loved him and wept with joy when he was returned to them. Isaac was still sailing, although in a letter she had had from him recently, Miriam said he was talking of retiring and spending his days as a land lubber.

And Rorie had not been missing, after all. He'd hidden himself away for fear of what might happen to him after Albert had got him alone and warned him he was going to put an end to him. Rorie had only revealed himself after Laura sailed off in the whaleboat. Of course, Leo had been furious with him and locked him up until the steamer came. They had never seen or heard from him again, and weren't sorry. As for what happened to Rochelle Munro's brooch, Rorie would not say. Leo wondered if he might have hidden it with one of the dead seaman they had buried, but it was unlikely anyone was going to dig up the poor souls again just to be sure.

Of Albert and Elsie there had been no word. They had vanished into the Victorian interior, and no one had seen them since. Laura often found herself wondering about them. Were they still together? A man like Albert … she was not sure she would ever completely trust him. Did he love his Elsie enough to stay with her as the years went by? He had killed once, hadn't he? Did that mean he would never kill again? She could not imagine them being very comfortable with each other. A glance here, a festering suspicion there.

The very thought made her shiver.

Laura had come to Bruny Island after leaving Benevolence, and a short stay in Hobart. The lighthouse station here was on the southern coast of Tasmania, and closer to civilisation, but still wild and windy. She had no regrets about not living a 'normal' life, as Miriam called it. She was happy with the solitude and her own thoughts. Perhaps the years on Benevolence had spoiled her for normality. All the same, she might be lonely if it was not for …

Warm arms slipped about her waist, hands resting over the bulge at her waist, and she leaned back with a smile. Her husband, her friend, the man she loved and trusted above all others, bent to kiss her cheek.

'Is the storm gone?' he said.

'I think so.'

'But there will be more?'

'No doubt.'

'Well, we shall weather them,' he said confidently. 'Together. Just as we always have.'

She settled against him, their child moving under his hands. It had been just Edmund and Laura since they had married seven years ago, a simple ceremony in front of the people she loved the most. She had almost given up on them having a child, but soon there would be another member of their family.

She would be going to Hobart for her confinement, something Edmund would not be moved on, and Miriam was coming down to keep her safe. Laura did not expect to be in Hobart long. She would miss the island, and her husband. This was her life and always would be. One day, perhaps her child would stand here; she hoped so.

A new generation to carry on the tradition of tending the lights, of protecting the ships that dared to sail in these dangerous waters. Another Bailey to love the solitude of the islands.

NINA

August 2020, Hobart

Nina cleared away the soup bowls, waving off offers of help. Jude and Lis had come for lunch, something that happened often these days. Paul and Arnie would have come too, but they were busy packing up. They were moving to the Sunshine Coast together. Putting the past behind them. Nina had a standing invitation to visit at any time.

Jude had finished filming his television series, not without difficulties due to the lockdowns that seemed never ending. Still, that was one good thing about making a show set on islands—there was no need for social distancing.

'So, what now?' Lis asked. 'Another series?'

'No.' Jude glanced up at Nina. 'At least … I want to talk to Nina about it first.'

Lis raised an eyebrow. 'You're not thinking of sailing around the world, are you? I still remember those conversations you two used to have. Bloody Pitcairn Island.' Suddenly she grinned. 'It was like you were two halves of a whole.'

Lis and Nina had become friends. It was difficult to believe, sometimes, when Lis had been a spectator of some of the worst moments of Nina's life. Nina liked to think that Murray had brought them together, unwittingly and certainly unwillingly. It was unlikely he knew or cared, these days. Murray had turned supergrass and no one knew where he was. A safe house somewhere.

She hadn't dismissed the possibility of one day pursuing the justice she deserved. It seemed more than likely that Murray would reappear, and when he did, she wouldn't be surprised if he brought himself to the attention of the authorities. When that happened, Nina would make a decision. Take him to court so that he could answer for all the pain he had caused, or let it go and live her life without that dark cloud hanging over her. In the meantime, she wasn't going to spend her days plotting vengeance. She had wasted too many already.

'I am so sorry,' Lis had said, during an impromptu visit after they'd returned from Benevolence. 'How can you ever forgive me?'

'You didn't know ...'

'I should have. I was just so jealous, I suppose. I loved Jude like a big brother and then you hurt him, and everything went weird.'

'Lis, please, let it go.'

Eventually she had.

'I'm writing a book about the sapphire,' Lis said now, grinning at them. 'Fact or fiction, or maybe some of both.' Then, with a sly glance at Jude, 'Have you told her yet?'

Nina sat down. 'Told me what?'

Jude smiled, that open, charming smile she had missed so much. 'Remember I said my great-something-grandparents were lighthouse keepers at Cape Bruny? Well, Lis did a bit of research for me, and their names were Edmund and Laura Bailey. They were here for a good few years, had some children. Turns out that Laura Bailey was actually Laura Webster, daughter of Leo Webster. The head keeper at Benevolence at the time of the wreck of the *Alvarez* and the missing sapphire.'

Nina stared at him, wide-eyed in amazement. 'Really? So, when you went to Benevolence you were walking in Laura's footsteps? Jude, that is remarkable.'

He nodded. 'It really is.'

They kept looking at each other. They couldn't seem to stop.

Lis sighed and rolled her eyes like the teenager she used to be. 'Thanks for lunch, Nina, but I think I'll head home. I have lots to do.'

Belatedly, Nina was on her feet. By the time she'd seen Lis out, she was beginning to wonder what Jude had to tell her. He was a busy man. Nina had left Island Heritage under her own terms, and these days she was concentrating on her health and was making great progress. The flashbacks were few and far between, but she was learning to manage them much better. She would always have problems, but she was a different person from the one who had arrived on Benevolence.

Jude was standing by the window, staring out over the city. The cold, clear air made everything appear magical, the old and the new juxtaposed, and the grey water of the Derwent slipping past. He had an expression on his face that she had always loved, as if his head was full of dreams.

She came and stood by his side and he took her hand in his, linking their fingers. When he twisted around there was something very vulnerable in his expression. As if he was about to open his heart and lay it out before her. And Nina found herself caught between wanting that more than anything, and being terribly afraid.

He leaned in and gently kissed her temple. 'I love you, Nina. I've never stopped loving you. I want to be with you.'

His eyes were full of tears, as if the emotion was overwhelming. 'Jude,' she whispered. 'Oh, Jude, I love you, too. I always have. But things have changed. You know they have. I want so much for us to be what we were.' Nina was crying now. 'I don't know what you're expecting from me ...'

'You're Nina.' He said it with steely determination. 'You're my girl. Anything else we can work through. If ... if that's what you want, as well?'

She did want it. More than anything. He must have seen the truth in her shaky smile, because suddenly his arms were tight around her. For a long time they just stood there, holding each other.

'The production company did offer me another series,' he said at last, smoothing her hair back from her face as she leaned out to look at him. 'I turned them down.'

'Oh, Jude, why?'

'Lis was right. I want to make a show about two amateurs sailing their way across the Pacific. From go to whoa. There'll probably be some frightening moments, but some funny ones, too. And some touching moments. It'll make for great viewing, but more than that, it will make for great times.'

That had been *their* dream.

'Will you come with me and make our dream come true?' he said. 'It's taken a while to get here, but I want to do this. So much. With you.'

'Yes,' she said. 'Yes, please.'

'Then that's what we'll do,' he said.

Nina tried to picture it, her and Jude sailing, the world before them. There would be long days, probably stressful days, but there also would be good times. Laughter and love. And that was when she knew everything was going to be all right.

Acknowledgements

Thank you once again to Selwa Anthony, my agent, and Alex Nahlous, my editor. Also to Laurie Ormond, and the rest of the team at HQ Australia. This is my sixth book with you, and I am grateful for your support over the years. I also want to thank friend and fellow author Sandy Curtis, who helped me fill some very large plot holes, and gave me the confidence to finish. Benevolence Island is a fictional place but it is based on Deal Island, part of the Kent Group in Northern Bass Strait. And I probably toned down the weather a bit… I made up my own version of the island but the help I received was invaluable. Jo Widdowson from Wildcare Friends of Deal Island told me about her time on the island, and how this important and remote place is maintained. She also shared 'An Historic Overview of Deal Island' by David Reynolds, which really was gold. Jo and her partner and son spent three months alone on the island, and her stories about that time gave me so much material for the book, as well as made me marvel at the courage of those who are willing to suspend their normal lives to look after these important environmental and historic places. So my heartfelt thanks to Jo! I read a great many books on lighthouses during my writing of the book, as I tried to get a feel for what it must be like to be a lighthouse keeper in a remote location, especially in the 1800s. There were many unsung heroes and heroines. Finally, thank you to my family for supporting me during the many months of writing, and thank you to my readers. You are the reason I keep writing my books.

talk about it

Let's talk about books.

Join the conversation:

facebook.com/harlequinaustralia

@harlequinaus

@harlequinaus

harpercollins.com.au/hq

If you love reading and want to know about our authors and titles, then let's talk about it.